WHISPER
IN THE
TEMPEST

ANNABELLE
MCCORMACK

Published by Annabelle McCormack

Cover by Patrick Knowles

Cover photography by Richard Jenkins Photography

Other images by Shutterstock

www.annabellemccormack.com

To Suzabelle Givings, who knew that writing was a lifelong passion, and to Ginger and Noah, who will always be a part of my heart.

Persistence perseveres.

ALSO BY ANNABELLE MCCORMACK

The Windswept Saga

A Zephyr Rising: A Windswept Prequel Novella

Sands of Sirocco: Book 2

Whisper in the Tempest: Book 3

The Brandywood Small Town Contemporary Romance Series

All This Time

I'll Carry You

Once We Met

Stand Alone Contemporary Romance Novels

See You Next Fall

To find out the latest about my new releases, please sign up for my newsletter or join my Facebook Reader's group! I love hearing from readers and have some great offers lined up for my subscribers.

WHISPER
IN THE
TEMPEST

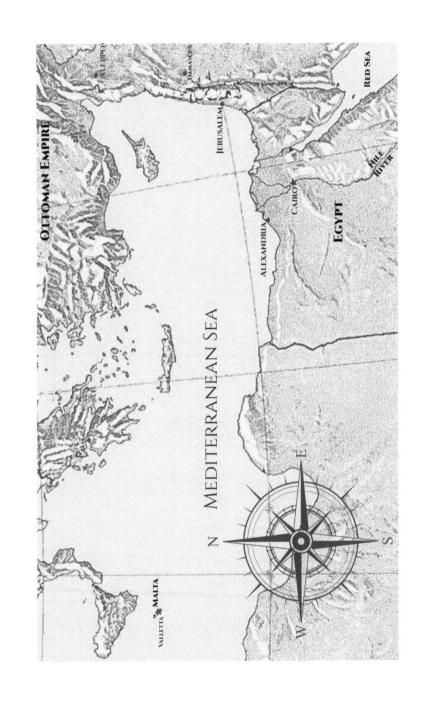

"[The war] is not a passing shower—it is a deluge ... It is a cyclone which is tearing up by the roots the ornamental plants of modern society and wrecking some of the flimsy trestle bridges of modern civilization. It is an earthquake which is upheaving the very rocks of European life. It is one of those seismic disturbances in which nations leap forward or fall backward generations in a single bound."

— DAVID LLOYD GEORGE, PRIME MINISTER OF ENGLAND, 1915

PART I

CHAPTER ONE

DECEMBER 1917

VALLETTA, MALTA

*A*lmost a dozen men and not one of them helpful.
How typical.

Ginger Whitman gritted her teeth as she made her way through to the alleyway off the crowded street of the harbor city of Valletta. She handed the packages she'd purchased to her companion and friend, Sarah Hanover. "I can help," she said, addressing the soldier who'd come stumbling onto the street, yelping for help for a snakebite. "I'm a nurse."

The soldier hovered over his fallen friend, who reclined against the outside wall of a stone pub. A few of their mates watched in concern nearby.

The golden glare of the late-day sun was bright in her face, the temperature warm and comfortable. Shadows of the people and buildings around her were long and extended, the light soft as dusk approached. She sat back on the heels of her boots, kneeling as she assessed the injured soldier in front of her. Her long beige skirt helped to cushion her knees and shins from the hard sidewalk—and probably kept them cleaner.

This close to the ground, she noticed the long cracks in the stone on the pub's façade, reminding her of how old Valletta felt. The fortified city of stone above the harbor was several hundred years old, a jewel in the Mediterranean. The stench of hot cooking oil and spices from the Is-Suq Tal-Belt, the famed indoor market that she and Sarah had just left, drifted from a nearby back alley. They were as close as you could get to the center of the city here, but that still meant a few minutes' walk to see the sea and get fresher island air and breezes.

Not that *all* men were unhelpful—her wonderful husband, Noah Benson, and his closest friend, Jack Darby, were certainly exceptions. But put a group of drunken young men together and give them an emergency and it was quite easy to sort the good ones from the rest. Especially in a time of war. Not every man who donned a uniform was a hero. Three years of serving as a battlefront nurse had taught her that lesson well.

A crowd had gathered around the soldier and Sarah edged past them, trying to stay close to Ginger. "Anything you need me to get?"

"I'm not sure yet." Ginger frowned as the wounded soldier held his swollen hand out to her, and she tugged it down, taking care to keep it low. "Give him some room," she said to the faces pressing in. She looked closer at the site of the bite. "What type of snake was it?"

The man grimaced, leaning back against the stone. "I don't know. Something venomous? We were playing a game with it." He was Australian, which wasn't surprising, given the number of ANZAC soldiers traveling through here to the Eastern and Palestinian fronts of the war.

Whatever game the man had been playing, it must have involved provoking the snake. *Of all the stupidity.* She'd seen soldiers in Palestine who'd received scorpion stings engaging in similarly foolish "games."

"Yes, but what kind? What did it look like?" *Someone must still have it.*

The wounded soldier shook his head. "Black. With yellow. I'm not sure."

Ginger tried to be patient. The Maltese locals had told her that venomous snakes on the island were a rarity. That likely meant that the soldiers had brought snakes with them from another country, like she'd seen so many do. Regiments, especially at the front, often had all manner of "pets" with them. Lifting her head, she asked more loudly, "Can anyone tell me what type of snake it is? I'm assuming the snake is still inside."

A murmur sounded from the soldiers who watched, then one of them went back inside the pub.

The men had clearly been drinking heavily, their slow reactions reflecting that. What would they have done if she hadn't been walking by—allow the man to die? The situation was ironic, too, as Malta was considered the hospital of the Mediterranean during the war. Other medical help wasn't far. In the absence of cooperation from the surrounding soldiers, maybe that was the best option.

Merchants lined both sides of the sidewalk at awkward angles. This wasn't a paved road where motorcars could find berth, but donkeys and horses seemed to come through, judging from the piles of manure swarming with flies—though there were none around at the moment.

A balmy breeze of the Maltese winter rippled against her lashes, bringing the relief of fresher air. Days of service during medical emergencies were behind her. She'd come to the island a month earlier while fleeing Egypt with Noah, who had been blamed for the crimes committed by Stephen Fisher, the man who had murdered her father.

Even now, thoughts of Stephen made a chill travel up her spine.

She blinked her attention back to the soldier.

"I can't feel my arm," he moaned, sweat dripping down his nose.

He flung his other arm back, and his fingertips hit a scrawny dog that yelped. The mutt went eagerly back to the pomegranate it had scavenged from a nearby fruit cart.

Ginger looked round toward Sarah, who had stepped back to give her some space. "See if you can fetch a carriage to take him to the hospital."

One of the soldier's friends straightened from his place beside the injured man. "I'll go with you, ma'am."

Sarah gave him a quirk of her brow, then touched the base of her blonde braid under her hat. "Ma'am? I must be looking older than I feel." She hurried off with the soldier in her wake, the crowd closing behind her.

Valletta had played host to British military units and medical personnel in the Eastern and Arabian fronts of the war, but with the Royal Army Medical Corps recently deciding to close most of the hospitals on the island, the numbers of nurses and doctors on the streets had gone down dramatically in the last few months. The war was moving, troops concentrating their focus almost entirely on France now that Russia had pulled out and the Germans were regrouping along the Western Front.

To Ginger, it felt as if the end of the war was imminent, but how many times had they all hoped that would be the case, only to have that hope dashed? *Maybe now that the Americans are finally on their way ...*

Their arrival was one last thread of a fragile hope, seemingly made of spider silk, for those who had been facing the onslaught from the beginning.

"Why can't I feel my legs?" The Australian soldier heaved. His anxiety was growing. She needed to keep him calm.

"The venom may cause numbness for a while." *Depending what bit you.* She gripped his good arm. "Look at me, Private—"

"Jenkins," he gasped, his face reddening further.

"Private Jenkins. Look at me. Right here, in the eye." She touched his cheek. "You must remain as calm as possible. It's going to hurt, of course. Your inebriation is speeding the flow of your blood and the venom. Take steady breaths. Breathe with me."

She lowered her fingertips to his wrist. His pulse raced. If she didn't calm him, he might have a heart attack. "Keep looking me in the eye. Breathe." Wasn't there anyone else here who could help her? "And someone fetch me boiling water and a clean cloth—and *please* find out what type of damned snake it was." Her exasperation with their incompetency was getting harder to hide.

She heard a mumble from a nearby pedestrian, followed by a scowl in her direction. *Yes, a woman swearing is such a scandal, but being utterly useless isn't.*

Private Jenkins struggled for composure, his gaze unfocused and darting from place to place. At last, his pupils settled on her. Even his eyes held a look of pain, one Ginger had come to recognize so clearly in so many of the men she had treated. She clasped his hand. "Keep breathing, calmly. The sooner you can get to hospital, the better." *Where is Sarah?*

From seemingly out of nowhere, a barkeep set a bowl of steaming water and a few cloths beside her. The cloths were stained, but they didn't appear dirty. *They'll have to do. I've worked with far worse.*

Ginger dipped one cloth into the boiling water to sterilize it as best she could, then cleaned the wound carefully. Tearing the other cloth into a few strips, she made a makeshift bandage for Private Jenkins' hand.

In her focus on him, she could almost forget the surrounding crowd, mostly Maltese locals, together with a few British soldiers that had come out of the pub. She recognized other Australians and New Zealanders, from their uniforms and regimental tabs. The market held the hurried pace of life that came toward the end of the day, when vendors packed up their stalls, eager to go home. The scents that were fresh in the morning—baking bread, newly lit fires, the early baked dust of dawn—had been replaced with grease, sweat, body odors from a day in the sun, and bad breath.

"You have pretty green eyes," Jenkins said, his face relaxing as she worked. "Like my mother at home—"

Realizing what was about to happen, Ginger thrust her hands forward as his eyes rolled back. His head lolled, limp, and he pitched forward. She caught his torso, his body heavy against her.

"Someone help me keep him upright. In case he vomits."

Another Australian soldier squatted beside her and pushed Jenkins back against the wall.

"Are you a lady doctor?" the Australian asked, seeming intrigued by her poise.

"No, a nurse on her day off." She grunted, holding Jenkins against the wall tightly to keep him from toppling forward again. *Or a month off. The truth wasn't necessary to give this stranger.*

Noah's status as a fugitive made the lie necessary, though. If he was found, he'd be arrested and probably executed. That had been Stephen's goal and his partnership with Noah's former superior in British Intelligence, Lord Reginald Helton, had ensured that the job they'd done in tarnishing Noah's name and making him look culpable for Stephen's crimes was thorough.

Ginger and Noah hid in plain sight as well as they could in the relative safety of Malta—he'd grown a beard and she'd tinted her recognizable red hair dark—but they were still at risk. If anyone recognized either of them, they'd have to flee again.

Of all the days not to have Noah and Jack accompany us to the market. Or to not have her medical kit accessible to her. She'd never expected to have to use her medical training when she'd left the hotel this afternoon.

"Did he hurt you?" The Australian searched her face as though looking for a bruise.

She shook her head. She'd been punched, slapped, and knocked over by patients before. This wasn't too terrible in the grand scheme of it all. For a fleeting moment, darker thoughts pressed in, of familiar light-blue eyes, a knife menacing ...

Stephen Fisher had done more than ruin Noah's good name. He'd wormed his way into both of their nightmares, having subjecting them both to torture, including carving his initials on Ginger's chest.

She snapped herself out of the horrible memories, looking back at the Australian soldier who'd come to her aid when the wounded man had fainted. "He needs to get to a carriage. Quickly, now that he's unconscious." *What on earth was taking Sarah so long?*

She searched for Sarah, then for anyone coming out of the pub. Looking at the Australian, she asked, "Do *you* know what type of snake it was?"

"No, the fellows who brought it in here made themselves scarce after the bite. I heard the venom was removed, but the private doesn't look too good."

"No, he doesn't."

A fly buzzed by her face. She waved it away and set her hand on the brim of her hat. The fly fled, circling in dizzy spirals around the curious onlookers. Even with the relative anonymity she and Noah had been enjoying in Malta the past month, Ginger shifted uneasily. She took what little comfort she could in the Australian soldier at her side, who didn't appear threatening. Two English Tommies had stopped on the street and watched from the crowd. She stiffened.

They don't know my husband is a fugitive from the law.

But she hadn't considered she'd be out after dark when she and Sarah had left the hotel earlier that afternoon. At this rate, they'd be back late, and Noah would be worried. He'd been growing more uncomfortable with their situation by the day, fearing that they might be discovered hiding here if they remained much longer.

She focused her attention back on the task at hand. The sooner she could get the injured soldier to a carriage, the sooner she and Sarah could be on their way back to the hotel.

She turned toward the Australian who had knelt to help her. "Do you think you can carry him?" The injured soldier was a thin man—little more than a boy. Like so many of the "men" she had treated. "If you can take his torso, I'll carry his legs. We'll find the closest hospital."

The Australian sized Ginger up. With dismay, she realized she was as tall as he was, though he was undoubtedly stronger. He gave a firm nod. "We'll give it a burl, eh?"

As she bent to get the soldier's legs, the English Tommies hurried out toward her. "No, no, ma'm. Best to leave us to it."

At last, someone who hasn't been drinking.

"I hear he has a snakebite?" one of the English soldiers asked.

Ginger nodded. "But the snake was defanged. Supposedly. Though, who knows, because no one seems to know anything." She glowered at the drunk soldiers who still hung by the pub. "Let's get him to a hospital, even if we have to carry him. There should be one within walking distance somewhere."

"We'll take him from here. We can ask. Thank you, Sister." The Tommies nodded toward the Australian who had been helping her.

The tension in Ginger's shoulders didn't settle as she watched them carry the unconscious form of Private Jenkins away. She wished she could do more for the young soldier, though she strongly suspected this would become a story of great gallantry for him for many years to come—if he lived.

What a tremendous shame, though. To have made it so long in this insipid war, only to risk death by snakebite while drunk.

Ginger searched the vicinity for Sarah. She hadn't returned yet. Noah didn't like for her to be anywhere alone, but given the emergency, it couldn't have been helped.

Of course, Noah might disagree. But his caution came from a place of improbable fear. Noah had never expected to be betrayed by Lord Helton, nor to be charged with crimes like smuggling, murder, and treason. Ginger had always believed her husband had a cynical side—but lately it had become significantly more barbed. They couldn't expect to hide in Malta forever and Ginger had felt Noah's increasing restlessness with the situation.

The shadows darkening in the marketplace increased Ginger's fears. The streets were already emptying of commerce, shops closing for the evening as their owners retired for the night.

When another couple of minutes passed without Sarah's return, Ginger went in the direction that she'd gone. Hopefully they'd meet somewhere in the middle. At any rate, the carriage she'd sent Sarah after was no longer necessary, and they could easily walk to the hotel from here.

Ginger's heels struck the pavement, where smooth stone served as the street. Valletta had been built so long ago that many of the narrow streets between the buildings could only handle pedestrian traffic. In some ways, the city reminded her of Florence, Italy, which she'd visited years earlier with her family.

Long gone were the days of traveling through Europe. Her father had been an English earl but one who had taken the family to visit many countries throughout the course of his work for the Foreign Office.

Days of luxury and comfort had ended when the flames of war had ripped their way through the fabric of European life. The war had spread its destruction and desolation over all aspects of everyone's lives—but, for her family, the effect had been particularly devastating. Her father, blackmailed by Stephen Fisher, had lost his integrity, his life, and the family fortune.

When her beloved brother, Henry, had ceded to Stephen's influence and tried to kill Noah for his investigation of her father, Ginger had been forced to stop Henry by killing him. And now her mother and sister would never forgive her for it—or for marrying Noah, whom they blamed for everything.

Ginger hastened her pace, not wanting to dwell on the images that came to mind when she thought of her family or her role in its upheaval. Sarah was still nowhere to be seen, and the daylight was quickly fading.

The sandstone that was used in the construction of most of the local buildings helped preserve the light somewhat. At sunset, the city practically glowed like gold. And even from where she stood, she could see the blue waters of the Mediterranean in the harbor, as though, if she continued right down the street, she'd walk right into it.

The buildings around here weren't as tall as the ones in other parts of the city—only a few floors—but most had beautiful balconies gracing the windows on the side, some made of wrought iron painted black and others of painted green wood. She wished she could crawl up into one of those balconies and look down, see if she could find Sarah from a better vantage point.

She regretted moving on without Sarah. Staying in the marketplace would have made it easier to find one another.

I should go back to the hotel. Sarah will be along.

Sarah was a confident and seasoned traveler. When Ginger had met her, she'd been wearing trousers and working her own archeological dig in Giza. If anything went wrong, Sarah would know to go back to the hotel without Ginger.

But would Noah be upset that Ginger had come back alone?

Ginger squinted toward the darkening sky overhead. It wouldn't be long before the strip of blue between the buildings turned a deep black. Nearby in a doorway, a doorknocker in the shape of a goblin growled at her. The city was known for its unique and fanciful knockers, which she'd appreciated many times while strolling through the streets, but right now they played to her fears.

She continued down the alley she and Sarah had used to walk to the market. She hadn't gone far when she heard Sarah's familiar voice from around the next corner. Sarah snapped in a bitter tone, "Don't you dare. Millard will never stand for it."

"Frankly, I don't give a damn about Van Sant's concerns. You've been given orders, Anderson."

Ginger stopped abruptly.

Who was Sarah talking to?

The man seemed familiar with Sarah. He knew and used her maiden name—and, from the sound of it, he was American, like her.

If someone had recognized Sarah, Noah could be at risk. By now, anyone looking for Noah or Ginger would know that Sarah had fled Egypt with them earlier in the month.

What was this about orders? Sarah was an archeologist. That she might be anything else other than how she'd presented herself made Ginger's skin crawl. She considered Sarah honest and a friend. *Is she being threatened?*

Ginger flattened herself to the side of the building, her breath growing shallower. She wished she could peek around the corner, see who was there. But if they saw her? This didn't sound like a pleasant conversation. And Noah had always told her that if one of them was recognized, it was better for them to split up. He'd worked in intelligence for too long for her not to trust his opinion.

"This isn't the solution you think it is. And I'm finally on the cusp of making progress on all my work, Charles." Sarah sounded angry. "Please trust me. Just give me—"

"You have twenty-four hours. And that's to follow orders. If you don't comply, we'll let you face the consequences of your actions." The man's voice was stern. Then, more gently, he added, "Don't be foolish. Please."

Approaching footsteps made Ginger startle, and she bent as though she were collecting something from the ground by her feet. It was a poor move to conceal herself, but better than running. Out of the corner of her eye, she saw a man in a light-beige suit and Panama hat walk past. She couldn't see his face, though.

Ginger straightened and paused, waiting until the man was out of view. Then she hurried around the corner, eager to ask Sarah what had happened.

She found Sarah standing on the street and she blinked at Ginger, as though lost in thought. Her blue eyes registered faint surprise, but then she smiled. "There you are. I was on my way back to you—I sent the carriage ahead of me with that soldier—did you get it?"

Strange. Ginger wouldn't have missed seeing the carriage and it had never arrived. Was she lying?

An uncertain tingle of pressure rose in her chest. "No. Some Tommies came out of the pub and took over the soldier's care. It was getting dark, so I came after you."

"Just stopped to catch my breath." Sarah adjusted her hat. "We should get back, though. Ready?"

She is lying. Why?

Ginger scanned her face, tempted to confront her. Confusion rippling through her, she nodded, and they hurried toward the hotel, the electric lights of buildings illuminating the darkening streets.

If Sarah wouldn't offer information, then she wouldn't ask. She didn't want to reveal what she'd heard to anyone other than Noah. He'd know what to do.

CHAPTER TWO

"And that's what you call a straight flush," Jack announced, setting his cards down with a smug look. Of course, it wasn't hard to mistake any of Jack Darby's looks as smug ones. Ginger smiled as they collected the playing cards together.

Not that Jack was as arrogant as he pretended to be. He was Noah's best and closest friend and confidant, and there was no one in the world other than Noah whom Ginger trusted more. But he had an American swagger that was both charming and disarming, the opposite of her more reserved husband, despite their similar dark hair and skin tones that tanned golden.

Noah stretched his shoulders, pushing his chair back from the wrought-iron patio table as Sarah wrinkled her nose at Jack. "I told you playing poker with Jack was a fool's errand," Noah said as Jack picked up the farthings they'd used to play.

"All these games are fool's errands when you're playing against a cryptographer. He's made a career out of playing." Sarah rolled her eyes, then extinguished her cigarette in the glass ashtray on the tabletop.

Ginger tipped her head toward Noah, avoiding looking at Sarah. The entire evening had passed without Sarah so much as saying a word about the encounter in the alleyway. The more time that passed, the more Ginger wanted to confront her about it.

But Ginger hadn't even told Noah yet—he and Jack had been waiting for them to go to dinner when they'd returned from the souk, and then they'd played a long after-dinner game with drinks, as they'd done all week.

They were at the café across the street from the hotel where they'd been staying since arriving in Malta earlier in the month—a place that now felt like a home to Ginger. Despite being married, she and Noah had never had the luxury of spending this much time together in the past, and she'd learned more about her husband the last few weeks than in all the time before.

He was fastidiously tidy, consumed books at a pace that seemed unimaginable to her, and he seemed to have a working knowledge of any topic she discussed with him. Most days, he was already awake by the time she blinked her eyes open, a cup of coffee in hand, and the daily newspaper finished. Noah's strong preference for coffee to tea was surprising, as he'd been raised by his English aunt, but perhaps it was the Egyptian blood of his mother that made him choose coffee. And while Jack and Sarah usually burned the midnight oil happily, Noah preferred to go to bed earlier.

She loved how predictable he could be now that she knew him better, how he seemed to thrive on structure. He was adventurous and exciting, and life with him had been anything but ordinary, but the routines he loved seemed to give their life a sense of stability that she also craved. She'd come from a life of order—both before the war and in the endless scheduling that came with being a war nurse with the Queen Alexandra's.

Ginger closed her eyes for a moment, enjoying the stillness of the evening. The winter air felt chill despite her thick woolen sweater. Even a few months ago, she couldn't have imagined doing anything like this. Most of her adulthood had been spent during this war, with a nursing matron's threatening consequences if she and her fellow nursing Sisters flirted too much with soldiers or wore anything other than their stern uniforms.

"Shall we retire?" Noah's voice was beside her ear, and his hand touched her shoulder gently.

"I don't know that my pride can take being battered much more at these card games with Jack and Sarah," she said with a laugh. Their friends were equally competitive and outrageous, but Ginger couldn't have thought of two better people to be spending this time with.

Sarah tossed a flirtatious smile at Jack, and Ginger's stomach clenched. She didn't want to be bothered by what she'd overheard earlier that afternoon, but how could she not? All she knew of Sarah was from Sarah's lips alone. Noah and Jack had encountered her on archeological digs in Egypt before the war, but the British government had recruited many intelligence agents from the archeological field. Had the Americans done the same with Sarah? And if that was the case, why hadn't Sarah been more forthcoming about it from the start?

I hate feeling like I can't trust anyone anymore.

Ginger and Noah said their good-nights and then headed back toward their room. The heady warmth from the wine she'd had during dinner flushed her body, and she leaned against Noah, relishing the feel of his hand in hers, the strength of his torso to keep her stable. He was tall and broad-shouldered, and everything about him, from his physique to his calm, helped her feel safe.

"Has Jack always been so adept at card playing?" Ginger asked as they climbed the stairs to their room.

"For as long as I've known him. Ironically, his father was terrible at gambling—and addicted to it. He'd occasionally take Jack along to help give him signals during games. The first time Jack ever had his nose broken resulted from that."

The first time. She couldn't imagine Jack as a young, carefree boy, given the descriptions she'd had of his family. The details of Jack's childhood had never been discussed, but she knew he'd lacked the care of his parents. The experience had contributed to his closeness to Noah, who had lost both his parents as a young boy in Ireland. But in Noah's case, he and his younger brother Neal had gone to live with a wealthy aunt in England after being orphaned.

Once in the safety of their room, Ginger went to the attached bathroom and ran water for a bath. The amenity was a luxury that she'd appreciated during their stay at the hotel, but she worried about how much the room was costing them. They had escaped Egypt practically with the clothes on their backs and, as a fugitive, Noah couldn't access most of his money. Jack's generosity helped them survive, but the more time passed, the more the situation became untenable.

She removed her hat, then plucked her hair from the tight chignon she'd pinned it into. As her hair tumbled down on her shoulders, Noah drew the curtain in front of the large balconied window. He gave her an admiring look. "Some of the tint in your hair is fading. I see a hint of red."

"I've been considering becoming a brunette for life," she teased, crossing the room toward him.

He placed his hat on the desk in the room and studied her. A mischievous glint shone in his dark-blue eyes. "Well, I have always preferred brunettes."

"You're absolutely rotten." She grinned, then tugged at the buttons of his vest. Thankfully, she knew he loved her red hair. But his words reminded her of her worries earlier that evening and the encounter she'd witnessed with Sarah.

She didn't want to bring up the situation with Sarah and break his good mood, but he'd be unhappy later if she didn't tell him right away. She'd learned her lesson well enough about not telling Noah information about suspicious activities.

As casually as she could, she said, "Have you ever wondered what Sarah was doing in Egypt when we met her? Other than archeology?"

Noah gave her a sharp look. "Why?"

He already knows.

Ginger stepped back from him, then set her hands on her hips. The way he'd given her that look spoke to something she couldn't quite put her finger on but gave her a certain enough feeling—Noah had kept something from her. "What do you know?"

"I won't start the game of 'I'll tell you if you tell me,' darling." Noah unbuttoned the cuffs of his sleeves and rolled them. "I know nothing—not with any certainty, at any rate. I suspect Sarah might work for the American government in a similar capacity as I served for the British, given her knowledge of Arabia, the language, and that the United States has now entered the war."

The news was blunt enough, its impact lost because of what she'd overheard that afternoon. "So, a spy?"

The corners of his lips twitched in a slight smile. "It's all less glamorous than that term conjures, you know. Gathering intelligence, typing it into reports, sending observations—it's all mostly desk work."

She laughed, knowing how far the reality of it differed from what her husband wanted her to believe. He'd spent countless days embedded with enemy troops, sneaking into foreign lands, even having been captured once when Stephen Fisher had betrayed him to the Turks. "What makes you think Sarah is a spy?" She pulled a scarf from her neck, then set it on the bed.

Noah gave her an impatient look. "I know you're not telling me something."

"And I know that drives you mad, but humor me and answer the question."

With a sigh, Noah sat on the edge of the bed. "She was armed to the teeth in Gaza, to start. Most of the Americans have abandoned their archeological concessions and haven't returned the last couple of seasons, but she was still there. Not to mention the fact that her late husband had business dealings with your father."

She cringed. Her father had been involved in intelligence, too, and worked for the Foreign Office for years before they'd transferred him to Egypt for the war. He'd been a loyal British servant until he'd lost his fortune and become indebted to Stephen.

Ginger bit the inside of her lower lip. "I overheard Sarah speaking with someone this afternoon. She left to find a carriage for that soldier I told you about—the one with the snakebite—and then didn't return. I went looking for her, only to find her engaged in a heated discussion with an American man I couldn't see, who told her something about having twenty-four hours to carry out orders."

Noah's gaze clouded. "What else? The most minute of details could be important."

She searched her memory, wishing she had perfect recall of the moment. "Sarah mentioned someone by the name of Millard having concerns. And the man said something about not giving a damned about what Van Sant wanted. Something like that. Do you think there may be something to it all? Or who Sarah might have been talking about?"

"Millard Van Sant is a famous archeologist—quite an old man, actually. I've met him several times. He's lived in Cairo for over forty years by now."

Oh. "So this could all be about archeology?" Perhaps this wasn't nearly as concerning as she'd thought.

"It could be." His face was somber, thoughtful. "I should talk to Jack. See what he thinks."

She wrinkled her nose, knowing this wouldn't help with the worry that had been weighing on Noah's shoulders—or his increasing insomnia. *Maybe I should have asked Jack myself, instead of troubling Noah further.* Attempting to inject some levity into their conversation, she asked, "Does that mean you won't be joining me in the bath?"

He smiled, his eyes perusing her figure with appreciation. "Don't tempt me." He plucked his jacket from the back of a chair, where he'd placed it minutes before. "I'll return soon."

The door closed quietly behind him, then Ginger disrobed and climbed into the bath and sank into it. As warm water sluiced over her legs, she settled back. Had she made too much of what had happened? If Van Sant was an archeologist, the most logical scenario was that this was about a dig.

But Noah already thinks Sarah could be a spy.

That thought bothered her, but not because of its implications. Instead, it made her stomach churn that Noah hadn't shared that suspicion with her. He hadn't lied to her, of course, but why hadn't he said anything? Surely, he must have known she'd find that information relevant. After all, Ginger had spent hours with Sarah the last few weeks, sharing stories—trusting her.

She was trying to be better about accepting that her husband had his secrets and stories from his past that he'd never share. And, illogically, it irritated her that this concealment bothered her. They were beyond this by now, and she shouldn't hold his silence against him.

After all, she kept her own secrets sometimes.

She lifted a bar of soap from a nearby window ledge and smoothed it over the flat of her stomach. The weeks had passed too quickly and, in some ways, too peacefully, given the circumstances they'd had to overcome to escape to Malta. Her marriage to Noah was the sole bright spot in the last year.

She'd been married for well over a month, with Noah arranging a secret wedding for them in the Coptic church in mid-November. They'd never had the chance after that to go to the consulate in Cairo and register their marriage, nor would they be able to while

Noah was a fugitive. Too much had happened, and all of it had been a whirlwind.

Then, this morning, when she'd woken, her one and only thought had been about how she couldn't remember the last time she'd gotten her monthly cycle.

She had said nothing to Noah, but the idea had planted itself in her mind and the cold, slick fear of the possibility broke out across her neck now. It was too early to know. Too early to go to a doctor for an examination, she imagined.

But would Noah even welcome the thought? Would telling him of her suspicions only add to his burdens?

Dropping back into the water, Ginger's breath vibrated against the surface of the water. The tops of her knees broke through the surface, her skin unnaturally cold there, and she didn't move, blinking slowly.

Skipping dates or months of her cycle altogether wasn't entirely unnatural for her—especially during some of the harder times of the war. When she'd been on minimal rations during the Gallipoli campaign and working fourteen-hour days in field hospitals, there had been several times she'd barely noticed a skip.

But could this be different? They'd tried to be cautious, knowing that a pregnancy wouldn't be ideal, but it wasn't always easy to do, given their attraction to each other. She was madly in love with her husband, and their time in Malta had been like a honeymoon.

Her bath was a short one, both the events of the day and the worry about a pregnancy making it difficult for her to tussle with her thoughts. She stepped out of the tub and dried herself, then pulled on a dressing gown. They'd fled from Egypt with practically nothing, and everything she had they'd bought in Malta.

What if they needed to flee again? How long would it be before their lives returned to any semblance of normalcy?

She didn't want fear ruling their lives. Hiding like this wasn't a solution—or a life. Every time Noah went out the door without her, she worried he'd be arrested. The uncertainty was wearing on her, like a pebble in her shoe, bound to blister and cause more pain. Something needed to change ... and if nature had its way, that change might need to come much sooner than either of them had expected.

CHAPTER THREE

*N*oah hesitated at the end of the hotel hallway, staring at Sarah's door. He'd been halfway to find Jack when he'd turned around. It wasn't Jack he needed to talk to.

For a moment, he considered going back to Ginger, joining her in the bath and forgetting that she'd introduced a moment of tumult into his otherwise peaceful evening.

But he wasn't truly at peace. He hadn't been for a long time.

And now that Ginger had witnessed Sarah having some sort of clandestine meeting in the alleyway by the Is-Suq Tal-Belt, it was finally time to confront her about his suspicions.

Oddly, he trusted Sarah—not that he could rely on his own instincts after the debacle in Cairo with Fisher and Lord Helton. But there was something about her that seemed genuine. And Jack clearly had feelings for her, even if he wouldn't admit how fond of her he was.

But he'd been misled before.

He wouldn't take that risk again.

Noah knelt and picked the lock, stealthily, noting the position of a nearly hidden matchstick, by the hinge of the door.

Clever woman.

She must have left it there to gauge if someone opened the door in her absence. The matchstick tumbled to the floor. He wouldn't be able to replace it from the inside, which was the whole point of it. The damned thing would give him away, but there was nothing to be done about it now.

Noah entered quietly, then turned on the light. In all his time sneaking into and out of locations for investigation, the peculiarity of entering a room in the absence of its dweller, had always struck him. The belongings, set in their place by someone's hand, felt frozen in time—an undisturbed glimpse of the individual's inner sanctum.

In response to his work, Noah had become meticulous with his own living space. Everything had an exact place, and the bed was always made precisely. Even objects that looked askew were set that way purposefully so that he could notice instantly if they'd been disturbed. He didn't mention the reason for the peculiar habit to Ginger when she laughed at his tidiness, though maybe he should have. But much of who he'd allowed himself to become felt tainted by the dark association of the work he'd undertaken during the war.

As he'd seen at her home in Cairo, Sarah seemed to surround herself with books—most of them about Egyptology. He regretted that they'd only recently become better acquainted. Her theories and insights about archeology were fascinating.

Since the matchstick had ended his hope of investigating Sarah without her knowledge, he used that to his advantage. He found her bags under the bed and pulled them out, searching the cedar-scented fabric for any hidden compartments.

Nothing.

Sarah might not opt for that obvious a hiding place, if she was hiding something.

He skimmed through her books, opening up her journals. They were written in that strange code of hers. A wry smile came to his lips. No wonder Jack liked her. He appreciated a good puzzle better than most.

He could ask her questions later. Now was his chance to see into her world without hiding. Much as he wanted to trust her, he'd been burned too badly by those he'd trusted not to do his own search.

Noah went through the drawers of her wardrobe, pulled the sheets from her bed. By the time he'd finished, he'd done a thorough job of ransacking her belongings, but the search had been fruitless. He'd seen nothing that was particularly interesting.

The click of the door opening interrupted him, and Noah glanced up as Sarah entered, her pistol already drawn in her hands.

"I surrender," he said in a mocking tone, then tossed a book onto a pile on the floor to join the rest.

"Noah Benson." Sarah's jaw dropped. "I should have known it was you. Ginger overheard me talking to someone, didn't she?"

"She did."

"She couldn't have heard much, though. She was too busy taking care of that soldier." Sarah put her pistol on a chair by the door, then shut it. "I hope you're planning on cleaning all of this up. Did you find what you were looking for?"

"I didn't know what I was looking for." Noah sat in an armchair near her bed, leaning back lazily. "But maybe you can tell me."

"I'm not a spy, if that's what you think. An informant, yes. The Americans don't have a lot of spies in Arabia. They want information about the area, but have no desire to be involved. Why do you want to know?"

"Because it affects me," Noah said flatly. "So you're an informant for the United States government." *Interesting. Not quite what I expected.*

"I was. But, of course, I ran away with you and Ginger, so now they're not very pleased with me. They tracked me here, and in the meantime they decided they're intrigued by this mastermind criminal chameleon I'm traveling with. Apparently, Helton's been doing a hell of a job smearing your name back in Egypt. You're looking like a mad genius that any government would love to talk to."

Noah grunted a scoffing laugh. "I highly doubt that."

"Doubt it or not, they want you. He found you through me. I'm a danger to you, Noah. To you, Ginger, and Jack. And the American government wants you. They want me to turn you over to them. And I have twenty-four hours to do it."

Noah stared at her, unblinking, waiting for her to expand on that thought. When she didn't he prodded, "Or ...?"

"Or they're going to let a few people who Paul wasn't too friendly with know that I'm here."

That Sarah's dead husband had enemies wasn't surprising. He'd clearly been mixed up with some people who lived outside of the law, like Ginger's father. He didn't want Sarah risking her life for him, though.

"But that's not all." A shadow crossed Sarah's face. "They're threatening to arrest all of us, including Ginger and Jack. By now, there's a good chance they could accuse both of them of something that will stick—mostly because of their association with you. The only reason Charles saw fit to warn me is because he's—he's got a bit of a soft spot for me."

"Charles?" Noah raised a brow. He wanted to know more about what she'd said, but asking the name of her associate seemed too important to skip it.

"Charles Pointer. He works for the State Department."

"And if you turn me in, they won't arrest Ginger and Jack?"

Sarah sank onto the bed, her face wan. "As far as I can tell. But you never know. They know they're important to you, so who knows how they'll use that information in the future? They offered me a chance out, but Jack will never accept that. He'd die for you, and you know it."

What was it that Helton had always said? *Love is a liability.*

"Listen to me, Noah, and listen clearly. They're not safe. You can't run forever. You know you can't. And when they have the first chance to use them against you, they will. If you want them to be safe, you're going to have to strike and strike hard."

Noah lifted his chin sharply, narrowing his eyes. "What do you have in mind?"

Sarah smirked, then went over to the pile of scattered books that lay on the floor. She sifted through them, then picked up a thin volume. "What do you know about Akhenaten?" She handed him the book, then grabbed another.

"The heretic pharaoh?" Noah gave her an amused look, unable to follow her logic. "He was an Eighteenth Dynasty pharaoh who tried to make Egyptians monotheistic, worshiping only Aten ... what else do you want me to know?"

"Good enough. Do you know about the clearing of his tomb, KV55 in the Valley of the Kings?"

"Is this relevant?" Noah sighed, thumbing through the volume she'd handed him.

She shrugged. "Do you want my help or not? Because if you do, you're going to want to know as much about Akhenaten as possible." She sat on the floor in front of him, holding some more books. "I'll give you everything I have. What you choose to do is up to you. But a few years ago, Millard Van Sant—you know who he is, right?"

"The archeologist? Yes, I know who he is."

"Right, well, Millard came to me and told me he had a problem. In the 1880s, before the tomb of Akhenaten was 'discovered' in Amarna, there were rumors that the locals had found it first. Stories of gold being carted off—even a sarcophagus—circulated among anyone in the know."

Noah crossed his arms, trying not to reveal his impatience. When would she get to the point of all this? He'd heard those stories, but never paid much attention to them. Not much was known about Amarna or the Eighteenth Dynasty royals. They had faded into obscurity.

"Anyway, Millard asked me for my help. He'd recovered some objects that he believed belonged to the royal tomb at Amarna. Artifacts that had been on the brink of being smuggling out. He wanted my help in investigating the smuggling ring, to see if I could find out who was involved and where the artifacts had come from." She seemed to sense his growing fatigue with her story. "So I did."

He smiled slightly. "It's not that you're boring me ... I'm trying to make sense of how any of this fits in with my situation."

"Okay, then I'll skip to the good part. More artifacts appeared on the black market. Lots of them. Enough that it was clear someone had probably found a cache of artifacts and was trying to get them out slowly without arousing too much suspicion. Someone good. Someone who had some level of authority in the British government."

Noah sat straighter, more attentively. He had a feeling he knew whom she meant. "Lord Edmund Braddock, Ginger's father?"

"Bingo. But then—there was something strange. The Amarna artifacts had led me down a rabbit hole into some shipping anomalies on British military liners—things Braddock couldn't possibly have access to. These were way above his head. I didn't know who it was, but now—now it all makes sense."

Another corrupt official in the British government with his hand in smuggling? As shocking as it might have been for someone else, Noah had spent too long interacting with government figures to be surprised.

"Lord Reginald Helton."

Sarah's words cut through the noise in his head, and he locked eyes with her, his chest tightening.

Helton had been involved in the smuggling trade?

Then fury bubbled up inside him with such force that his hands curled into fists, his nails digging into his palms as he tried to control himself. He felt as though someone had punched him in the gut, the air knocked from his lungs.

He'd been used like a fool.

Lord Helton was nothing more than a criminal, a mastermind who had used Noah to eliminate his enemies, and Noah had destroyed Ginger's life and that of her family's in much the same way that a paid assassin would have been expected to. Helton must have been working with Fisher the whole time. Perhaps even directing Fisher.

He pictured Victoria, Helton's sultry daughter, who had claimed to be in love with him. Helton had proposed Noah and Victoria use a false engagement as a ruse to allow Noah more direct access to Helton without arousing suspicion. But had there been more to it?

Victoria had been an eager participant in their fake romance—attempting to seduce him on more than one occasion. A further manipulation?

"Are you certain?" Noah managed, his throat tight.

"Yeah, I'm positive. And I've been checking some records since I got here. Edmund Braddock made a lot of trips over here—always within a few weeks of when the Amarna artifacts showed up on the black market. I have a hunch he got nervous and moved his cache here."

"Braddock has a house here. It would be a logical place to look."

"Agreed. Especially because I think there's a way to catch Helton at his game and expose him for the crook he is. And I think it's going to take a large cache of undocumented artifacts to fool him."

Noah still couldn't quite understand the way her mind was working, but he would be mad not to pay attention to her. She knew more about this than most. "In what sense?"

"Okay—so Millard has been digging in the Valley of the Kings. He started digging there recently because KV55 had so many random artifacts, but especially the ones from the Amarna royals."

"Including Akhenaten."

"We think." Sarah smirked. "But who knows? And he thinks he's on the verge of finding something—something big. That something is hidden close to KV9, the Ramesses tomb. But he's old and he's tired, and Howard Carter has been irritated with Millard's poking around in the valley."

The image she painted was entertaining. She spoke so casually of the archeologists in Egypt that Noah knew they were all well acquainted with her. Carter was known to be extremely secretive—if Millard had been disturbing his process, he wouldn't be pleased. "Go on. If I'm not responding, it's because I'm too busy trying to absorb it all."

Sarah gave a chuckle before picking up a few more documents and books. "I think there's a good chance that the right person, with the right treasures, could come into the Valley of the Kings and make a claim of an undisturbed tomb—something big, like the tomb of Nefertiti or Smenkhkare or Tiye. Maybe even Tutankhamun or another tomb of Akhenaten. After all, if Akhenaten was buried in Amarna but then moved to the Valley of the Kings to KV55, his treasure could have been moved too."

"And the right treasures would be the ones from a certain Amarna cache?" Noah raised his brow, sudden understanding dawning on him.

"Exactly. Just a few things, to get things started. Proof that an antechamber or something significant has been found. Millard could vouch for the claimant—he has every desire to see the smuggling ring stopped—and then a trap could be set. The Egyptians would be eager to see those treasures preserved and kept in the country, so—"

"If Lord Helton was offered an opportunity to invest in exchange for unfettered access to the tomb before artifacts were documented, it might be too tempting an opportunity for him to pass over." Noah leaned forward, the wheels of his mind spinning.

Sarah looked pleased. "I knew you were a quick one, Benson."

Noah bit the inside of his lower lip, thinking as his eyes shifted through the room. "And Fisher?"

"Well—I don't think Helton actually has enough money for the investment required for a dig of the type we're describing. He has the government access, but the money has to come from somewhere else."

The scheme wasn't a bad one, but it would require diligent planning. "I could have Alastair—"

"No." Sarah's face darkened. "No, Noah, you aren't understanding me. This isn't something you can involve anyone you know in. If they get the slightest clue that you're a part of it—or anyone you're associated with is—they'll never go for it. You have to do it alone."

Noah looked away, aware of how hard his heart hammered in his chest.

She's right.

"You'll only keep putting your friends—and your wife—in danger if you involve them. You can't say anything to anyone. Not even Jack. Not Ginger. Send her back home and go get your name cleared."

Noah stood, cradling in his hands the books she'd given him. He would start reading them tonight, if possible. "You're not going to turn me over to the Americans, then?"

"No, of course not. I wouldn't ever knowingly endanger my friends." Sarah pushed her fingers over her scalp, her blue eyes growing sadder. "I'll figure something out. It'll be fine."

CHAPTER FOUR

$\mathcal{T}$he wind howled through the sunbaked sandstone of the ancient megalith temple, and for the third time since she'd arrived at the cliff, Ginger checked over her shoulder, certain she'd heard a footstep around the corner. Her ability to see to the other side of the stones was limited, and there were many reasons for the noise. Malta offered no shortage of gusty wind that could carry with them pebbles or whipping foliage.

Or maybe the sound had come from another tourist.

Still, a nagging feeling crept up her spine.

"You have twenty-four hours."

The warning that the man had given Sarah rang through Ginger's mind, as it had many times in the last two days. She'd held her breath most of the day yesterday, wondering if she should await some great calamity.

Yet nothing had happened.

Noah and Jack had spoken, but Noah hadn't shared all of what they had discussed. Just that whatever the circumstances were, they needed to proceed with caution.

Ginger hung back on the path into the temple at Hagar Qim, leaning forward to peek around a fallen lintel.

A soft scraping sound followed, and her heart thudded in response. Someone—or something—watched. Ginger leaned further forward. A burst of feathers fluttered, a bird escaping from the other side of the stone, startling her into a muffled scream.

Oh, dear God. Heat crept up her neck. She was becoming utterly gutless.

Noah turned back toward her. He lifted a dark brow, amusement in his eyes as his gaze swept over her blush. "What is it?"

"I'm making a ninny of myself over a bird." Ginger released a nervous breath, her heart rate returning to normal. Sheepishly, she explained, "I thought I heard something behind that upright stone."

Noah glanced to the other side, as she'd done, then a smile twitched at his lips. "Yes, I've heard the avian species on Malta are murderous." He took her hand in his, drawing her to him. "Well, Mrs. Benson, I'll have to do a better job protecting you from such deadly forces."

She laughed, slipping her arms around his neck. "You know, I didn't *have* to give you the means by which to mock me."

He dropped a kiss to her lips that made her knees weaken. "Ah, but you did," he whispered. "Which tells me you rather enjoy my mockery."

She chortled against his lips, a giddy feeling of bliss swelling within her.

Part of Ginger wanted to keep going and leave everything behind, so long as she and Noah were together. She shifted comfortably into his arms, enjoying the sound of his heartbeat beneath the shirt that covered his well-muscled chest. Being on the top of a remote cliff in the countryside, overlooking the sparkling blue Mediterranean, it felt as though they'd stepped away from everything and were free of the cares of the world.

But when Ginger thought about it too long, her happiness was fraught with guilt in knowing the world was still swept up in the chaos of war. Christmas approached quickly, and the troops fortunate enough to be alive continued to be separated from their anxious families. One more holiday marked by absent place settings at the table and with grief and mourning.

She didn't want to think about that, though. She wanted to nestle in the arms of her husband, then later go down the rocky terrain along the cliffs and sit with their friends for a picnic lunch by the sea. Pretend that nothing concerned her.

Go back to the way things were two days ago.

The sound of Jack clearing his throat interrupted the moment. "You know, if I didn't know any better, I'd say someone has badly influenced you. Aren't you English against public displays of affection?"

Ginger and Noah stepped away from each other, and she shook her head at him. "Oh, stop it, you. I'm certain I spotted you and Sarah wrapped up in more than one amorous embrace while we were at Mnajdra."

They'd gone to the adjacent temple before this one, and Jack and Sarah had been arm-in-arm. It thrilled Ginger to see them so happy. Sarah deserved to find love again—her late husband had been a liar and philanderer. And Jack seemed to be smitten with her.

But given the calm manner with which Jack and Noah seemed to handle whatever concerns Ginger had mentioned two days earlier, she couldn't help but wonder if Jack's judgment was clouded. *Shouldn't he be more worried about Sarah?*

Even Noah seemed irregularly calm about it all.

"Yeah, well, all that honeymooning between you two has me jealous, what can I say?" Jack winked at Ginger as they caught up to him. Sarah was a few feet further down the path, her head bent at an angle as she analyzed the divots in the stones in front of her.

"These are fascinating, aren't they?" she said, beckoning Jack with a curl of her forefinger. Her eyes glimmered as she set her bag down and pulled out a notepad.

Jack and Noah joined Sarah, examining the prehistoric art with similar enthusiasm.

They'd decided the day before to explore some of the ancient megalith temples of Malta, having spent most of their time within the city of Valletta, save for a few day trips that Noah and Ginger had taken to the countryside. But going to the archeological sites with three people who had studied and worked in the field had proven to be more than Ginger had bargained for. She'd quickly found herself the odd man out in every conversation, nodding along mutely as they exchanged theories and spoke of studies she'd never heard of.

She wandered a few feet away again, surveying the fields that surrounded the temple. The brim of her hat shaded her eyes. Few trees dared to grow on the rocky hills, and both the sun and the reflection of the Mediterranean nearby made her eyes water with the brightness.

Noah sidled up beside her after a few minutes, setting his hands on her shoulders from behind. "You're bored," he whispered in her ear, tucking her back close against him. His lips grazed her jawline, the dark hair of his trim beard tickling her, and goose bumps rose on her arms.

"Mmm. What gave it away?" She turned her face to give him a warm smile. "Truth be told, I'm not sure I can tell the difference between this pile of rocks and the other one we just visited, but that's not to say I'm not enjoying myself."

"The dark look on your face would say otherwise." He curved his palms over her shoulders. "Still worried about that bird by the entrance?"

She sighed. *I don't want to be the only one who seems to be worried about Sarah.* She gave him another reason for her seriousness instead. "I suppose I can't help feeling like I'm carelessly on holiday while others are hard at work. I started nursing so early in the war, and it's been a good month since I've even been in a hospital. Christmas was always one of those times that it felt necessary for everyone to do their bit. Don't you think we ought to resolve our situation once and for all so we can return to our normal lives?"

A shadow crossed his tanned, handsome face. He gave a curt nod. "Lately, I keep dreaming of your father. And Henry. On the day they died."

"My father and brother?" She held his gaze, resisting the urge to let his words have their impact. *Henry.* Her heart twisted whenever she thought of him, especially.

"Yes, I can't quite understand why my mind keeps taking me to that moment, but it occurred to me the other morning—we may have erred by not going to your father's property in Malta, seeing what he may have kept there."

The conversation had taken a turn she hadn't been expecting. Her father's property? When she'd discovered that her father kept secret properties in Egypt and one in Malta, Ginger's first impulse had been to explore them. It was Noah who had felt strongly that the risk wasn't worth satisfying her curiosity.

She gave him a puzzled look, and a strong breeze forced her hand away from his to hold her hat down. Her skirt lashed against her legs. "But didn't you say you thought going back there could be dangerous? That someone might watch the house? We've stayed out of harm's way so far. What could be there that would be worth risking our anonymity?"

"I don't know." Noah sighed, adjusting his own hat. "It's a nagging feeling. We know your father sent other secrets here. Malta would have been a more logical place to hide incriminating things than his home in Cairo. But Jack thinks I may be right. We were discussing it the other night."

Ah.

She pressed her lips to a firm line, wanting not to be bothered by his silence about what he and Jack had discussed. *Let him keep his secrets. You trust him.*

"So Jack thinks you should explore my father's house?" she asked as casually as she could.

"I think I heard my name." Jack interrupted their quiet discussion once again, this time with Sarah at his side, her arm linked with his. "No doubt discussing my good looks."

"Of course. It's our most frequent topic of conversation." Ginger turned toward him, setting her hands on her hips. "What's this about going to my father's property in Valletta?"

Sarah scanned her face, her blue eyes sympathetic. "It's not a terrible idea, Ginger."

Ginger's gaze flickered back to Noah, her stomach pitting into a knot. "I suppose I'm the only one who thinks it's terribly foolish to even consider going there. And dangerous?"

No one answered.

Ginger sighed, annoyed that she was alone in her belief. She was the one they'd had to talk out of going—how had this flipped on her? "Then I suppose I've been outnumbered regarding this subject. Again. Shall we move on?"

She strode away without waiting for a response, back toward Mnajdra, suffocation pressing in on her. What had changed? Weeks earlier, when Ginger had said she wanted to visit her father's property, they'd all discouraged it and she'd felt foolish. As she hurried down the steep slope to the other temple site, Ginger wasn't surprised when Sarah hurried to catch up to her. "Are you okay?" she asked.

"I'm fine." Ginger gave her a terse smile. "I promise I'm not upset at anyone. Just worried. If my father's house was too dangerous to visit before, I don't understand why that's not the case now."

"Maybe it's not that the danger has changed." Sarah glanced over her shoulder, back at Jack and Noah, who followed at a distance. "More that the potential benefit in going has increased. Noah needs to do *something*, after all. His life won't get any better just sitting here."

Sarah's words chastened her, and she wrinkled her nose. She didn't want Noah or her friends to think she was throwing a temper tantrum. And she was grateful Sarah had followed her to soothe her. Only a few of her friends had ever been so refreshingly honest or willing to challenge Ginger's tendency to be rash. Though they'd only known each other for about a month, Sarah had quickly become one of the closest confidants Ginger had ever had. "I suppose you're right."

"Oh, you know I am." Sarah grinned. She looped her arm through Ginger's. "The fact is, you can always trust me to tell you when you're wrong. And, in this case, you are. I know—" Sarah held up a hand—"you wanted to go there before now. But things changed. Don't hold it over his head. The man has had everything torn away from him, his reputation ruined, and is being hunted for crimes he didn't commit. I say it's about time he tries to take his life back. I can't imagine he's happy."

Ginger nodded and gave Sarah a chagrined expression. "I'm trying to temper my overreactions. I wish I could be as cool-headed as you are."

Sarah laughed. "Now you're making me sound like Solomon or something. Don't forget that it took me marrying a rat to even meet you." She patted Ginger's forearm. "Go talk to him. I'll see you up ahead."

Ginger stopped and waited for Noah and Jack to join her as Sarah continued down toward Mnajdra, closer to the cliff side. She gave them both an apologetic look. "I'm sorry if I was being difficult."

"You're a peach, Red." Jack winked. He resumed walking.

"Wait, Jack," Ginger called, and he paused, looking back.

Ginger glanced from Noah to Jack. "Do you really think there may be something in my father's house in Malta worth looking for?"

They exchanged a look, and Noah nodded.

"Then can't Jack go by himself—or even with Sarah—to see? Wouldn't that be safer?"

"Maybe. Maybe not. Anyone looking for Noah is looking for me, too," Jack said. He scanned the path ahead. "I should go find Sarah."

As Jack walked away, Noah and Ginger fell into step some distance behind him. "Still angry?" Noah asked.

"I wasn't angry." The open air of the cliff side near them made her wonder if their voices would carry in the silence. "But I shouldn't have been so annoyed, either." She released a slow sigh that took with it a knot of tension in her chest. "If going to my father's house is something that feels necessary, then of course I want you to do it. I trust you, Noah. And your judgment."

She reached for his hand and rubbed her thumb over the wedding band she'd given him a few weeks earlier—a sight that still made her heart melt. "And I want you to have your name back. I want the world to know I'm Mrs. Noah Benson."

The warmth in Noah's eyes as he returned the gentle pressure against her fingers made her heart settle. Then, a cry caught their attention.

Noah and Ginger looked toward the stones of the Mnajdra temple, which were coming into view.

Jack had broken into a run ahead of them. "Sarah!"

Ginger lifted her skirts and hurried down the hill, Noah at her heels. Noah quickly passed her, but Ginger did her best to keep up.

"Jack?" Noah called out.

They drew closer to the stones and Ginger's heart raced. *Why aren't they answering? Do they not hear us?* She didn't see Jack or Sarah in the ruins. Where had they gone?

The rocky terrain of the fields surrounding the stones gave way to the cliff, pebbles crunching beneath their boots. Then Noah caught Ginger by the waist, holding her back, his eyes scanning the vicinity.

A man lay sprawled near the edge of the cliff. *Jack.* Sarah kneeled beside him, leaning over him, but Jack didn't appear to be moving.

Ginger's heart slammed into her ribs.

No!

What had happened?

Ginger tore away from Noah, running. "Sarah!"

Sarah turned slowly, as though dazed, and then Ginger saw what she'd been unable to see before: her hands were feebly pressed near her diaphragm, blood seeping between her fingers as her blue eyes sought Ginger's. Her face was pallid, her gaze unfocused.

"Oh my God. Sarah, no!" Ginger cried, barely aware of Noah's hand on her arm.

Sarah stood, appearing to stumble on the rocks.

Too stunned to process what was happening, Ginger focused only on Sarah's face, dimly aware of Noah speaking. A buzz in Ginger's ears filtered out all other sounds, the unbearable sun beating down upon them. Noah grabbed her, pulling her into cover near one of the larger boulders in the ruins.

There hadn't been a gunshot—they would have heard that. So why was Sarah bleeding?

Sarah's gaze locked with Ginger's as a slight smile came to the corners of her mouth. Then she fell, tumbling over the side of the cliff and out of view.

"Sarah!" Tears slid from Ginger's eyes, and she crawled to her knees. "No! No, please, God, no." *Not Sarah. Please.* She tore herself from Noah's grip. "Let me go. Let me go to her."

"Ginger, anyone could still be here—" He looked over his shoulder, scanning the vicinity, but they appeared to be alone.

Who? Could someone have stabbed Sarah and then vanished?

How was that possible? They had seen no one.

Ginger's thoughts didn't feel lucid, and her head was spinning as she ran.

Noah followed behind her and grabbed her arm, but she pushed forward, rushing over to the edge of the cliff, beside Jack. Blood shone from the rocks and grass there. And, below them, water lapped against the edge of the rocks. The fall would have been straight into the water, not land, but Ginger didn't see Sarah anywhere. Could she have survived the fall?

She's gone.

A soft groan came from Jack's lips, and he sat up groggily, holding his head. "Where's Sarah?" he managed.

Ginger broke down, a sob ripping from her throat. Noah knelt beside Jack, checking on his injury. She turned toward them, too much in shock to think clearly.

As she looked toward the surrounding stones, Noah's warning that someone dangerous might still lurk made goose bumps rise on her skin. They were vulnerable here in the open. But the ruins appeared desolate, exposed to the heavens on a day that seemed too beautiful for such shattering heartache. A black bird in the crystal dome of the heavens circled them and then soared away, a mournful call filling the air.

CHAPTER FIVE

Of the lessons Noah had learned during his time in the clandestine service, the most important one was to never make decisions out of panic—a lesson Jack had taught him. Jack had taught Noah more than his superiors had, as Jack had already had his fair share of adventures before the war.

But even Jack Darby had his breaking point, and Noah was worried that his friend might be nearing it.

Jack sat at the end of a bar, staring at a clear glass of amber liquid —whisky, Noah presumed. When they'd come back from Hagar Qim, Noah and Jack had packed everything in their rooms while Ginger had bathed, her hands still covered in blood from tending to the blow Jack had received on his head.

Ginger's emotions were in tatters. She'd sobbed in Noah's arms, and he'd hated forcing her to gather her things rather than nurse her pain.

As soon as she calmed enough, they'd moved to another inn, where they planned to stay only temporarily. They weren't safe here and needed to leave the island as soon as possible.

They'd moved with enough speed and caution that Noah hoped

they'd bought themselves a day or two before they could be found. But whoever had killed Sarah clearly had superior skills at tracking. And when Jack had disappeared from the room he'd rented across the hall, Noah felt obliged to go looking for him. He'd left Ginger with a gun and strict instructions not to open the door for anyone.

Jack hadn't gone far. That he'd drowned his own sorrows in whisky wasn't out of character—but it was surprising, given the circumstances. Jack was more cautious than this.

Noah surveyed the bar. Only a few patrons were seated inside: a gruff-looking octogenarian with white hair that contrasted starkly with sun-stained skin, a plain middle-aged man dully sipping a drink and writing in a book, and a younger man, perhaps in his early twenties, who appeared already drunk.

Jack didn't flinch as Noah sat beside him and ordered a gin.

"I didn't love her, if that's what you're wondering," Jack said at last, lifting the glass to his lips. His words were bitter, tinged with a churning anger. Noah studied Jack's profile as Jack tossed the rest of his drink back into his throat then asked for another.

"I know." But whatever Jack might say, Noah also knew he'd cared more deeply about Sarah than he had allowed himself to care for any woman recently, which was also probably what was bothering Jack the most.

"She was a pain in the ass." Jack sucked in a breath through his teeth. "We got into a three-day argument a couple of days ago about whether Smenkhkare was Nefertiti, and she danced circles around me with how much she knew about the subject. Read every damned book on the subject. Like you would, actually."

Noah settled his forearms against the bar, clasping his hands together. "Would it be so terrible if you let yourself admit you may have loved her?"

Jack's eyes narrowed at his glass. He frowned, running his thumb over the edge of the glass. "You think you're an expert on the subject?" Jack's lips curled. "Far as I remember, you used to claim you wanted nothing to do with love. That you were incapable of being around any one woman for too long and not finding yourself bored."

Noah swallowed back a sigh. Jack was clearly more drunk than Noah had guessed he would be by now. "Yes, back when I was a fool."

"Love makes fools out of anyone willing to take a chance on it—young or old." Jack slung back another drink. "For the sake of our friendship, my advice would be to leave me alone tonight, Noah. I don't want to talk about Sarah." His glass thudded against the scarred wood of the bar top.

"All right, then. We won't discuss Sarah. But we need to plan—"

"We'll go to Cairo, then burn everything down together. This has gone far enough, wouldn't you say?"

Noah set his palms on the edge of the bar top. A glance over his shoulder revealed that no one new had arrived or watched them.

Stick to the plan.

"I was offered a chance out, but Jack will never accept that. He'd die for you, and you know it," Sarah had said.

He hadn't needed for Sarah to tell him he was risking both Jack and Ginger. That had always worried him. And when he'd gone to speak to Sarah the other night instead of Jack, she'd told him everything. Including the name of the American spy who had ordered Sarah to turn Noah over to him: Charles Pointer.

But had Charles murdered Sarah for not following his orders? And if he had, why would he have killed Sarah and then left him free and the others unharmed?

They'd stayed in Malta too long and this was the consequence. But with Jack recently having recovered from malaria and still weak, Noah hadn't wanted to push him to leave. And Noah's own feet were still healing from a vicious foot caning he'd received at the hands of one of Stephen Fisher's henchmen when Noah had been captured in November.

And, if I'm honest, I selfishly wanted some time with Ginger, too.

Noah cleared his throat, the weight of what he had to do hanging over his head. "I didn't spend the last month forcing everyone to live incognito just to turn around and race back to Cairo now. There's a good chance whatever Sarah was doing died with her." Noah snuck a look at Jack's unwavering expression. "Unless she told you about it."

"That depends." Jack's eyes glittered in the dim light of the tavern. "Are you going to help me or not?"

It wasn't like Jack to not be forthcoming. What had Sarah told Jack? They'd been close. Most likely lovers. If Sarah had told Jack as much as she'd told Noah, then Jack would be in Noah's way. The last place Noah wanted Jack was in Cairo—because that was where Noah intended to go himself.

Jack needed to be safe. To be away from the threat Noah posed to his life, for once and for all. Noah couldn't be the type of friend and husband that continued putting the lives of those he loved the most in danger.

But maybe if Jack believed Noah didn't want to go to Cairo, didn't want to help him avenge Sarah's death, he'd get angry enough to be driven away from Noah. After all, Jack had always selflessly helped Noah, no questions asked. He would feel betrayed if Noah refused to help him in return.

"I can't go with you, Jack, not this time. It's not that simple. I have a wife to think of—"

"I get it." Jack pushed back his stool abruptly, the legs scraping against the wooden floor. He stood, wobbling. "You're not in intelligence anymore. Not a soldier. I'll go back to Egypt and do it myself. You sit pretty and … you know what? Forget it. Forget I said anything."

Tossing money at the bar, Jack's booted footsteps resounded against the stone walls of the small tavern. Noah paid for his drink, then followed Jack. He couldn't leave him to wander the streets, not when he was drunk like this.

The air was heavy with humidity, the smell of rain hanging in the air and mixing with the evening scent of wood smoke. The residents of the local street were settling into their homes for the night, but a few English soldiers and other young men milled in the streets.

Noah caught up with Jack as he turned into an alleyway. "Jack—"

"I can take care of myself, Benson. Been doing it my whole life." Jack didn't slow, but Noah fell into step with him, anyway.

"You're drunk."

"I'm fine. Going to meet up with a friend of mine who's still on this island and might help me get the hell off it."

Noah had seen Jack this angry before and far more drunk. Usually a good night's sleep was all it took to bring Jack to his senses, but something about Jack's words hinted at a bitterness that went far deeper. As though he was angrier at Noah than anything else.

Good. Stoking Jack's anger would be helpful in driving him away.

Doubt immediately rushed in, Noah's mind warring with itself. *I've always been successful with Jack as my confidant and ally—is this necessary?*

Noah thought of Sarah's fall over the cliff. *Yes, it's necessary.* Jack was in this too deeply. As was Ginger.

He had to protect them both. Keep them both from knowing any more details that could kill them.

Noah grabbed Jack by the bicep, drawing him to a stop. "You're not in any condition to—"

"If you won't help me, then you're in my way." Jack's shoulders fell with a tense breath.

"What's your plan? Go find her killer and … what? Take your revenge? It won't bring her back."

Jack swung a hard look at him. "Just because you weren't man enough to kill the man who tried to hurt the woman you say you love doesn't mean I'm the same as you."

Jack's words struck like bullets ricocheting from the sandstone walls of the surrounding alley, burying themselves in Noah's gut. The image of Fisher flared immediately and his visceral reaction of anger burned in his chest.

Fisher, who had carved his initials into Ginger's skin, to torment them both. Who'd stolen his good name. Jack had meant to provoke Noah and it had nearly worked.

His plan to make Jack angry and drive a wedge between them was working better than expected.

Noah's hand dropped to his side, and he raised his chin, swallowing his anger. "Is that so?"

Without dropping his gaze, Jack stepped toward him. "That's what all of this is about, isn't it? If you had just killed Stephen Fisher when you had a chance, none of us would be here, would we? We'd all still be in Egypt, and Sarah would be alive."

One more barb, aimed with precision, meant to wound in the deadliest way possible.

Ignore him. He's drunk. And I need him angry with me.

As though the weather sensed their argument, a flash of lightning filled the shadows of the alley, followed by a sharp crack. Just as quickly, the sky burst forth with heavy drops of rain.

"If I forgive you for that, it's only because I know you cared about Sarah, even if you won't admit how much." Noah's voice was clear, despite the pounding of the storm.

"Go back to your woman, will you? With the rate people are dying around you, who knows how long you'll be able to hold on to her."

Neither man moved. Rain dripped from Noah's face, and he pictured himself in that desert the previous November, when Jack had tried to convince him to shoot Fisher and be done with it.

Noah's loyalty to Lord Helton had stayed his hand. Then Lord Helton had betrayed him.

Jack's imprisonment had come about because of Noah's hesitation. Noah had lost everything. A stabbing pain ripped through him. From anyone else, the criticism would impact less. But Jack? Noah stiffened, narrowing his eyes at his friend. He sensed he was losing whatever semblance of control he had felt over this fight and that it was becoming altogether too real. But he still needed to push Jack further. "As I recall from years of knowing you, I'm not the only one capable of making mistakes that hurt the people I love. Or should we ask Alice?"

The mention of Jack's sister, who hadn't spoken to him in several years, was enough for Jack to flinch. Then he balled his hand into a fist, throwing a punch at Noah's face so quickly Noah didn't duck. Jack's fist connected painfully with Noah's cheek, sending spots dancing in his field of vision. He narrowly avoided another swing, then tackled Jack to the unforgiving stone ground, pinning his arms to his sides.

"Get off me!" Jack swore, his shoulders heaving, trying to escape. Thankfully, Jack's drunkenness was to Noah's advantage, as the men were equally matched in size and stature.

Noah's face throbbed with pain and he blinked hard, trying to think clearly. His instinct was rarely to suppress his opponent rather than fight back, so holding Jack down took both mental and physical strength. He sucked in a shallow breath when Jack stilled, then released him, stepping back.

Jack sprang up, looking around for his fallen hat, then scooped it up. He ran his fingers through his wet, dark hair and shook his head at Noah. "You're a real son of a bitch, you know that?" Then he turned and continued down the alleyway, his stride somehow steadier.

This time, Noah didn't follow him. He watched Jack until he disappeared out of view, listening to the rain do battle against the sides of the buildings. When Jack was gone, Noah sank against the stone wall closest to him and rubbed his cheek, feeling numb from the chilly rain. Goose flesh had broken out on his arms.

He'd made Jack angry, that was for certain.

Noah had pushed Jack hard, and his response had been equally reactive. Jack was raw, seething with anger and grief over Sarah, unwilling to admit how much she'd meant to him.

Had he pushed hard enough, though?

Jack might still want to see this through and find Sarah's killer.

"Listen to me, Noah, and listen clearly. They're not safe. You can't run forever. You know you can't. And when they have the first chance to use them against you, they will. If you want them to be safe, you're going to have to strike and strike hard."

Sarah was right. But every uncertainty Noah felt about her came back now, in full force.

Sarah's voice was loud in his mind. *"You have to do it alone."*

He'd known that. And how many times had he not listened to his own instincts?

He *should* have killed Fisher long ago. Noah's failure to kill him had spilled into so many things. And he'd had more than enough reason to kill Fisher long before Noah had even met Ginger— starting with when Fisher had betrayed him in Aleppo the year before, leaving him to torture at the hands of the Turks.

Noah had been blind to Lord Helton's deceptions. A fool.

He couldn't continue to be a fool any longer. He'd endangered everyone. He could never do that to anyone else again.

Strike and strike hard.

Noah wiped the rain from his eyes and stood, his shoulders taut, his legs heavy. He'd lingered in Malta long enough.

CHAPTER SIX

For the third time that night, Noah rose from the bed, causing Ginger to rouse from fitful sleep. She rolled her cheek onto her pillow, peering into the darkness as Noah's figure sidled beside the window of the cramped room. He looked out from behind a slit in the curtain, his gaze lingering on the street in the alley below the inn, then pulled the curtain back.

Ginger sat, drawing her knees into her chest. "He's still not returned?"

"No." Noah turned his back to the window but didn't return to the bed. He leaned against the wall beside the window, and Ginger wished she could see his features more clearly, gauge his worry for Jack.

The day's ordeal had left Ginger utterly exhausted, but each time she closed her eyes, she relived the moment Sarah died. Her eyes burned with the tears shed throughout the day.

Ginger didn't fully comprehend what had happened, and Jack couldn't remember the moments before he'd been knocked unconscious. The last memory he'd been able to recall was seeing Sarah lying on the ground. But *someone* had killed Sarah—that much was indisputable. This was connected to the conversation she'd over-heard two days earlier, she was sure of it. Guilt clawed at her chest.

And she was still bothered that Noah had returned to their room earlier in the evening, soaked and with a fresh bruise on his cheek, which he'd told her Jack had given him while drunk. Noah seemed to brush it off as inconsequential, but Ginger would be sure to give Jack a piece of her mind when she saw him.

Ginger swung her legs around the bed and set her feet on the floorboards. She pulled her dressing gown from the chair beside the bed and donned it with a shiver, then crossed the room toward Noah. As she reached him, his hand curled around her waist and she nestled against him. Tension radiated from his body. "Jack will be back, I'm sure of it."

Noah's palm flattened against the small of her back. "Yes, I know. He's been at this sort of thing for too long not to."

"Then what are you worried about?"

Noah was silent for a few moments.

"I'm worried about how Sarah's death is going to affect him." Noah nuzzled the crown of her hair, resting his chin against her head. "Jack doesn't let many people in easily—especially not women —and he seemed to care genuinely about Sarah."

Despite her bleakness, Ginger couldn't help but choke back an ironic laugh. "Spoken by the blackest of pots."

"And, yet, I married you. That only goes to show how much more reserved Jack is than I in that way."

Jack didn't seem reserved, but Noah knew him better than Ginger did. Noah wouldn't mention concern like that facetiously. The thought of Sarah being dead was incomprehensible, but Ginger had been so absorbed in her own heartache over the matter that she hadn't thought of the toll it might take on Jack. "Was he in love with her?"

"I don't know. He doesn't fall in love easily. If he was, he may not handle it well. But he certainly seemed to be taken with her."

Ginger's throat thickened with tears, a lump forming there. The happy days they'd spent over the last few weeks, strolling through the beautiful stone alleyways and buildings of Valletta, admiring the views, sharing laughter—how had it all come to such a horrifying, abrupt end?

"Do you think we're safe at this inn?" Ginger asked. She'd watched Noah place a gun under his pillow when they went to bed earlier.

"Safe enough, hopefully. We can't stay long." Noah kissed the top of her head and then released her. "You should go to sleep, _rohi_. I'll keep checking for Jack. We don't know what we'll be up against tomorrow, and it'll be easier for you if you're rested."

She stepped back but didn't go to the bed. "Was Sarah murdered because of us?"

Noah rubbed the back of his neck. "I don't know."

"But what else could it be?"

Noah's voice sounded tired. "It seems the most likely option."

"But why kill Sarah? She was just our friend." She mused about the questions rhetorically, hugging her arms to her chest.

Noah released a deep sigh, his face darkened by shadows.

"I don't know. But what I know is I'm risking the safety and well-being of both my wife and closest friend every day. And it's driving me mad. I refuse to have your deaths on my hands."

She'd pushed him too far. Ginger cringed, then took his hands and led him to the bed. "None of this is your fault, my love." She sat behind him, gently massaging the tight muscles of his shoulders which were bunched with tension. "You didn't kill Sarah any more than I did. Sarah wanted to be here with us. She chose to come. And we don't even know—"

Noah turned toward her, gathering her in his arms. His lips descended upon hers and stopped her from speaking further as he kissed her passionately. In his fervor, he communicated something else that Ginger hadn't expected: his own fears and sorrow.

Her seemingly stoic husband was shaken by what had happened to Sarah.

She broke away and wrapped her arms around his neck, drawing him to herself.

"If I lose you, I'll never forgive myself. I should have killed Fisher so many times, but I did what was 'right' and 'decent.'"

Then he thought Stephen must be behind it. Ginger tightened her arms around him. She kissed the curve of his neck, the scruff of his beard tickling her cheek. They'd lost everything but each other. And while Ginger's losses had been partially by choice, Noah had been a victim of Stephen's treachery. "You won't lose me, darling."

She pulled back, pressing her forehead against his and closing her eyes. She thought of Sarah bleeding to death, likely stabbed in her abdomen. Ginger curled a hand reflexively over her own belly. *What if it had been me instead of Sarah?*

"If we go on the run, Noah, let's make it the last time." She sat away from him, then drew her legs up under her, sitting back on her heels. "Let's go to America. Start over. I'll always miss my family, but my mother and sister don't want to see me. They're never going to forgive me for shooting Henry, and especially not because I saved you by doing so. They've probably convinced my other relations that I'm a lost cause by now. We'll have each other. And that's more than we need."

Noah's guttural sigh revealed his frustration. "What am I supposed to do in America? How can I provide for you? My money, my education, everything I worked for is tied to my name. What little property I have is too."

"Maybe Jack can help us—"

"If Jack wanted to be in America, he would be. And I can't continue to turn to my friend with my palm outstretched," Noah snapped. He drew a sharp breath, then rubbed his eyes. "Forgive me. I don't want my pride to get in the way, I promise. But I won't stake our future in Jack's fortune and generosity. He's sacrificed enough for me. What sort of man would I be if I continued to put my safety above that of my friend and wife? Not one that could ever look anyone in the eye."

Ginger bit her lip. She knew it wasn't about pride—Noah's concerns were legitimate. *And if he finds out that I might be pregnant, he'll be even more upset.* She didn't want the news of a child to be like this. Telling him would do nothing but deepen his fears.

A soft knock at the door broke her chain of thought. Noah practically leapt from the bed, his bare feet padding softly across the floor. "Who is it?" he called in a low voice.

"Guess," Jack answered.

Noah unlocked the door, and Jack came in. The stench of cigarette smoke and whisky wafted in with him. Noah closed the door behind him as Ginger turned on a lamp beside the bed.

Jack removed his hat, his eyes looking bleary. He turned the hat in his hands, scanning the room for a place to sit. The only chair was beside the bed, a small rickety one where Ginger had placed her clothing.

"Are you all right?" Ginger asked, her brow furrowing.

Jack rolled his shoulders back and slung a bag over his shoulder. "There's a ship bound for Alexandria, the HMT *Aragon*. It's currently anchored at Marsa Scirocco and should be there for a few days. I think they'll sail right after Christmas."

Christmas. The thought of the holiday, only a few days away, seemed bleaker than ever. Ginger swallowed hard, then looked from Jack to Noah, then back again. "Are you suggesting we should try to board the *Aragon*?" *Why on earth would we go back to Egypt?*

"She's here in Malta, she's British, and she's heading for Egypt— where I'm going." Jack peeled his smoking jacket off and draped it over his forearm, leaving him in a shirt and vest. "The bulk of Noah's money and possessions are also in Egypt. Not to mention the son of a bitch who probably orchestrated this attack on Sarah.

It's time to put a stop to this. I don't care what it takes—I'm putting a bullet in Stephen Fisher's head once and for all."

Much as she understood Jack's hotheaded, boiling sentiment, the idea of going back to Egypt appalled her. She sat on the duvet cover on top of the bed, feeling unsteady.

"But won't we be in even further danger in Egypt?" Ginger appealed to Noah with a glance, thankful that the orange light from the lamp let her see his face now. He stared at Jack, as though lost in thought, not meeting her gaze. "Noah, you can't be considering this. They're actively looking for you there. And not just to arrest you. If you're caught, you'll be hung. Or worse."

"Going to Alexandria might not be the worst of options," Noah said. "From there, we can get on another ship to England. And at least we won't be stuck here." Noah glanced at Jack. "Your contact can help us all get on the *Aragon*?" he asked Jack.

"Yes. No questions asked. Which is the best we could hope for." Jack stretched, then ran one hand through his chocolate-brown hair, which was still matted down from his hat. In that moment, Ginger noticed the swollen knuckles on his right hand.

She cocked a brow at him. "That hand looks painful."

Jack scowled. "You should see the other guy."

"I already have." *You bastard.* She narrowed her eyes at him but said nothing more. Considering Jack was offering them a way off the island, she didn't want to be catty.

"Anyway, think about it. We'd probably want to leave before dawn, so that gives me a good couple of hours to get some sleep." Jack gave them both a nod, then slipped back out the door.

Noah followed behind him and locked the door again. He placed both hands on it, his shoulders tense. "Is there any way I can convince you to sail on to England alone?" Noah's voice was quiet.

Her heart fell. Ginger folded her hands on her lap, swallowing hard. How many times had he requested something similar? Each time he'd begged the question, it seemed to be before he was about to plunge headlong into danger.

He wants to go to Egypt.

Ginger's last conversation with Sarah came hurtling back to her. *"I say it's about time he tries to take his life back."*

Oh, Sarah.

The weight of the day nearly crushed her lungs, making it hard to breathe.

Her hands lifted to her abdomen as she sucked in a breath, squeezing her eyes shut.

Noah would never let her go with him if he even suspected she might be pregnant.

But he'd also be furious with her if he knew she'd accompanied him to certain danger while that remained a possibility. Even if she couldn't tell him anything yet, she had an obligation to him—and to their child, if there was one—to be responsible.

But if she went back to England, where would she go? Her mother and sister, if they'd listened to her and gone home, would certainly not accept her. Would her grandmother or aunt? Or maybe one of her old friends?

She cleared her throat and drew another, more calming breath, then looked at Noah. He hadn't moved. "What are you suggesting?"

Noah was silent for a few moments, then he turned, taking a few steps toward her. He watched her closely, as though trying to guess if she might go, and then came toward her wearily. "I'm suggesting that we get on the *Aragon*. But when we arrive in Egypt, we find you another ship heading home. I want you as far from Egypt as possible."

The thought of being separated from him was a painful one, which cut deeply through her core. But how many wives were separated from their husbands right now? How many women had said their good-byes to the men they loved, never knowing if they would see them again?

The last few weeks had been like a dream, one that she'd known couldn't last.

If Stephen hadn't convinced the world that Noah was guilty of treason and murder, Noah would be out on the battlefields right now. They might have spent a few days together in Cairo while he was on leave, but then he'd have gone back.

Right now, her husband needed her to let him go, to enact whatever plan he could to save his name. To make a future for them. The seemingly easier route of running once again was something he couldn't be happy with.

She sighed, knowing what she had to do but unwilling to do it yet. Desperate to drive out the gloom that had settled in the darkness, Ginger crossed the room to him. She leveled her chin at him. "If I agree to think about it, will you tell me why Jack punched you?"

Noah grimaced. "He was angry about Sarah."

She lightly ran her fingertips over the bruise, and he didn't flinch. "I hate always seeing you banged up like this."

"I think it bothers you more than it bothers me." Noah caught her fingers in his hands, leaning his forehead against hers. "But you will consider going back to England, then?"

If she didn't know better, he seemed amazed that she wasn't protesting loudly.

"I promise I won't dismiss the idea without giving it thought." She squeezed his hand. "I love you. Now come to bed with me. If we go on the *Aragon*, it might be the last time we share a bed for some time. Especially if you insist on leaving me on my own."

"Thank you." Noah nodded, then lifted her hands to his lips, kissing the back of her hands gently. "Never on your own. I'll always find my way back to you, *rohi*. Always."

CHAPTER SEVEN

*D*ressed in the uniform of the nurses of the Voluntary Aid Detachment, Ginger shifted in the small vessel. She'd chosen to keep her rings on her fingers—the Claddagh ring Noah had given her that had been his mother's and the gold ankh wedding band from their wedding in the small church ceremony in Coptic Cairo. She prayed no one would question her about them, but she wasn't willing to take them off, either. Nurses weren't allowed to be married.

For now, Noah kept all their official papers safely hidden away in the lining of one of his military jackets. Jack had somehow produced papers for them with aliases, and she was to be Diana Clayborne. Noah had shaved his beard, but a thick walrus-style moustache remained above his lip, which oddly enough made him look like an entirely different man. He would use the alias of Captain Eugene Brooks.

Jack, now traveling as Lieutenant Harry Nelson, sat in the stern of the small rowboat, his gaze fixed on the *Aragon*, still about two hundred feet away. The vessel gleamed in the sun, and no smoke came from its one large funnel in the center of the ship. A Union

Jack waved wildly from the mast, caught in the bay's wind. The ship wasn't the largest Ginger had seen, but it crawled with troops and nurses, who hung near the rails on the boat deck.

Noah had told her the ship carried troops to Palestine. In early December, General Allenby had been successful in capturing Jerusalem, providing the Allies with an unexpected victory that had raised morale and now the British military wanted him to press on to Damascus. That meant more troops and more medical personnel flooding Egypt.

It also meant more German submarines patrolling the waters of the Mediterranean. The attacks on Allied ships had escalated over the last few months, with headlines in the newspapers weekly of ships being torpedoed and sunk. Whatever safety the *Aragon* provided them from whoever had killed Sarah, they risked as much danger by boarding the ship.

Ginger glanced over her shoulder, back at the shore. She wished they could have stayed on the island for Christmas the following day, but Jack had insisted they board the *Aragon* as soon as possible, since it was likely the ship would leave port once the holiday was over. She felt little desire to celebrate. The chill of Sarah's death hung over everything.

But being on board the *Aragon* would force her to be isolated from Noah and Jack for the next week. Depending on how strict the matron aboard the ship was, she might spend time with Noah occasionally, but they would have no freedom to show much affection. And Ginger knew all too well how lonely a hospital or ship like the *Aragon* could be when you were surrounded by a group of women who'd spent the last few days or weeks together.

They reached the side of the ship where a rope ladder swung. Jack paid the fisherman, then handed their papers to the soldier who'd dropped the ladder. As Ginger started the climb up to the deck on the rickety ladder, she tried not to look at the waters of the choppy sea glistening below her. Heights had never scared her, but recently they'd bothered her more. Her palms grew slick, and she focused on Jack's booted feet.

Or maybe it was because climbing onto this ship felt unnecessarily dangerous, where all it took was a single suspicion or inconsistency in their aliases to threaten Noah's freedom.

Noah followed behind her. The rope swayed, the fibers of it creaking and clanking against the steel hull of the ship, and she imagined tumbling down, falling into Noah, and the two of them dropping into the cold sea. She shivered, her neck moist with perspiration under her nurse's cap. Dressing in her uniform this morning had been an odd comfort.

Ginger glanced down the length of the deck as she climbed over the side. A sea of khaki uniforms greeted her eyes. Jack was talking in low tones to the soldier that had greeted them, and Noah followed behind her.

The ship's soft pitching in the waves forced her to steady herself on the rail. One second on the damned ship and nausea wrung her stomach. She scrunched her nose.

"Sister Clayborne." The officer who had brought them aboard approached her from several feet away. "If you'll follow me, I can take you to Matron."

Ginger nodded. As she followed him, she glanced back at Noah, not wanting to leave him. He held her gaze for a moment and then looked away. Sadness clamped itself over Ginger's heart as she followed numbly, keeping her gaze low. Several nurses who had seen her climb aboard gave her curious looks as she filed through the deck.

The CO led her to the matron's quarters. She turned out to be an unsmiling, grim woman similar to the one she'd worked with when she'd first started nursing in Egypt. She assessed Ginger with a sharp look, her brow furrowing. "I didn't get notice that you would join us," she said, scanning the papers that Ginger had provided her.

Hopefully the papers Jack had obtained would hold up under

scrutiny. Ginger gave her a congenial smile. "The hospital they assigned me to in Malta closed. The RAMC is assigning many of us to Egypt." Fortunately, she hadn't been that long out of nursing and was still up with the war effort. The Royal Army Medical Corps had indeed started sending many of the nurses and doctors from Malta to Egypt to help with the campaign in Palestine.

Matron frowned. "Yes, well. We all came from Marseilles. I'm not sure why the RAMC would send a single VAD while we're anchored here, but I'm sure we'll find a use for you." The matron folded the papers and handed them back to Ginger. "It may take me until later this afternoon to scrounge up a room for you, so you're welcome to leave your bags here in my office in the meantime. I've been invited to an excursion on the shore for the evening with a few of the officers."

Matron's eyes flickered to Ginger's bags, which comprised a single suitcase and her kitbag. If Ginger's limited possessions surprised her, she said nothing. Then again, many nurses traveled lightly. "In the meantime, you're welcome to familiarize yourself with the ship. The well deck is for NCOs and troops only—I'll remind you that you are not to fraternize with the soldiers."

Ginger kept her expression blank as the lecture continued.

"At all times you are to behave with the utmost decorum and in a manner which is befitting your station. Remember, you are a lady. I advise you to stay away from some of these VADs who don't seem to know how to stop flirting with the officers. Meals are segregated from the officers at the mess, an hour before them. You're to be at the first-class saloon for the nurses' dinner exactly at six. And there will be a Christmas Day service tomorrow, which I expect you'll attend."

Much as the rules had taken on a sense of absurdity since she'd married, Ginger nodded somberly. Rules were familiar and gave her a framework. "What about work?"

"Oh—" The matron scanned her chart. "You can start the day after Christmas. Our incidence of illness has been high, particularly seasickness. A good deal of the troops and Sisters were positively green on the trip over from France. I was even taken ill for a few days." The matron leaned down and pulled a life belt from beside her desk. "This is for you to wear at all times once we leave the safety of the harbor. At night you shall sleep with it beside you, understood?"

Ginger took it and nodded, grasping the bulky material in her fingertips. She had spent little time at sea since Gallipoli, but the life belts had been one of her least favorite aspects of life aboard ships. When the matron had finished lecturing her, she dismissed Ginger, who left the life belt with her suitcase. If she was going to wear it all the way to Alexandria, she'd start when they left Malta.

Wandering up to the boat deck, Ginger strolled slowly hoping to see Noah, her footsteps light against the floorboards. She felt aimless and apprehensive. Wearing the uniform of a VAD was odd —she'd been a trained and high-ranking Sister of the Queen Alexandra's Imperial Nursing Service. Known for their red capes— and their snobbery toward the volunteer ranks—Ginger had at least felt that she fit better with their level of experience. But, normally, nursing matrons usually put her to work immediately, knowing she could handle most tasks given to her.

She set her hands on the rail, taking in the view. The deck had been stripped of chairs when the British Navy had outfitted it as a troopship, but it appeared the officers and nurses had taken to sitting in the lifeboats instead. She smiled at their ingenuity.

Nearby, a group of VADs had gathered inside one lifeboat and laughed, chatting amongst themselves in a carefree manner. Their camaraderie made her miss Sarah more than ever. For the first time since Beatrice Thornton, her nursing friend whom she'd grown distant from because of Henry, Ginger had felt she had a genuine friend. That wasn't something she took lightly. An ache in her chest seemed to widen at the thought until it swallowed all the joy she might feel.

"Would you like to join us?" a woman's voice called cheerfully, and Ginger snapped to attention.

Glancing over, Ginger realized she'd nearly completely ignored the friendly wave of one nurse in the lifeboat. Feeling her cheeks warm, Ginger took a few steps toward them. The nurse stood and offered a wide smile. "Come, sit with us." She pointed to the lifeboat. "It's the most comfortable place on the deck. I'm Kit. Kit Dodsworth This is my sister Eve." She pointed to one of the other VADs directly across from her. "And the rest of the gang."

As the other women in the boat introduced themselves, Ginger sat on the benched seat inside the lifeboat. "Diana Clayborne," Ginger said, ducking her chin. "I've just come aboard from Malta."

"Oh, you're so fortunate," Kit said, eyes wide. "We've all been dying to go to shore, but they say we have to stay aboard the ship. One officer went out yesterday, though, brought us back some pastries, the dear brick."

"*Pastizzi*," Ginger said with an eager smile. "Yes, it's one of the local specialties."

"It's divine," another nurse piped up. Ginger didn't quite remember her name—or any of the other nurses except for the Dodsworth sisters. Perhaps Anne? She didn't want to ask again and seem like she hadn't been paying attention.

"Are you joining us on the trip to Alexandria, then?" Eve asked, looking up from a notebook in which she was sketching. "Just in time for Christmas."

"Yes, it's going to all be rather exciting. We'll be allowed to have Christmas dinner with the officers," Kit said, beaming. "Eve is designing the menu cards. And one of the men is going to play the piano so we can dance! Here, grab a pair of scissors. You can help us cut them out if you'd like."

As the nurses went on about their plans for Christmas dinner,

Ginger settled quietly into the background, answering questions when they posed them but mostly listening to them chat gayly. Their enthusiasm was infectious, and Ginger appreciated them putting her to work rather than let her stand idly by, drowning in her own sorrow. They brought Ginger a cheerful comfort that reminded Ginger of some of the best times she'd spent in the hospitals of Egypt. Often even the most war-weary nurses were bricks, still providing the men with smiles and color in their grey and somber worlds.

Eve Dodsworth had skillfully drawn plum puddings and sailors and boughs of holly on the cards, along with other Christmas symbols, and some of the other girls were coloring in the backgrounds. It occurred to Ginger that she'd never once in her life done anything like this—tasks like these had always been required of the many servants at her family's estate of Penmore, in England. The daughter of an earl wouldn't have ever expected to do something so menial, and her parents would have been appalled if she'd befriended the staff.

While in the QAs, many other nurses had known of her background. But here, no one knew her mother was a countess or that she'd gone to finishing school. A freedom existed in her anonymity that she hadn't realized. She no longer had to be Lady Virginia Whitman, daughter to the Earl of Braddock.

Occupied by her shore excursion, the matron wasn't available "to prowl the decks," as Kit put it, and the result was that an amiable crop of officers and admirers kept dropping by to visit them. Ginger did her best to demur from introductions, but in time, the girls started prodding her.

"It looks like you have an admirer, Sister Clayborne." They gestured meaningfully toward a figure a few feet away.

Ginger hesitated to look. She didn't want to give any encouragement to the flirtations she'd been witnessing. Still, she snuck a glance.

Jack.

He raised a dark brow at her.

Her fingers fumbled with her scissors. "Oh, if you'll excuse me for a moment." Ginger set down the menu card she'd been cutting and then stepped out of the lifeboat. Her legs wobbled from being aboard the ship, and she smoothed her hands on her apron as she approached Jack.

"Making new friends?" Jack asked in a low tone. A smile teased at his lips but didn't quite make it to his eyes. He'd been quiet all morning, not that she blamed him.

"It seems everyone on this ship is occupied with Christmas tomorrow." She walked a few paces away, wanting to increase the distance between herself and the nurses she'd been spending time with. Much as she liked these nurses, they might gossip about her. She'd been seen coming aboard with him, after all. "Where's Noah?"

"Settling into his cabin. A-36, in case you need him." Jack's handsome face was somber. He'd shaven also and made no effort at a disguise, even though Ginger knew he was traveling with an alias. Taking her by the elbow, Jack drew her closer to the railing. "We need to be on the lookout. When we boarded, I thought the ship wouldn't be allowing the crew or officers off the ship while at anchor. But they've informed me since then that they're allowing some officers. Your nursing matron, too."

"Yes, she told me about that." Ginger studied him, then rested her fingertips on the railing, gripping it as she tried to quell the unease in her stomach. "Why is that a problem?"

"Someone has apparently invited them to dine somewhere on the island. Either way, if there are other people coming and going from the ship, we need to be prepared for the possibility that someone malicious could come aboard as well."

Malicious? "But Noah said he doubted we'd been traced to the inn last night."

"Well, Noah lied—what can I say?" Jack's voice was hard, his eyes flat and humorless.

She blinked at him, shocked at his reaction. *Jack has never talked about Noah like this.*

Jack's expression softened, and he continued, "He was probably trying to make you feel better, Red. He wants to keep you safe, but he's worried. He gave me a gun for you. I'm going to hug you, slip it in your pocket."

"If you hug me, it may force me to slap you, Jack. I'm sure those women are curious about you. I'd rather not have them thinking you're a beau."

Jack smirked. "Then slap me. I'm just following orders." He leaned forward and pulled her into a sudden embrace, and Ginger felt the weight of the gun slide into her dress pocket.

She wrenched away from him. "Lieutenant Nelson!" She slapped him, harder than she'd expected, across the cheek, the sound echoing against the deck boards.

Jack winced and touched his cheek, then gave a slight bow. "Sister Clayborne." With a wink, he strode away, a mocking bounce to his step.

Jack Darby. Even when he wasn't trying to make her laugh, she couldn't help but chuckle at his antics.

She turned slowly, back to the stares of the group of nurses she'd been with.

"You have an admirer already?" one nurse asked with surprise.

"I met him last spring. I suppose he was happy to see me, but I'd rather not have the matron witness something like that and have me reported the very day I've arrived."

"Oh, and she might just do that. She scolded me the other day for 'collecting men,'" Eve said with a laugh.

"Yes, but unlike you, Sister Clayborne gives powerful slaps," Kit cut in with a giggle.

Ginger managed a smile and slipped back into her seat, the

weight of the pistol against her thigh. She hoped no one would notice it.

Noah wants to keep me safe.

But in the back of her mind, she pictured Sarah dying amid the ruins she'd loved so much. *And she had a warning.*

How on earth did Noah expect Ginger to survive—gun or not—when she didn't even know what to be on the lookout for?

CHAPTER EIGHT

*R*ain battered the sides of the ship, and Noah tightened the collar of his trench coat as he made his way from the boat deck to the officers' mess. Setting his hand on the cold rail, his gaze flickered toward the group of nurses on the other side of the deck who'd been pulled from their afternoon tea for a lifeboat drill. He hadn't seen Ginger among them and couldn't help wondering if she was still so terribly seasick that she'd received special permission to skip the drill.

He wished he could do more for her. As it was, they were stuck at port in Malta, waiting for the storms to pass before they set out to sea. But, as each day passed, he worried that their chances of being traced to the ship were increasing, especially for someone savvy enough. Too many loose ends existed for Noah to relax his guard.

He held the door open for a nurse exiting the mess, then went inside, brushing the rain from his shoulders. Jack was already inside, in a corner of the room, and appeared to be playing poker with some unlucky sods who didn't know what they were in for. Noah had made that mistake only once.

His lips twitched in a smile and he took some tea, then sat in the opposite corner of the room. The book he'd stowed in the inner pocket of his officer jacket would provide enough entertainment until Jack finished his game, and then they'd talk.

Trust Jack to continue to stick by Noah's side, even after an ugly argument. If Jack couldn't be persuaded out of going to Cairo, Noah didn't know what he would do. The only option left to him was to *ask* Jack not to go, which, while reasonable, usually meant Jack would only insist on helping him. Jack's loyalty was fierce, but Noah didn't want that loyalty to result in his death.

As he opened the book, he felt the familiar tightness in his chest, the strain in his throat that had been creeping in since he'd boarded the ship days earlier. He recognized the symptoms as the onset of claustrophobia, and he squeezed his eyes shut for a moment, surprised to find his heart pounding. He drew a shallow breath through his nostrils, wishing all at once to tear off his jacket, loosen his collar, and jump off the ship.

Remain calm.

With his pulse still pounding in his ears, Noah opened his eyes again and sipped his tea. After years in Arabia, he'd grown to prefer the deeper, bitter flavor of coffee, something that made him an outsider when he was with English officers. Truthfully, he'd spent most of his childhood trying not to be an outsider—to fit perfectly with the English boys he'd gone to school with and be the ideal nephew for his English uncle and his aunt.

A lifetime of blending, only to have a few newspaper articles and Stephen Fisher's sabotage now undo everything. Noah curled his fingers into a fist, letting his knuckles pop, then uncurled them. The solace he normally found in books felt distant. In the last month, he'd let Ginger's presence distract him and console him. He could lose himself in her love. She had a way of looking into his gaze and sensing when to press and when to wait for him to bring up whatever bothered him.

Between the unmistakable feeling that he might be watched, the constant nightmares, and the utter helplessness, there was too much for him to share right now. He'd never had the gift for verbalizing his troubles. Not discussing them was preferable. The only option, really. Talk was a useless exercise.

He trained his eyes back on the book, the words blurring. Turning to a photograph of Millard Van Sant and Georges Daressy inside KV9, he blinked at it for a moment, memorizing their faces. He'd read the volume Sarah had given him three times now, trying to commit it to memory.

If only he'd had more time to discuss it with her.

He peered at the photograph. KV9 was one of the most spectacular royal tombs he'd ever been inside. Theories abounded that Ramesses VI had built several other tombs for himself—some perhaps still left undiscovered and filled with gold—but Noah knew from speaking to Van Sant that Ramesses hadn't been his focus.

Van Sant had long been obsessed with a more obscure figure in Ancient Egypt, one that he often referred to as his muse—Nefertiti. Two years before the war, German Egyptologists had found a spectacular bust of Nefertiti in Tell el-Amarna, which had brought even more focus to the excavations there. The Germans were long gone from the digs—so many of the archeological concessions had been abandoned during the war—but Van Sant had continued digging, looking for more of the Amarna Egyptian royals. He'd stumbled into a smuggling ring that had become the focus of Sarah Hanover's work.

He kept his mind occupied just enough to pass the time until Jack's shadow fell over his book. "How much did you win?" Noah asked without bothering to look up.

"Enough." The legs of the chair opposite him screeched as Jack pulled it back, then sat.

"Enough that they all left?" Noah quirked a brow at the now-empty table. "There's a difference between giving your opponents a rousing game and a thrashing that chases them away."

Jack chuckled sardonically and tilted his head. "Maybe I didn't feel like being merciful today."

Jack's mood had improved little since they'd argued, but at least he wasn't drinking. Which was a start. Drinking seemed to bring out his worst side. Noah didn't comment and then turned the book toward Jack, with the photograph of Van Sant open. "So tell me, how much do you know of the Eighteen Dynasty?"

"I was wondering where Sarah had put this." Jack closed the book. "How did you get your hands on it?"

Noah lifted his cup, intrigued that Jack hadn't told him about being in possession of Sarah's belongings. "She gave it to me."

Jack drummed his fingers on the book cover, then sighed. He put the book in his jacket pocket, rather than offering it back to Noah. "So you talked to her, did you? What did she tell you?"

"A few things." Noah set his cup on the table. "But if I'm going to Cairo, I need to know what you know."

Jack met his gaze, then gave a curt nod, the news that Noah planned on going to Cairo clearly sinking in. Then a more apologetic look crossed his face. "For what it's worth, I didn't mean what I said—"

"The apology isn't necessary." The bruise on Noah's face had faded, but a daily glance in the mirror reminded Noah of more than their ugly brawl.

Noah had never believed Jack would go away easily, but now Jack seemed to have his own motivation, his own quest for revenge.

Even if Jack apologized, Noah couldn't help feeling that Jack *had* meant every word he'd said in the argument. The fissures between them were like the thin veins on a block of ice, just waiting to break with the right blow.

"I'm no good at apologies anyway." Jack rubbed his jaw. "But I know you don't want to be going back to Egypt, so I appreciate it."

Oh. Jack thinks I want to go to Egypt to help him. He was in for a difficult discussion, then.

Jack sank back into his chair, a hint of a boyish grin on his tired face. "It all seems far away, doesn't it? Digging by day, green with envy at the men who were pulling up jewels and treasures while all we kept on finding were more mummies. Nightly adventures at Shepheard's, pissing our money away, or that place in the Khan you used to drag me to. Seems like another world away. And nothing's ever going to be the same, is it?"

Noah scanned Jack's face. The same ... *between us? Or in the world?*

He ignored the tug at his chest at the first idea. "I don't think Egypt's going back to the way things were in the khedives' time, no. Your president Wilson has too many people on the streets of Egypt talking about the right to self-determination. This is their moment to break free—from the Turks, from the British."

Jack rolled his eyes. "Except you and I both know the Brits aren't about to let the Suez go without a fight." He rolled his shoulders. "I'm not gonna lie to you, Noah. When we were in Malta, Sarah"— his gaze focused on the tabletop between them—"asked me to work with her for the US State Department. I said I would consider it. With you out of the picture, my place with the British military is tenuous. And she thought that with my expertise in the area, I could help her build a stronger case to push for American support of Egyptian independence after the war."

So Jack *had* learned more from Sarah than he'd wanted to share. It didn't surprise Noah that Sarah had wanted to paint a favorable picture of Egyptian independence to the Americans. She'd loved Egypt in much the same way that Jack and Noah did.

They were getting off track, though.

"So what did she tell you about Van Sant?" Noah raised a brow. The idea of the Dutch archeologist operating an investigation into a high-level smuggling ring was interesting, but not out of character.

Van Sant had always been a strong, vocal opponent of antiquities being taken out of Egypt.

Noah could picture the grizzled old man sitting across from him on a braided rug in a Bedouin tent on one trip he'd taken with him years earlier. *"The Egyptians have every right to resent it when we take their treasures,"* Van Sant had said. *"Would any Englishman be happy to see the bones of Henry VIII or Queen Elizabeth ripped from their crypts and carted off to display in a museum halfway across the world?"*

And though Noah hadn't known how to respond to that, or the other progressive concepts Van Sant had espoused, he hadn't dared to argue with the man either, his words resounding in his head.

Jack's voice brought him back to the present. "Van Sant was helping Sarah track a ring of smugglers at the highest levels—one that included political figures and important men in the government." Jack cringed and hesitated. "Men like Lord Reginald Helton."

A slick sweat broke out on the back of Noah's neck, and he stared at Jack for a full minute, not speaking.

Then Jack knows. And he didn't tell me.

That Sarah and Van Sant had been tracking Helton as a smuggler was one thing. But why had Jack kept it to himself? He would have known Noah would be interested.

Anger bubbled inside Noah, spewing inside him with such force that he drew a sharp breath to steady himself. Sarah had already told him this and the last piece of the puzzle had hurt when it had clicked into place. But time was doing nothing to decrease Noah's fury about the matter.

Lord Helton had hired Noah to investigate Ginger's father under the false pretense of protecting the British Empire. The reality was that Helton wanted Noah to eliminate the competition. He'd lied to Noah, manipulated him repeatedly, sought to control and keep a tight rein on him.

For the second time since he'd sat down, the pressing feeling of claustrophobia weighed down on Noah's chest, his heart racing so fast that he thought he might be sick. He wanted to finish speaking to Jack, but he also needed to get out of this space. "I need some air."

Standing bolt upright, Noah grabbed his trench coat and stalked from the mess without waiting for Jack, his mind spinning.

Rain pounded against his face, the storm churning in the depths of the dark and foamy sea. His footsteps pounded against the slick wooden boards, and he hurried down the deck toward the bow, where he stopped by the rail.

"Noah." Jack stepped beside him.

Noah's shoulders tensed as he struggled to breathe, feeling ashamed by this weakness in his mind. "Why didn't you tell me?"

"Well, first, because I didn't know Sarah had told you. We agreed you didn't need one more thing to torment you. It wasn't the right time."

Was there ever a *right* time for news like this? He didn't want to accept the explanation, but the words made the sting of Jack's silence feel less barbed. Noah turned toward Jack, his expression hard. "What else do you know?" Noah had hoped Sarah would be more discreet.

Jack turned his back to the rail and leaned against it. "Of a cache —maybe something more—from the tombs of the heretic pharaoh. Van Sant started hearing of treasures showing up on the black market, bearing the names of Nefertiti, Tiye, Akhenaten—even Tutankhamun."

Noah wiped rain droplets from the long fringe of lashes around his eyes and looked back at Jack. With a sardonic chuckle, he asked, "I suppose I should ask what Sarah *didn't* tell you?"

Jack set his hands on the rail. "I'm wondering the same thing." He let out a slow, long sigh. "So I take it you're not just heading back to Egypt for my benefit?"

"No. I'm going back to put an end to this. Once and for all."

"And you have a plan?"

Noah nodded curtly.

"Am I part of it?"

Noah avoided the weight of Jack's gaze. "No. And neither is Ginger. She needs to go home, Jack. I want her safe. That's all I care about. And if you give a damn about our friendship, you'll take her back to England for me. Ensure she gets there and is taken care of."

He removed his officer's cap, the band feeling unusually tight around his head. *Please, Jack.*

"If I know Red, she's not going anywhere. Not without you."

"Then help me convince her. Help me. Please," Noah said gruffly, feeling the torment inside him building.

Jack scanned his eyes, his expression growing somber. "What are you planning to do, Noah?"

The details would only put Jack in further danger.

"Whatever I have to do to get my life back." His eyes narrowed. "I don't want you there either. I have to do this alone."

"You don't look good, Noah. Are you all right? We should go to Ginger, have her help you."

"I'm fine." Noah drew a sharp breath that burned as though his lungs were collapsing. "I need my wife safe. And my friend. And I can't think of a better person to take my wife to England, actually. Two birds with one stone."

He closed his eyes, not wanting to beg, his heart pounding.

Silence hung between them for several seconds. At last, Jack nodded. "You could have told me what you wanted from the start, you know. It would have been easier. We've both been dancing around the same truth."

"I could say the same." Noah gave Jack a pointed look.

Jack sighed, then held out his hand for Noah to shake. "We'll part as friends, then?"

His words brought Noah unexpected relief. The pressure in his chest lifted, and he breathed deeply, his heart rate beginning to slow. Then he shook Jack's hand. "As brothers."

This time, the smile Jack offered reminded Noah of days long past. Jack released his hand. "And, Noah—"

Noah met his gaze.

"I *am* sorry. For punching you. And what I said."

With his list of allies growing thin, how could he afford grudges? Noah pulled his hat down, shadowing his eyes. "I know. Good luck, Jack."

CHAPTER NINE

"Do you want some tea?"

Ginger startled on her bunk, then rolled over to face the door, still hugging her sick bucket. She hadn't heard her cabin mate come in—or had she been sleeping?

Doubtful.

She'd been sick for days, barely able to leave her cabin. Sleep, when she could find it, helped her escape the nausea for a time, but there had been little relief once they'd left Malta. With other people around her complaining about seasickness, it was easy enough to blame her own malaise on that. But every day she grew more certain that her sickness was something else entirely.

She had no way of confirming a pregnancy yet, but her heart told her it was true.

Christmas had come and gone, with general merriment and festivities—and Matron in tears threatening to report the misbehavior of the nurses and the officers, like the Dodsworth sisters and their friends, who danced the night away and hung mistletoe to steal kisses. Ginger had yearned to dance with Noah, but they'd agreed it wasn't worth the risk.

Instead, she'd barely seen Noah—or even Jack. Once nausea overtook her, most of the opportunities to see Noah had passed.

Storms had raged for days following Christmas, making it impossible to weigh anchor at Malta for several days and driving Ginger's nausea to a tipping point. She wasn't the only one so ill, which made her feel less embarrassed over her weak stomach. Many of the nurses and soldiers were running for sick buckets or leaning over the rail. Fortunately, the lack of duties aboard the ship allowed her to rest.

She met Dorothy's awaiting stare, her mouth feeling dry, her tongue stuck to the roof of her mouth. She was grateful for her bunkmate, who'd been attentive and watched over her. "Tea would be lovely, thank you."

"I'll go and see if I can scrounge some up for you. Everyone is busy getting ready to sail into port in Alexandria. Half the deck is nothing but suitcases." Dorothy gave her a cheerful smile as she headed to the door. "If you're up for it, go and get some fresh air yourself. It may do you a world of good to see land again. I'll leave the tea on the armoire if you're not here."

Ginger groaned a response. Dorothy had even done her the favor of helping her pack, thank goodness. She hadn't given Noah a conclusive answer about going back to England, but the last possible thing she could imagine was taking another sea voyage now. Or staying on this infernal ship.

Of course, the week-long stay on board hadn't been all bad— they'd spent most of it at anchor, only traveling by sea for three days. The time in bed had given Ginger a chance to grieve Sarah and kept her from working with sick men. She couldn't help wondering if Noah and Jack were any closer to learning who had killed Sarah, though she imagined any progress on that front would have been limited by being on the ship. More than anything, she yearned to talk to Noah freely once again.

Seating herself, Ginger scooted toward the foot of the bed and crawled from the bunk. She stood and stretched, then tucked her sick bucket under her arm to look out the round porthole of the room. They'd anchored off the coast of Egypt, awaiting transport into the port of Alexandria. Her breath fogged the glass, and she wiped it away. It would all be over soon.

Ginger grabbed her dry toothbrush from her kitbag. A stale taste lingered in her mouth. She needed water. Maybe Dorothy was right. Maybe some fresh air would help her. As it was, she felt suffocated from having to always wear the bulky life belt.

She opened the door to the room and headed down the passageway, her knees feeling weak. Even the soft sways of the ship as it rolled over waves made her grip the walls.

Opening a door to the deck, she blinked in the sun. She hurried to the rail, gripping it tightly. If she vomited now, it would land on the well deck below.

She grimaced and sucked in a deep breath, hoping it would offer her some relief. Every spot on the deck seemed to be filled, nurses and officers stationed by the rail down the length of the starboard deck, laughing and talking in animated voices. She envied them. She envied anyone who didn't seem to be affected by the sea. "We've made it safely," one nurse she passed said, pointing to the channel in the distance. "I suppose all those lifeboat drills weren't needed after all." Many of them were already dressed and ready to disembark.

Ginger pushed further forward, wishing she could go up to the boat deck like she'd done while in Malta, but during the voyage it had been limited to the crew and officers of the ship, with only a few men stationed there on guard. The bow of the ship seemed crowded, so she moved toward the stern instead. Finding a clearer spot by the rail, she gripped it, her knuckles white, knees weak.

At least the storms had calmed. The azure waters were choppy, but they were almost into the safety of the port. They were in view of the harbor, the buoys to the channel close by. The ship had stopped though, awaiting transport into the channel.

She jumped as Noah settled beside her, his back to the rail. "Excuse me, Sister, is this spot taken?"

So happy to see him, she managed a grin. "The matron better not catch you talking to me."

"She can't stop an entire ship of nurses from talking to the officers—what's one more?" Noah turned and rested his arms against the rail, clasping his hands together. "How are you feeling?"

"Awful." She reached over and placed her hand on his forearm. "Please don't ask me to get on another ship. I can't bear the thought of another voyage."

He stared out over the water. "I was afraid you might say that." His jaw clenched. "But it's safer for you not to be with me. You can't possibly imagine how much I wish it weren't the case."

Her gaze traveled over the waters. Two Japanese Imperial destroyers and a transport ship, the *Nile*, had sailed beside the *Aragon* convoy. Strength in numbers. But what good would it do against a torpedo or mine? Even as close as they were, U-boats could still be out there or be laying mines in their path. "Do you think the other ships have helped? My bunkmate said we'd been traveling at a zigzag pattern and that she thought it had only made the journey longer."

"The Japanese naval convoys make it harder for the U-boats to have direct aim. But what else can we do? The Germans have sunk thousands of ships. It's too dangerous for us not to have convoys."

She supposed that was true. It was hard to see what difference the convoys made while out on the sea, but their safe passage here might be evidence of their usefulness. Taking another deep breath of fragrant sea air, Ginger set her hand over her stomach, trying to fight the nausea. She nodded toward the troops below their deck. "I'm surprised to see how many troops they're committing to the region right now."

Noah frowned and leaned closer to her. "That's because of Allenby's victories at Beersheba and Jerusalem. The prime minister wants him to keep pushing to Aleppo and Constantinople—see if they can't capitalize on the advance."

He didn't make it sound like a positive thing. She tilted her head toward him. "And you think it's foolish?" She gave him a sidelong glance. "I can tell from the way you said it."

His smile showed in his eyes without quite reaching his mouth. "The war won't be won on this front. They have other reasons for pushing that far. Syria is a pretty prize, no matter what promises we've made about who will control her after the war. And the rumors of oil fields north of Baghdad might change our minds about relinquishing control there."

Sacrificing all these troops for such an ulterior motive seemed so wrong. The men of their generation were war weary and wanted to go home. But his answer gave her an unexpected feeling of appreciation and warmth in another way. "You know what I've always loved about you?"

"What's that?" Noah scanned the churning sea as though unaffected by her words, but the hint of a smile touched the corner of his lips.

"You don't treat me like I'm too stupid to understand the mechanics of war, just because I'm a woman."

"Anyone who makes the mistake of underestimating you is an imbecile."

"I recall a certain husband of mine underestimating me." She gave him a sharp-eyed, knowing look.

Noah chuckled. "I never said I wasn't an imbecile in my youth."

A long peal of laughter left her, and she slid her hand toward his, the outer curve of her palm barely brushing his. He responded by extending his fingertips, just slightly over her pinkie and ring finger, and she closed her eyes, overwhelmed by the rush of feelings she felt at his touch. *Goodness, I've missed him.*

Tears pricked her eyes unexpectedly, and she glanced at his

profile. "I've felt such an emptiness the last week, especially knowing you were on this ship and I couldn't even speak to you."

His eyes stayed trained on the sea, his expression serious. *He's preparing for me to tell him I won't go to England.*

She gritted her teeth and went on. "I want you to be free to do whatever reckless, dangerous thing you feel you need to do to get your good name back." The salty air stung her lungs as she sucked it back. "I'll get back on a ship, even if I'm seasick the whole time. And then I'll wait for you back home—even if I don't have one right now." She gave him a teary-eyed smile. "But please, don't take too long to come back to me. You're right. I'm impatient. And I'll be impatiently waiting for you with my every breath."

Noah gave her a smile, one that didn't quite meet his eyes. "I'm not planning on dying yet, *rohi*. And I have some money put aside to help you find a house. When we disembark in Alexandria, I'll send a message to a friend in London to have something waiting for you when you arrive back in England. It'd be easier if I could make all the arrangements myself, but that's precisely why I need to clear my name. It may be a small flat, not the luxury you've been used to—"

"You know I don't care about that," she said with a shake of her head. They appeared to be moving again. She leaned forward as the Japanese ships and the *Nile* left their side. "Where's the convoy going?"

"We must have received the signal to move into the channel."

Land couldn't come fast enough. Ginger swallowed, the back of her throat clenching as she felt herself tempted to vomit once more. As she eyed Noah, she considered once again telling him about the possibility of a pregnancy. But would he receive the news with gladness, or would it only cause him further worry?

"I've been looking all over for you." Jack's voice came from a few feet away. Noah and Ginger both looked back at him as Jack came and settled beside Noah. "I just heard they got a message from the trawlers. Mines in the channel."

Ginger straightened with alarm, her eyes widening. "What? How did you hear? Doesn't that put us at risk?"

"They're trying to figure it out right now. But, yes, it's serious." Jack set both hands on the rail. He frowned, looking out at the water. "They're talking about sending us back out, but I'm not sure if that makes any sense."

"Not just talking about it." Noah nodded toward the distant shore. "It appears we're turning."

A sudden cry of alarm went up from the passengers on the *Aragon*.

Ginger peered over the rail. A long, thin trail in the water was speeding toward them.

A crash resounded, the whole ship shaking and groaning. Ginger clung to the rail, ducking into Noah's arms as he pulled her against him. Dust and wood flew into the air over the well deck, glass shattering from windows.

The *Aragon* had been torpedoed.

CHAPTER TEN

Time seemed to pass in a slow, exaggerated fashion as Ginger straightened, still holding onto Noah. She met his gaze and, for the briefest moment, worry flashed in his eyes. Then it dimmed, and he straightened, setting his hands on her shoulders. "Are you all right?"

"Yes, I'm fine, I'm ..." Ginger scanned the deck. Everyone around them seemed to be in a similar state: disbelief that their worst fear had been realized, but calm, prepared. This wasn't a group of civilians, after all. They trained for situations like this, however harrowing. A momentary pulse of pride swelled in her, a strange feeling when contrasted with the racing of her heart. Their calm was awe-inspiring.

The same group of Sisters who, moments before, had laughed and joked on the deck, hurried toward the boat deck, officers falling into place to escort them. The ship began an immediate list to the starboard side, and Ginger looked back at Noah and Jack.

They had to get off this ship.

"My—my things." And Dorothy. Had she been in their cabin,

waiting with the tea? Guiltily, Ginger thought of the soft-spoken girl. "And my cabin mate. She was getting me tea."

"Leave your things. They aren't important. Your cabin mate should know to go directly to the lifeboat." Noah took her by the elbow and hurried forward, walking at a brisk pace along the deck.

"But if she doesn't?" Ginger looked toward the cabins. Nurses were streaming out of the door.

"I'm certain she will. But I can go back and check if you'd like," Noah said, then looked behind him at Jack, who followed them only a few feet away. "You have everything you need, Darby?"

"I was ready before this," Jack answered, raising his voice to speak over the din.

Despite the calm and orderly fashion in which the evacuation seemed to proceed, she couldn't help the fear clawing at her. She glanced at Noah. His eyes, usually a dark blue, seemed to reflect the light from the sea, making them strangely light. "Where are we going?"

"To the lifeboats. You're getting on one."

The lifeboats? It didn't sound like he planned on getting on board with her. She dug in her heels and pulled him to a stop. "They aren't evacuating the officers yet. I'm not getting on a lifeboat until you're in there with me."

Noah shook his head. The clamor on the ship seemed to increase. He pointed back toward the officers' quarters. "I can't leave yet. I have to go back to my quarters for my bag."

His bag? He'd said her things weren't important. But she didn't want to be parted from him. That was the reason he was leaving her? Her mouth opened. "You're abandoning me to go back for your bag?"

He seemed to sense her frustration and looked sheepish. "I have some papers there that I can't allow to sink to the bottom of the sea."

"What on earth could you possibly have to go back for?"

"Our wedding certificate, to begin with. As well as papers I'll have a difficult time replacing given the warrant for my arrest."

She lifted her chin. "Then I'm staying with you. You're my husband. I'm not letting a sinking ship separate us."

His eyes warmed at her words. He cupped her face with his hands and kissed her.

She pulled away, knowing they could be seen, and stopped. It seemed an odd thing to kiss in the middle of a calamity, but she kissed him back, ignoring the reality of their situation. She needed the comfort of his embrace.

Noah broke the kiss and held her hand. "You are getting on that lifeboat, Ginger. Jack, will you get her to the lifeboats?"

What? Then, it had been a good-bye kiss for him. "You aren't hearing me—"

"No, darling. I'm not putting you at risk for even one extra second for my papers. Get on the boat. I'll be on one as soon as possible." Noah continued tugging her forward.

How would she find him among the other soldiers? She needed a good way to spot him, especially if he went into the water. Among the blues and whites and greys of the sea and the ship, little stood out.

"Noah, no!" Ginger scanned his face, her knees feeling weak. "I want to stay with you." The boat was taking on water quickly.

"But you can't." Noah held her shoulders. "Get yourself to safety. I'll find you in Alexandria."

When Noah dropped his hands to his sides, Jack took her by the elbow. "Come on, Red, let's get going."

"Take care of my wife." Noah dipped his chin, then turned to go. Already, the stern sank lower, forcing them to climb at an angle back toward the lifeboats.

"Noah—" Ginger raced back toward him and grabbed his arm.

"Promise me. Just get the bag and then get off this ship. No heroics."

He scanned her gaze. "I promise."

She gave him another hurried kiss. "I love you."

"And I love you. Now go."

Before she could stop him again, he pivoted on his heel and left, disappearing into the crowded deck.

The ship gave an awful groan as it listed to one side and a terrible cacophony sounded of men shouting orders, footsteps pounding against the deck boards, splashes of water. Lifeboats were already being lowered and cables screeched as the boats dropped closer to the sea.

Ginger struggled to catch her breath as she lost sight of him. Jack was beside her in an instant, his warm brown eyes sympathetic. "He'll be fine. But if anything happens to you, he'll never forgive me, so we should get going."

She nodded mutely, then let Jack lead her to the lifeboats. They passed nervous chatter, nurses wondering out loud if they should take their bags, while others shouted things like, "Come on, hurry along!"

The troops on the deck below them were rowdier. Disembarking would be a slower process for them, and that increased the likelihood of drowning. The *Aragon* was sinking at a stunning speed.

As they arrived at the lifeboats, Jack gave her elbow a squeeze. "Stay alive, you hear?" Jack gave her a wink, then handed her over to the officer in charge of loading the nurses.

"Find Noah, please. Make sure he gets to safety." As she climbed on board the large boat and sat, she released a slow breath. The boats could all hold about sixty people, and this one was at capacity. But she'd never felt more alone.

Somehow, she didn't feel alone in that emotion, though. The stunned looks from the other nurses portrayed the dismay and shock, the incomprehension. The threat of submarines, torpedoes, and mines had always been abstract. Something that might happen to some other poor soul's ship, but never one's own. And yet it *had* happened to them.

Tears formed in her eyes, and she blinked them away. She desperately wanted to jump out of the lifeboat and stay until Noah came back from his quarters.

Jack continued to stand where he'd left her, watching her closely. He gave her a salute, his eyes locking with hers.

"Everything I own is in my suitcase," one nurse on the lifeboat said, looking wistfully back at the deck.

Another other nurse appeared distressed. "Mine too. I got my papers, but nothing more."

Ginger pressed her lips together. She'd barely had any possessions with her on this ship, but the things she'd brought were important to her. The only other things she owned were in a trunk at Alastair Taylor's house in Cairo. But what could she do about it now? They would go down to the bottom of the sea.

As the officers lowered the lifeboat, she looked up. Jack still stood by the rail, gazing down at her. Unlike Noah, his emotions were more clearly written on his face: he was worried.

What was he still doing there?

"Go." She cupped her hands over her mouth, not caring who heard her. "Go! Don't just stand there!"

He gave a slight wave before pushing back from the rail and walking away.

The lifeboat continued swaying against the ropes, which squeaked and screeched as it brought the group of Sisters closer and closer to the water. With the number of storms that had come through in the morning, the sea looked choppy and dark. Alexandria had frightening storms in the winter.

Ginger imagined sharks and whales and any number of vicious

sea creatures with sharp teeth below the surface of the water. Or, worse yet—the German submarine that had torpedoed them. She shuddered. Any ship that came to rescue them could be at risk. The submarine couldn't have gone far.

At last, the lifeboat hit the water. It bounced, one side dipping low into the water, the other bucking in response, and sent everyone in the small vessel flying. Ginger reached out to grab hold of the edge of her seat but instead grabbed the hand of a fellow nurse. The other nurse clasped her hand with as much fervor. They exchanged horrified glances.

Water dripped from their faces and clothes, the salt stinging their eyes.

Hers was the last lifeboat containing nurses. Ginger squinted against the sun and back toward the *Aragon.* The starboard side was now listing to such a degree that the men on the decks had to grasp the rail to move back and forth. They seemed so far away—it was hard to imagine she'd just been on board. She felt small compared to the giant ship. Lifeboats dotted the surface of the sea in front of it, all of them watched in mesmerized horror.

Noah, get off that ship. If ever there was a time in her life she'd wished she could have the power of telepathy, it was now. *Get off, get off.* She imagined him in his room, combing through his things. If anything happened to him, she'd never forgive herself.

"Look!" someone said from the boat. "The other ship is here to save our men."

The sight of the Union Jack on an approaching destroyer made Ginger choke back a sob. Her country's flag, flapping in the wind, sparked ineffable relief.

A few of the nurses clapped.

Ginger swallowed, her hands shaking. She looked back to the *Aragon.* Where was Noah?

She could no longer see the faces on the ship clearly enough to tell. "Dammit," she whispered under her breath. Still, she couldn't tear her eyes away from the sinking ship. It was going down so fast. How was it possible that an entire ship could sink so quickly?

"Take the water," voices called from the ship. The cry had grown so loud that it rung out across the sea.

Rafts continued to drop into the sea from all sides of the decks. Lifeboats weren't properly filled, though—there wasn't enough time. Men were jumping from the rails. Some jumped from boats that had been lowered midway but could no longer be put into the sea. Within minutes, the sea seemed to be covered in flailing khaki figures, both in and out of the lifeboats and rafts.

As the other ship pulled alongside the *Aragon,* men attached ropes from one ship to the other. Thank God. Lives would be saved by having the other ship so close.

"How many troops did we have on board?" Ginger asked the nurse sitting beside her.

"I think just over two thousand."

Ginger covered her mouth. There would be no way two thousand men could escape the ship. Not as quickly as it appeared to be sinking. Men would die. Not everyone would get off. A pang struck her in the chest, and she struggled to breathe.

I shouldn't have left without Noah.

The sounds of singing voices reached the lifeboat. The troops still on board seemed to sing in one voice. "Keep the home fires burning, while your hearts are yearning..."

She'd heard the song so many times before, but never like this. A profound ache formed in her chest.

The nurse beside her grabbed her hand. "We should pray."

Ginger shook her head, mute. She couldn't pray. She couldn't speak. Her every heartbeat seemed to pulse Noah's name, but how could she possibly see him? Everyone left on that ship was going to drown. They needed to get off or they would be sucked under. Was it possible Noah and Jack had already made it onto a lifeboat?

Ginger stood, her feet unsteady, scanning the water for Noah.

How would she ever be able to spot anything at this distance? The men in the water swarmed and writhed, swimming away from the ship and toward the rescuing destroyer. At least in the water they had more of a chance of survival than those who were still on board.

The *Aragon* now rose high in the water, its stern well below the surface. She scanned the decks of the ship, feeling as though she might vomit at any moment. A sudden rush to the water by the men still remaining on board made it clear the orders had been given to abandon ship. Men seemed to pour from all sides, looking more like bees escaping a hive than human beings.

Those who had not made it off the ship now took to jumping. From the height at which they stood, Ginger knew many must be jumping to their deaths. Oil burned on the surface and with the amount of debris in the water, they were likely to hit something—or worse, another person. At that speed, they would kill or maim anyone they hit. And if they were injured, they wouldn't swim away from the ship in time to avoid being sucked under.

Her horror grew. Between uncertain suicide and certain drowning, life fought for even the smallest speck of hope.

As the *Aragon* slipped below the waters of the Mediterranean, an awful churning of water sounded, drowning out the shouts of men still clinging to the decks, trying to find a clear spot in the water to jump to, which was an impossibility with the amount of men and debris bobbing in the waves.

Ginger sucked in her breath, her heart pounding in her ears. The ship was nearly under, the devastation unimaginable. Blood churned in the water.

The sea seemed to suck the mighty ship beneath its surface, the explosions of boilers and the screech of twisting metal reverberating through the air.

Then, silence.

The ship was gone. Ginger gripped her life belt, her eyes brimming with tears. The sea bobbled with hundreds of men, some injured, some dead. Was Noah among them? Or had he made it onto the other ship?

A soft, mournful tune carried over from a few men standing on a raft. "... where me and my true love will never meet again ..."

Ginger gritted her teeth. "Loch Lomond" was the last song she wanted to hear right now.

A crack and a boom splintered the water.

Ginger gasped as cries left the nurses in the lifeboat with her. The destroyer that had been taking on survivors split in half.

A scream left her, the boards below her feet feeling wobbly as she stood. "What happened?" She grabbed the arm of the nurse closest to her.

"They torpedoed the rescue ship," she answered, her face pallid.

The crew of the lifeboat and the nurses stared at the destroyer, horror written on their faces. Some held their heads, some covered their mouths.

Ginger nearly threw up.

She turned toward the water, which now shone black like a mirror. The torpedo appeared to have hit the destroyer's oil tank, and the water was slick with oil. Men and debris floated in the water, some completely covered with oil.

Ginger searched blindly for Noah or Jack. She couldn't focus. Where was he? The oil covered so much she could hardly distinguish the men from the water.

"We need to hurry and get to shore," one of the crew said. "It's not safe here."

"No!" Ginger was pulled down to her seat by some of the surrounding nurses. "We can't just leave those men floating in the water. We should go back. Collect as many men as we can."

"We can't stay here."

She didn't even know who had answered her.

The wreckage of the destroyer was vanishing at astonishing speed. There was no way the men on board had time to disembark—or even jump. Ginger pushed her way to the edge of the boat.

Gasps sounded behind her. "Sister!"

Noah had to be in the water. One way or another. She wouldn't rest until she reached him.

She jumped into the Mediterranean. The cold water hit her, shocking her senses. She bobbed for a moment before sucking in a deep breath. She was a reasonable swimmer. But she hadn't reckoned with how cold the water would be. Or how much her uniform wasn't meant for swimming. The life belt helped, but it made her feel immobile.

She sucked in a deep breath and headed toward the bodies in the water. As she drew closer to some rafts and lifeboats, she shouted, "Noah!"

Would he be able to hear her above the noise of the men in the water?

"Noah!"

She swam further, dragging herself with each stroke. Her dress weighed her down, nearly drowning her. When she stopped to tread water again, she struggled for deep, labored breaths.

A hand grabbed her bicep. A lieutenant on a raft, near to her, hung over the side. "I have you, luv. You're safe now."

She attempted to pull her arm back, and the raft wobbled. The man's grip felt like iron. "No, let me go—I have to find someone."

The lieutenant's eyes widened. "You're going to tip the raft."

"Then let me go." She fought against him.

"I can't let you head toward a sinking ship. You could get sucked under. Anyone near there will."

Even more reason to find Noah.

She yanked her arm until the lieutenant released her. "Have it your way," he said.

She swam away from his raft and turned in the water, scanning the bobbing heads, but it was impossible. There were too many people. Too many men covered in oil.

No, God, no. Don't you dare take him from me now. Not now.

Her skirts weighed heavily. If she wasn't careful, she would drown from exhaustion before she found Noah, even with the ridiculous life belt.

Another two men, clinging to an upturned raft, floated by. "Hang on here with us," one of them said. Before she could move away, an oar came in front of her face.

"Grab onto the oar," an officer from a lifeboat commanded her.

"But—" She turned to glance at him.

He wasn't asking. His uniform told her he was a colonel. "Don't make me climb into that water to save you, Sister. Get on the oar, and I'll pull you in."

She grabbed the oar, hands trembling.

He pulled her back and then helped her climb into the lifeboat. As the men on board made a space for her, she sat, trembling. Her skin was numb, her breath ragged.

"What were you doing in the water, Sister?" The colonel leaned over her. "I saw you jump from that lifeboat."

The lifeboat she'd leapt from was closer than she realized. She hadn't swum that far, despite her efforts. She felt foolish and impotent.

"My husband—he was on the destroyer." She looked back to where the other ship had been. It was gone.

The men exchanged looks.

"We need to get you onto a trawler. You'll have more of a chance of finding him once you're on shore than you will in this mess." The colonel squatted beside her. "Have you ever gone into the water with exhausted, wounded, and drowning men? They'll drown each other trying to find something to hold on to."

Ginger pushed away the hair matted to the side of her face. She clasped her hands together and nodded. Water droplets dripped from the tip of her nose.

She gazed over at the men in the water and squeezed her eyes shut. Her heart continued to scream his name. She kept replaying the sight of the destroyer after it had been struck.

Noah.

CHAPTER ELEVEN

ALEXANDRIA

*I*n a room in the Khedivial Hotel, Ginger ran her fingertips over the rough fabric of the striped pajamas the nurses had been issued after arriving. They'd each been given scrambled eggs, bread and tea, aspirin and a toothbrush, and ordered to go to bed. Though hours had passed since she jumped into the water, she couldn't shake the chill.

The nurses had worked tirelessly on the survivors as they'd been brought in from the sea, but Noah and Jack hadn't been among the wounded. With each new patient that Ginger treated, she searched for Noah's face, only to have her hope crushed. Guilt had mixed with numbing exhaustion. She didn't want to be taking care of these wounded when her own husband might be wounded elsewhere.

Before the ambulances had taken the nurses from the dock, she searched each of the trawlers that came in loaded with survivors. Noah wasn't on any of them. Nor Jack. The men on the docks whispered many bodies would never be recovered. They estimated the dead and missing to be almost seven hundred men.

Was it possible that Noah and Jack could be together? She hoped Jack had listened to her and gone after Noah. But if they weren't found, what hope could she have that they would be alive? The boats had all come in. No more survivors would be found.

Unless Noah is so seriously wounded that he can't reach me. In which case, she would have to comb the hospital wards.

The three other nurses sharing a room with Ginger stood at the open bedroom windows, staring down at the street, solemn expressions on their faces. Their attention appeared to be occupied by raucous noise down below, on the streets of cosmopolitan Alexandria. Despite not having been interested in it, Ginger rose to see what they saw.

Life pulsed with energy and enthusiasm on the streets. Troops sung and danced in celebration.

She understood the other nurses' expressions. The celebrations were a jarring contrast to what they'd been through and what they'd seen. Joy felt so distant to all of them—it seemed wrong that the troops down below weren't as solemn and mournful as they were. But, then again, they likely hadn't been on the *Aragon*.

Ginger's heart ached.

"What are they celebrating?" Ginger finally asked one nurse, blinking numbly.

"The New Year," one answered.

The New Year. One more year beginning with the world at war, with death around them. None of her companions smiled or seemed to take any pleasure in the sight of festivities. From here, Ginger could see other nurses who'd survived standing at similar posts at the windows in their rooms. Tears streaked their brave, tired faces.

Ginger crept back to bed, too exhausted to remain standing. Her eyes stung, and she wiped tears away, settling onto her side on the bed.

He has to be alive.

She closed her eyes, trying to think of a solution. She couldn't wander the hospital wards in pajamas looking for him. Her uniform hung over a chair in the room, still soaked. For the time being, she and the other nurses weren't permitted to leave these hotel rooms, as they had strict orders to rest.

But if he was alive, wouldn't he try to find her?

That he hadn't found his way to her yet struck a chill in her heart. Noah always found a way back to her. He wouldn't leave her wondering if he was safe. She would be easier for him to find than the reverse. All he had to do was ask where the nurses had been taken. Their numbers were far fewer than the rescued men, even if they weren't all in the same hotel.

Would he be wondering if she had perished? Only a handful of nurses were unaccounted for.

She hugged her knees to her chest.

Her gaze focused on the rings he'd given her. Stripped of her uniform, they'd become her only possessions. They meant more to her now than ever before, and she thanked God she hadn't removed them. The few possessions she'd accumulated after fleeing Egypt were now at the bottom of the Mediterranean, and all her happy memories seemed gone with them.

We should have stayed in Malta.

Unreasonable as the thought was, her mind had been screaming the phrase repeatedly.

The other women in the room left Ginger to herself—they were strangers to her, anyway—and she hadn't seen the nurses she'd met aboard the *Aragon* in the hotel.

As they retired to bed and lights went off, Ginger struggled to sleep. She curled onto her side and a sea of horrible images poured over her in waves, of men dying, missing their limbs, the air burning with oil, the carnage of men drowning. Then she sat, body trembling, her lips dry and cracked, her mouth parched.

Her eyes, heavy-lidded, struggled to find anything and anyone in the dark.

Noah, please find me. Please, God, let him be alive.

* * *

THE DAWN WAS DEATHLY QUIET, the streets emptied of all of those who had been making merry for the New Year two days earlier as Ginger slipped out of the hotel. She'd had to make do with her damp shoes, which hadn't dried since her plunge in the Mediterranean.

But she couldn't stay at the hotel doing nothing. The Sisters had been offered every comfort possible, but it felt elusive to Ginger. Neither Noah nor Jack had found her, despite her staying in one place. She couldn't rest easy while they were separated.

The first thing Noah would have done was look for her—she was certain of it. Jack too. That neither of them had appeared was damning.

A dog on the street growled at her as she passed it, as though she threatened his meal of rubbish in the gutter. She edged her way around it. Street dogs weren't always friendly, and rabies wasn't something she needed to add to her list of troubles.

As the grey light painted the surrounding buildings with more color, Ginger felt as though she walked in a numb dream—or nightmare, really. She was in Egypt again, but it was all different now.

When she'd fled to Malta with Noah, she believed she had nothing, but truth was a stark, unkind friend. Now she only had the clothes on her back, the shoes on her feet. She'd left behind the pajamas they had issued her, having no way to carry them. The only thing she'd brought was the toothbrush, which fit in the pocket of her apron.

A toothbrush. I own a toothbrush.

She had no friends, no allies, no money, no food. She'd been asked for her name when she arrived at the hotel, but who knew how long it would be before Diana Clayborne was discovered to be a fraud?

And, unfortunately, Lady Virginia Whitman and Mrs. Noah Benson were no help to her either. Her name had helped her in the past, but now it condemned her.

Fortunately, she was familiar with Alexandria, having spent the summer and early fall at a hospital in the city. The hospitals treating the injured from the *Aragon* would most likely be those closest to the harbor. Men had been brought in soaked in oil, missing limbs, with deep puncture wounds from wreckage that struck them in the sea. Finding a trace of Noah and Jack meant starting at the hospitals.

But if they were injured, how long would it be before they, too, needed to go on the run?

By the time she reached the first hospital, her shoes had worn blisters on her heels. She limped inside, gritting her teeth as she walked, and asked a passing doctor about the wounded from the *Aragon.*

"They're everywhere, Sister," the doctor answered with a frown curling under his thick moustache. "We found beds for them where we could. Them and the poor souls from the *Osmanieh.*"

"The *Osmanieh?*"

He gave her a grave look. "Didn't you hear? It hit a mine in the harbor days ago. Two hundred souls lost."

Good God.

When would it all end?

Despair crested in her chest. How on earth would she find Noah and Jack among all this?

The doctor pointed her toward the ward with the most *Aragon* patients and she started off toward it, trying to keep herself from limping as the pain of the blisters grew. She hadn't gone far down a hallway when a deep voice called out, "Ginger?"

Hope rising in her, she turned and met a familiar gaze—that of her former fiancé, Dr. James Clark.

She choked back a cry, a mixture of disappointment and strange relief in her chest. James didn't deserve to know of her disappointment at seeing him instead of Noah. Their relationship had ended because of her romance with Noah. Despite that, James had been honorable enough to save Noah's life after Ginger's brother had shot him.

"James. I-I'm stunned to see you. I heard they had sent you to France." Not even a year earlier, she would have rushed to embrace him, but she stayed firmly rooted and clasped her hands in front of her.

James came out of the doorway where he'd been standing. "I wasn't certain if it was you at first." He scanned her hair. "You tinted your hair?"

She wanted more than anything to have someone to trust, to tell of her troubles. But she didn't have that relationship with James anymore. She nodded, pressing her lips to a line, her heart heavy.

When she gave no explanation, he adjusted his glasses and said, "Yes, I was supposed to go to France. But with Allenby making a push into Palestine, the RAMC thought my services should remain here, as I've been in this region most of the war."

Because of me. He'd requested to serve in Egypt after they'd been engaged, just as her father had arranged for her nursing service to be centered on this front of the war.

"I'm certain you're the expert in the field here by now." She bit her lip. *That's true.* James was an expert and respected, most likely a senior officer, with access to information and people that she could never hope to have.

It positioned him perfectly to help her find Noah and Jack.

"How are you?" James said with a tenuous smile. "I didn't expect to see your familiar face. You're still in service, then." He nodded toward her uniform.

Well, no. Not exactly.

She didn't want to lie to him. Especially not if he might find out more about the casualties from the *Aragon*. But did she dare ask him for help? She had no right to, and Noah was a fugitive, which could put him in a compromising situation. Knowing anything about Colonel Noah Benson's last known whereabouts was dangerous information.

But Captain Eugene Brooks?

James was too intelligent not to guess who the alias was for. And if he'd read the newspapers at all—which she knew he did—he would know of Noah's troubles. But what choice did she have? She needed to find her husband, and soon.

She took a step forward, wringing her hands. "James, I—"

"Yes? Is something wrong?" He gave her an earnest look. "We were friends once, Ginger. I'm happy to help you."

Tears stung the back of her throat, her relief more palpable now. She gave a brisk nod, then scanned the area to make certain no one would overhear. "I'm looking for two men who were on the *Aragon* with me. They seem to have gone missing after the sinking, and I desperately need to find them."

James's eyes widened. "You were on the *Aragon?*" He replaced his shock with a quick nod. "Yes, of course. I'm happy to help you. I'm uncertain if they've compiled a complete list of survivors yet, but we'll find what we can, yes? There are quite a few souls unaccounted for, unfortunately."

She followed him to a room that turned out to be his office, and within a few minutes, James was on the telephone making inquiries into Captain Eugene Brooks and Lieutenant Harry Nelson.

Would Noah and Jack have continued using the aliases if they'd been wounded? They had no reason not to, but that also depended on how wounded they'd been.

James hung up the phone, a deep frown between his eyes. "I can't find any record of them, Ginger. They're not on the lists." He cleared his throat, then wrote something on a scrap of paper. "But this is the address where I'm living in Alexandria. You can phone or telegram me—I'll keep asking."

Not on the lists. Officially …. *unofficially?* How on earth was she supposed to find two men that didn't exist, according to the military?

But the fact that they weren't listed could also be further proof that they weren't among the known survivors, wounded or not.

He handed the paper to Ginger, and his fingertips brushed hers. A sad look came into his eyes. "Is there anything else you need? Any other way I can help you?"

She fought the temptation to ask him for more. She needed so much, but James couldn't possibly provide it. And he had to know that Noah was one of the men she was looking for, even if he was too polite to say so.

She had done enough damage in the past—she wouldn't endanger James.

"No, thank you. This is the best help I could have asked for." She transferred the papers to her other hand, then squeezed his warmly. "I owe you so much already. Good-bye. I'm so glad to have seen you."

If she didn't know better, the hint of a blush showed on James's cheeks. "I know you'll succeed in your quest, Ginger. I've known no one as tenacious as you."

A hopeless feeling returned the moment she left the hospital. As the morning turned into afternoon, Ginger made her way toward the harbor, her feet throbbing. The blisters on her heels had broken. Her throat clenched, holding back tears as she realized she should have asked James to help her find some bandages for her feet, at least.

The elegant buildings marking the cosmopolitan area of downtown Alexandria came into view as she walked, watching life hum at its normal pace around her. Few people noticed her and if they did, gave her no attention. She looked like a nurse, and there were plenty of them in the city. Their stomachs weren't turning sour and growling with hunger. Their needs weren't ignored. A part of her wanted to laugh at herself: the spoiled, wealthy woman that she'd been, fretting about a missed meal or two.

And then there was the quieter, more desperate side—the one telling her she had no meal awaiting her. She might go back to the Khedivial or a hospital and finagle a meal whilst still in uniform, but that was a short-term solution to a long-term problem.

The warm and humid sea air was thick against her skin as she reached the crescent-shaped quays that provided a walkway around the harbor. Low, dark clouds threatened a coming storm, but a band of brighter sky gleamed off the waters of the Mediterranean beyond the short beach on the other side of the road.

The same sea that had swallowed hundreds of men while she watched.

Was Noah there? Did the watery grave of the *Aragon* now mark his resting place? Anything less than certainty about his death would only lead to a lifetime of feeling as though she'd somehow abandoned him. She couldn't leave Egypt if there was a chance he was still here in a hospital somewhere. Even if she was destitute and hungry—

You must stop thinking of yourself. The admonishment came from the back of her mind and warmed her cheeks. She pressed her hands to her face to cool her skin.

The genuine possibility existed that she was carrying Noah's child.

What a terrible mother she'd make. What could she possibly give a child?

She had nothing.

Her family didn't want her, and she'd be rejected from society.

While she had some education, how could she possibly expect to work as a nurse while raising a child? And beyond those skills, she had none. She was raised for a life of luxury and civil service through fundraising for and supporting charities. She knew how to host a party and the basics of running a household as the lady of a house. Jobs that now seemed ludicrous.

But no one would hire her for even the most basic job in service with a child. Without her marriage certified by the consulate and no paperwork to prove that she'd been married by the church, would her child even be legitimate?

Ginger sank wearily onto a bench on the quays, feeling unnaturally cold despite the warm winter air. Egyptian winters were the most seasonable time of year in the country, as opposed to the summers when the heat became intolerable. But the sun didn't warm her, and, for the first time, she wished for the harsh rays of summer to thaw the chill.

She knew no one in Alexandria. She had to go to Cairo. Her family might still be there. Even if she had to strip whatever shred of pride and dignity she had, it was the best option she had. Noah had told her he'd left their marriage certificate at his friend Alastair Taylor's home in Old Cairo. Retrieving that certificate was her only chance of proving that she'd been married in the Catholic church.

Her stomach felt as though she'd swallowed a rock.

And now, whom could she turn to for help?

Cairo could be dangerous for her, too. The last time she'd seen him, Stephen had been in Cairo. And Lord Helton lived there as well.

Noah had emboldened her. Given her strength in the freedom from her family's expectations. Made her feel that she could be something other than what she'd been raised to be.

But she was a woman. The world was a cruel place for women, especially those without money or influence.

She'd go to the train station, get to Cairo, continue searching for

Noah in whatever capacity she could. Alastair Taylor might even help, and Noah counted him among his closest friends. She could continue to contact James Clark from there if he found something.

Without Noah, she didn't know how to go on. Whatever independence she'd once felt seemed to have shriveled in the light of her circumstances … *and the child I might be carrying.*

Her throat thick, Ginger closed her weary eyes, her soul aching.

This wasn't the time to crumple and fall. She had everything to lose if she did.

CHAPTER TWELVE

*T*he train station in Alexandria had never seemed so threatening. Ginger's heart pounded in her chest as she moved from where she'd been watching beside a lamppost as a hospital train finished loading.

Go now.

She had to will her feet into action, which was difficult enough, given the aching of her limbs and the fear that clamped her chest. Hurrying, she lifted her chin, trying to stay calm as she walked with a sense of purpose and belonging. She'd never had to stow away like this.

She reached the train and boarded it, her ears ringing, and avoided eye contact with a medical orderly as she passed. The platform of the train seemed to sway under her feet, her every step unsteady.

"Sister?" She heard behind her.

Swallowing a breath, she froze in place. If questioned, would she have the strength to stick to the story she'd concocted?

She turned and glanced over her shoulder to see the orderly stopped by the doorway to the adjoining train car. He gave her a friendly smile. "The nurses' cabin is three carriages down. That way." He pointed in the direction he was going.

Relief flooded her, and she nodded, her breath shallow. She didn't want to have to follow him or seem as if she hadn't known where to go. "Thank you. I'll find my way back there shortly."

She hurried forward, clasping her hands to keep them from shaking. The nurses' carriage wouldn't be a good idea. Any nurse with even the slightest observation skills might notice that her uniform wasn't entirely correct and how bedraggled she appeared. She pushed forward, passing through the carriages outfitted as hospital wards, trying to put distance between herself and most of the medical personnel. At last she reached a supply car. She helped herself to a few bandages and clean linens, then nearly dropped them as she spotted a wooden crate with rations.

Holding back a cry, she dug into the crate and pulled out a few tins of bully beef and biscuits—field rations she'd had to eat while in clearing stations. Despite having joined in complaints about them with other nurses, now they appealed like heaven-sent manna. She also had to find water to eat the hard, tasteless biscuits and to quell her thirst.

Now she just needed a tin opener. These crates normally came with a few openers. She sifted through the contents, removing some cigarettes and chocolate, until she found an opener at the bottom of the crate.

Thank God.

She made a makeshift sack with some linen she'd found, then helped herself to a few tins, some chocolate, matches, and cigarettes —the latter she'd always found useful as a trade item.

The door to the train car opened, and she straightened. She would be spotted quickly enough, even though she was in the middle of the train car.

Trying to keep her composure, she fished out a stack of linens from a shelf.

"You there," a male voice rang out. "What are you doing in here?"

She lifted her chin to see an orderly striding toward her. He wore a deep scowl on his face, his expression wary.

"Making beds. But we're out of linens," Ginger said, then smiled.

"Yes, well, you can't just come taking what you like from the supply car. That would be chaos. Things have to be done in the proper fashion." He stopped near her, then reached out for the linens.

If Ginger had learned anything over the years, it was that nothing made a man more uncomfortable than an emotional, verbal woman. She sniffed loudly, holding the linens to her chest. "I'm so terrible at this. My mother said joining would be a terrible idea for me. I'm always the one who burns the food and spills tea on the floor, as though being clumsy is something one can help. God doesn't seem to hear my prayers. I rather wish I could be useful without mucking everything up. And now the matron will be upset with me once again. Is it so wrong to want to do my bit and want to make my family and my country proud, when—"

"It's all right. It's all right, luv." The orderly shifted, taking one step back. "Go on ahead. But next time, look for help, yes? You best get on with it now."

She thanked him profusely, wiping her eyes, then hurried out of the train car, her heart in her throat. Half-certain he'd call her back there, she held her breath until she'd gone through two more cars. Then her relief turned to worry. Getting on the train had been only the start.

Where could she sit and be unnoticed?

The rations she'd stolen weighed heavily in her arms, and she tried not to think about the morality of her actions. It was stealing, after all. She'd spent years dedicating her service to the troops, but she'd been summarily dismissed from that service for having the imprudence of choosing to save the life of a wounded soldier rather than a deserter an officer wanted her to "patch up" for a firing squad.

At last, she dodged into a bathroom compartment near one of the operating theaters and slid the door shut, then latched it. At this hour and with such a brief ride to Cairo, it was unlikely many—if any—surgeries would be performed.

She sank down onto the floor and her hands started shaking heavily, as though the simple act of sitting had released all her nerves. Her throat stung with tears and she hugged her knees to her chest, trying to catch her breath. Would her mother help her when she arrived in Cairo? What if her family had already left?

One day truly on your own and you're already failing and running back home.

But what was she supposed to do?

The potent scent of urine came from the nearby latrine and she covered her nose, her stomach gripped by both hunger and nausea. She didn't dare look for an electric light—not wanting to attract any more attention to herself.

She struck a match, the sulfur a welcome relief to the smell of refuse. With trembling fingers, she dug the opener into the tin, then extinguished the match. She lit one more to help her open the tin. The light extinguished quickly, the soft wafts of smoke tempting her to light a cigarette to distract from the fetid smell.

The first time she'd ever been issued bully beef in a tin had been in Gallipoli, when rations had been as scarce for the nurses as they had been for the soldiers. Ruefully, she recalled her ineptitude, how little she'd known of survival, even then—her friend, Beatrice, had shown her how to open the tin, teasing Ginger about her lack of knowledge.

Where was Beatrice now? Had they maintained their friendship, Beatrice would have been a source of consolation and help.

But she was gone. Like her father. Henry. Her mother and Lucy. Sarah. Jack ...

Noah.

Everyone she'd believed she could rely on.

She had to survive.

One day at a time. One moment at a time.

I just need to get through today.

The train gave a shuddering lurch forward. She was on her way to Cairo.

CHAPTER THIRTEEN

From the first time that Ginger had come to Cairo in her childhood, then again with her return as a young woman, she'd always sensed a pulse to the city. Cairo's continued existence seemed to be inextricably linked to humanity itself, like an unbroken chain without which the story of mankind could not exist. Even Alexandria couldn't compare to it. The baked dust, the ancient streets, the mixture of civilizations—Egyptians and conquerors—that had all left their mark on the stones.

Her family's house, in one of the smarter neighborhoods in the Anglo Cairo, wasn't a long walk from the train station, but not a single light greeted her as she approached it.

Even at this hour of night, she could see that the house was shuttered, the gate closed and bound with a chain. Her mother's rosebushes, which had been tended to with care, drooped.

Her family wasn't here.

Much as that was a relief, it meant she needed to find help elsewhere.

She hoped that meant her cousin William, the new Earl of Braddock, had kept his promise and taken them back home to England.

Despite the way her mother had ousted Ginger from the house, she only wanted the best for her mother and sister. Ginger had confessed to killing Henry to save Noah's life and had exposed Stephen's crimes to her sister, Lucy. Lucy's secretly harbored romantic feelings for Stephen had only made the revelation worse.

The worst part of it was that she understood their anger and hurt toward her. She'd hoped, foolishly, that explaining herself would help. But they had rejected her outright instead.

Stopping at the front of the house, she leaned against the gate, gazing inside. She pictured her family gathered on the verandah for tea, a memory from that time she'd been on leave a couple of years earlier.

If she could only turn back the pages of time, tell her father not to buy an oil concession that had cost him his fortune. His desperation for money had led him to treason and smuggling and—worse still—Stephen manipulating and controlling him through bribery and threats.

She couldn't help but wonder how different her life might have turned out. Would she even have met Noah? Lord Helton had tasked him with investigating her father.

Then again, Noah had been friends with Henry. Maybe they'd have met through her brother.

She didn't want to think about what could have been. A knot seemed to form in her stomach, and she stepped back from the gate.

There was nothing for her here. If she was honest, she didn't want to be here, anyway. In some ways it was a small mercy that she didn't have the option to go to them now, hands outstretched.

The night was bitter, a blaze of stars trumpeting the late hour.

She took care to stay on the main road as she walked toward the heart of Anglo Cairo, where Ezbekieh Gardens and Shepheard's and all the most talked-about social gathering holes existed. As she drew closer to it, she hailed a cab that whisked her away toward Old Cairo, where Alastair Taylor lived.

She left the cab waiting near the back alley that Alastair used as a main entrance. Before she could knock, the door opened, and Alastair himself was there, a frown between his dark eyebrows as he studied her appearance. "*La belle femme.* My dearest, come in."

He must have noticed her bedraggled appearance and how little she had with her.

Ginger set her hand on the door, feeling weak at the sight of him. "I couldn't pay the cab I hired—"

"Don't give it another thought. I'll send someone immediately." Alastair offered her his arm. "Can I offer you tea? Or a hot bath? Soup and a bed?"

Ginger choked back a cry and gave him a teary-eyed smile. "All of them. Noah has gone missing. Jack too. We were aboard the *Aragon* and it was torpedoed. I've searched everywhere for them, but I can't find them anywhere and hundreds of men died."

Alastair stared at her in stunned silence, his face growing pale.

"I had nowhere else to go," Ginger managed. Would he be upset that she'd stopped searching and come here?

"Well, of course." Alastair seemed to recover, but his hand trembled as he smoothed his hair into place. He led her up the stairs to the main level of the house. "I assumed you wouldn't be here otherwise." He patted her hand with his, giving her a gentle smile. "But you can give me every detail later. I'm honored you thought to come."

Alastair's reaction was subdued, but he was clearly shaken. He cared deeply for Noah and Jack, and Ginger doubted he'd display much more emotion than he had. Noah had told her Alastair was deeply private, an enigma even to most of his friends.

"I still have your trunk," Alastair said, taking her to the next level of the house. "But if there's anything else you can think of that you need, you only have to ask for it." He stopped in front of the room where she'd stayed the last time she'd been here—right before she and Noah had gone on the run.

Ginger stepped inside, holding her breath as Alastair turned on lamps. Noah had found her here, and they'd made love in the large four-poster bed. She didn't want to remember it all right now.

Alastair went back to the doorway and waited there. She turned toward him, unable to keep her eyes from filling with tears. "I think he may be dead. I think they both may be."

Sadness filled his eyes. "We'll see what we can find out. In the meantime, you're alive and you're here, and I'm going to see to your every need. Noah is more than a friend to me. He's saved my life on more than one occasion. And you're his entire world. So now you're more than a friend to me too, my dear."

"Thank you, Alastair." Ginger didn't want to melt into a puddle of tears in front of him, and she gave him a tight-lipped, heart-broken smile.

He nodded. "I'll have a bath drawn, get you a meal and a bracing cup of tea. We're still English, yes? Tea always makes everything better."

Tea did sound wonderful. It wouldn't solve her troubles, but it was a sign that she had help now. "Just the tea and food. I can take a bath later. I'm exhausted."

"Whatever you need, dear." Alastair left, and she went over to her trunk and opened it. The familiar sight and smell of her things was unusually emotional, and she sank on the floor in front of it. Did Alastair also have Noah's possessions? He had to have some things, she imagined. Noah had checked out of Shepheard's Hotel before they'd left Cairo.

Right now, she wasn't certain she could bear the thought of going through Noah's personal possessions. But she would ask Alastair when she saw him again.

She eased out of her shoes and then pulled out her familiar medical kit to clean and bandage her blisters. Finding a warm pair of wool socks, she tugged them on, feeling a strange relief in them.

Then she dressed in pajamas and a dressing gown and crawled into the bed, brushing her hair as she walked.

Sleep came the moment her cheek touched the top of the pillow, and when she opened her eyes next, morning light streamed through the gaps around the window curtains. She turned her head, then noticed a cold cup of tea and a bowl of soup on the nightstand beside her. She sat, her mind in a fog.

Then she caught sight of a familiar figure seated at a chair near the foot of the bed, dozing.

Jack.

Ginger gasped, which caught Jack's attention. "Jack."

He looked up, blinking blearily.

Ginger tossed the covers aside. "Jack!" Hope and joy unfurled within her. "You're here. Oh, thank God." Seeing his face was more wonderful than she had imagined, her relief at his presence indescribable. She scrambled toward him, unconcerned about decorum or being in her pajamas.

"Red … you're awake." He held out a hand toward her. "How are you feeling?" He was in civilian clothes, a fedora on his head.

"I'm … fine. Well enough. When did you get here?" Whatever means Alastair had of finding and reaching Jack, Ginger felt more assured than ever that coming here was the right decision.

"I got in a couple of hours ago from Alexandria. Alastair sent for me."

Is Noah here, too?

"Where's Noah? Did you come alone?" Her voice sounded like gravel, and her lips felt dry and chapped. She hadn't meant to sound so accusing, but her tone seemed to condemn him.

Jack rubbed his jaw, then swallowed hard, his gaze darting away. "The thing is …"

"Jack, what's happened? Where's Noah?"

Jack shifted his eyes to hers for a moment, then looked away again. He removed his hat. "I haven't found him."

Lifting a hand to her throat, Ginger struggled to remain calm. *Then he really is missing?* "Wh-what do you mean? What happened? Didn't you go back for him?" She grabbed his arm.

Jack set his hat on the bed. "I went back for him, like you asked." He cleared his throat. "Only, I—I didn't find him. And I searched for as long as I could, but by then the ship was about to go down. I managed to grab onto a line for the *Attack* but ended up in the water when they cut the line as the *Aragon* was going down. I got on the *Attack*, but then after they torpedoed it, I ended up in the water again. Didn't make it to shore until close to five o'clock."

The thought of his ordeal made her feel ill. There had been so many dead in the water—he must have been surrounded by dead and dying men. "Were you in the water for long?"

"A boat picked me up after what felt like an hour, but we went around looking for survivors for a while." He met her gaze, his voice dull. "I've been searching for him ever since. For both of you. I found out where they'd sent you yesterday, but you were gone. I went to every hospital where the wounded were taken, and I've got friends combing through the records. Ginger—I …" He gathered himself slowly.

"Don't say it." Ginger's eyes pricked with tears. Jack's hand reached for hers again, and she pulled it away. She might not have noticed the subtle shift in his demeanor if she hadn't had years of practice writing to families about their dead sons.

He thinks Noah is dead.

"Over six hundred men are dead or missing, Ginger."

"But not Noah." She gave him a stern look, her eyes burning with tears. "You know him, Jack. He's good at surviving. And a strong swimmer. He promised to get off that ship as quickly as possible." *Not Noah. He can't be dead. I would know, wouldn't I?* Somehow, she felt certain she'd feel it.

"Yeah, I do know him. That's why I think the worst might have happened. He would have found a way to get to you by now, or at the very least, contact me. There are only a few people Noah trusts enough to reach out to in a circumstance like this and no one has heard from him."

She noticed the shadow of a beard on Jack's jaw right then, the redness of his eyes, the signs that he hadn't slept well for several days. "But anything might have happened. He might have—hit his head ..." Her voice cracked. She cleared her throat and went on. "Or be at a hospital you haven't checked yet. He might be injured and unable to find us."

Jack seemed to sense he shouldn't push, and he scanned her eyes, then nodded. "Yeah. Maybe. I haven't given up. I just don't have anywhere else left to look."

"Good, I'm glad to hear you haven't given up." Even though she knew Jack wasn't her enemy, she couldn't help but glare at him. "Because he would never give up on you so easily."

"Ginger, I—" Jack stared at her, his face drawn. A long, thin scab showed on his forehead, and she wondered if he'd received it while escaping the ship. *Poor Jack.* She should be nicer to him. He'd been nothing but a kind and caring friend. And if he really believed Noah was gone, he'd be devastated. He nodded at last. "No, you're right."

A light seemed to have gone out of Jack's eyes, his spirit crushed. Maybe Sarah's death had done it first, but this certainly hadn't helped. He looked weary and out of fight. He dropped back, lifting his hat from the bed. "You're right. I'll keep looking."

She strode toward her trunk. "I'm coming with you."

For a moment, the Jack she'd become friends with over the last year was there. Humor glinted in his eyes, a smile curving at his mouth. "Of course you think you are." He crossed his arms. "You know, they told me what you did. How you threw yourself in the water after the *Attack* sank. They were all shocked, of course. Didn't surprise me though. Sounds just like you—charging into battle without a plan."

She cringed sheepishly. "I thought—"

"That you could drown yourself? One of these days, you're going to have to learn that being heroic means standing down when everything inside you is screaming to move forward."

This wasn't about being heroic. Jack needed to understand her desperation.

"Jack, I think I'm with child. I have to find Noah."

Her revelation seemed to make the reality of it stronger. She'd never intended for Jack to be the first person she'd tell, but now here she was and he had to know.

Jack lifted his chin sharply, his eyes narrowing. "What?"

She rubbed her forehead. "I think I may be pregnant. I don't know for certain, but without Noah ..."

She didn't have to finish. Understanding dawned in Jack's eyes, and he stared at her without a word.

"Get dressed," he said at last. "Then come downstairs—Alastair will have breakfast set by now. And then we'll figure out what to do next."

She nodded and he left. Closing her eyes, she set her hands on her belly.

Was it a mistake to tell Jack?

What if he now refused to allow her to come with him?

Should she have told Noah her suspicions about a baby? In her heart, she was more certain of that reality than ever before. Maybe he wouldn't have gone back to his cabin when the *Aragon* had been struck. Maybe he would have stayed with her.

She'd have to find a doctor she could trust and who would be discreet to examine her.

Jane Radford, her surgeon friend, came to mind. They hadn't parted on the most cordial of terms, but Ginger had liked her and she was here in Cairo. She also seemed trustworthy. Going to her for something like this might be the best way to settle the matter once and for all.

And then Ginger was going to find her husband.

CHAPTER FOURTEEN

*I*t hardly seemed possible that it had been two months since Ginger had last been in Jane Radford's medical office in Cairo. So much had changed since then. They'd been friends, but Ginger's work for Cairo Intelligence had interfered and given Jane a negative view of her. When Ginger had been forced to choose between concealing Noah's participation in the assault on an English officer and her integrity, she'd chosen the former. In the end, Jane had realized Ginger's deception and had dropped her because of it.

Not that Ginger blamed her, really. She didn't know enough about Ginger—or Noah—to understand how extreme their circumstances had been. Jane was an excellent doctor and a woman of good moral character. Her assumptions about Ginger made sense.

But as Jane settled behind her desk, she offered a pleasant smile. The office in the Cairo hospital was sparsely decorated, but clean and brightly lit, with the requisite certifications on the walls and bookcases of medical reference books.

Ginger twisted the handkerchief she'd taken out of her handbag in her hands, a flutter of nerves in her stomach. She felt exposed and fought the urge to fidget more. She was certain she already knew the answer to her question: her nausea, level of exhaustion, and the tenderness of her breasts had already confirmed it in her mind. The medical examination had gone quickly enough, and Jane had said nothing when Ginger had requested it—or when she'd examined Ginger.

"You're expecting," Jane said, without ceremony. She raised a dark brow. "But I'm assuming you already knew that?"

Expecting. Such a foreign sound to such a concrete reality.

Yes, I knew.

She'd never really envisioned how this moment should be. So much of motherhood felt like a mysterious unknown to her. But she'd expected it would be joyful, with visions of a chubby-cheeked infant and pushing a white pram.

Instead, she felt strangely hollow, uncertain. Even fearful. Awful, because her husband was missing and, instead of being here with her as he should be, or even being able to share this news with him, she was instead facing a future where her child's father might be dead.

Just breathe.

The news wasn't something she could easily absorb. But, then again, Ginger had spent the last month with the idea firmly planted. Her body had known, even if her mind hadn't completely accepted it. She'd been a daughter, lover, wife—*mother* had a very different feel to it.

"Ginger?" Jane asked, bringing her back to the present moment. "Are you quite well? Do you need a glass of water?"

Ginger winced, pushing dozens of other thoughts and questions from her brain. "I thought I was with child, yes." She smoothed her hands over her lap.

Jane gave her a wary look. "If you're hoping I can help rid you of the problem—"

"No." Ginger gave a firm shake to her head, horrified that Jane would assume that was why she'd come. "No. It's my husband's child. But ... he's missing."

"Your husband?" Jane's eyes widened, and she stared at Ginger, a shocked expression on her face. "I didn't know you were married."

"Yes, I've been married since November, when I was working with you."

Jane touched her temple as though the news was difficult for her to process. Nurses for most official organizations weren't, by rule, married women. "I-I suppose I knew little about you, did I?"

"But you did." Ginger gave her a tight smile. "I ... I wish I'd been more forthright than I was, but I was in a difficult position. Almost everything you knew about me was true. Except that I was married. To Colonel Noah Benson, whom you met one time when I asked him to call for your help. I expect you've read about him in the papers."

Jane stiffened, then dipped her chin in a nod. "Yes, I have." She gave Ginger a wary look, as though trying to assess if Ginger was involved with Noah's purported acts of treason and murder.

Although she didn't owe Jane an explanation, Ginger felt the need to defend Noah—and, perhaps, herself. Clarify the truth once and for all.

"He's not the criminal they have accused him of being. I know who framed him. But regardless of that, the ship we were on—the *Aragon*—was torpedoed off the coast of Alexandria. He's been missing ever since."

Was it dangerous to tell Jane? With each day of Noah's absence, Ginger didn't know what was safe to say or not.

Jane blinked a few times, then set her hands on her desk. "I want to believe you, Ginger. I really do. But I ..." She dipped her aquiline nose as she examined the desktop with sudden thoughtfulness.

But you don't.

Jane, like most, believed the worst about Noah. That was

Stephen's triumph—convincing the world that Noah was truly a villain.

Sighing, Ginger stood. "I only came for the examination, Dr. Radford. And I appreciate you doing it. And for your silence about my visit here. Thank you. I wish you well."

Ginger turned and started for the door, feeling glum. This was a good-bye she wasn't sure she had needed. They had parted on frosty terms before, and nothing would ever bring back Jane Radford's good opinion of her.

"Ginger, wait." Jane came out from behind her desk, pulling her stethoscope off her neck and setting it on the chair Ginger had previously occupied. "Where will you go?"

Ginger rubbed her forehead. She was tired, her mood bleaker than ever before. "I'm not sure." She adjusted her hat. "I'll stay in Cairo for a while, see if I can find my husband. Then go to England, I suppose. I have some family there, though I'm uncertain they'll see me."

"Do you have any money? Any means to survive?" Jane crossed her arms. "To be honest, finding your husband may not do you much good, considering who he is. And you were an excellent nurse. Your talents shouldn't be … " She cocked her head to the side to allow Ginger to answer her previous questions.

Ginger straightened, clasping her handbag. Jane's questions were highly inappropriate, but perhaps Ginger had invited them by discussing the details of her private life. She felt her face flush with embarrassment and drew a sharp breath in through her nose.

"I don't feel right about setting you on the street in your condition," Jane said at last, seeming to sense that she'd gone too far. She studied Ginger for a moment longer, then rubbed her brow.

"I may regret this, but I'm hoping I don't." Jane walked back to her desk and wrote something on a slip of paper. "This is the name and address for Dr. Louisa Garrett Anderson. She's a close friend of mine. She's currently working at the Endell Street Military Hospital in London. Should you decide to go back to England, consider looking her up. You can tell her I sent you, and I'll write a letter to her recommending she help you complete your training as a physician. I'm sure you're well on your way with what you've studied. And Louisa has far more connections than I do."

Complete her training as a physician? Ginger gaped at her, stunned.

For years, she'd contemplated the idea. But now, becoming a physician had been the furthest thing from her mind. Jane held out the paper, and Ginger took it from her. "Thank you," she managed. Her eyes threatened to mist over, but she successfully controlled the impulse. She'd been doing enough crying as it was.

Jane's kindness was overwhelming, though, and Ginger fought the urge to hug her. Even though she hadn't been in England for several years, Ginger knew the name of Louisa Garrett Anderson. Her mother, Elizabeth, had been the first woman to qualify as a physician in England and had founded the London School of Medicine for Women. Her aunt, Millicent Fawcett, was one of the most well-known suffragists in the country. To say Louisa had connections was an understatement.

"No one can take an education from you," Jane said with a taut smile. Her hand dropped to her side. "It's the smartest thing any woman could do for herself. And you, my dear, are a smart woman."

As Ginger left the hospital where Jane worked, she stepped out onto the pavement, a strange pressure in her chest. From the steps, she pictured the motorcar Noah had driven to pick her up from the hospital a couple of months earlier. The city had broken out into riots because of the publication of the Sykes-Picot agreement, the locals protesting at the way the British government had promised to parcel out the lands of Arabia and the Levant after the war between themselves and the French.

Noah had been worried about her and come to pick her up.

Then he'd driven her to Coptic Cairo, and they'd married in secret.

She couldn't stop the tears that formed now, her hands clutching her tight, flat stomach. She couldn't see her pregnancy yet, but she knew it wouldn't be long before her belly would grow. Her body was already changing in ways she hadn't quite expected, her level of exhaustion seeming worse than when she'd worked fourteen-hour shifts on the front.

And in a few short months she'd have a baby and have to learn to be a mother, all alone without his hand to hold or his encouragement. The thought of being a parent was frightening enough. But without Noah?

He wouldn't have ever left her.

Never, never.

Either he was alive, and she'd find him …

Or he's dead.

She glanced up as a motorcar stopped by the pavement. The door opened and Jack, who'd brought her here, came toward the curb. She hurried toward him, pushing back the rising tide of grief.

Jack lifted his eyebrows expectantly.

"It's what I believed."

Jack's expression clouded, then he rubbed his eyes. "All right. Then I'm taking you back to England. It's what I promised Noah I would do, anyway, and he wouldn't want you here in Cairo."

"I'm not leaving without Noah."

The brim of Jack's hat shaded his eyes as he turned his back to the motorcar and leaned against it. "I've been to every hospital in Alexandria, Red. Scoured the lists of known casualties. He's not there."

"What about the unidentified or unconscious among them? Cases of amnesia, perhaps? There are still possibilities we haven't explored—"

"He's not here!" Jack stopped and faced her, his face a mixture of agony and impatience. "We can't keep hoping more injured will come in from a ship that sank four days ago. A third of the men that went into that water didn't come out." He pulled a flask from his jacket pocket, unscrewed it, and took a sip. "There's nothing else we can do. He's dead. Just like Sarah."

Her eyes narrowed, and a spark of fury churned through her. "And this is your solution? Get drunk and forget about it? We're talking about my husband. To hell with your sorrow, Jack Darby." She snatched the flask out of his hands, then hurled it toward the street, where it bounced against the side of a passing cart. The flask landed on the dirt road with a thud.

"Goddamn you!" Jack scowled at her, his face dark.

"Well, Goddamn you too!" She squared off with him, her shoulders thrown back, her chest tight.

Their gazes continued locked for several moments until Jack shook his head and walked away, to gather his fallen flask from the street. Then he shook his head at her as though he was finished dealing with her, his hands balled into fists.

"Fine, just go, you miserable louse!" she called after him. She ignored the looks of passersby who probably thought she was an ill-mannered, lower class, and vulgar woman. She couldn't care less.

His broad shoulders knitted with tension.

Damn the day my husband went missing, and I was stuck dealing with this insufferable drunk. Ginger clenched her jaw, trying to tell herself not to cry. She couldn't afford to be this way with the people who were helping her.

Closing her eyes, she pulled out a handkerchief and dabbed at her eyes.

Noah was nowhere to be found.

She released a slow breath.

How in the world would she make it through without him?

A gentle hand on her shoulder startled her. Jack stood beside her stiffly, dully looking out at the crowded road.

Sniffling, Ginger didn't look him in the eye. Her fingers curled around the handkerchief he held out, and she noticed the embroidered monogram in the corner: SCH. *Sarah Catherine Hanover.*

Her tears grew thicker.

She'd loved Sarah, but she hadn't been as close to her as Jack had been.

And Noah was his best friend.

He's suffering, just like you.

Ginger knew she should be grateful for his friendship, not fighting with him in public because he'd accepted the horrible news that she couldn't let herself accept. Ginger sighed. "I apologize for throwing your flask."

"Yeah, well, I probably deserved it." Jack squeezed the back of his neck. "I'm sorry for snapping at you. I'm exhausted. It's been a long time since I got more than an hour or two of sleep. Every night I lie awake in my bed, staring at the ceiling and wondering why I'm still here when Sarah and Noah—" His jaw clenched and he looked down.

Are dead? Ginger didn't complete the thought out loud, the words hitting her hard in the chest. She'd wondered the same thing. Sarah and Noah were infinitely more athletic, more talented, more resourceful, and prepared than she could ever have been.

Jack's voice was a low, conciliatory growl as he offered, "We can keep looking. Wherever you want. But I can only give you a week and then I'm taking you back to England—deal?" He rubbed his hands together. "I'm worried Noah ran into trouble on the ship. And the only reason he was on that damned ship was because—"

Ginger waited for Jack to finish, but he lapsed into stony silence.

She hadn't even considered that possibility.

The magnitude of the shipwreck had dwarfed the idea that Noah's disappearance could have anything to do with the spy in Malta or whoever had killed Sarah.

A lump formed in her throat and she squeezed her eyes shut, not wanting to entertain the myriad of unknown options that could exist with that possibility.

And yet, what if she was ignoring the most obvious reason for Noah to be missing?

A rattling cart, laden with goats, passed on the street and she watched them go by, their faces staring out from behind the enclosure that held them tightly packed inside, reminding her of prisoners being led to their execution. Noah's face flashed in her mind at the thought. If Sarah's death was connected to this, then she needed to broaden the possibilities of what might have happened.

That means thinking of who would have wanted Noah to disappear.

She lifted her chin. "What if they captured Noah? Lord Helton or Stephen could be holding him somewhere."

Jack rubbed his temple, his face darkening. "Alastair is already looking into that possibility. But the truth is we both know what would happen if they got him. Lord Helton wouldn't hesitate to announce his capture and have him executed—or to shoot him before he even gets a trial. And Fisher wouldn't hesitate to kill him, either. Noah being alive is a liability for them both."

She didn't want to admit how right Jack was. The thought of Noah being in Stephen's or Lord Helton's control made her ill.

"But we should talk to someone. Maybe even them. You know them both—you can probably tell if they're lying. Or even Victoria might know something. Victoria is in love with Noah; she's bound to want to find out what happened and be on our side."

Jack shook his head. "If you think Victoria isn't her father's puppet, then you don't know her at all, Ginger. She's married to Fisher now. You're right—she's not like them. I don't think she's even a bad person. But Lord Helton has been manipulating her for years, and he holds those purse strings tightly."

What on earth? Victoria had *married* Stephen?

Acid burned in her chest. *Poor Victoria.* "How do you know?"

"Like I said, I already thought of the possibility that Helton or

Fisher got ahold of Noah. The first thing I did when I couldn't find her was to find out everything I could about their current status."

"But doesn't Helton know what a brigand Stephen is? Why on earth would he want his daughter to marry him?" Ginger set her hand on the frame of the car to steady herself, feeling shaky at the thought.

Jack held the car door open for Ginger. "If Noah had been here, he'd probably have tried to talk some sense into her, but the fact is that Victoria is always going to choose her own comfort over everything. Who knows what arrangements her father has made? Fisher's rich enough to tempt him, that's for sure. But I think there's a higher chance Fisher trapped her into that marriage."

Ginger climbed into the motorcar, dazed. She couldn't imagine what Stephen could offer Lord Helton to allow the marriage or what could possess Victoria to move forward with it. Blinking hard, she surveyed the city street.

Jack was right; Noah *would* have tried to talk sense into Victoria.

Much as Victoria's relationship with Noah had always bothered Ginger—particularly the fact that they'd used an engagement as a ruse while Noah investigated Ginger's father—she knew Noah had also genuinely cared for her.

And if Lord Helton or Stephen knew anything about Noah, Victoria would be the one Ginger might persuade to help her.

As Jack climbed back into the driver's seat, she gave him a sidelong glance, clasping her hands tightly. "Jack, we have to go and talk to Victoria. Please. She might know or be able to find out about Noah."

Jack gave her a skeptical look. "You really like to go from the frying pan to the fire, don't you? She's never going to help you, Ginger."

"Please, Jack. Please help me. I need to explore every possibility."

Jack's eyes returned to the road. "I couldn't live with myself if I took you within two miles of Fisher knowingly. The answer is no.

I'm sorry. I might go myself, if that's what you really want, but I'm not taking you there. I know you don't want to listen to me, Ginger, but the best chance we have right now is Noah finding us and not making you the bait for his enemies—if he's alive. Between Alastair and me, we won't leave any stone unturned searching for him. But, so far, there's nothing. No one has any information to share."

Ginger swallowed hard, trying to temper any desire to lash out at Jack.

The midday sun burned brightly against her skin, the warm air was suffocating, and she blinked dully at the blur of passing buildings.

If Jack wouldn't take her, she might have to take matters into her own hands.

Sweat burned Ginger's eyes as they passed by the front of Shepheards' Hotel. The outdoor space was always packed with military officers and ladies from Anglo Cairo, taking tea and gossiping, making merry. The dragoman guides stood at the entrance, and she could practically hear the clink of porcelain and smell the fine perfumes.

She no longer belonged to that world, did she?

With a child, she wouldn't belong to many worlds, though. Without a husband, people would shut both her and her child out from most of society.

Unless I attempt to make peace with my family.

"One of these days, you're going to have to learn that being heroic means standing down when everything inside you is screaming to move forward," Jack had said. That was what he wanted her to do. Stand down, accept that Noah was gone.

She knew what Noah had wanted—for her to go to England. To be safe.

And that was without him knowing I'm carrying a baby.

The palm trees in Ezbekieh Gardens swayed in a breeze, and her drive through the famed streets of Cairo felt like a procession—or a good-bye.

How many times had she charged into battle without listening to others? She was headstrong and obstinate. Stubborn.

But she wasn't in charge of simply her own life now. She had something—*someone*—more to consider. And her child had no one else as an advocate.

Not even a father, it seems.

She wanted to scream, to stomp, to wail.

Noah ....

Could their love just end like this? This wasn't like the death of her father or brother—or anyone else she'd known.

He can't be dead ...

She drew a shattered breath, and despite the roar of the engine and the winds of the moving car as they drove, Jack seemed to sense her distress. He glanced over, alarm on his face.

A part of her soul felt as though it had been ripped from her body and thrown into the abyss, gone forever.

She might never again see Noah's smile, bask in the warmth of his embrace. She could never recover, never heal from his absence. But throwing herself at the mercy of Lord Helton and Stephen wasn't what Noah would have wanted, either. And if he was alive, he'd promised to find her.

He would find her if he were alive.

He's dead.

The thought made her squeeze her eyes shut, struggle for composure.

Jack pulled over to the side of the road and turned off the engine. "What is it?"

She stared at her hands tightly clasped in her lap, the rings Noah had given her on her fingers. The ankh ring.

One night, while they'd been in their room in Malta, Ginger had been in Noah's arms, holding his hand.

"What exactly does the ankh mean?" she'd asked, her fingers tightening against his.

Noah kissed her temple. "The ancient Egyptians saw it as a symbol of life. Or, more accurately, that death is never the end. Just the beginning of a new life."

Here in Cairo, on the edge of the Sahara, the ancient world had placed its graveyard in the dust and stone that would never fade. The lush banks of the Nile, green with life and vegetation, were for the living.

The desert was for the dead.

A breeze carried the scent of that dust and distant smoke and baked earth. Scents she lived and breathe in during her time as a nurse in this war.

But no more.

Noah wouldn't want her to break herself trying to find him. He'd want her to carry on. In Jack's words, maybe the heroic thing was doing the most difficult thing of all: sacrificing her own bullheaded desire to keep searching against hope and accept that she had a new life to take care of now.

Ginger turned toward Jack and put a hand on his arm. "Take me to England, Jack."

CHAPTER FIFTEEN

FEBRUARY 1918

LONDON, ENGLAND

*T*he last time Ginger had stood at the doorstep of her aunt's home in London had been late in 1914—and somehow it still looked the same. The creamy white exterior of the modern Edwardian home seemed unsullied by the German bombardments that had been occurring in the city, the hedges still perfectly trimmed behind the black wrought-iron fence.

Yet, Ginger no longer felt like the naïve girl that had charged up those steps shortly after the war had been declared, bubbling with the idea of being a nurse. She felt like a worn shoe that had once been advertised as sturdy, necessary, and smart but had still succumbed to shabbiness, holes, and a threadbare sole after an arduous journey.

Ginger waited for the cab driver to put her bag onto the curb, nerves tingling at the back of her neck. After taking a ship from Alexandria to Marseilles, she and Jack had gone back to England through France, which had taken longer than expected. She couldn't have asked for a better friend than Jack Darby, if she was honest, though he'd sobered since Cairo—in more ways than one. His amiable smiles and jokes seemed to have become rarer.

When they'd arrived in Southampton, Ginger had dared to call her Aunt Madeline, who lived in the fashionable neighborhood of Knightsbridge in London. She thought Madeline might be the only source of support she'd get from her family and a good way to test the waters to see how she might be received. To her surprise, Madeline had invited her to come up to town at once.

But now, staring at the façade of her aunt's elegant home, Ginger felt out of place. She reconsidered Jack's offer to help her get a hotel room until she could get situated. A lump formed in her throat. She couldn't continue to take advantage of Jack's generosity—or think that it was limitless. Not when she owed Jack so much.

At one point or another, she was going to have to make it on her own.

Before Ginger could start up the steps, the butler opened the door to the house. "Lady Virginia," he said with a polite smile. "How good it is to see you." A footman hurried out to fetch her belongings.

Ginger tried not to notice the poor footman's surprise when he saw only one small carpetbag on the curb. She'd made do with two dresses and two nightgowns for the trip home, washing her soiled clothing while she wore the other. It was easy to not care when a black dress for mourning was her everyday choice.

While she'd traveled, her dresses hadn't mattered. She was in mourning and no one knew her to ask. But here it might present a problem, since her aunt might not even know she'd been married.

"Likewise, Giles." Ginger returned the butler's smile and then shuffled into the house, feeling as though she had to force one foot in front of the other.

Before Ginger could even peek around, her aunt rushed into the foyer, hands outstretched. "Ginger Eleanor, my dearest darling niece, let me look at you!"

Of all her extended family, Ginger had always felt she fit the best with her mother's younger sister, who was as warm and lively as she was enthusiastic about politics and social reform. Like Ginger and her mother, Madeline also had red hair and green eyes, though her hair was a darker auburn hue. Madeline's daughter, Meg, had always been amused that strangers often thought Ginger was Madeline's daughter. Like her father, Hugh, Meg had dark-blonde hair and brown eyes.

Ginger straightened as Madeline reached her, her self-consciousness growing. Madeline pulled her into a tight hug, though, and Ginger sagged against her. At once, the nerves and worries vanished, replaced by a crushing feeling of relief. Ginger hugged her aunt tightly, her eyes filling with tears.

Madeline wiped her own eyes and held Ginger's cheeks, scanning her eyes. "My goodness, you've grown up so beautifully. I always thought you were the family beauty, but you're a stunning woman now."

Ginger's cheeks warmed as Madeline pressed her forehead against Ginger's, brushing the tears from her face with her thumbs. "But what have you done to your hair? Tinted it?"

Cringing, Ginger nodded. The red roots had been growing in longer. "I'll have to see about fixing it. It's a long story."

"Yes, I miss my *ginger* Ginger. I am so happy you're back." Madeline stood straight and reached for Ginger's hand. "What can I get you first? Tea?" She surveyed Ginger's dress. "And I can see about scrounging some dresses from Meg's room. She's still in France—and she'll be devastated to hear she missed seeing you."

Ginger set her hand on Madeline's wrist. "Before you do anything, I need to tell you—I may not be the most welcome guest. My mother and Lucy—"

"Oh, they'll be along for dinner. Mama too. I haven't had the chance to tell any of them you're here. They'd all gone out for the day by the time you called."

Her family was here? And it didn't sound as though her mother had told Madeline anything about the estrangement or what had happened in Egypt. Ginger's face fell. She had to tell Madeline now. She might not want her here if she knew the truth and silence would be dishonest.

Ginger glanced over her shoulder at Giles, who still stood in the vicinity, then fidgeted with her gloves. "I'm afraid Mama isn't likely to be as happy to see me as you are. Nor Lucy. We didn't part under the best of circumstances in Cairo."

"Well, I should say not. Your father and brother are both victims of this war—it's been a terrible time for all of you." Madeline shook her head with sympathy. "Speaking of which, I'm eager to hear what on earth happened with your dear Dr. Clark. When you left for Egypt, you were an engaged woman, with an admirable and intelligent young man on your arm. I was so sorry to hear that your engagement had ended."

James. Yet another person who hadn't been able to help her find Noah. Ginger had sent him a message before leaving Egypt, but he had replied with no news to share. Ginger smiled sadly. Just what should she tell her aunt about Noah?

The truth would likely come out soon enough. Faster than Ginger might be comfortable with. But soon there would be no hiding her pregnancy—and that was *if* Madeline allowed her to stay after she learned of Ginger's involvement in her family's misfortunes. If her mother and Lucy were staying here with Madeline, she had to know some of their difficulties.

But how could she share all that had happened with Noah without bringing up Stephen and her father and Henry?

She glanced again at Giles. This wasn't the type of conversation to have in front of a servant, no matter how faithfully he served.

Madeline followed Ginger's gaze, then looked back at Ginger.

"Yes, let's have tea. It might be good to get a decent cup. Lucy's told me all about how you developed the habit of putting sugar in it because of the horrible taste of the tinned milk—simply atrocious." She gave Ginger a serene smile. "Giles, will you please have tea brought to the library? There's a nice cozy fire going, and the sofa there is much more comfortable than the sitting room."

Ginger followed her into the room, glad to be out of the purview of curious eyes she knew would watch in the hallway. The library might be Madeline's idea of a comfortable room, but it made Ginger chuckle to herself. Two long walls had wall-to-ceiling bookcases, including a ladder for the books on the topmost shelves. The other walls boasted enormous oil portraits of her Uncle Hugh's ancestors. Every detail of the room spoke of luxury, from the ornamental plaster and medallions on the ceilings, to the beautifully uphol-stered sofas and armchair—all of which seemed too expensive to sit on.

She sat on the sofa, careful to set her handbag in front of her. She wasn't showing much yet, but every day the slight bulge of her belly seemed to grow, a reality that still felt so distant.

Sharing the news with anyone else right now still filled her with dread. The tiny life inside her provided the only speck of joy and hope she felt—but also would turn her world upside down. She wasn't prepared to have the only light within her be a source of struggle and pain yet.

Madeline sat across from her, worry lining her brow. "What is it, my dear? You look as though you're carrying a tremendous weight on your shoulders."

Ginger pulled off her gloves and set them on her lap. "I met someone else. An officer who worked for Cairo Intelligence." A lump formed in her throat.

She could practically picture Noah the first time they'd met, in an abandoned ramshackle hut in Palestine. Or the next morning, when she'd really had her first good look at him. Sometimes she'd wondered if she'd fallen in love with him at that first sight, ridiculous as it sounded. She hoped her mother and Lucy hadn't already prejudiced Madeline against him. "Colonel Noah Benson."

Madeline's eyes warmed. "A real, passionate romance, I take it? The love you'd always said you were dreaming of?"

Then she hasn't heard of him.

Ginger nodded. "Yes, it was wonderful." She ran her fingers over the fabric of her gloves. "But I made some mistakes along the way. And then we married in secret, last November. After which, Mama asked me to leave. We went to Malta for a month, then boarded troopship *Aragon*. It was torpedoed off the coast of Egypt, though, and I believe my husband went down with the ship."

Ginger barely met her aunt's gaze. Even though it had been a month since the sinking, the reality of her situation was still hard to verbalize. Would Mama and Lucy be glad to hear of Noah's death? That might be even worse than having to tell them.

Madeline was silent for a while, her expression sorrowful. She left her spot across from Ginger and sat beside her, taking her hands. "I'm so very sorry, my dear." She touched Ginger's cheek. "Elizabeth didn't tell me any of this."

That her mother had shared nothing about the scandals and trials that had rocked their family wasn't surprising. But Ginger had expected that somehow her family might have heard whispers of it all through gossip. Maybe the lines of communication between Anglo Cairo and London were narrower than she'd imagined they might be.

"She doesn't know that Noah is most likely dead," Ginger said, feeling her shoulders tensing. Even though she'd wanted to be cautious in what she shared for the sake of her family, she couldn't help but feeling duplicitous. "His disappearance prompted me to come back here ... because, unfortunately, there's a bit more to it." Ginger couldn't meet her aunt's eyes, feeling her cheeks redden further. "We didn't legalize our marriage at the consulate. We married in the Coptic Catholic church and then didn't have time to go to the consulate. And … I'm with child."

Madeline paled. "Oh." She gripped Ginger's hand tighter, looking down at their clasped hands. A slight flush spread across the freckled skin on her chest, above her neckline, a physical response that Ginger had dealt with often enough to understand what it meant. She was flustered.

When Madeline didn't speak, Ginger went on. "I intend to raise my child, of course. I won't be considering a quiet adoption or any other option. I loved my husband, and this baby is all I have left of him. But I know that—"

"You'll be seen as an unwed mother." Madeline frowned deeply, a line forming between her eyebrows. "And I'm assuming you're intelligent enough to have considered the impact this will have on your mother and, especially, your sister. The family honor is at stake."

"I don't know how to tell them," Ginger whispered, staring dully at the fireplace.

"Are you planning on staying in this country?"

Ginger closed her eyes, the subtext of her aunt's question clear enough. Moving away would avoid disgrace to her family.

A servant chose that moment to come into the room, carrying a tea service.

Madeline directed the servant gracefully and seemingly unperturbed. As the servant left, she handed Ginger a teacup.

She sighed. "Leave the matter of telling your mother this news to me. I take it we won't be having a joyous reunion at dinnertime." A sad look crossed her face. "Would you prefer I ring Mama and tell her not to come? I know she'll be terribly disappointed, but it may be one less person to face."

As much as her grandmother had always been an ally in the past, Ginger doubted Gran would find much sympathy for Ginger in this case. Gran was old-fashioned enough to be appalled at Ginger's behavior.

Still, she hadn't seen her grandmother for years. And once her mother found out about the baby, Ginger's access to her family might be even further limited. Ginger shook her head. "No, let her come. I'd love to see her."

Madeline nodded, then paced the room for a moment. She stopped near the fireplace and gave a heavy sigh. "You know we all admire you a great deal, darling. You gave Meg the push she needed to join the Voluntary Aid Detachment, and while Hugh might still be sick to his stomach about it, I'm proud of our girl, out there serving our Tommies."

Ginger nodded, feeling chagrined. If only her aunt knew how terribly and humiliatingly things had ended for Ginger in her service as a nurse. "Meg was always brave. She needed little encouragement, I'm sure." She missed her cousin. They'd been close as young girls and were only two years apart. But keeping in touch during the war had proven especially difficult. Ginger couldn't remember the last time they'd exchanged letters.

Would Madeline and her Uncle Hugh want Ginger to have much to do with Meg once Ginger's name was fully sullied? She doubted it. They were far more liberal than her own parents had been, but they still had to be a part of society.

"And you're sure there's no way of proving your marriage was legitimate? I'd imagine you're owed a pension if you can, at the very least. How do you plan to survive without that?"

Did she dare tell her aunt that Noah had been charged with killing her father and brother—as well as a laundry list of other horrific crimes? She wanted to. It would be better that Madeline heard about Noah from her instead of her mother.

But she hesitated. Madeline might be Ginger's ally now, but it wasn't entirely fair to pit her mother against her own sister. And if Ginger's mother and Lucy had come to Madeline and Hugh's for shelter and help, what right did Ginger have to make their lives more difficult?

I've done enough to ruin their lives already.

Ginger turned her attention back to Madeline. "I don't think I can prove anything or get a pension, unfortunately." Her best solution was to take the reference Jane Radford had offered for Dr. Louisa Garrett Anderson. But training as a physician would require money she didn't have and would also be sure to displease her family.

Madeline shook her head. "That's a shame. Well, leave the matter to me. I'm sure, between us all, we can think of a way to get you out of this mess."

CHAPTER SIXTEEN

The closer the clocked ticked to dinner, the more acid burned in Ginger's throat. After she'd taken a bath and napped, Madeline had sent a lady's maid to help her dress for dinner and fix her hair. The luxuries of her youth seemed so distant that the poor maid's tending to Ginger flustered her. A lady's maid wasn't likely to be part of Ginger's future, and she wasn't at all sorry about that.

But Ginger was certain that, by now, her mother and Lucy must have already arrived and been informed of her presence. That neither of them had come to see her in her room spoke volumes. She hoped maybe Madeline had told them she was resting, but she doubted that was the reason they kept away.

Pacing in her room, Ginger glanced at the full-length oval mirror in the corner. Her cousin's black dress wasn't a perfect fit, but the maid had done her best and stitched Ginger into it, which had helped. Being tall would help Ginger hide her pregnancy for some time, and it might be necessary until Madeline told her mother. And the dark dress was forgiving.

The doorknob to her room turned without warning and Ginger

startled, turning. Her mother came into the room, shutting the door behind her quietly. She stood back to the door, her shoulders taut, face drawn.

She's not happy to see me.

"Mama—"

Her mother lifted a hand to stop her, and it surprised Ginger to see Mama's fingers trembled.

Ginger's heart gave a painful lurch. She wanted to go to her and embrace her, beg for forgiveness. She was the prodigal daughter, returned, but unlike the Bible story, her mother took no pleasure in her presence.

"Why did you come?" Her mother's voice was startlingly quiet.

Tearful emotion thickened Ginger's throat, but she kept her eyes from misting. Only absolute honesty could help her here. "I had nowhere else to go. I was on board the troopship *Aragon* with Noah when it was torpedoed and he's been missing ever since." She stepped forward, then stopped, clasping her hands. "I didn't know you and Lucy were here either."

Her mother tightened her lips to a firm line. She continued to stare at Ginger for a full minute, then came further into the room, as though only to speak in a whisper. "Madeline has informed me of your ... *condition.*"

The way her mother said it, with revulsion, made a spark of anger crest inside her. Her fingers curled into her palms. "It's not a disease, Mama. I'm going to have a child—your grandchild. A child that was conceived within the bonds of marriage to my husband, who—"

"Do not speak of that man." Mama came closer. "Thank goodness he's dead."

Ginger held back a strangled gasp. Her mother's words were flat, without ceremony, and cutting. Ginger hadn't expected sympathy, but she'd never known her mother to be cruel, either.

"You'll find I haven't changed my opinion of him at all. I loved him. With all my heart. And I'm sorry that he wasn't what you wanted for me. But if I hadn't been forced to hide my love for him, I wouldn't be in this position either."

"No, darling. If you'd done a better job controlling your lust, you wouldn't be in this position." Her mother went over to an armchair and sank wearily into it. "I understand the mechanics of how you got this way quite well enough. I did mother three children."

Humiliating as it was to have *that* conversation with her mother, she needed to redirect the conversation. Still, her face flushed. "That's not what I meant—"

"I know." Her mother drew in a sharp breath through her nose. "And I know you were in love with the man."

Dull pressure at the back of her head thrummed with her pulse. She closed her eyes.

"He was my husband, Mama. Not some random ill-bred stranger who seduced me. You know so little about him, of what he did for me." The words came out in a rush. She cleared her throat and went on. "In Palestine, he rode out into the desert and rescued me from a group of Ottoman Turks that had taken me as their prisoner. He protected me time and time again. He loved me." Tears splashed onto her cheeks, and she finished in a whisper, "And I loved him."

Her mother stared at her, unblinking. Her mouth fell open, as though she couldn't think of how to respond.

Ginger touched the wedding ring she'd given him, which hung around her neck. "This is all I have left of him. I have no pension, no money. You know what Stephen Fisher did to Noah—he took everything away. The lies the newspapers in Cairo printed about Noah, you knew—*knew* Father was to blame for some of those crimes. You know what Stephen is. And you don't have to forgive me for taking Henry away from our family ..."

The hurt in her mother's face showed plainly enough.

Ginger cringed. She could only imagine the pain her mother must feel upon hearing this. "But Henry had thrown his lot in with

Stephen. Father had brokered a deal with Lord Helton to save himself from some of the worst charges, but Henry didn't want to abide by that. He blamed Noah for everything and thought that if he simply killed Noah, life could go on merrily. Noah had done nothing to—"

Her mother pressed her lips together. "Colonel Benson was no saint. His reputation was that of a rake, and he was clearly a gifted liar. And look what he did to poor Lady Victoria Everill—ending their engagement so publicly and breaking her heart. Everyone whispered it was your fault, after that scandal. You were still a sullied woman. You *are* a sullied woman. And you'll never be accepted in polite society anywhere."

Ouch. Her mother wasn't hesitating to let her know how she felt. "Mother, I don't care about that. And Lady Victoria and Noah were never engaged. That was part of Noah's cover while he was investigating Father, so that Father wouldn't suspect Noah's constant, direct communication with Lord Helton."

Her mother's face colored, her green eyes blazing with anger. "This is …" She rose to her feet. Pacing to the window, she glanced out to the street below. Her face seemed thinner than Ginger remembered. Her mother pulled the curtain back as though to block others from hearing their discussion. Turning back to Ginger, she hissed, "If you insist on raising Benson's bastard child, you'll be disgraced. Forever."

Ginger's jaw dropped open with outrage. Was that how her mother thought of her baby? "My child isn't illegitimate."

"A wedding no one knows about. Not to mention you *were* legally required to go to the consulate. Your child will be a bastard before everyone." Her mother wrung her hands, the heels of her shoes clicking on the wooden floorboards as she paced. "We will need to consider what to do next to fix this problem."

Ginger jerked her chin. She knew the hidden meaning in her mother's words. This situation needing "fixing" of the variety that brought the least amount of discomfort for her family members rather than herself. "There isn't any problem for you to fix here, Mother."

For the first time, Ginger saw her mother with fresh eyes. For so long, she'd suspected her mother of being complicit with her father's crimes, unwilling to show moral opposition because it benefited the family. But now she wondered if her mother's desire to maintain the family status—an attribute Ginger had long associated with Lucy—hadn't partially driven her father to do the unthinkable.

"How can you be so selfish?" Her mother narrowed her eyes at Ginger.

"Selfish?" The irony of her mother's accusation made her recoil. "How dare you accuse me of that? I'm not the one who is desperately trying to cling to a social construct that has failed me."

Her mother's fingers instinctively went to the pearl necklace hanging low down her chest. One of the last vestiges of the former grand role she'd played as a wealthy countess. "When you decided you wanted to go to nursing school, I said nothing. I encouraged it, in fact."

Ginger didn't respond, and her mother went on. "When you served in the most horrific places, I said nothing."

Her mother's shoulders dropped. "Then I saw you throw away a perfectly good match for a man without connections and, worst of all, one who was determined to bring your father to task for the things he had done for our family. Well, you got your wish, Ginger—your father never came home. And you *killed* Henry, leaving us with nothing. And, even then, your cousin William proposed to you, offering you one last chance to save us all, and you brushed him aside for the man who had facilitated our family's ruin."

Ginger clenched her jaw. Her mother would never forgive Noah or her. *Which is why I came for Madeline's help, not hers.*

Coming here was a huge mistake. She needed to leave before her family tried to control her and her "situation" for their own purposes.

Her mother turned, her eyes blazing. "If you do this, Ginger—if you decide to have this baby under the circumstances you've chosen —you won't just be ruining your own life, you'll be ruining your sister's. In the sight of the law, you're an unmarried woman. Who will want to marry Lucy with such connections? Her name will be tarnished by yours."

"What choice do I have, Mother? This is my husband's child."

Her mother's face hardened. "Your dead husband's."

"My *missing* husband's. I may hold out the thinnest hope imaginable that he's alive, but there's still hope." Ginger cut her eyes at her. How long had her mother been stewing in anger that she couldn't even manage the slightest shred of sympathy? "How can you be so cruel? Have you nothing kind to say at all? Can't you understand my pain? You aren't the only person to have lost, Mama. I lost Father and Henry too—and their deaths haunt my nightmares because I saw them both die. I've lost beloved friends and now Noah. I've lost everything."

A tired expression crossed her mother's face. She sighed and came toward Ginger. "I don't know that I can forgive you, Ginger. Not yet. You took my son from me. And you'll soon learn that you can't help but love your children, flaws and all."

Ginger nodded, wiping her eyes. "Mama, I'm sorry. I promise you, I have lived every moment of my life since then, wishing that I hadn't killed Henry. That was the most painful choice I ever made in my life. If you want to send me away again, so be it, but now I'm here. And I'm your child too."

Her mother reached up and put her hands on each side of Ginger's face. "Yes, you're my daughter. And you're in trouble. We don't have time for feelings right now. Believe me, I'm angry ..." Her mother's voice broke with grief.

Ginger's tears came harder now. "I'm sorry, Mama. I am—I am so very sorry—"

Her mother inhaled sharply. "We have lost almost everything. If we fold now, we will lose it all. I have an idea how we can deal with this. But we have to be strong and stand together, my darling, because we are women and we can survive the cruel things life throws at us with ingenuity, no matter how unfair it may seem."

Ginger squeezed her eyes shut, her sobs shaking her shoulders. She ached for her mother to embrace her, to forgive her, but it was a fool's hope. Despite how justified she'd felt in her actions, her mother would always believe Ginger should have chosen differently. Wiping her eyes, she stepped back. "What's your plan?"

"Marry William."

From the matter-of-fact way her mother said his name, Ginger stiffened. Mama had a resolute look on her face that worried her.

She wants me to what? I'm already married. Shivers traveled her length.

"William fell madly in love with you. You know that. He would have gladly married you in Egypt if you hadn't rejected him. And I think you two developed enough of a friendship that there's some mutual trust there."

"Some." *Not much, really.* Ginger had discovered that William had a habit of lying to make himself look better.

"Fortune is on your side—William will be here at dinner tonight. If you go to William in your grief, let him console you, I think we can convince William to propose to you still. Marry immediately."

Ginger felt choked, as though the walls of the room were closing in on her. *I need to flee. Get out of here and get help elsewhere.*

Where could she go? Could she still reach Jack?

Or maybe she'd take a cab to Dr. Louisa Garrett Anderson. Though, if she was going to present herself as a competent professional nurse, showing up in a state of emotional distress might not help.

With her throat dry, Ginger managed, "I doubt William will want to marry me when he learns I'm already pregnant."

"Your pregnancy is still early enough, isn't it? You can just surprise him with an early baby."

Ginger's jaw dropped. How could her mother possibly suggest such an unscrupulous lie? She wanted Ginger to pass the baby off as William's? Then another, more revolting thought occurred to her. For that to happen, she'd have to be intimate with him. The idea of allowing another man into her bed was awful enough, but while pregnant with Noah's child? A shudder echoed through her. "I could never do that. That would be horrible, Mother."

"Well, you don't have a lot of options, Ginger." Her mother's visage darkened. "Let's get your face washed up for dinner. You can spend some time thinking about it tonight. But remember, either we stand together, or we don't stand at all."

CHAPTER SEVENTEEN

*T*he news that William Thorne would be at dinner was the last thing Ginger had expected as she'd prepared for the evening, but her mother's demand that Ginger win a proposal from him was infinitely worse. As Ginger walked down the sweeping and elegant spiral staircase in her aunt's home for dinner, she fought the temptation to go to bed and avoid her family.

She wanted to run, but she also didn't want to be rash. No one had the power to force her to do anything, ultimately, and she needed to remember that.

Her mother had said, *"... we are women and we can survive the cruel things life throws at us with ingenuity, no matter how unfair it may seem."*

But her mother's version of ingenuity didn't feel strong or ingenious. Machiavellian.

Now, more than ever, Ginger missed Sarah. If Sarah had been alive, Ginger doubted that she would have ever been alone through this. Not only did Sarah know how to be independent and resourceful, she had also been one of the best friends Ginger had ever had, even in the short time they'd known each other. She had been a strong woman, one who knew how to survive in a man's world and wasn't afraid to do what she felt to be right, no matter the opposition.

Her mother's plan meant once again falling back on the mercy of someone else. Nothing about it was strong.

The soft murmur of voices from the sitting room fell silent as Ginger stepped inside, where her family had gathered before dinner. Mama was seated by Lucy and Madeline on a sofa, with her uncle Hugh and William Thorne standing by the lit fireplace. Across from Lucy sat her grandmother in a stiff, cream-colored armchair.

Gran was the first to move. She stood, holding on to the arm of the chair for support. "Ginger, my darling." She hurried toward Ginger, a smile on her face. "I can't tell you what a wonderful surprise it was to hear you were here with us today."

"Hear, hear," William said, coming away from the fireplace. He wore a white tie ensemble, his dinner jacket finely tailored. In Cairo, he'd seemed awkward and unaccustomed to her family's ways. Whether it was Lucy's influence or being back in England, he seemed to be more comfortable now in the role of the Earl of Braddock.

Ginger gave him a taut smile, then leaned in to press a kiss to her grandmother's cheek. She tried not to notice the way Lucy averted her gaze and didn't move to greet her. Gran held her by the elbows, inspecting her with her sharp eyes. "You should have let us know you were coming. I'm certain Madeline would have sent the car for you."

Ginger searched her grandmother's gaze. She doubted her mother or Madeline had been indiscreet, but she couldn't help but wonder what her white-haired, wizened grandmother would have to say about her pregnancy. Ginger had grown unexpectedly close to Gran while studying nursing and had lived with her in London during that time. Ginger's fiancé at the time, James Clark, had been very fond of Gran, calling her one of the "smartest" women he'd ever met. And even though Gran wasn't vocally supportive of the suffragettes the way Madeline was, Ginger had always suspected her sympathies were much more aligned with them than she'd ever said.

After all, Gran had been left a widow at the relatively young age of thirty-eight and had never remarried. She lived comfortably in a house only a few streets away from here, with limited servants, but dedicated herself to charitable endeavors and was a patroness for several organizations.

If only Gran would allow me to live with her again.

But who knew what Mama had told Gran about Egypt? Her grandmother's sympathies for behaving independently had its limits.

Ginger pulled away from Gran and turned toward William, who'd approached with an eager smile. "How are you, dear cousin?" William took her hand and squeezed it. Ginger lifted her chin. The last thing she wanted was to feel that she'd come here, tail tucked between her legs, to beg for scraps from William's table.

And, yet, that was what her mother seemed to want.

Is this what life is like for single mothers everywhere? Humiliation and desperation? The castoffs of society, left to live a life of survival.

"I'm well." She tried to give him a more earnest smile. "Thank you so much for accompanying my family here to England, William. But I must admit I didn't expect I'd see you here tonight. How is Penmore?"

Her family's estate in Somerset, entailed to William after the death of her brother, was several hours away by train. Just what was William doing here?

Lucy rose from her seat, as if on cue, and sidled up beside William, setting a hand on his forearm. "William comes to visit us at least once a week. Isn't he a darling?" She gave Ginger a hard look, a warning in her dark eyes, clearly claiming William for her own. "How's Colonel Benson, dear Ginny?"

Ginger averted her gaze, taking a moment to gather herself.

Leave it to Lucy to be so wildly inappropriate if it meant injuring Ginger. She had to know that bringing up Noah would only cause controversy. Going into detail about Noah would only raise questions from people like her uncle and grandmother, who might not know as much about him. She swallowed the lump in her throat and answered in a low voice, "He went missing, and we believed he perished aboard the troopship *Aragon*. A month ago."

That was enough information to silence Lucy on the topic and tell William she was now most likely a widow. The astonishment in Lucy's eyes was clear enough, and she stared at Ginger, frozen in place, as though the news had been the last thing she expected.

William cleared his throat. "I'm so sorry to hear it," he said in a low voice, stepping closer to Ginger and away from Lucy. He reached for Ginger's hands again. "Is there anything I can do?"

"What's this?" Hugh asked, sniffing from his place beside the fireplace. He was a kind uncle, but much more oblivious than Ginger's own shrewd father had been.

Her mother stood. "Oh, no one of importance. Just an old friend of Ginger's." She placed a firm hand on Ginger's elbow. "I'm sure William and Ginger have catching up to do. Should we go through to dinner, Hugh?"

Hugh flinched at her mother's forwardness. "Yes, of course."

As Ginger tried to step back toward her grandmother or Madeline, her mother practically pushed her toward William. She shot her mother a hard look, then fell into step beside William. She could feel Lucy's presence lurking behind her. Lucy wouldn't take to Ginger's presence kindly. Just a few months ago, Lucy had confessed to hoping that William would turn his attentions to her. It had hurt her when William had proposed to Ginger instead, but if she continued to hope for William's attentions, then she'd see Ginger as a threat again.

Mama had known of Lucy's interest in William. She'd probably even encouraged it. Why wasn't her mother worried about that now?

"To answer your earlier question, Penmore is wonderful. Really lovely. I'm glad to be learning the lay of the land at last. I'd tried to convince Lucy and your mother to come and stay there until the dowager cottage is ready, but I think family here in London may be what they really needed."

As Ginger sat at the dinner table, her appetite left completely. William sat beside her, with her grandmother on her other side, thank goodness. Gran's ability to see the poisoned daggers Lucy shot in Ginger's direction from the other side of the table might help curtail them.

Lucy's thinly veiled contempt was so unsurprising that it saddened Ginger. They'd never particularly gotten on as sisters, but there had been a few times the previous November that Ginger had a rare glimpse of what it might be like to be friends with her sister. That relationship now seemed more elusive than ever.

Thankfully, her grandmother dominated most of the conversation, peppering Ginger with questions and stories of air raids and bombings in London while they'd been in Egypt. The idea of her poor grandmother having to take shelter during bombings ignited Ginger's anger. She'd seen German bombers ignoring the neutrality of the hospitals on the front lines and read accounts of bombings in London. But it was one thing to hear about and another for her elegant elderly grandmother to recount having to hide in a cellar.

Even William seemed muted, which Ginger was grateful for. She couldn't bear the thought of trying to lure him into a marriage using deception. That her mother had come up with such a plan so quickly after learning of Noah's death gave Ginger chills.

With dinner at last over, Ginger made polite excuses to avoid the after-dinner gathering and hurried back toward the shelter of the guest room, eager to be alone. She'd just removed her shoes and sat on the bed when a tap on the door sounded. Her grandmother opened it, then stepped inside.

"I'd hoped to have the opportunity to speak to you alone this evening," Gran said, clasping her hands in front of her.

"I'm sorry for leaving so quickly." Ginger rose to her feet, unable to will herself to smile. "It was all a bit much on my first night here, I suppose."

Gran looked over her shoulder, then shut the door. She came further inside the room toward the bed. "You know, your mother has told me all about your adventures in Egypt. And how Henry and Edmund really died."

Gran knows I killed Henry? Ginger blanched, a dizzying feeling cresting over her. She reached unsteadily for the bed behind her, and Gran crept closer. "I didn't know you knew."

The beading in Gran's dark-blue evening gown sparkled in the dim yellow light that came from the lamp on the bedside table. Diamonds bobbed at her ears and glittered on her necklace as she nodded grimly. "Elizabeth told me everything. How Edmund risked all his money on a foolish oil concession. How that brigand Stephen Fisher blackmailed him into smuggling and treason. And how Henry involved himself in it all, too." Gran's blue eyes locked with hers. "And of your colonel."

The revelation that her mother had told Gran so much sensitive information made Ginger feel exposed. Goose bumps rose on her arms and she sank onto the bed, hands folded in her lap. "I don't know what to say. Mama is—"

"She understands what you did better than you think. But if she doesn't—what difference does it make, darling? Would you have done any differently?" Gran quirked a grey brow at her.

It was a question Ginger had often asked herself. "No."

"That's right." Then Gran's eyes misted. "Because you are a woman of integrity. I'd like to say you got that from the Lennox side of your heritage."

Ginger let out a tearful laugh. The Lennoxes were her grand-mother's Scottish side. "Perhaps."

Gran shook her head. "You'd best believe it. That father of yours always had a scheming side to him, but would Elizabeth listen to me? Henry too. Now"—Gran ducked her chin—"are you going to tell me what's troubling you? You look quite done in. Is that from travel or something else?"

"My husband is most likely dead." Ginger avoided Gran's gaze. "And I'm with child. We didn't legalize our marriage through the consulate, and he was a fugitive from the law—wrongly accused, I might add—when he died."

A few beats of silence hung in the air as Gran absorbed the news. She sat beside Ginger, staring at the fireplace opposite the bed. After a minute, she asked, "And your mother is aware?"

Ginger nodded. "I told Madeline, who told her. Mama wants me to … turn my attentions to William and then convince him the child is his, procuring a hasty marriage."

"That *would* be a solution your mother would think of." Gran cleared her throat, then took out a handkerchief to wipe her nose delicately. "I'm old, Ginger, and my advice comes with bias, but I'm not certain what you expected by coming here. You knew the world you came from, my dear, did you not?"

Ginger frowned, uncertain if she should feel shame in her grandmother's admonition.

Gran reached over and set her cool hand on Ginger's forearm. "When you left this country a few years ago, you didn't leave to continue taking part in the life you knew. You left because you wanted something else. That took courage and tenacity, Ginger dear. You are capable of a great deal more than you give yourself credit for. It seems to me it would be a shame to forget that now."

Reaching up, she patted Ginger's cheek affectionately.

Her words brought to mind the reference that Jane Radford had provided for Dr. Louisa Garrett Anderson. But the possibility also existed that Dr. Anderson would look into her background, believe she was an unwed mother, and then reject her outright. She, like the rest of the world, may not have any use for women who found themselves unexpectedly pregnant.

Closing her eyes, Ginger tried to think clearly. But her mind felt muddled, her thoughts incoherent. She relished her grandmother's gentle touch. "I sometimes wish I was a girl again," Ginger said, blinking tears from her lashes. "And I could just curl up on your lap. You were one of the few people who let me do that."

"I've always loved you. Always been proud of you." Gran dropped her hand, then winked. "And I know you'll make the best choice—not only for your child, but for yourself. I'll work on your mother the best I can, though she can be just as stubborn as you are. In the meantime, this is for you." Gran reached up and removed her necklace, then pressed it into Ginger's palm. "Either as an heirloom to wear or in case you find yourself in need of some possessions."

Ginger's eyes widened. "I can't take this." Her mother would be furious if she felt Gran had interfered.

"Yes, you can and you will." Gran stood. "Now, I should get back downstairs, before someone thinks I've wandered off and locked myself in a water closet again." She hurried toward the door, then slipped out, a spry swish to her steps.

The necklace in Ginger's hands was still warm from having been around Gran's neck. It was heavy—and expensive. Just what on earth was she supposed to do with it, though? Sell it?

If she didn't do what her mother wanted, it might be the only family heirloom she'd ever have.

CHAPTER EIGHTEEN

The feeling of malaise that had started the night before when Ginger had seen her mother had continued through the night and into the morning. As Ginger walked down the sweeping and elegant spiral staircase in her aunt's home the next morning, she fought the temptation to go back to bed and avoid her family. She needed the extra sleep, anyway. These days she never felt as though she could get enough, thanks to her pregnancy.

But her pregnancy also meant that she was ravenously hungry. In the end, that was what had forced her to leave the bedroom. But a late breakfast also meant, as she reached the bottom step, that she was feeling nauseated. Of course, her mother's loathsome suggestion about William didn't help the matter.

Mama would never accept her raising a child that was viewed as illegitimate. That she even had appeared to offer some sort of olive branch had stunned Ginger—*but what an olive branch.*

She could never try to deceive William in such a horrible way. He was a kind man and had tried to be honorable. He'd even kept his word to Ginger to bring her mother and sister back to England.

The only way she would even pretend to agree to her mother's plan was if she told him the truth about her pregnancy first, at which point he might not want her anymore.

Ginger paused in the foyer, hand resting on the banister.

But can I marry again?

She doubted she would ever marry for love again—or that she could love again. All her protests over the years ... her rejections of both Stephen and James Clark had been in the name of wanting to marry someone she truly loved. But she'd never thought about the risk she'd taken in doing that. The heartbreak of losing Noah was so much worse than anything she could have possibly imagined.

She drew a sharp breath, unable to continue thinking about it any longer. Hurrying to the sitting room, she found her mother and Madeline inside, along with Lucy and Gran. Lucy lifted her gaze sharply as Ginger entered the room, then she took in the black dress Ginger wore. "Black again?" she asked as a greeting.

"Of course she's back again," Gran said with a twist of her lips. "She's finally here where she belongs at last." She held a hand out toward her granddaughter. "Come over here and let me look at you in the windowlight. You're so beautiful, dearest."

"I think Lucy was referring to the color of my dress, Gran," Ginger said with a smile. She came toward her grandmother, disregarding the proximity it put her to Lucy. Lucy shifted uncomfortably, as though having to be near Ginger was tedious, and patted her dark hair. "I'm wearing it because I'm still in mourning."

Ginger met Lucy's awaiting gaze, and her dark eyes reflected her disinterest in Ginger's heartache. *Why bother to try?* Ginger sighed. "Good morning to you too, Lucy. Any fun plans for the day?"

"I hear that dashing William Thorne is to visit us again later this evening," Gran said, her eyes flat. "Apparently, he stayed in town for the night."

Ginger looked back at Madeline and her mother, alarm trickling up her spine. Did Mama have something to do with this?

From the pleasure that flushed Lucy's face, it was clear Lucy didn't know what her mother was planning. Which meant that if Ginger agreed to her mother's plan, she'd only alienate her sister further.

She had to leave her aunt's house. As much as she appreciated her aunt wanting to help her, Madeline had inadvertently placed her in an even more difficult situation—one which meant someone in her family would inevitably end up resenting her further. "I think I may go out in the morning. There's a hospital on Endell Street—"

"Surely you've spent more than enough time in hospitals, Ginger," her mother said, an edge to her voice.

Lucy didn't appear altogether upset at the possibility. Her face seemed to have brightened. "Oh, you know Ginny could never stay away from nursing long, Mama. She longs to be in the midst of it all, doing her bit."

"We are still at war." Ginger leveled her gaze at Lucy. "And I'm still able to help."

"Oh, for goodness' sake, you can't be serious. Nursing, again?" Her mother rose from her seat beside Madeline. "It's high time you settle down."

"Really, Mama, I couldn't possibly imagine sitting idly by doing nothing. I may not have many options but—"

"Lucy, why don't you take Mama to work on the florals for tonight's dinner?" Madeline said in a smooth voice. Then to her mother, she said, "No one knows how to do florals the way you do, Mother."

Gran rolled her eyes. "Yes, go on pretending I'm so old I can't see through your attempts to redirect my attention. You'll fare wonderfully when they're reading my will." She rose slowly, reaching for her cane. "Come, Lucy. Let's go and see those florals that are probably quite finished."

Ginger held back a snort of laughter. Her grandmother always had a way of speaking her mind in a manner that made Ginger feel refreshed. Gran was a pillar of strength—a force to be reckoned with when she wanted to be. But even Gran followed the carefully delineated rules of the society to which she'd been born. In the privacy of a bedroom, she might show herself to be Ginger's ally, but she wouldn't speak up for her here. Ginger had gone too far beyond the pale even for Gran to support her publicly, no matter her sympathies.

As Lucy and Gran left the room, Ginger turned toward her aunt and mother. Ironic, how she wished for Lucy's presence now. She had a feeling a stern lecture awaited.

Madeline gave a peaceful smile. "Why don't you have a seat, dear?"

Ginger groaned inwardly, then approached them, sitting across from them on a stiff, unyielding sofa that Ginger imagined Madeline had purchased only to flaunt how expensive it looked rather than for comfort.

"Have you been giving any thought to the idea I suggested to you?" Mama asked, closing a book that had been at her side.

"I've been thinking about it a great deal." Ginger set a cool hand to her burning cheek. "But, Mama, I couldn't possibly lie to William like you're suggesting. It would be immoral and outrageous to take advantage of him like that. And, at any rate, I doubt he'll want to marry me tomorrow. Even if he was dull enough to believe I could have a full-term baby at six or seven months, I think we've passed the point where I could realistically fool him."

"Oh, Ginger, sweetheart. Then you … take your comfort from him in a more physical manner. As soon as you can," her mother said with a straight face.

She wants me to seduce William immediately? Ginger's ire grew. She'd never known her mother could be *this* conniving.

Madeline winced. "Elizabeth, do be reasonable. If Ginger doesn't want to—"

"I am being reasonable." Her mother's eyes narrowed. "What

other option does she have? Do you see any other men hanging around, waiting to rescue her? Half the eligible men of this country are crippled or dead, and the other half are still embroiled in this godforsaken war. Her child will be labeled a bastard—"

"But he won't actually be a bastard." Each time her mother said it that way, Ginger felt sick. *Especially because she's right.*

"But it won't matter. The child won't escape the label. And you'll be ruined." Her mother's face reddened. "But if you can convince William to marry you, he can claim the child as his own. No one will know. You'll be safe, your name untarnished, and your child's future secure. You hopped into Colonel Benson's bed easily enough. What's another man if it means saving yourself and your child?"

Her remarks made Ginger flush with guilt and betrayal. Noah had been her husband. She didn't deserve to be spoken to like this. But her mother's anger stemmed from a place of deep resentment, one that only time would assuage. "Mama, I loved my husband. Very much. I don't love William. I'm not a whore."

Madeline shifted in her seat, looking uncomfortable. Even she seemed to understand that the topic was fraught with a deeper issue, and no matter how much she might disagree with her sister, she wouldn't quarrel with her in front of Ginger. *That isn't the way things are done, after all.*

Mama moistened her lips. "There's only a limited time available to us before it will become impossible for William to claim the child as his own. You're right—we're pushing the boundaries of believability. But time is of the essence. You cannot beat about the bush on this. A decision must be made immediately."

"And I've made my decision." Ginger's head felt light. "And what about Lucy? Don't you even care about how she feels about this?"

Mama blinked. "What about Lucy?"

"Lucy is still hoping William will marry her, Mama. Don't you see the way her face lights up when she's around him? If I took your suggestion—which I'm not going to—Lucy would hate me forever."

Ginger could hardly believe she was having this conversation. When had her mother become so cold and calculating?

Mama rubbed her chin. "Lucy is a sweet girl, Ginger, but you're the one William prefers. And she wouldn't say a thing because we haven't told her about your pregnancy. She already thinks you're unscrupulous enough to seduce William. Remember, your disgrace risks her future, too. Unlike you, Lucy is much more tied to the idea of maintaining the life she was born into. You can always make amends—"

Ginger held up a hand. "I can't." She shook her head. "I won't do that to William. Or to Lucy. That's all there is to it."

Her mother threw up her hands and turned toward her sister. "Say something, for goodness' sake."

Madeline paled, looking toward Ginger with a sympathetic and stricken expression. She drew a slow breath. "Ginger, darling, did this man you married love you?"

Ginger nodded. Would she ever reach a point when she didn't want to cry at the memories of him? "Desperately."

Madeline left her seat and squatted in front of Ginger, taking her hand. "If he loved you like you claim, he wouldn't want you to be sullied. You're too wonderful, too beautiful—"

"Please don't." Ginger shook her head, her shoulders knotting with tension. "Just don't."

"Your mother's plan may not be the most morally acceptable one, but it isn't a bad plan. God knows you wouldn't be the first woman to keep such a secret."

Ginger gaped at her. "How can I possibly build a marriage on such a lie?"

"All marriages are built on lies in some manner. No one truly is who they pretend to be when they marry, even if it's completely unintentional. The pretense only falls away after years of commitment."

How very cynical.

Ginger pulled her hand back. "If you want me to do this to get Penmore and the family title back, you're speaking to the wrong daughter. Just encourage Lucy in her infatuation with William. He may come around. I'll just make it on my own."

Her mother's eyes filled with tears, and she left her seat as well. She stood in front of them. "I want you to do this because I would prefer to meet my grandchild. And because I want my daughter in my life. What you're asking is for me to choose between Lucy and you, Ginger. If I accept your child under the circumstances you want to bring him into the world, I condemn your sister to a life of scandal. You could go to the United States or Switzerland or somewhere else and give the child up for adoption, but you won't. And I know you—once you hold that baby in your arms, you'll never let him go."

Ginger's chest felt so tight it hurt to breathe.

"I'm a mother, Ginger. And you're my baby. Think about your unborn child. If you think you love that child, you have no idea. No idea how that love grows once you've given birth to the child, raised him, heard him laugh. There is no love like a mother's. I will do anything to protect my family."

Her words brought Henry's gruesome death to her mind.

This is why she'll never completely forgive me.

Her mother leaned forward and kissed her cheek. "I'm asking you—as a new mother—to make the choice that is best for your child. What would Colonel Benson want you to do?"

She couldn't know what Noah would want her to do in the long term. Noah wasn't here. But one thing was certain: Noah would *never* want her to do this. He'd always been proud of her sense of honor.

The door to the sitting room opened, and Giles came through. "There's a Mr. Jack Darby at the door, asking for Lady Virginia."

Oh, thank God. She didn't know or care why Jack was here; she was just thrilled that he was. Ginger sniffled, taking out a handkerchief. She'd been on the verge of tears, but the announcement was enough to help her take a much-needed breath. She stood. "Can you see him to the library, Giles? I'll be there directly."

Ginger excused herself from her mother and Madeline. She paused by a mirror to check her face—sure enough, her eyebrows and nose looked red. But she'd never be able to hide her emotional state from Jack.

Hurrying out of the sitting room, her heels struck the tiled floor hard. She was nearly breathless when she reached the library, and relief flooded her as Jack turned toward her.

"I don't think that I've ever been more relieved to see you." Ginger rushed to him and, before she could overthink it, she embraced him, a cross between a laugh and a sob choking from her throat.

"Red." Jack's voice held a note of surprise, then his arms tightened around her, returning her hug. "You know, we just saw each other yesterday morning."

Much as she'd thought they were driving each other mad while they'd been in Egypt, his familiarity provided more comfort than any of her family members had. She stepped back, wiping her cheeks, when she noticed the uniform he wore—that of an American officer.

"You—" Her heart thudded. *He must have enlisted.*

Jack removed his hat, turning it in his hands. "I came to say good-bye. I got you here, and now I can move on. But I can't sit back and let other Yanks outdo me." He tipped a grin, one that reminded Ginger so much of happier times. "I'm going to France."

She flattened a hand to her chest, surprised how much his news sent arrows through her body. "You said nothing—"

"I didn't want you to think you were holding me back somehow. Getting you here was too important." Jack smiled warmly, then set a hand on her shoulder. "You okay?" His expression sobered. "Your family giving you trouble?"

Ginger turned away, covering her mouth with her hand. Her eyes scanned the wall of gilded book spines. Books, like so many things, reminded her of Noah.

Why did you have to leave me?

Swallowing hard, she nodded. "Yes—I didn't—" *How to say this?* She set her hand over her belly. "But my mother isn't happy about the news. With my marriage to Noah never having been legalized, our child won't be legitimate. So she wants me to marry William Thorne, the new Earl of Braddock. Convince him the child is his, eventually."

"What?" Jack's face filled with disgust.

"Because if I don't, I'll be ruined completely. They won't have anything to do with me. I've said I won't do it, of course." Ginger shook her head. "But I don't have many recourses, Jack. I don't have any money. And even with my skills as a nurse, I won't be hired if people think I'm an unwed mother."

"For God's sake, will you just take my money?" Jack swore, stepping back from her. "I'll make sure you have what you need."

"And if something happens to you?" Ginger gestured to his uniform. "I know you mean well, Jack, but so did Noah and look what happened with him. He's gone. And I have nothing. No pension. No home. No way to raise my child. And I can't live by holding out my hand to you for the rest of my life. What if you find someone to love and marry? Surely, she won't want you supporting another woman and her child."

Jack ran his fingers through his short, dark hair, which had been recently trimmed. He gave a frustrated look. "Then Goddammit, marry me."

What?

She gripped the back of the chair closest to her, giving him a stunned look. "What are you saying?"

"You need a single man with money to marry you, save you and your baby from being destitute—I just happen to be a single man. If you really don't have any other options, then marry me. I'll give your baby a last name, even if it's not the one it should have." He shrugged as though it were nothing.

For the briefest moment, she felt the temptation of his proposal. She trusted Jack more than anyone.

But, no. It would be wrong on every level.

Yet it cut to the heart of the issue: Jack must truly believe Noah was dead. Jack wouldn't offer otherwise.

She couldn't possibly ask that from him. He'd done more than enough already. Asking him to involve himself in her problems—for the rest of her life? That went far beyond the bonds of friendship.

"I can't marry you, Jack." Ginger squared her shoulders, then gave a firm lift to her jaw. "It wouldn't be fair. I will never love anyone the way I love Noah, and you deserve better than that. You're a good man and I'm extremely fond of you, but there's no reason for you to shoulder the burden of my struggles." She stepped closer and touched his cheek, grazing it with her fingertips, then let her hand fall to her side. "Thank you. Good-bye, friend. Please write. And stay safe."

As she started for the door, her feet felt as if bricks were attached to the bottoms of her shoes. Only Jack could understand the depth of her despair, the pain she felt when she thought of Noah. But she couldn't take away his future while he was so emotional. He wasn't thinking clearly.

"I was in love once, and it wasn't with Sarah." Jack's voice was a whisper.

Ginger slowed, then stopped. She turned toward him and found him standing right where she'd left him, in the middle of the library. "What?"

"I fell in love with her at sixteen." Jack gave her a sidelong glance, his eyes narrowing. "And that was it for me. She was the only one I had eyes for. The only one I wanted."

She released a slow, aching breath and struggled to suck in

another. She didn't know him well, but he was a passionate man, just as Noah had been. Maybe even more private in some ways, because he wore his bravado like a suit of armor.

Jack held her gaze unflinchingly. "I lost her. And it's why I left America. But there isn't an ocean wide enough to put that behind me. I'll never love anyone the way I loved her. And I don't expect you to love me. This world isn't fair to women, especially mothers. And we both know the assumptions that are going to be made about you. You don't deserve that. Neither does that baby."

Tears pricked Ginger's eyes, and despite her best effort, she felt her chin quiver.

Jack cleared his throat and came closer to her. "I couldn't live with myself, knowing I left you to fend for yourself. Hell, I'm pretty sure Noah might come back from the grave and haunt me if I did. He was my best friend, Red. The person I trusted the most in the world."

A tear slid down her cheek, the aching of her chest making it hard to breathe. Jack brushed her tear away with his thumb, his voice gruff as he went on, "I can't offer you what he did, but I can protect and take care of you. Love that child you're carrying as if it were my own. I have money. I'll see that you both never want for anything. And who knows?" He set his hands on her shoulders. "Maybe in time the mutual respect we have might turn into something more. Or not. I leave that in your hands."

She squeezed her eyes shut, breaking the penetrating eye contact that threatened to undo her resolve. Jack didn't want intimacy? Or was he just saying that to convince her?

Noah had even had a platonic engagement with Victoria, for appearances. If she married Jack solely out of convenience, Jack could be free to have discreet romantic trysts without guilt.

Drawing a deep breath, she stepped back from him. Agreeing to marry Jack would mean something more, something she didn't want to admit to herself. If she married him, it would mean accepting Noah wasn't coming back. The thought of that made her feel weak.

She had no desire to return to the life she'd had—but that was what waited for her if she did what her mother wanted. And if she didn't ... what choice did she really have? Leave the world she knew, pretend to be someone else entirely, hope that people would believe she was a war widow, struggle to provide for herself and her child?

Her throat clenched, preventing her from speaking. When she opened her eyes, Jack's warm brown gaze still searched hers. Then, with a resigned look, he ducked his chin and dropped his hands. "You know where to find me, Red. For what it's worth, I won't be marrying anyone else. The offer stands, but I'm leaving for France soon. You can always write to me, though. I'll make sure you have a way of reaching me."

He started toward the door, and Ginger's heart already ached in his absence. Only Jack knew what she'd been through.

Only Jack will ever know.

She choked back a sob, then turned toward him. "Jack ... wait."

PART II

CHAPTER NINETEEN

FEBRUARY 1918

JERUSALEM

*F*or those first blurred moments of consciousness, Noah was back on the floor of the *Aragon*.

The ship was sinking, seawater now spilling into the cabin where he'd gone to retrieve a few documents. Under a couple of inches of cold water, against the floorboards, the only photograph he had of his mother stared at him. Her pose was formal, a hint of a smile at her mouth. He'd always thought of his mother as beautiful, something inquisitive and intelligent in her eyes.

He hadn't known it was the last moment he'd ever see that image.

His blood was in the water, trickling from the back of his head, where he'd been hit when the wall of the cabin had collapsed on him. His leg felt pinned, and he couldn't seem to command his body into action.

Ginger. He'd kissed her and promised to find her again. He had to get up.

But I can't.

Panic closed around his heart.

He had to get off the ship …

A great cracking sound turned into a buzz—sharp, piercing, and blanking his mind with white.

Then he blinked, and the buzz of a fly by his ear was the first thing he noticed as he opened his eyes, the sunlight so bright that he squeezed them shut again. His eyelashes felt encrusted with sleep, his mouth dry.

His head ached, the buzzing reduced now by awareness but still ever-present.

The sound of someone taking a step prompted him to fully open his eyes again, try to sit.

A firm hand held his shoulder, and a man's face swam into view.

Young—most likely in his thirties—with brown eyes and light-brown hair. A trim moustache above his lip, an oval-shaped face. Panama hat.

The Panama hat felt significant, but he couldn't remember why.

"Don't move too much yet, Benson. You're weak. It's been over a month since you were last awake."

He has an American accent.

A month? Where was Ginger? And Jack?

Despite the man's warning not to move, he tried to sit and found he couldn't. His arms and legs felt heavy, useless, and he lifted his fingers from the surface of the bed before curling them into loose fists.

His inability to move speeded his heart to a gallop. *What is happening? What's happened to me?*

He swallowed, his tongue sticking to the roof of his mouth, dry like sandpaper. "Where am I?" he managed. He scanned the spartan space. He was in a bed that was so small it barely fit one man, but it smelled clean. A crucifix was the only ornament on the wall, and one window was the source of the sunlight.

"Jerusalem. In a friary." The American stepped back, clasping his hands in front of him. "I'll be back. Your care is far outside my level of expertise. I should fetch someone now that you're awake."

"A friary?" Noah blinked again, scanning the barren space. No wonder it didn't look like a hospital. He'd awoken in hospitals before and there it was always noise and wards filled with other patients. He was alone in this room.

The American nodded. "You had quite a serious blow to your head, I'm afraid. They thought it might have affected your spine. You may not walk again, Benson. You spent a week in a Red Cross hospital until I believed it was too dangerous to keep you there, and then I brought you here. The monks have been caring for you ever since."

Noah breathed slowly, but his heart continued pounding.

"...over a month..."

"...you may not walk again..."

His back hurt, as did his hips. He wanted to shift on the bed, to relieve the pain, but found he couldn't. Sweat broke out on his forehead and on his neck, his chest so tight that it felt as though someone had wrapped a belt around his lungs.

The buzzing sound in his head came on strongly once more, to the forefront of his thoughts, blocking out everything else until the pain seemed to radiate from his skull.

"You may not walk again, Benson."

As the pain in his skull increased, he groaned, clenching his jaw. He couldn't think, couldn't see, couldn't move.

The American must have thought the news was too much, because he opened the door and called for help.

"My head," Noah gritted through his teeth, the pressure increasing as his breath grew shallower. "Where am I? Where's Ginger?"

Where was his wife? Was she still alive? Why wasn't she here with him?

His pulse felt more erratic still.

"Try to calm yourself, Benson."

"No, m-my ... my h-head." A sharp feeling crested in the top of his head, his heart so fast that he cried out. *Move, God damn it, move your arms. Your legs. Get out of this bed!*

A barrage of images flooded his mind, but he couldn't focus on any of them, the pain robbing them of any meaning and memory.

"I'm going to give him morphine," the American was saying, though Noah didn't know to whom.

Then a cool feeling ran through his veins, stilling him, the muscles he'd held taut slowly releasing, numb. The buzzing sound receded once again.

"Kill me," Noah mumbled, then closed his eyes.

CHAPTER TWENTY

MAY 1918

One hundred days.

Noah scratched the mark onto the wall and then dropped the pencil. As a child, he'd read the *Count of Monte Cristo* and remembered vividly a passage about Edmond Dantès, the eponymous count, going mad while imprisoned, trying to keep track of how long he'd been there.

Noah had once possessed the ability to remember passages he'd read as if they'd been yesterday. Often, when he closed his eyes at night, he thought of those books, spent his days recalling the stories, the words on the page.

Now those memories were gone.

The pages had blurred, replaced by that insufferable ringing and a blankness everywhere his memories used to be. Just ... *nothing*. No memory. No color. As though someone had snipped out portions of his life and hidden them in a place he could no longer access.

He'd spent hours trying to conjure any line of Dumas's book, until Brother Wagner—the monk who tended to him most often—had brought it from the monastery library, an exercise that was nearly as useless. He didn't seem to possess the ability to focus on the words on the page, the infernal pain in his head blocking his concentration.

Brother Wagner had read the book to him out loud instead. As he'd reached the last line, he'd said, "Wait and hope," then closed the book. A kind smile had lit his light-blue eyes. "Maybe God is trying to send you a message."

A God that either didn't exist … or had abandoned Noah.

He ran his tongue over his teeth and found them smooth. In his first few days after he'd awoken, the filmy feeling on their surface had preoccupied him. Perhaps boredom. Perhaps because there was little else to preoccupy himself with.

To his great relief, sensation and strength had started returning to his limbs only a few days after he had woken up. Now his days were an endless cycle of lying in bed, eating, drinking, grunting with pain when he needed help to relieve himself, or when Brother Wagner insisted on exercising him around the room or—worse still —outside.

Now that the winter rains had ended, outside was Wagner's preference. He'd conjured a wheelchair from somewhere, insisting on pushing Noah around the grounds of the Basilica of the Dormition, which was part of their abbey. Unlike most other places Noah had stayed whilst in Jerusalem, the abbey was modern, built just before the war after the land had been acquired by Kaiser Wilhelm.

The place had been named Dormition because Catholics believed the Blessed Virgin Mother's life had ended near this spot … whether by death or "falling asleep," as the name indicated. It seemed an apt place for Noah to find himself in—he preferred sleep now. It wasn't restful, but better than the torment and humiliation of his situation.

In his fitful nightmares, he revisited the *Aragon*. Sometimes he dreamed he was in a water-filled cabin on the ship, drowned souls all around him. Other times he dreamt he was in his cabin, just as he had been, when he'd lost consciousness.

He saw faces, which morphed into others. Fisher. Lord Helton. Lord Braddock, too. Jack. More rarely, Ginger.

Noah swallowed, his throat aching.

When he let himself think of her, his lungs burned, feeling deprived of air. Charles Pointer, the American spy who had dragged him, unconscious, from his flooding cabin aboard the *Aragon* and contrived to transport him here, had told Noah that both Ginger and Jack had survived the sinking. Did she think Noah was dead?

He'd wanted to send her a message, but Pointer had given the monks strict orders. No messages, in or out. In time, he accepted Pointer's orders as a blessing in disguise. As much as he'd immediately wanted to contact her or Jack, if he did, he could endanger himself *and* them. Helton and Fisher were still out there, and Noah was still a fugitive.

Though maybe it's better if she thinks I'm dead.

She didn't need to be connected to a wanted man—not to mention an invalid—for the rest of her life. The life he'd wanted to give her was impossible now.

He pictured her smile, her gorgeous face, the intelligent glint of her eyes ... making love to her in the desert and on that soft bed in their hotel room in Malta. Helton was right—Noah had lost all reason when he'd met her.

Wait and hope.

For what?

The time had long since passed when Noah had any hope.

All he had been was dead.

Charles Pointer hadn't needed to leave a guard at the monastery to restrain Noah. He knew, just as Noah did, that Noah's body was a more effective prison. His mind. His ruined legs. The headaches that crippled him.

Brother Wagner believed Noah had merely lost his strength after lying in bed for so long and pointed to the mobility Noah had regained in his arms as evidence. But Noah wasn't fully convinced of it. The weakness was overwhelming.

The door to Noah's room squeaked open, and he propped himself up on his elbows.

Brother Wagner limped inside, his tall, thin frame swathed with his black robes. He wore a clean work apron laden with tools. He paused at the doorway as though surprised to see Noah give him attention, then smiled and bowed his head. "May I enter?" His deep voice, with its thick German accent, always held a certain softness, velvet in quality, which strangely calmed Noah.

Noah raised a brow. "Would you really leave if I told you not to come in?"

"No." Brother Wagner shut the door behind him. He set the tray in his hands at the foot of the bed, then inspected the empty bowls on the sturdy wooden table beside Noah. "You ate your breakfast well." He looked pleased.

Noah grunted, then settled back against his pillows. "Warm porridge is infinitely preferable to cold porridge."

Brother Wagner had spent months coaxing Noah to eat. At first, when food made him sick, then later when food no longer held any interest for him.

"When your bowels are stronger, I will bring you *Brot und Honig*."

"Bread and honey sounds like an improvement."

The monk smiled, then removed the bowl, replacing it with a steaming soup. "And your bowels will be strong when you use your legs more. Which means today we will go for a walk, yes?"

The utter humiliation of discussing his bowels with this middle-aged monk still made Noah cringe. He'd rather confess his sins. But he was too melancholic to argue with Wagner—about the food or the walk.

He ate in silence while Wagner pulled back the sheets on Noah's bed, exposing his bare legs. From his work apron, he pulled a jar of salve, then uncapped it. Noah didn't know what was inside it, nor did he truly care. Like most things, his opinion on whatever treatment Wagner deemed necessary was irrelevant.

After weeks of Wagner rubbing the salve on his legs, Noah had felt sensations once more. It had started with a cool tingle on his skin, one that spread to his muscles. A toe twitch. Wagner had been delighted.

To Noah, it had been a cruel taunt.

Maybe it was the salve. Maybe it was the way Wagner exercised his legs to keep him from bed sores.

Maybe it was nothing.

Wagner, Noah had learned, had been a scientist in a Benedictine monastery in Germany before he'd come here with his brothers in 1906. They were all Germans here. Charles Pointer's rationale for keeping him with German monks in Jerusalem had been that he'd be less likely to encounter the British.

Whatever Charles's reasons for keeping Noah from the British, or even saving his life in the first place, were even more unclear.

He wished he knew more about the mysterious American who had rescued him, other than that he'd been the man who, in Malta, had ordered Sarah to turn Noah over. That had made Noah believe Charles had been the one who killed Sarah as well, but he'd denied being involved.

Noah wasn't sure he believed Charles. But the man seemed to go to some considerable trouble to keep Noah alive and safe from capture. He didn't know what Charles had planned for him, though.

Noah finished his soup without complaint, then set the bowl on the table. The monk went to the wardrobe in the corner and pulled out a fresh pair of trousers, then brought them to the bedside. "Brother Schneider has made you a special walking frame. Inspired by St. Anthony." He helped Noah to sit, then scooted him toward the end of the mattress.

He bent and pulled the trousers up over Noah's legs, then stood in front of him. "Arms around my neck."

Noah knew the routine by now. He relived daily the helplessness of draping himself against the monk's torso while he pulled the trousers over Noah's hips. His bare feet were cold against the stone floor, and he drew a deep breath as Wagner leaned forward, setting his arms around Noah's waist.

The intimacy of this forced relationship wasn't lost on Noah. Wagner tended to his every need, and in return, he required Noah's absolute trust—whether Noah wanted to give it or not.

Wagner's cowl smelled of sage and thyme and sandalwood, and Noah's cheek pressed against the rough woolen fabric. He closed his eyes, gritting his teeth as Wagner heaved him up—no small feat, considering Noah wasn't a small man—and pulled the waistband of the trousers up. Then he lowered him to sit once more and tied the waist cord tight.

"You have spent long enough in this bed, *mein Freund*. You're wasting away." Wagner brought forth a simple pair of sandals out of the wardrobe and knelt at Noah's feet, then slipped them on.

"What crime did you commit to have to pay your penance by caring for me?" Noah asked, noting the grey hair that touched the corners of Wagner's temples. His brown hair receded badly, giving him a wide brow.

"All have sinned and fallen short of the glory of God," Wagner answered, not meeting Noah's awaiting gaze.

"Some of us more than others, though, wouldn't you say?" Noah stretched, straightening his back, which ached with a dull throb.

Wagner sauntered to the doorway once more. He rolled in a wooden frame enclosure that was a little more than waist-high, with wheels on the bottom of the legs. There were no sides to it, the frame just made an open rectangular-like box. "Schneider saw something like this in the portrait of *The Temptation of Saint Anthony* by Bosch. When he was in Spain, long ago. He thought it might help you."

Noah raised a brow at the contraption. "What am I supposed to do with that?"

Wagner lifted one of the wooden slats on the frame to open it, then stepped inside. He set his hands on two of the opposing sides. "Hands here. And you brace yourself. I'll help. If it goes poorly, we'll work on your arm strength."

The thought of attempting to walk inside this thing made Noah's pulse erratic. The constant reminder of his ineptitude made the pain in his head worsen, and he yearned to do everything in his power to drive Wagner out of the room.

He narrowed his gaze at the monk. "I used to kill your country-men, you know. I took pleasure in it."

Wagner made no response. "Shall we try it?"

"Women too." Noah folded his arms. "German spies."

"Soldiers must kill the enemies given to them. It is part of war." Wagner came closer to Noah, dragging the frame with him.

"I was nothing more than a mercenary. I know that now." The words were out of Noah's mouth before he realized how deeply he felt them. Lord Helton had used him as a mercenary, after all. Used him to protect his own fortunes, to do his bidding in addition to the Crown's. Whether Noah had known about it made little difference —he'd never questioned his orders. That made him complicit.

"Forgiveness from God, *mein Freund*, begins with forgiving your-self." Wagner set a hand on Noah's elbow. "Now up. Up we go."

Noah jerked his arm away. "I destroyed the life of a man. His family too. Seduced his daughter. They lost everything because of me. *She* ..." The words choked in his throat. *Ginger. My beautiful* ... he'd taken everything from *her*. "All because I wanted to be blind to the truth. What forgiveness do I deserve?"

Wagner folded his hands in front of him. "*Mein Freund*, how many men have died in this war?"

"Millions."

"And you are here. Why?" Wagner's gaze pierced Noah's.

Noah's jaw clenched. "There's no reason, Wagner. No purpose to any of it. You seek to find God in the confines of four walls so isolated from the world that an entire war can come to your doorstep and yet you remain unaffected. And God is no more in here than he is out there in the unforgiving desert where the blood-soaked sands erase the memory of us all. Just as they have for thousands of years."

"Well, perhaps you should have been a poet instead of a soldier, *mein Freund*. But if you're right, and there's no purpose, no meaning to this existence, then you have a choice to make. Spend whatever remaining days you have languishing in this bed, or attempt to stand and regain your strength. Only you can determine the degree of your own misery. But you might consider that God put you here to speak to your heart."

"If God is speaking, then he may want to raise the volume."

Now Wagner laughed. "Don't you remember the story of Elijah? He looked for God's voice in the winds of a tempest. Then an earthquake. At last, a fire. But no ... God's voice was not there. God speaks in a gentle whisper, *mein Freund*, but you must be listening."

Noah looked away from Wagner. Trust a monk to turn every opportunity into a chance for a homily.

The frame in front of Noah threatened his equanimity and he closed his eyes, the pain of a headache snaking in around the orbits, throbbing at his temples.

What do I want?

"Stay with me." Ginger's voice rang through his memories. A cloud of red hair, fair skin, the greenest eyes he'd ever seen. His head was in her lap, and tears streaked down her face, leaving trails along the dust on her skin from the *khamsin* they'd ridden through the night before.

"You can't leave me here, Noah. Please."

The agony he'd felt then had been unimaginable. Every breath from the bullet hole Henry had shot into his chest sent searing pain through his body. For the first time, he'd believed he was dying, on the precipice of *something* else.

How he loved her.

Her courage, her indomitable spirit, even the damned headstrong stubbornness that could be reckless and maddening. She'd given him her heart, her body, her love.

And what had he offered her in return?

Nothing. I have nothing to give her.

But he loved her. With every fiber of his being. If he ever had faith in anything, it paled compared to his certainty that their souls must be knitted forever together.

"Listen to me. Fight. For me. Because I'll be damned if I'm waiting for this war to end to marry you, Noah. You hear me? I've decided that's how this ends between us. You don't get to die yet. I don't want to live without you."

Her words had found him slipping away, like a handhold, gripping him tightly.

"Fuil de mo fuil ..." You are blood of my blood, my darling Ginger.

Noah drew a sharp breath, pulling himself back from the memories that seemed so hard to access, the torment in his aching head worse now from the mental exercise.

He reached out a shaky hand and rested it on the frame.

CHAPTER TWENTY-ONE

*N*oah shifted the cane in his hand, squinting into the sun as he leaned into the grapevine. His fingers were stained red from the harvest, which Brother Albert, who oversaw the vineyard, had been carefully inspecting each time he passed by. Noah cut the grapes from the vine, then dropped them into the basket at his side.

Late July in Jerusalem was hot and dry, but over the course of the last few months, Noah appreciated being given tasks outdoors. The more Brother Wagner saw Noah occupied, the more Wagner left him to his own devices. After all, Wagner delighted in Noah's progress. He'd graduated from the contraption Brother Schneider had made him to walking with canes in each hand, then a single cane.

As his leg strength came back, so did his appetite. He no longer protested any food, and the monks had invited him to eat meals with them. He attended their masses, sat in the church while they did vespers, gained their trust.

Trust that would bring him freedom.

Soon.

Other than the fact that the monks were, effectively, his prison guards, he enjoyed his time with them. He'd asked them why they were taking orders from an American spy, but they didn't answer. Whatever Charles Pointer had said to convince them not to allow Noah to leave intrigued him, but while he'd been physically limited, it hadn't mattered as much.

But once his agility was returned, he would leave at night. He knew better than to go without his strength and a plan—especially with British troops everywhere in Jerusalem now. He might be unrecognizable now and could pass for an Arab with the right clothing, but there were more laws restricting civilian movement and checkpoints than ever before, and Noah needed to be careful. The monks told him that more forces seemed to arrive now, which didn't surprise Noah. War in this region had always slowed in the summer months, when the heat was too brutal for even the most enthusiastic warmonger. But it wasn't a bad time to bring up extra troops for when the fighting resumed.

The winter rains that were equally miserable wouldn't begin until late November, which meant that the British would most likely be on the move up the coast of Palestine into the Trans-Jordan in late August and September.

Noah needed to be gone before then.

He felt robbed of information here within the walls of the abbey, where the monks preferred their prayer books to newspapers and their gardens to the marketplaces that Noah had once combed for information. Peaceful, yes, but separate. Too separate. If it bothered them they were enemy citizens in a city now overrun by soldiers from the countries at war with their own, they said nothing.

But if Noah could escape and find Fahad, one of his most trusted friends who lived in Jerusalem, he could be on his way back to Ginger before the troops mobilized for an autumn assault. Checkpoints would be easier to navigate before then. The desert—while harsher—would still be viewed as unmanageable for the soldiers, which would give Noah berth.

He longed to see Ginger. She'd been right. They should have run away to America together from Malta. Even if he could never use his name again, at least he'd had her by his side, and that was all he needed. And friends like Jack could help him get started once again.

But he still didn't trust his body. He wasn't sure-footed, and his balance seemed off. Just three days earlier, he'd fallen over while trying to put on his sandal. The cane was still a necessary evil.

And his headaches were still barely manageable.

Morning was the best. But by night, the pulsating in his head brought all thoughts to a standstill, sometimes with the severity of the pain so strong that he'd vomit. As a man who'd lived his life at night for years while in intelligence, Noah's frustration bubbled hotter with each passing day.

While Wagner's treatments for Noah's legs seemed to have been effective, none of the solutions the monk had created for the headaches had worked.

Noah popped one of the grenache grapes into his mouth, the sweet flavor settling his stomach. The monks used these to make wine, but their fruit harvest was so plentiful that Noah had been eating like a king compared to his days in the military.

He folded the knife and slipped it into his apron, then picked up the basket of fruit. He limped over to Brother Albert, then set it down in front of the elderly monk, who looked through his spectacles that sat on the bridge of his hawklike nose.

"This will do." He didn't smile, though Noah knew he meant it warmly. Albert was content in his curmudgeonly ways, but he had a good heart—on more than one occasion Noah had overheard him having friendly conversations with the birds and insects that came through the garden.

"There you are." Wagner's voice came down the row of vines. He was one of the younger monks in the abbey and, compared to his companions, he seemed to walk with a bounce in his step. He stopped in front of Noah, winded, then let out a deep exhale. "You have a visitor."

Noah furrowed his brow. "A visitor?" *No one knows I'm here.*

"Yes, yes. The American who brought you here to us. Come." Wagner offered a hand to Noah. "I can help you."

Why had Charles returned? Would he have news? Noah doubted it was to free him.

Shrugging off his offer, Noah started in the direction Wagner had come. "It may be slower than he wants, but I can walk there myself." He fatigued easily, which caused no end to his annoyance with himself, but relying on help had only slowed his progress. If he'd taken the time to listen to Wagner earlier, instead of being caught in melancholy, he might not have lost so much strength.

He was intrigued to speak to Charles Pointer. When he'd last seen the man, it had been February, and Noah's condition had distracted him too much to ask him anything of significance. That Pointer had kept him alive and hadn't turned him in to the British spoke volumes—a fragile trust, though, given what had happened to Sarah Hanover.

The walk from the vineyard to the abbey was uphill—the abbey itself was on Mount Zion, near King David's tomb and the Cenacle, which Christians believed was the room of Jesus's last supper. The freedom granted to Noah had struck him more than once when he'd walked the path from the vineyard to the abbey. If he had two perfectly working legs and his full faculties, escape would have been easy.

He was outside the walls of the Old City, which meant that once he could leave, he'd have one less obstacle in the way. Last November, he'd become trapped in the Old City with Jack, as it had still been under Ottoman control. An encounter with Fisher had saved them both from capture, but set them on the path of Fisher's nefarious plans.

Sweat was dripping from Noah's brow by the time he reached the abbey, the cool shadows of the interior a welcome relief to the heat, his hips aching from the strain of the hurried pace. Wagner led him to Noah's room, which seemed a surprising place for a meeting.

Pointer stood when Noah and Wagner entered, removing his Panama hat. He'd occupied the solitary wooden chair in the room, which was at the foot of the bed, and Noah nodded toward him, then sank onto the neatly folded coverlet of the bed. His pulse thrummed through his veins and skin, and he reached for a glass of water at the bedside table.

"You're doing well," Pointer said, genuine surprise on his face. "I expected to find you still lying here in bed—but I suppose the physicians in Alexandria were mistaken about your diagnosis."

"I told you there was nothing wrong with his spine," Wagner huffed. "His reflexes were sound. It's being bedridden that has robbed him of his strength, I tell you."

"Thank you, Brother." Pointer's lips pursed under his thin moustache. "Would you mind leaving us for a few minutes?"

Wagner bowed his head, then exited, closing the door behind him.

Silence settled between the two men as Wagner left. Noah took a moment to sip his water, using the pause in conversation to better assess Pointer. He had a worn expression on his face, his skin tanned darker than Noah remembered.

That Pointer may have saved his life was the only reason Noah felt at ease, especially unarmed as he was. He had the knife in his apron he'd been using to pick grapes, but having spent so many years with a gun readily at hand, it felt like a poor mechanism for defense.

"You've been in the desert?" Noah asked, breaking the silence at last.

Pointer gave one nod. "How can you tell?"

"You have that look about you." Noah settled back onto the bed, swinging his legs onto the surface of the mattress. "I'm intrigued by your presence in the area. Didn't your president Wilson make it clear he wants no entanglement with the Ottomans? War was only declared against Germany."

"There are Germans still in Syria, are there not? We're near there." Pointer's expression hinted at amusement. "Besides which, it's in our interest to know what happens in this region of the world. Which is why I'm here, coincidentally. I have a few questions for you."

"Unofficially, of course."

Pointer crossed one knee over the other and set his hat atop it. "Of course."

Noah smirked. He doubted anything Pointer was doing was official. Even when Noah had been involved in the political scheming of the intelligence world in Cairo, the Americans had been loath to involve themselves with the goings-on of the Arabian world. Those who were involved, such as William Yale from the State Department, hadn't been given official titles by their own government. American caution in this war had been clear from the start.

"What do you want to know?" Noah crossed his arms, feeling listless. Was this why Pointer had kept him alive? To question him about British intelligence in the region? It seemed an illogical move —most of Noah's knowledge was eight months out of date. What little he'd learned was from newspapers Brother Wagner brought him that were a few weeks old. And even then he could only read in the early morning, before his headaches became unbearable.

"I'm interested in your opinion of the Zionist question." Pointer scanned his face. "I've spent the last few months amongst the Arabs, both in this region and in Egypt. They're seething with rage."

"Because of the Balfour Declaration."

Pointer nodded.

Noah rubbed his fingertips against his full beard, which felt wild and untamed. How long had it been since he'd looked in a mirror?

The monks didn't keep them in the dormitories. "What's your question?"

"A Zionist committee arrived in Jerusalem in April, with several prominent men in its midst. They claim they have no desire for a Jewish nation here—just a homeland where the Arabs and Jews can peacefully coexist."

Noah studied Pointer. He still hadn't asked a question, which intrigued Noah. It was as though he wanted Noah to react, but he'd offered little of substance to react to. Noah waited for Pointer to continue. When he didn't, Noah raised his brows. "I'm a disgraced British officer accused of treason and murder. What difference does my opinion make?"

Pointer chuckled. "I had it on good authority from Sarah Hanover that the charges against you were false. Not to mention the fact that, before all this, you were quite the expert in this region, were you not? Perhaps rivaling only T. E. Lawrence himself in his intimate knowledge of the Arab world?"

"There are others," Noah said flatly. *Not to diminish Lawrence's accomplishments.* But Noah knew firsthand that often the glory all fell to one man when the exploits were the work of many.

"Perhaps. But I don't have *them* at my disposal." Pointer shifted in his seat, as though uncomfortable. "Of course, I could return you to the British. Allow you to face those charges you mention. I certainly don't have any reason to believe in your innocence. Or you could share some of that extensive knowledge with me. Give me a better understanding of the situation being faced here in Palestine."

Of course. He should have expected blackmail. Noah sat straighter. "Not until you tell me where my wife is."

Pointer gave him an exasperated look. "I don't know that, Benson. I had trouble enough finding out if your wife's name appeared on the list of the rescued. If I dig too deeply, I may as well announce to anyone looking for you that you're alive and well."

"I can give you her family's name in England. You could make inquiries, I'm sure."

"Yes, but that would be problematic and, possibly, a waste of my time."

"And that would be problematic to whom? You? Or me?"

Pointer's eyes flickered with surprise. Then displeasure crossed his plain features. "I've gone well out of my way to prove my good faith to you. Kept you alive and brought you to a place of safety. Do you know the trouble I had bringing you here from Alexandria?" He shook his head. "I'd hoped the pains I took would be worth it. Don't think I haven't noticed the freedom with which you wander these halls. When I left, you were in a bed. I didn't think you needed guarding. But I'll remedy that as soon as I leave here today."

Noah's shoulders bunched with tension. Pointer's arrival was quickly becoming the most irritating obstacle he'd encountered in months. Most of what he could share had to be common knowledge by now, wasn't it? And even if it wasn't, the Americans were allies. *If* Pointer wasn't working for the other side.

But Noah's own loyalties no longer felt as clear as they once had. He'd seen enough of the scheming between diplomats to be sickened by it. Maybe there was a way to share his knowledge with Pointer that wouldn't pose a real danger to anyone. "I need some reassurance you'll try to learn the whereabouts of my wife."

Pointer rubbed his eyes. "If I promise to see what I can learn, would you do me the favor of answering my question?"

Where Noah might have once found dry humor, all he now felt was bristling annoyance. "Until you actually ask one, Mr. Pointer, I won't be able to answer."

"Call me Charles." He leaned forward, tugging at his collar. "And what I want to know is your opinion of the Zionist claims to the area. Your government doesn't seem to have a very clear policy on the matter—everything we seem to hear from those in the know is contradictory."

"They have a policy," Noah snapped. "They laid it out clearly with the Balfour Declaration. The problem is that they're only beginning to understand the problems they created for themselves with that ill-advised document. The Arab world is furious, convinced more than ever that the only intent of the British in this part of the world is further colonization and cementing the Jewish nation state—which is the aim of the Zionists, no matter what they claim. And there is no population more opposed to governance by the Jews than those found in Palestine, Moslems and Christians alike."

Noah took a breath, then continued, "The Egyptian nationalists who have been simmering under the strain of strict martial law and conscriptions *will* revolt, and the Syrian nationalists—who have no more desire to be led by the Bedouin king Hussein or Ibn Saud and his Sunni extreme Islamists—aren't likely to coalesce easily under colonial powers they deeply distrust."

Charles stared at him, then smiled slowly. "Sarah didn't exaggerate the depth of your understanding of the region, did she? You'll be very useful indeed."

Noah scowled. The thought of Sarah Hanover brought him little peace. Her secrets, shared under duress, were now his to keep until he was free to use them. They did him little good here, though. He was still a prisoner.

"You want me to work for you? To tell you what I know, to help you as you learn the secrets of this land? For how long?"

Charles tapped his foot impatiently. "For as long as I deem necessary."

That wasn't good enough. This war had already dragged on for nearly four years. And Ginger was out there, most likely frantic to know what had happened to him. He couldn't abandon her indefinitely. "I can give you two months. In exchange for my freedom." Escaping in September would be more difficult, but it would be far easier than waiting till the autumn, when the desert was crawling with soldiers and patrols.

Charles guffawed. "Two months hardly seems worth the price I paid to purchase you, Benson. A year, perhaps. Anything less would be out of the question."

It had already been seven months since he'd last been with Ginger. But maybe if Charles found her location, he could at least try to send her a message—let her know he was alive. They'd always discussed the possibility of being separated by the war, but not under circumstances such as these. "Six months. Which will make me your prisoner for a year. I won't give you any longer than that."

"I think you'll give me as long as I require." Charles seemed amused at Noah's words. "Because if you don't, I'll simply turn you over to the British authorities and tell them exactly who you are and what they have accused you of. Don't be foolish, Benson. This is simply a business transaction. No hard feelings."

Noah leaned toward him, his gaze menacing. "I could just simply kill you. You stand in the way of my freedom."

Charles nodded and turned his palms up. "You could. But I've been authorized to do this by the men I report to. They know I have you. They wouldn't doubt you murdered me. If you are an innocent man, do you really want to commit a crime that you'll never be able to erase? Work with me and one day, you may be free. But if you don't or if you kill me, let me be very clear: you will always be hunted."

CHAPTER TWENTY-TWO

SEPTEMBER 1918

AZRAQ, SYRIA

*T*he remote desert castle of Qasr Azraq loomed in front of Noah and Charles as they rode on horseback into the settlement just past sunset. They'd set off from Jerusalem a few weeks earlier, as soon as Noah had felt that he could make the perilous trek through the arid region, but by now he was exhausted. His strength wasn't nearly what it had been before the *Aragon* sank, and the daily headaches drained him of whatever reserve he had remaining.

Charles was nearly as unrecognizable as Noah was, both dressed as warriors of the Rualla Bedouin tribe of Syria. In August, Charles had intercepted intelligence that the leader of the Rualla, Nuri al-Shaalan, had promised his warriors to be a part of the Arab contingency for the upcoming British offensive. With Noah's expertise, the American had seen an opportunity—a chance to sneak into the Arab effort and have concrete knowledge of the British plans.

Noah squinted at the fortress, moonlight gleaming against the thick black basalt stone walls. The surrounding area was choked with tents, and the British had even built an airfield in the vicinity. It would be easy enough to assimilate themselves with the Arab warriors gathered here. They came from all corners of Syria and the Trans-Jordan, men who had all been drawn together by a promise issued by the British and French in June: fight for the British and find their support in gaining emancipation from the Turks at the war's end.

By now, Noah had grown too cynical of that promise, too beleaguered by the scheming he'd witnessed in Cairo.

He was equally suspicious of the man at his side.

Whatever interest the Americans had in this region, they hid their motives by sending attachés and embedding informants. Everything Charles did was 'unofficial.' Every time he asked for Noah's opinion, Charles made no comment, as though the Americans had sent him solely to observe and report back.

Noah slowed his horse, ready to dismount. The first steps on the ground gave him the most trouble lately, his legs feeling like jelly after a ride of this length. He tugged the reins, bringing the horse to a halt, then gritted his teeth as he swung his legs around the creature's side.

As his sandaled feet hit the pebbles of the rocky terrain, it reminded him of how little desire he had to be here. He'd spent years sneaking in and out of Turkish camps in this region— sneaking into a British one seemed even more absurd, like a strange paradox of fate from which he couldn't escape.

The chances of being recognized here were remote. Only a handful of English officers were here, including T. E. Lawrence himself, and Noah doubted any of them would remember him. If, by chance, any of the Arabs that he had met in the past were here, the fact was that Noah was unrecognizable, even to himself. He'd lost considerable weight during his recovery, and both his hair and beard had grown untamed. He still used a cane to assist with the limp he had from aching pain that started in his lower back and traveled down his left leg—though that might not be possible now.

He shifted the rifle slung around his back, a bandolier of ammunition belted around the long *thobe* robe he wore. A *ghutra* head covering helped obscure the sides of his face, slung under his chin and tied with an *aqal* headrope around the crown of his head. Yet, despite the elaborate disguise, he felt more exposed than ever.

Noah had never gone in disguise anywhere that he wouldn't have been killed if he was discovered, and it was no different now. If found, he'd be arrested and most likely executed. Charles would also face a steep penalty—he wasn't supposed to be here either.

But whereas Noah had once felt a sense of confidence in his ability to survive, now that didn't seem as certain. He'd fallen behind one too many times. In November he'd chosen to allow Ginger, Jack, and Sarah to escape and been captured as a result, which had led to his torture and a foot caning that had started his physical decline. The fear of pain didn't bother him nearly as much as the fear of helplessness.

The camp outside the fortress teemed with soldiers, a vast array of people gathered for the battle. Besides the Rualla Bedouin horsemen, which Charles's intelligence intercept had estimated numbered close to three hundred, there were also thousands of tribesmen on camels. And that was just the one tribe, besides countless others. Faisal Hussein would be here with his men, as well as the Egyptian Camel Corps, Indian sepoys, and British troops.

They found a place to make camp and water their horses, then went to wash their faces and hands in the waters of a nearby oasis. Men still swam in the oasis, the mood jovial rather than tense with the apprehension of the upcoming battle. No matter how much Noah might long for a bath, that would be impossible under the circumstance: both the regimental tattoo he'd foolishly had inked onto his back upon first joining the army and the scorpion brand on his left forearm could give him away.

"Aren't they being too loud?" Charles muttered as they bent toward the water.

Noah smirked, splashing the cold water on his face. It brought with it refreshment and respite, and he considered dunking his head to see if it would aid with the pounding ache in his skull, but then decided against it. Charles wasn't British, but in this manner, he was taking his direction from them. "They're not like us. Somber silence before battle is as foreign to them as is their laughter and noise to us. The biggest blunder any of us makes is to assume our ways are the most logical."

Standing, Noah wiped his hands on the rough fabric of his *thobe* and nodded toward the fortress, where he knew the English officers would take shelter for the night. "If you go up there, I'm certain you'll find sober darkness."

He started back toward the camp, Charles at his heels. "And which world are you from? Your mother was Egyptian, wasn't she?"

The moon was a thin crescent fingernail, making the sky seem to vibrate with even more stars than usual. Noah rubbed his eyes, his pulse throbbing in his temples. "I don't belong to any world. Not anymore."

Ginger's face flashed through his mind, his heart squeezing painfully. *She's the only world I have left.*

"By choice?" Charles fell into step beside him.

Noah glanced at his profile, intrigued by Charles's sudden curiosity about him. In the last two months, every time Charles had come to the monastery—which was several times a week—their discussions had been about troop movements and foreign policy. What was General Allenby's likely plan of attack? When did Noah think the offensive would begin? Why the interest in taking Damascus? Would the Syrians join the battle now that the British and French had given them incentive to do so?

Never anything personal.

Charles had yet to relay any news about Ginger, claiming he

couldn't locate her. Jack, he had learned, was in France, having joined the US military as an officer, which meant whatever relief Noah had felt in hearing news about Jack had been replaced by worry for him.

Noah didn't doubt that Jack was still working in intelligence, but it had surprised Noah that Jack had gone into the disaster that was the Western Front. All he could do was pray that Jack had kept his promise to deliver Ginger to England—any sort of cable or message to Jack would be too dangerous to risk sending, as the military censors would comb through all communications.

Noah had lapsed into silence in his thoughts, and a peal of laughter from a nearby Bedouin warrior brought him back to attention. Charles was still awaiting a response. "I'm not so different from most men," he said at last. "My place was decided by birth. An Irish Catholic married to a Moslem Egyptian—my parents broke the rules of their worlds and expelled themselves from them. My aunt saw their deaths as an opportunity to assimilate me to the English, and, thanks to my father's appearance and name, I could for years. But I'm not truly English, am I?"

"So, do you sympathize with the cause for Arab independence? That's why you were accused of treason, right?"

"Not entirely." Noah lowered his voice further still as they drew closer to where they'd made camp. "I was accused of treason because a pair of traitors in Cairo drew me into a scheme. But, yes, I do sympathize with the nationalist cause. Not by default, mind you"—he nodded toward the valley, filled with Arabs readying for the battle—"but because we issued a call to arms with a promise, and these men answered the call. And we promised the Egyptians we wouldn't use their lands or men for our war and then did precisely the opposite. Whatever you've heard about me, I believe in honoring my word. I lie to my enemies, but never my friends."

Charles's eyes glittered, reflecting the light of a passing fire. The smell of dust and sweat mixed with the rich aroma of brewing coffee. "We're not so different, then."

"Aren't we?" Noah's eyes bored into Charles's. "Sometimes I'm not quite certain just what side you're on, Pointer. Especially after what happened to Sarah in Malta."

"If you're going to accuse me of that again, I'll have to remind you I had nothing to do with what happened to her. My orders were to have her hand you over or risk accepting the full consequences of having run off with you. My superior informed her former husband's enemies of her presence after she failed to turn you over and we believe one of them, regrettably, took his vengeance out on her. But I was against exposing her. Sarah was a good informant in Egypt and served an important function, but she was careless by leaving the way she did."

Sarah had told him what Charles wanted when they'd spoken in Malta. *"He found you through me. I'm a danger to you, Noah. To you, Ginger, and Jack. And the American government wants you."* Noah shook himself from the memory. "Sarah had to flee Egypt with us. My enemies would have killed her in Egypt."

"She could have come to me. I would have protected her."

If Noah didn't know any better, Charles sounded bitter.

"There wasn't time. We were being chased."

Charles grunted. "What she wanted was to be with Jack Darby. They had a history of run-ins."

Noah couldn't deny that either. Jack hadn't told him much about any past encounters with Sarah, but they certainly had seemed to have known each other better than just passing acquaintances when they'd first reunited. But that Charles seemed to know so much about Sarah *and* Jack was intriguing. "Do you know Jack?"

"Of him. We share some friends in common but haven't ever formally met." A tired expression crossed Charles's face. Or possibly regret. "I knew Sarah for about ten years. We met studying archeology before Paul Hanover whisked her another world away."

For as little as Charles had told Noah about himself, this information seemed to put him in a new light. Sarah had the sort of enigmatic beauty and allure that most likely had won her a long list of suitors—no doubt Charles had been among them. But before Noah could ask anything else, Charles stopped, abruptly. "I think I'll go peek around the fortress. See what I might overhear. I'll return within ten minutes."

He started in the other direction, and Noah watched him go. For as much as Charles looked the part of a Bedouin warrior, he didn't entirely carry himself in the same manner. He'd slip past unnoticed to the untrained eye, though.

As he stood there, his left leg ached with a deep pain, one that he knew would keep him from sleeping. Instead of going back to the tent, he also continued walking, wanting to get away from the noise of the camp, which was only worsening the fog in his brain.

He climbed the slope of a gentle hill, then sat, the pebbles of the ground crunching into the sand. In some ways, he was freer than he'd been at the monastery here. He could run, if he wanted to, go back and find Ginger and be away from this mad war. But Charles never left him for longer than ten minutes.

In some ways, that was the beauty of Charles's arrangement, wasn't it? Charles had dragged Noah to a region of the world that wasn't easy to survive in. If Charles thought Noah had run, he could have British troops trying to track him down before Noah had even gone a mile.

Charles knew Noah needed him to survive now.

They were captor and prisoner, simple as that. It was better that Charles remained cool and distant instead of showing flashes of humanity as he'd just done when they'd discussed Sarah. Noah didn't need—or want—that feeling of kinship with Charles. Whether he was an ally to the British cause was immaterial to the larger control he was commanding over Noah's life.

The distant howling of wild dogs reminded Noah of the stories he'd heard of Azraq, of demon dogs that guarded the ruins, searching for their masters—the Beni Hillal who had built the fort. Goose flesh rose on Noah's arms as he listened to the cries, despite his disbelief in the legends.

Still, in the whispers of the wind and the desolation of the desert, he could hear Ginger's voice. It had only been a little over a year earlier when she'd practically bewitched him in a Bedouin camp, dancing in the Dabke and tempting him to kiss her.

He missed her with a totality that was inexplicable. Every pulse of his heart seemed achingly aware of the loss of her proximity, the emptiness he felt to the depth of his soul.

Each time he'd tried to send her away to keep her safe, she'd fought against it—until that last time, when she'd agreed to go and neither of them had known just how a severe a separation it would be. He wished he'd never left her, that he'd listened to her pleas to go to America. But he'd allowed his pride to get in the way.

The soft scrape of a camel's hooves against the ground pulled Noah from his reverie, and he lifted his chin. A figure approached on a camel, dressed in white. A slight man with a thin frame and short of stature blinked at him, dreamily, then stopped a few feet away.

Noah knew who he was in an instant—he'd met him before, but only briefly, in the offices of the Arab Bureau in Cairo. In some ways, they should have met long before that brief encounter—T. E. Lawrence had belonged to the world of archeology before the military had recruited him, just like Noah.

Lawrence spoke to him at last, in soft Arabic. "You've wandered away from the fold."

That Lawrence had defaulted to the native tongue made Noah relax. He believed the disguise.

"Azraq is crowded now," Noah said in Arabic, standing and dusting his hands. "I wanted to breathe the air without the stink."

A slow smile spread across Lawrence's tanned face, his white teeth gleaming in the moonlight. "I understand. I've just returned from Ain el Essad, for much the same reason. Come." He lowered the camel to its knees, then climbed off. "We can return together."

Noah hesitated. Lawrence was a man of exceptional intelligence and perceptiveness. If anyone might see through Noah's ruse, he seemed the man for the job. If Noah pretended not to know the identity of his companion and rejected the offer, he would appear both foolish and ungracious—neither of which would serve Charles's purposes in being here.

Then again, T. E. Lawrence was arguably the most important British official here at Azraq. If Noah could gain his trust, he might prove his usefulness to Charles faster than expected, convincing him that the deal was complete.

He started forward, with Lawrence by his side.

Lawrence studied him. "Have you come with Nuri Shaalan?"

"Yes. We've only just arrived."

Lawrence nodded, his gaze settling distractedly out into the desert plain. "On horse or camel?"

"Horse." Noah's gaze flicked toward the beast lumbering behind them. At night, camels were practically shadows, moving with a stealth that only desert creatures possessed. Lawrence was smart to use one, and he seemed as comfortable with the camel as he did in the robes he wore.

"The Arabian stallions of the Rualla are magnificent," Lawrence said with an appreciative gaze. He gave a tense little smile, and Noah sensed Lawrence held something back, his free hand clenching and unclenching.

It was strange, conversing in Arabic with someone when they could more easily have a conversation in their native tongue, but there was something poetic in it too: Lawrence had done his best to align himself with the people whose cause he now championed. Lawrence's actions might represent the greatest deception yet perpetrated on the Arabs. Like Noah, the British had asked him to befriend these people and then abuse their trust. Given the strain that appeared to lie thick on Lawrence's face, Noah wondered if the deception had taken its toll on him, too.

Proving his competency to Lawrence was crucial. Since the beginning of the war, Noah's most important asset had been language. A person able to communicate was worth his weight in gold.

His pulse speeded. English was a risk, but the reward might help secure his freedom sooner. At minimum, it would give him something to add to his credit with Charles, or maybe a bargaining chip if he could gain Lawrence's trust. Timorously, in a voice that sounded as though English was not his native language, Noah said, "I speak English."

Lawrence blinked at him. Then he scanned Noah's face once again, and Noah was grateful for the dark. Despite his ability to blend and his confidence in his disguise, he felt exposed.

"I spent a few years in England. Before the war," Noah added, hoping the explanation would suffice.

Let it be enough.

At last, Lawrence looked back toward the horizon. "We have a long few weeks ahead of us. Do you think you'll fare well with that leg?" Lawrence nodded toward Noah's left side.

Noah had tried to obscure the limp, but it must have been clear enough. "Yes." A smile curled on his lips. "Do you think you'll manage with that boulder on your shoulders?"

Now Lawrence laughed. "You see through me. What's your name?"

"Aziz." Noah bowed his head.

"It suits you." Lawrence tilted his chin, inspecting Noah's clothing. "Have you ever worked as a sapper, Aziz?"

As an English military man, Noah knew exactly what Lawrence meant. But he doubted an ordinary warrior of the Rualla would. *Maybe he's testing me?*

Noah raised an eyebrow. "Sapper?"

"Demolition. Exploding bridges and railways and such. It's what we must do in the next few weeks." Lawrence gestured toward the fortress in the distance. "I'll need a few Rualla guides to lead some of my men through the night. You seem well suited for it."

He gave a grateful bow. "It would be my honor. My friend, Selim—"

"He can go with you, too." Lawrence waved a weary hand. "Meet me in the fortress within the hour. We'll see you off with my men."

Noah said his good-bye, then parted from Lawrence, just as they approached the edges of the camp. A dark and anxious pressure encircled Noah's chest, mixing with a strange sense of excitement.

For the first time in months, he felt as though an opportunity might open for him. But it was one more way he was being drawn into a conflict that was no longer his. Once he might have been captivated by the idea of a thrilling ride through the night, setting charges on Turkish lines, weakening his enemy—but no more. With each step forward, he felt further than ever from the man he'd been.

Run.

To what? He'd never make it in the desert alone.

And if he was captured, his fate would be sealed. Charles wouldn't rescue him twice.

Run anyway.

The voice in his head was strong, making the back of his neck break out into a slick sweat.

He didn't want to be here. His soul felt tightly wound, about to snap. The winds of the desert swept past him, colder now that night was settling in. Once again, he heard them whisper in the voice of his beautiful wife.

Run, Noah.

Pushing the voice away, he started back toward Charles. He had to see this through. He'd never forgive himself if he didn't.

CHAPTER TWENTY-THREE

An aeroplane circled the sky above the valley. Noah looked up from his resting place in an olive grove in Sheik Saad. He'd been drifting off to sleep, exhausted from two weeks of making his way up the road to Damascus with Lawrence and Faisal Hussein's army, sometimes riding through the night, demolishing the Turkish line as they went.

The olive groves and palms and fruit trees in Sheik Saad were a veritable paradise, with a stream cutting through the earth, giving them a place to water their horses and themselves—and rest. The offensive had been grueling, mainly due to brilliant planning from Lawrence's council, which seemed to work in tandem with General Allenby to deliver a decisive and smashing victory to the British in Damascus as they pushed the Ottomans and Germans further north each day.

Beside him, Charles squinted into the sky. "Is it one of ours?"

Noah nodded, understanding his concern. The Germans had bombarded them on the plains more than once, where there was little cover. "It appears as though they're trying to decide what side we're on, given the way the pilot keeps circling. He probably has a message to drop from Allenby."

Charles rubbed his eyes. "You might see what it's all about, then." He plucked a ripe olive from a nearby tree and shook his head with disgust. "I'll stay here with the useless fruit."

Noah chuckled and stood, dusting himself off. When they'd first arrived, Charles had been thrilled that they were in an olive grove. He'd been sorely disappointed to learn that olives were practically inedible when first picked—curing was crucial in order to remove their bitter flavor.

Noah's first step was painful, but the pain dulled as he headed toward the old Roman ruins in the village and to Lawrence, where he knew he'd be welcomed. Over the course of the last few weeks, he'd found a place of usefulness beside Lawrence. As they'd made their way through the villages emptied of Turkish and German control, the locals had come in throngs, some joining their forces by the hundreds. Many had eager news to share about the enemy.

Sorting through the sudden barrage of information had been an arduous task, especially considering that the newfound "loyalty" these locals enthused about the British cause was hardly believable. Lawrence didn't seem to be under any illusion about that, though— he'd confided to Noah that he was well aware these villagers would welcome and help whichever force was most likely to leave them unharmed. Not that Noah blamed them. They were simple peasants whose goal in life was not so dissimilar to his own: survival.

Not that there hadn't been a risk in befriending Lawrence. Noah had been careful to avoid Nuri Shalaan, who was frequently at Lawrence's side. But the chief of the Rualla could also expose both him and Charles—he was more likely to recognize that they were strangers and not his tribesmen.

Noah found Lawrence with a few members of his personal bodyguard and Tallal, the sheik of Tafas, an imposing Arab chief with a thick black beard and bright, energetic eyes. Like

Lawrence, he wore white, and the two men were deep in conversation. About forty feet in front of Lawrence and Tallal, a small group of English officers sat in canvas chairs, and one of them held out a hand toward Noah, indicating that he shouldn't proceed any further.

The Englishmen paid little attention to Noah and resumed their discussion in low tones, careful not to let Lawrence overhear them. "We never should have come here in the first place," one of them muttered, a dour expression on his face. "We've fulfilled our mission and destroyed the Hejaz railway. But would he listen to me? Now there are thousands of Turks pouring from Deraa and coming toward us. We should go back to Azraq until further orders from Allenby."

"Lawrence has been making sound calls all along. Who are we to question what he wants?" one of the other officers said. "He isn't rash. We should just take orders and follow."

"What Lawrence wants is Arab honor and Arab freedom—not the interests of the British," the other man snapped coolly.

"Aziz, my friend," Lawrence said, his voice strong. He had paused in his conversation with Tallal and looked directly toward Noah. "Come here."

The English officers looked up, their eyes widening with alarm as they realized Lawrence was beckoning Noah in English. They exchanged glances amongst themselves, and Noah avoided their gazes as he moved past them, trying not to smile to himself. It never failed to amaze him how often men used language as though it was an impenetrable shield to discuss things aloud that they ought not to.

As though Lawrence had known exactly what his subordinates had been saying about him, he gave them an amused look, his bright blue eyes gleaming. He set a hand on Noah's shoulder as he approached, then nodded toward the horizon. "Heavy smoke coming in from Deraa. The Germans are setting fire to their stores and readying the evacuation. What say you, Aziz? Are you ready for a rout?"

Lawrence's exuberance was startling. They had smashed the Turkish defense faster than any of them had expected, but could he be right? Could they be nearing the end of Turkish resistance in Syria? Given the way the war had worn on so interminably for years, hope had seemed distant.

Lawrence seemed to sense Noah's skepticism. "Bulgaria has surrendered to the Allies. The Germans have lost the ground they've gained in the spring … and we are on the cusp here, too."

Tallal shook his head, interrupting Lawrence at last in Arabic. "And what of those six thousand Turks?" Worry wore lines into the crinkles near his eyes.

"If we demolish them, our purpose here will be at an end." Lawrence was calm, as though unperturbed by the threat of six thousand enemy soldiers. "There are two columns. We'll allow the larger one to pass and concentrate our strength on the smaller." He looked back at Noah. "Have you learned anything of significance from the locals who came carrying news this morning?"

"Nothing helpful," Noah said. The scent of acrid smoke grew heavier, and Noah could imagine the hasty retreat. Apprehension gripped him. He'd seen the Turks in retreat before—they weren't predictable and could be cruel to both civilian populations and animals in their path. "But if they are on the move, we should be too."

Tallal nodded vigorously. "The ones from Muzerieb are moving toward Tafas. My people will not be safe."

Lawrence looked between Noah and Tallal. "I'll speak to the others. Aziz, you and your man go on ahead, scout the road to Tafas and report back. Your horses have the speed necessary."

The irony of Charles being Noah's "man" in this scenario wasn't lost on him, and he kept his expression even. Noah bowed his head and left Lawrence.

"Who is he?" He heard Tallal ask as he walked away.

"One of the Rualla."

Noah almost slowed to hear Tallal's response, but he felt the eyes of the English officers still on him, besides Lawrence's and Tallal's. He'd never wanted to be so far out in the open, this exposed, but he kept getting drawn in further and further. But if Lawrence was right and the defeat of the Turkish army was around the corner, then maybe he could at last be free of Charles's grip.

He found Charles dozing where he'd left him and roused him from sleep. Charles sat, scratching the welt of a mosquito bite on his cheek. "We have to hurry. Lawrence wants us to scout the road to Tafas." Noah knelt by his rug. He rolled it, then tied it to his horse.

Charles scrambled from his own rug. "What's in Tafas?"

"What's left of the Turkish army—or, at least, it's headed that way." Noah glanced over his shoulder at Charles. "According to Lawrence, we may be near the end of this offensive. Maybe even the end of the war with the Ottomans." He adjusted the headstall on the horse. "In which case, I think I've more than fulfilled my word to you."

The fasteners on Charles's saddlebag snapped shut. "There's still more to be done in Egypt. The Wafd party is growing in strength, and I need someone with your experience to—"

"My obligations to you end after this offensive." Noah gave Charles a hard look. A black fly swarmed near his face, then moved onto the mane of his horse.

"Your obligations to me end when I say they do."

Noah set his hand on the pommel, then swung up onto the horse. A sharp pain shot through his leg as he did, and he squeezed his eyes shut, missing the ease of his movements before all this. His frustration with Charles was mired by the conflict he regarded him with: the fact remained that Charles had saved his life. But at what cost? And for what—to keep him in indefinite servitude?

"I suggest if you want help understanding the Wafd party, that you find yourself a different Orientalist. My interest in this part of the world is at an end. In the future, my interest will only reside within the four walls of the home I make with my wife."

Charles ducked his chin, leveling his gaze with Noah. "And you're certain she'll be there waiting when you return?"

Noah struck the fly away from his stallion with annoyance. "As certain as I am that the ground beneath my feet is dust and rock."

Charles mounted his horse. "Women can be fickle, Benson. They look for comfort in their sorrow. And then opportunists swoop in."

Noah had the feeling that Charles spoke from experience—he had probably been in love with Sarah Hanover. But Ginger and Sarah were nothing alike. "Not my wife." He pulled the reins, directing the stallion away from the grove. "But that's beside the point. The point is, you owe me my freedom. You never would have got this close to T. E. Lawrence without me and you know it. If I can't do anything to earn my freedom sooner, then what motivation do I have to give you the best results possible?"

After a few moments, Charles gave a lengthy sigh. "Fine, Benson. When the Ottomans surrender, you will have it." Charles brought his horse into step beside Noah's. "You're right. You've exceeded my expectations, particularly with this work with Lawrence. Your superior was an idiot to let you go."

"Letting me go was precisely the problem." Noah couldn't keep the bitterness out of his voice as he spoke. He had tried to avoid thoughts of Lord Helton as much as possible recently. "He found me too useful and demanded my full focus and attention."

As they left Sheik Saad, Noah took his horse from a canter into a gallop, riding southward toward Tafas.

Noah nearly closed his eyes at the rush of the wind against his face. He could imagine he was free here, the brilliant cerulean sky nearly cloudless, the earthen scent of dust rising under his horse's hooves.

But he wasn't rushing to freedom. A shiver rose in his spine, the fabric of his headscarf whipping against his cheek. The powerful muscles of the horse were taut, moving with a fluidity and purpose that made him feel the creature understood his urgency. Tafas would see death and destruction at the hands of the Turks.

The desolation gave way as the distant forms of humans took shape, their accoutrements gleaming in the sun.

All along the road there came peasants, fleeing the path of the advancing Turkish column. Lawrence had severed the Turkish line, cutting the approaching soldiers off from the bulk of the army. The Turks were still too distant to see, but Noah didn't trust that there wouldn't be Turkish scouts or aeroplanes able to spot him in the middle of the day, this far out in the open.

The Rualla Arabian stallions were amongst the finest horses in the world, known for their speed. Between them, the pair of Rolls-Royce motorcars that the British Army had given Lawrence for his use in the desert, and the aeroplanes that had minimized the threats of the German planes, Lawrence's men appeared vastly superior in equipment and strength compared to the besieged Turks. Noah looked over his shoulder at Charles. He was only a few lengths behind Noah, but he did a fair job of keeping up.

They had only gone a few miles when they encountered a few boys, no older than twelve, bleeding and barefoot. The boys fell to their knees, begging them for mercy. "What is it? What's happened?" Noah asked them in Arabic.

"Djemal Pasha's men entered Tafas and attacked us," one of them said, clutching a rag wound round his bleeding head.

Noah looked south toward the village, a knot of tension forming in his gut.

If Pasha's men are there, it's already too late.

These bleeding boys, despite their state, were already safe. Noah turned the horse back around, without waiting for Charles, and dug his stirrups into the stallion's flanks. He broke into a gallop once more, a sickening feeling rising in him.

He had seen what the Turks did to their enemies, witnessed the cruelty unleashed upon the Armenians. Tallal had been right to be afraid.

They could never save the people of Tafas.

Charles followed behind in hot pursuit, no doubt aware of the gravity of the situation. Noah didn't have time to explain it to him.

The world passed by in a blur of tan and orange, sweat stinging Noah's eyes as he drove the horse to its top speed. Lawrence's men were tired, and even if he'd mobilized them as quickly as Tallal had wanted, it would take time to get the weary troops there, too late to spare the village of Tafas from the worst of the plunder.

At last, Lawrence and his men appeared as a mirage on the road ahead and Noah slowed, his heart racing. He found Lawrence easily and rode straight toward him.

Lawrence sat straight on his camel, alert. "Well?"

"They've taken the village of Tafas." Noah saw Charles come up behind him out of the corner of his eye.

Beside Lawrence, Tallal uttered a groan, perhaps a prayer, and Lawrence stayed him with a gentle look. "We go on. If we make haste, we'll arrive within an hour."

The afternoon was too bright, too quiet, too beautiful for war. The stillness of it conjured an ominous feeling as Noah and Charles fell back into line with Lawrence's troops. Their horses were tired and needed water, but it would have to wait. The noise of the animals' hooves filled the air and Charles brought his horse closer to Noah's. "What now?" he whispered in a low voice.

Noah caught the fear in his eyes. Whatever function Charles served for the US government, he likely wasn't a soldier. During the last two weeks, he'd been able to avoid the conflict by taking a subordinate role to Noah, whose primary function had been assisting Lawrence in the demolitions. Charles had faced bombardments and the occasional spray of bullets with field guns but had never faced the Turkish soldiers head-on.

"Stay close to me. You have a rifle. Do you know how to use it?"

Charles nodded, moistening his lips.

"You may need to." Noah wiped the moisture from his brow, praying that the Turks would be merciful to the villagers. But he was certain they knew Tallal was one of Lawrence's men—most of the Arabs loyal to the British were well known in this region.

The slower pace of the troops gave Noah and Charles's stallions some time to rest but did little to comfort Noah. Desperate men were often the most brutal, and the Turkish columns bore the weight of their imminent collapse.

What was worse, the villagers were mostly defenseless old men, women, and children. Tallal had the bulk of his tribesmen with him. Ginger herself had endured torture and nearly been raped when she'd been captured by the Turks—Noah had barely saved her in time. The memory of it was something Noah didn't dare allow himself to dwell on. He'd taken his revenge savagely when rescuing her and in the day that followed, acting with a brutality that was difficult to remember.

As the village of Tafas came into view, smoke and ash greeted them. Lawrence's troops drew to a halt, a hush over them all.

The air smelled of death.

The villagers who had escaped stood huddled on the side of the road, standing among the brush and thistles that dotted the hills. Their faces were wet with tears, their clothing dirty, many of them bleeding: women holding babies, barefoot children, bent men with grey beards. Their cries were unbearable, shrieks of mourning, of inconsolable pain.

Rage built inside Noah at the sight of them. They were mothers, fathers, sons, daughters. All beloved to someone. All punished in a war that they'd done nothing to create. A conflict so devoid of meaning that humanity had filled the earth with the blood of the innocent. And it was still not enough.

When will it be enough? When will the men who order us all to slaughter see their goals met?

Flames licked the air above the burning houses. Villagers rushed toward the approaching troops, seeing Tallal at the forefront, their cries filling the air, babbling about the destruction and defilement. Noah cursed his ability to understand. He didn't want to hear, didn't want to see.

But he was a part of this now.

The Turks were leaving in a column, just beyond the burning houses. A few of the Arabs with Lawrence opened fire toward them. In an instant, Lawrence was giving orders, and the infantry took their position. Noah followed them, with Charles at his side. Neither could stay behind here—nor would they want to. The sight of death was everywhere, murdered women and children lying in distorted heaps on the rocky ground.

The infantry started forward on their horses, and, as they did, a little girl—only a few years old, bleeding and dirty—rushed toward the soldiers from among the dead. She cried out as one of Tallal's men jumped from his camel toward her. Noah's gut twisted as the soldier caught the girl in his arms. "Don't hit me," she cried, shielding herself from Tallal's man.

Noah's heart slammed against his chest as he imagined the brutality she must have witnessed for that to be her reaction.

Don't hit me.

A precious little girl. Her life just begun.

Don't hit me.

Noah's hands tightened into tight fists around the reins of his horse.

Then the girl fell to the ground. Tallal's man cradled her in his arms, but she was motionless.

"God have mercy," Charles whispered beside Noah. His face was pale, his eyes wide.

"Try not to look," Noah told him in a low voice, not listening to his own advice.

How could they not look? They couldn't look away, their souls branded by the fire that ripped through the village. The surrounding soldiers were still and voiceless, the village itself eerily forsaken. They rode closer toward the horrific destruction and a shudder went through Noah, the muscles of his forearms drawing tight as his anger built.

His entire body screamed at him, and his eyes felt as though thorns were being driven into them. But he still couldn't help but gaze upon the massacre, the coldhearted evil that had been handed to these poor people. The Turks had set out a group of mutilated bodies in a gruesome tableau near the village walls, a pregnant woman among the most prominently displayed.

The way they'd disfigured her would haunt him, he was certain of it.

Lawrence's voice came from the front of the line, shaking with fervor. "The best of you brings me the most Turkish dead. We take no prisoners today."

Tallal, who had been taking in the atrocity with tears streaming down his cheeks, gave a cry, shaking. He straightened, then dug his heels into the sides of his horse, galloping away.

His pain drove him forward, his despair written in his sobs.

There could be no consolation for Tallal. He'd brought this destruction on his people by trying to free them. Noah clenched his jaw, sitting straighter on his horse.

Tallal rode downward, at full speed, toward the retreating Turkish line.

The Turks turned, watching him as though in amazement, and Lawrence's men stared in somber silence. "Tallal, Tallal," Tallal cried out at last, in a whooping, fearless voice.

The Turks fired their rifles, the echoes of their shots snapping across the grim, flaming ruins, followed by the endless blasting of their machine guns. In an instant, Tallal and his horse fell, their bodies pierced through.

Goose bumps rose on Noah's skin as they all absorbed the fall of Tallal against the earth, a signal.

Lawrence's infantry cried out, then rushed forward. Charles didn't move. Noah grabbed the rifle at his side, yanking it from the saddle.

"Now you see why I didn't want to return to this war, Pointer." Noah smacked the rifle into Charles's chest, who caught it with shaking hands. "It changes you. You find yourself in the middle of the goddamned Arabian desert, killing men you've never met, and it doesn't bother you at all. You may even want them dead for what they did to other people you've never met. Go take your vengeance. The enemy won't think twice about taking his."

Charles stared at the rifle in his hands, looking unsteady. "I've never killed anyone before."

Noah scanned his face. Charles seemed genuinely disturbed by the thought. "I'll be right beside you." He swung his own rifle around from his back, loading it. He preferred to be off the horse, but didn't trust that it wouldn't get lost in the chaos of battle.

Instead, he came up the flank of Lawrence's men, riding straight for the Turks. The sharp whiz of bullets and the constant crack of gunfire pelted Noah's mind until it had worn a numbness to his skull, a dull deafness that made thought difficult. He concentrated on firing his own weapon, shooting to kill. If there would be no prisoners, then wounding the enemy was not an option.

At his side, Charles appeared to have fallen into the same steady rhythm as the Arab soldiers around them. They attacked with fervor, with a rage that showed in their own lack of mercy, even as hands raised in surrender and enemy soldiers cowered in front of them.

Death, everywhere. Thousands of Turkish troops, small groups of German soldiers, a clash of horses and camels, infantry and vehicles. Gunpowder hung so heavily in the air that it burned Noah's nostrils, a hell on earth that was indescribable. Though the flames from the village were more distant the further they pushed into the Turkish column, Noah's throat stung with the pungent tang of the fumes.

The aching in his head, once intolerable, pushed him forward now and he yelled as he shot, bayoneted, and charged. Blood covered his clothes, his face, his hands. He clenched his jaw, sweat dripping down his cheeks, his body burning with exhaustion.

Time became nonexistent, caught in some haunting ethereal melody, where gunshots replaced the beating of hearts and sunlight faded without notice.

By nightfall, the Turks were all dead, blood and bodies littering the plain where they'd fought. They had won and obliterated their enemy. Their forces had not only been superior, they'd wanted to kill their enemy more.

Charles and Noah found water for their horses and Noah dismounted, his legs so weak he had to grip the pommel of the saddle to stay upright.

Charles was filthier than ever, bloodstains splattering his *thobe*, his face encrusted with dirt. He turned around in a full circle, his eyes roving over the dead.

For the first time in a battle, Noah felt immediately haunted by the souls of those whose lives had been so brutally cut short. Normally the battlefield was a moan of cries, of wounded men begging for water and mercy.

But they had killed them all.

"My God, what have we done? Are we any better than them?"

Massacre had begotten massacre. Noah put a hand on Charles's shoulder. "There's a difference between killing women and children and killing the men who committed those crimes."

Did he really believe that though? They'd killed men begging for surrender. His hands were stained through.

He felt no satisfaction in this victory.

The faces of the dead villagers swarmed through his head. The little girl. The pregnant woman. The babies.

Their deaths would haunt him forever.

Charles didn't appear pacified by Noah's answer, either. His eyes were round, pupils wide in the dark. "Enough. It's enough. Let's go back to Sheik Saad. In the morning, we can make a plan to get back to Jerusalem. Free you for once and for all."

CHAPTER TWENTY-FOUR

*T*he gloom of the macabre events of Tafas had made sleep nearly impossible, and Noah rolled his cheek into his rug. The olive grove that he and Charles had used for a makeshift camp at Sheik Saad had been quickly snapped up in their absence, and when they'd arrived after midnight, they'd forgone the comfort of privacy and slept in the open, near the stream, where their exhausted horses could be watered.

Noah imagined Charles had wanted to wash himself, too, though the night had been too frigid for that.

The first streaks of light were creeping into the horizon as Noah sat, rubbing the palm of his hand over his dry lips, then over his scalp. His hair was longer than it had ever been—it had been almost a full year since he'd cut it—and it was thick and uncomfortable. He reached for his head cover and pulled it on.

Every muscle in his body ached, though it wasn't entirely unwelcome. He'd been able to ride into battle, fire a weapon with ease. The soreness of his limbs was akin to some strange progress—a return to what he'd been before. His memory still wasn't fully restored, and the headaches were life-draining, but if he could even be three-quarters recuperated, he would be pleased. He despised his weakness.

His throat was parched and he reached for his canteen, noticing just then that Charles's rug was empty. His horse was still nearby, tied to a tree with Noah's. Perhaps he'd gone down to the stream to bathe and drink.

Struggling to his feet, Noah tested his weight against his left leg, then stood to his full height, stretching.

The familiar click of a pistol being cocked made him freeze.

From behind the tree beside his horse stepped an English officer, holding a pistol. He aimed the weapon directly at Noah, his eyes narrowed. "Hands up. Now."

Noah blinked blearily at him, complying with the order. He was one of the English officers Noah had seen near Lawrence the day before—the one who had been speaking critically of Lawrence's orders.

"I've been watching you," the officer said, his face hidden by shadow. "Come with me."

Noah's eyes darted at the surrounding space. Had they been in the olive grove, he might have considered overtaking the man, dealing with the consequences later if necessary. But they were here in the open, with other men sleeping and stirring only ten feet away—in plain sight. He couldn't run without being stopped.

Where was Charles?

Charles had promised him his freedom, and he expected they'd be leaving for Jerusalem soon.

Had Charles betrayed him?

The English officer prodded him forward, and Noah stretched his shoulders as he walked, trying to loosen the stiffness in his back. If he needed to fight, he wanted to be as limber as possible. "Who are you?" Noah asked in his accented English, risking a glance back at the man.

"Lieutenant Ross Burke. Now walk."

"And my companion?"

Lieutenant Burke smirked. "Already on his way back to Azraq, then to catch a plane to see General Allenby. He claimed diplomatic immunity, demanded to see the American attaché with Allenby, who vouched for him."

Noah slowed. Charles was gone? What did he mean, Charles had claimed diplomatic immunity? None of this made any sense. Had Charles gone to them and surrendered himself?

What has he told them about me?

Anger flushed through him, his shoulders stiffening. At the first sign of trouble, Charles had easily broken. Had he thrown Noah to the wolves in the process?

He gritted his teeth, his clothing stiff with sweat and grime as Burke led him onward. "I want to see Lawrence."

"I'm sure you do. Sadly, he's gone on to Deraa—and it's doubtful he'll return. So I'm afraid you're out of friends here, whoever you are. Your American friend refused to tell us anything other than that you were a Rualla man. At any rate, I'm certain Lawrence will be far less inclined to be your ally once he learns you've been spying on him."

That Burke didn't seem to know his identity gave Noah hope. If Charles hadn't told him, maybe Charles hadn't gone to them.

"I don't understand," Noah said simply.

Lieutenant Burke smiled cruelly. "I think you do. You assisted that American in spying on us, didn't you? I monitored you both when you returned to camp last night, heard him speaking to you. Once he opened his mouth, I knew he wasn't supposed to be here. I doubt you are either."

Then Burke must have captured Charles shortly after Noah had gone to sleep.

The best-case scenario, under the circumstances, was that Charles had simply claimed Noah was a local he'd employed as a guide. But without knowing what Charles had said, it was better to remain silent.

They walked until they arrived at the location where Noah had seen Burke the day before, where Lawrence had made his camp. Whatever the chain of command here, Noah doubted Burke had many obstacles in his way to doing whatever he wanted. If Lawrence had gone to Deraa, he'd probably taken a handful of his most trusted advisors with him, along with the members of his bodyguard.

A few Arab warriors waited in the camp, whom Noah recognized as Rualla tribesmen. He didn't meet their gazes, knowing what was likely coming. Burke stopped him, then pushed Noah to his knees. "Arms behind your head, hands on your head."

Small, sharp stones dug into Noah's knees through the lightweight fabric of his *sirwal* trousers under his *thobe.* He put his arms back. He squinted as sunlight filtered in through the shade of a palm tree, the light dappled on the ground where he knelt. A beetle made its way across the ground near him and Noah watched it as it crawled, allowing the insect to be his distraction while he waited for Burke to make his move.

"Is he one of yours?" Burke asked the Rualla men.

They stared at Noah with stony faces. None of them would vouch for him, that much was certain. He wasn't one of them.

He didn't belong here. And if he told them anything about who he really was, he would soon find himself on the way to execution.

When the Rualla men said nothing, Burke frowned. He nodded toward the Rualla warriors. "Strip him. Make certain he isn't carrying any other weapons."

The command was a wise one. Noah always kept a knife at his waist and a pistol strapped to his ankle, which were soon recovered as the men stripped Noah naked. The early morning air was cold against his skin, causing an involuntary rush of goose bumps. He didn't doubt that disrobing him was also meant as a humiliation, and he kept his eyes down. If he survived this, the first thing he'd do was rid himself of any marking that could identify him.

Burke inspected the regimental tattoo Noah had inked on his back when he had first joined the army and Noah once again cursed his poor judgment. It identified not only the regiment he'd enlisted with, but also where he'd first been assigned. Burke's eyes widened. "Gloucestershire?" He studied Noah's profile. "You're a Tommy." Then he stepped backward, rubbing his neck uncertainly.

Noah didn't answer. Kneeling was more difficult now that they had stripped him of his clothing, the rocks digging into his skin. He raised his chin, his arms aching from holding them up on his head. He reeked of ammonia and body odor, his uncovered skin looking unnaturally pale compared to his arms.

"What are you doing here?" Burke demanded again, clearly frustrated by Noah's lack of response. He stroked the bare skin of his closely shaven jaw, his bafflement showing through. No doubt, he didn't know what to do with Noah.

Noah met his eyes again. He didn't drop the accent, because it wouldn't do to change anything about how he'd presented himself right now. "I want to speak to Lawrence."

Burke's jaw clenched. He wasn't in charge, but no doubt if he did something too far out of order, he'd face censure for it. At last, he grunted and motioned toward the Arabs. "Tie him up. Give him his trousers. Then we'll see about taking him to Deraa."

* * *

THE GERMANS and Turks had evacuated Deraa just the day before, and signs of their hasty exit were everywhere. What hadn't been burned had been plundered by the incoming troops, and the streets were a mixture of debris and spoiled goods, ash and charred remnants of fallen buildings.

Noah walked beside Burke's camel with his hands bound in

front of him. Burke had left him bare-chested—as a punishment, Noah suspected—and the sun had baked his skin, leaving it a bright red by the time they entered the town. The walk had been arduous, taking most of the day—a trip a camel could have easily made in a quarter of the time. But because Burke had wanted to punish Noah by walking, it was already dusk, the light quickly fading.

The pain in Noah's lower back and leg had intensified, making his limp more pronounced, and his lips cracked from thirst and sunburn. All along the route, the peasants had stared at him as he passed, and that intensified in the town. He was clearly a prisoner, and his special status in his being escorted like this probably increased their interest in him.

Burke led the way toward what remained of a burned-out aerodrome, and as they drew closer, Noah recognized some men of Lawrence's personal bodyguard keeping watch. By the time they were within a few feet of the place, Lawrence himself had exited. His eyes were trained on Noah, but his expression gave away little of his thoughts.

Burke halted his camel, then lowered himself from it and left Noah standing about twenty feet away. He directed some of the Arab bodyguards to keep their eyes on Noah and then pulled Lawrence away for a private conference.

The sharp sting of a mosquito on his forearm forced Noah to jerk his hand back, and the dromedary turned his head toward him, blinking with curiosity. If only he could simply hop on the creature and ride away. He didn't doubt that the members of Lawrence's guard would shoot him, though.

As much as Noah wanted to trust Lawrence, he couldn't. Lawrence was a military man, after all. If Noah was fortunate, he would only hold Noah in prison, which would give Noah more time. Maybe even Charles would return to help him. Hopefully Lawrence's familiarity with him would make him more merciful.

Within a few minutes, one of them approached, then cut the

rope attached to the camel. He grabbed the edge of the rope and tugged Noah forward. The blisters on Noah's sandaled feet screamed in response, and he clenched his teeth.

The man led Noah into the aerodrome and then toward a solitary chair. He pushed Noah into the seat and, despite the force, Noah almost sighed with relief. A moment later, he kicked his sandals away, preferring the freedom of being barefoot. The guard stepped away, within view of Noah, but silent.

Time passed slowly as Noah sat there and, in his exhaustion, his head lolled forward with sleep. He jerked his chin up, trying to fight the drowsiness, his thoughts unclear. As he did, his gaze fixed on the scar on his chest.

"Thank you for your attentions, Sister Whitman. I should go."

"Don't." Ginger's voice was barely audible.

Noah held his breath, gazing into those beguiling green eyes. He wanted to believe she was nothing like her father, that somehow she'd simply been mixed up in this business by accident.

Ginger drew closer to him and he ached to feel her in his arms, taste her lips once again. "I'm tired of being underestimated. Don't treat me like another stupid woman who doesn't know exactly what you're doing."

Do I even know what I'm doing? He wanted her and she was intoxicating, blocking out all other thought.

The corners of his mouth tipped in a smile. He encircled her waist with one arm, the palm of his hand against the small of her back, strong and purposeful. His words were a fierce whisper. "I wish you were any other woman. Then I could force myself to stay away."

"Aziz."

The voice startled Noah awake, and he squinted into the light of a torch.

It was night.

How long had Noah been asleep? He had no way of telling the time. The march to Deraa during the day had exhausted him and they'd arrived at dusk ... Noah estimated he couldn't have been sitting here for more than a couple of hours.

Lawrence pulled the light back from its offensive direction and straightened. He folded his hands behind his back, relying on the light of a nearby oil lamp on the ground. Burke wasn't in sight, nor was Lawrence's bodyguard.

Noah lifted his eyes to Lawrence, whose lips twitched, his face an unhappy scowl.

"Tell me, friend, why a warrior of the Rualla was acting as an informant to an American spy. Or, better yet, illuminate me as to that regimental tattoo, worn by our Tommies assigned to Egypt." Then Lawrence squatted, his eyes narrowing. "Or are you an Egyptian nationalist? You wear the brand of the Aleaqrab national-ists from Egypt, yes? I believe they're Wafd men now."

Noah swallowed, his throat aching from thirst. "And if I'm none of those things?" He made no attempt to hide his English accent this time.

Lawrence tilted his head to his side. "English then?" He shook his head. "No, that's far too simple. *Bist du Deutscher?*"

"*Nein.*" Noah pursed his lips.

"How many languages do you speak?"

"Six, fluently. But I can do well enough in several others."

"I'm certain you can." Lawrence's eyes glinted. "But who—more importantly—are you? And why should I bother keeping you alive? Besides the fact that you genuinely fascinate me."

For a moment, Noah considered telling Lawrence the truth. But even Lawrence had sold his soul to the British military, just as Noah once had, no matter how much he loved the Arabs he'd fought beside.

Noah stretched his shoulders back. "I'm no one of consequence. All the names I've used are the names of dead men, including my own."

"Yet you fought the Turks with us at Tafas. Helped with breaking their line. Why?"

"I fought to survive. It's that simple. The most basic instinct of any man or creature."

"So you have no side?" Lawrence leaned back on his heels, crossing his arms. "I don't think I believe you."

"I had a side once, but I was expelled from it. Because I dared to fall in love. Dared to have an opinion that went against what others wanted me to have. Dared not to hand over the last bit of my humanity as a soldier. That's what we do, after all. Tell kings and leaders that we'll allow them to control our every action and that we'll do it in the name of fealty and service, no matter our morality, conscience, or eternal damnation."

Lawrence stood. "There's a part of you that feels as though I'm looking in a mirror." He smiled. "A very tall mirror, of course." Then he sighed. "But, of course, much as I wish I could simply let you go, that's not the way things go around these parts. And I have no assurance that you won't use those marvelous skills you possess and the knowledge you have and then turn up on the other side of the line. So, a firing squad then? Something quick and painless."

His footsteps echoed as he walked away.

"Wait," Noah called after him.

Lawrence turned back to look at him.

"I have a wife. Can I entrust you to send her word of my death?"

Folding his hands, Lawrence sighed. "Well. Wouldn't that require you giving me her name? And, therefore, your own."

Noah shook his head. "I'd give you the name of a friend who could tell her. I wouldn't want to endanger her by contacting her directly."

Lawrence came closer once more. "I wish you would just tell me who you are. I hate to kill you, Aziz. You seem a good man."

"If my enemies know I'm alive, I endanger the lives of those who love me—innocent ones. Satisfying your curiosity isn't worth that."

Scanning his face, Lawrence gave one brisk nod. "Tomorrow, then. At dawn. Rest easy."

This time, Noah said nothing else. He bowed his head, his body feeling beaten and bruised, defeated. One more night. Then it would be finally over.

CHAPTER TWENTY-FIVE

$\mathcal{F}$or a week, Noah had gone to sleep each night believing he might die in the morning.

Instead, Lawrence had put him to work in his group of bodyguards and taken him to Damascus for the army's triumphant entrance into the city. Noah had no illusions that his every move hadn't been closely watched by Lawrence's most trusted friends. They hadn't spoken to him outside of giving him orders, and any of the friendly communication he'd had with Lawrence was gone. Noah rarely saw him, and Lawrence never looked his way.

If Deraa had seemed disrupted by the Turkish and German evacuation, Damascus was in shambles by comparison. The first few days had been a flurry of reestablishing an interim Arab government under Faisal Hussein, reviving infrastructure, clearing the wreckage off the streets, feeding the population, and—perhaps most horrifically of all—tending to the Turkish wounded in their hospital, who had been all but abandoned in such a state of filth and disease that the Australian doctors who had entered the city were pleading for help from every official they found.

Then, abruptly, in the middle of it all, Lawrence had left the city, an extended leave granted to him. He'd taken Noah with him in a Rolls-Royce, without saying a word, and in the middle of the desert he'd had the driver stop and directed Noah out of the vehicle.

His face was as hard as flint, his eyes veined with red and dark with sorrow. "I think I may at last understand you, Aziz." They hadn't spoken since that night in the aerodrome, and Noah didn't quite know what to expect.

"How's that?" Noah shifted his weight. He'd been barefoot the last five days, allowing his blisters to heal.

"That bit about selling your soul. And now I've come to the end of the road, and I find myself nothing but a traitor. To my country. The men who called me friends. The promises I made." A distant look swelled in his eyes as he looked beyond Noah toward the desert. "King Hussein spoke of a pan-Arab kingdom, a utopia where all could exist in peace, and in my dreams, I think I saw the possibility. But I forgot that humanity is the destroyer of dreams."

Noah didn't have to ask what had devastated Lawrence—he'd seen it coming for some time now. Lawrence, if he was honest, had probably seen it too, but held on to hope. The British had promised a kingdom and independence to King Hussein. His son, Faisal, and their warriors had fought bravely for it. And then they'd parceled those lands up between themselves and the French, in secret.

"The Sykes-Picot Agreement is more intact than they tried to pretend?" Noah said in a low voice.

Lawrence nodded, then met Noah's eyes once again. "I can't kill you, you know. You've disturbed my last few days here in Syria. Reminded me of the man I no longer am." He reached into his robes and pulled out a pistol, then handed Noah a canteen. "There's one bullet. And enough water, perhaps, to last a day. Use them both wisely. Best of luck to you, Aziz."

Then Lawrence had left him there, in the desert's desolation, and driven away.

One single bullet for Noah to kill himself with, should he find himself desperate.

Water, for a fool's chance of survival.

Noah watched the dusty trail left behind by the motorcar until he could no longer see it.

For a few minutes, he sat, too numb to think straight. He curled his knees up, his bare feet flat against the rocky desert, the sand between his toes. The sun was hot against his skin, his headscarf long gone.

The two possessions Lawrence had given him were in each hand. His sole possessions on earth.

For the first time in almost a year, he was free.

No more war, no more doing the bidding of others.

But he had nothing.

He could forage what he needed for now. Supplies might be found along the abandoned Turkish line, though he knew the locals by now would have scavenged the best of it. Still, an odd rope or something he might fashion into a knife could help.

Water would be the hardest obstacle. His life depended on it, in a land where it wasn't plentiful.

Traveling by night might be best, to keep himself from freezing. Sleep could wait until the sunrise. He no longer worried about being recognized—no one would give half a blink to a dirty, ragged peasant—but he would be wise to avoid most settlements and villages. The journey to Jerusalem, where he might find help from the monks in the abbey or Fahad, would most likely take weeks and be miserable. One of the hardest things he'd ever done.

But he still didn't move, the gun in his hand heavy.

Or I could end it all now, spare myself any further pain.

Suicide. A gentleman's offer. But was he really that desperate?

He might find himself that desperate after not eating much for days or if he couldn't find water.

He scanned the ground behind him, looking for scorpions, then lay back on the ground.

I'm free.

When Charles had offered him freedom, he'd allowed himself to hope. He'd find a ship in the closest harbor, get back to Ginger. If Jack had joined the army, he was certain his friend had returned Ginger to England first. She might be with family, but once he got to England, he was sure he could find her easily.

A bird's cry caught his attention, then a buzzard flapped down on the sand close by, ready to examine him. He chuckled to himself.

I'm not dead yet.

He sat, the creature giving him a hard, beady-eyed stare, then flapping its wings back. It didn't leave, because it likely thought he'd be dead soon enough and he still had enough meat on him to be worth the trouble.

Noah stood and shook the sand from his garments, taking the ominous bird as his cue to move. Glancing at the gun in his hand again, he pulled the chamber open and dislodged the bullet. He rolled it in his hand, then tucked the bullet away between the canvas lining and the metal exterior of the canteen.

He tossed the gun at the buzzard and, at last, it flew away, circling the sky above him.

The gun lay on the sand, glinting in the light.

Better to rid myself of the temptation.

Then he started forward.

* * *

Bright light shone against Noah's eyes, making the back of his eyelids glow red.

He shifted with a groan, then the feeling of a hand against his forehead made him startle.

With a sharp intake of breath, he awoke, his eyes wide, his hand gripping the wrist of the person touching him. He reached for the shank he'd been carrying the last four weeks, but he felt a smooth rug below him.

Then his eyes focused on the woman in front of him, the glow of sunlight from an open window behind her. *Nasira.*

The wife of his friend, Fahad al-Najjar.

She murmured soothingly and Noah closed his eyes once more, trying to remember how he'd gotten here.

Weeks through the desert. Brutally cold nights and the threat of the winter rains and snows pushing him forward. Only to arrive in the hills of Mount Zion and find that the German Benedictine monks who had brought him back to life had been interned. He'd made his way to Fahad's home, then collapsed.

Nasira set something hard against his lips—a bowl of broth. The scent was intoxicating.

"Drink it," she instructed, tears in her eyes.

He did as she commanded, and the salty, warm broth radiated down his body. He took the bowl from her weakly, drinking until it was empty, then set it down. The canteen he'd carried all this way from Damascus sat at the foot of his rug, thank goodness.

Fahad appeared in the doorway. *"Akhy Nuh."*

How long had it been since Noah had seen anyone he truly considered a friend? A knot formed in his throat as he struggled to sit. "Fahad. I don't know if you're real or if I'm just dreaming."

Fahad laughed, his voice loud and clear. "I'd hope you would have better dreams than of me. Then again, you stink of piss. I can see why women would avoid you."

Nasira stood and joined her husband and clucked her tongue. "You should let him rest, Fahad. He's obviously been through a tiresome journey."

Noah chuckled, drawing his long hair out of his eyes. "I can't stay here long, just enough time to get my wits about me."

She gave him a scolding, hard look. "You are young enough to be my son, *Nuh*. You will rest. Understand?" She left the room with a shake of her head.

Fahad lifted his thick brows, then came further into the room. "Pay her no mind. You should have seen her when I dragged you inside. She was weeping for you. We had heard you had perished. Again. It seems you have more lives than the average man."

Noah drew his legs up. How long had it been since he'd bathed? He hadn't allowed himself to dream of it, but the thought of a bath now seemed to make his skin throb with the need of it. He felt grimy and covered in dust, as though the stench he carried couldn't be washed away. "It's been a long year." He cleared his throat, his eyes stinging with exhaustion. "And I dare not risk your safety by being here for long."

"My safety. Bah." Fahad sat on the carpet beside him. "My family hasn't known what the word *safety* means for years. And they may never, now that the war has ended and it appears we will be under the rule of the Zionists soon enough."

The war is over?

Noah's shock must have shown on his face.

"Ah, you didn't know." Fahad smiled.

"When?" The idea of the war being over was incomprehensible. Just months earlier, he'd been reading in the newspapers that some thought it might last two more years.

"The Turks signed the armistice at Mudros, and the Germans surrendered nearly two weeks later. There has been rejoicing and dancing on the streets throughout the world, friend. I'm sorry you've missed it."

Noah rubbed his eyes, the reality of it seeming so distant. *The Germans had surrendered?*

Which meant that they'd won. His country had been victorious, after all.

"At what cost?" Noah said at last, his throat aching. "Millions dead and horror forever written upon the souls of those who remain? The price has been dear."

Fahad nodded gravely. "And Death has not yet been satisfied. Thousands are dying by the day of a plague that is speeding throughout the world."

"That sounds horrible."

"Maybe it is Allah's punishment for what we have done to each other." Fahad's eyes reflected sadness. "But I'm glad to see you, my friend. That has brought me joy. I hardly recognized you at first. Nasira was the one to see your face beyond all that hair."

"I hardly remember stumbling into your garden. It was late at night and I was exhausted. I didn't want to wake you in the middle of the night."

"You shouldn't have worried." Fahad sighed. "Where will you go now?"

Noah shook his head. "I'm not sure." He combed his fingers through his beard. Much as he wanted to shave, his long hair and beard offered protection that none of the fake beards and wigs he'd used over the years in disguise could offer. "I need to contact Jack. He's one of the few people I can trust to help me and to relay a message to my wife." Fortunately, Fahad and Jack were also friends, which meant Fahad could facilitate that communication.

Fahad raised a brow. "Your wife?" For many years, Fahad had teased Noah about marrying one of his daughters, and Noah thought he saw a glimmer of disappointment in his face.

His beautiful Ginger. Thoughts of her had been his motivation to continue walking during those brutal nights in the desert. And now, for the first time, he had hoped that he might be on his way back to her. "I married her a year ago. And then we were separated by the war. My hope is that she's at home in England."

"Then you'll go to her." Fahad gave an encouraging smile.

"Yes, but it may take some time. I have no papers and few people I trust. I don't want to endanger my friends."

"Either way, it sounds as though you'll need Jack." Fahad stood, rolling his shoulders. "Though you may have trouble getting him to join you on another adventure. He wrote to me recently. He's arrived in England on leave, as his own wife will give birth any day now."

Noah stared at Fahad, his brow furrowing. Jack was married?

And soon to be a father?

Poor, foolish Jack. Noah had always told him to be careful—that he might end up accidentally fathering a child and find himself bound to a woman. Noah doubted Jack could ever be truly happy with any woman other than his first love, but he was an honorable man and if he'd put a woman in a compromised position, he wouldn't hesitate to make it right, either.

"So some cunning vixen forced Jack Darby to settle down, did she?" Noah gave a hearty laugh. "She may end up regretting it."

"He may have the last laugh. I think it was for love. They married in February. If she hasn't had the child yet, then I doubt he compromised her honor. Besides, she's some highborn lady—a Lady Virginia Whitman. Now he has even more connections, the bastard."

Noah's breath caught, his heart pounding with such force that he could hardly breathe.

Jack and Ginger ... are married?

"What did you say?" he whispered, his voice choking in his throat.

"I said—"

"No." Noah scrambled to his feet, feeling like a caged animal. He shook his head. *It can't be. No, no. She wouldn't.*

Ginger would never have moved on to Jack, especially so quickly.

But there was a child.

It can't be mine, can it?

He closed his eyes, his mind racing, trying to think. He and

Ginger hadn't been intimate since last December. Any child resulting from their union would have been born by now.

Oh, God, no.

"Can I see the letter?" He barely heard the words come from his own lips.

Fahad sensed something was wrong and gave no protest. He slipped out of the room, leaving Noah to his own thoughts.

Ginger would never betray him like this. She would never marry if she believed Noah could still be alive. *She must have thought I was dead.* But to marry again, so quickly? *And Jack?*

Maybe if she'd been pregnant already.

But the baby would have been born by now.

Noah drew a shaky breath, trying to make sense of it, but failing.

What could have possessed Jack to marry Ginger? His loyalty to Noah had always been unwavering—hadn't it?

The image of Jack in that alleyway of Malta bubbled up from the furthest recess of Noah's memory. *"If you had just killed Stephen Fisher when you had a chance, none of us would be here, would we? We'd all still be in Egypt, and Sarah would be alive."*

But no, Jack had just been drunk and angry. He hadn't really meant it.

Except it was the most hurtful thing he had ever said to Noah, and Jack knew it. *And it was also true.*

Had Jack's resentment toward Noah been stewing? Noah's actions had caused the death of the woman he had cared about.

But he never would have stolen the woman I loved.

And even if Jack had been angry, Ginger wouldn't have moved on from him so quickly. She loved him. He was sure of it.

Fahad returned, his face grave. He held a well-worn envelope out to Noah and Noah checked the post date, stamped on the back. *November 2, 1917.* Jack's familiar script was on the outside and Noah's heart gave a thump.

He tugged the note out and unfolded it, the paper trembling in his hand.

Skimming the letter, Noah reached Jack's words,

"I MARRIED Lady Virginia Whitman this past February, which I'm sure will come as a surprise to you. She's an exceptional woman and I'm happy to tell you she'll be soon giving birth to our child. The doctors expect the baby to be born in mid-November and I've requested leave to go and be by her side."

THERE WASN'T any way the child could be his. Acid rose in Noah's throat.

Why?

How could it be?

Had Jack seduced her? Had she been so distraught that she'd taken comfort in him? He felt sick.

Noah covered his face with his hands, aware of Fahad's careful scrutiny. "No, it can't be."

Fahad set a hand on Noah's shoulder. "Do you know the woman?"

Noah couldn't remember the last time he'd felt the sting of tears in his eyes. Not through torture or pain, through fear or rage. Not after his body had failed him in the *Aragon* sinking. Not after Tafas or Charles's disappearance.

But tears filled his lids now, his body shaking because of all those things—and more—because even in the darkest of those moments, even when hope seemed most frail, *he'd had her.*

"She's my wife," Noah whispered, nearly collapsing with the words. Fahad caught Noah's trembling form in the sort of embrace that only a father could give to a son, holding him upright against him.

Noah wept, the wail that left him sounding like a wounded animal.

She betrayed me and our love.

He betrayed me.

Even if they'd believed Noah was dead, they married after what? One month? A little more?

A child ...

The thought of Jack putting his hands on Ginger made Noah physically ill, and he pulled away from Fahad and vomited on the floor. He wanted to go find them both, punch Jack square in the face.

But none of that would erase the presence of a child.

If he went back now, he would only be in the way of *their* family. *Their life.*

"I'm sorry, *Akhy Nuh.*" Fahad didn't recoil at the sick smell, but reached out over Noah's bent form, placing his hand on his shoulder.

Noah wiped his mouth with the back of his hand. "Not *Nuh.* Never again. You must swear never to tell Jack that I'm alive."

He had been through hell trying to get back to her.

A hellfire that had killed his faith, tested him to his limits, and transformed him.

The person he'd been was dead and would remain that way, even if he took his name back from the demons who had robbed it from him.

And I will get my name back.

Then he would be truly free.

He straightened, his eyes burning with tears that flowed freely down his cheeks. "Everything I ever had has been taken from me, Fahad. *Everything.*" Rage filled him, rising like a tide through his core, spreading through his body until his fingertips clenched. "And now it's my turn to strike. Noah Benson may be dead, but he can still have his vengeance."

PART III

CHAPTER TWENTY-SIX

SEPTEMBER 1919

LONDON

"*W*inston Churchill is an insufferable wretch," Dr. Flora Murray muttered under her breath as she thundered into her office at Endell Street hospital, her hands shaking visibly. She spotted Ginger in the corner, finishing a practice exam and reddened. "My apologies."

Ginger looked up from her writing, amused. Dr. Murray was far more expressive than she probably ought to be—everyone at Endell Street watched her with an equal measure of fear and admiration—but she wasn't always quite so blunt. "Jack is having dinner with him in a few days," she said, the corners of her eyes crinkling. "Should I tell him to relay the message?"

Flora scowled, then shook her head with a chagrined laugh. "I wish he would."

Ginger set the pencil down, pulling her papers together into a neat pile. Flora's office was one of the few spaces in the hospital that wasn't filled with crates and boxes. Despite her request that the hospital be closed during the Spanish flu epidemic, the government had kept the hospital open for nearly a full year after the war, which had been a relief to Ginger. Endell had been a second home to her since she'd come to live here after arriving in England. "What's Churchill done now?"

"Besides making it clear that every female physician has outlived her usefulness? He's declined to reconsider giving us the equal rank we deserved during the war." Flora crossed her arms. "No matter how many soldiers sang our praises during the war, or how many lives we saved, all they see us good for is running a women's or children's hospital until maybe our zeal for medicine dies and all those old codgers can go back to their pleasant lives where women didn't dare to ask for a seat at the table."

It wasn't the first time the women at Endell Street had grumbled about their treatment after the war. As abruptly as the war had ended almost a year earlier, the men in positions of power in the English government had reverted to their long-held beliefs that women should simply go back home to their husbands, their homes, their children, and their frocks.

Everything they'd worked for in the last five years was quickly fading away, as though it had never happened.

Ginger stood and placed her papers on Flora's desk. "I suppose we're both left condemned to half-lives, always fighting for what we want and never quite finding satisfaction. In the meantime, I have a test to take." Ginger arched a brow. "*And* a son to go and feed supper to."

"I didn't mean to interrupt you. You have more important things to worry about than my rantings." Flora gave her a warm smile. "I'm proud of you, Ginger. Both Louisa and I are. You hardly look like the same bedraggled young woman who came crying to our doorstep a year and a half ago."

Ginger smiled, knowing the compliment was kindly meant. And Drs. Louisa Anderson and Flora Murray had given her life back to her. They knew the facts of her situation and had accepted and helped her despite that. She'd been honest with them, telling them about her church wedding that had never been recognized, her widowhood, and her marriage of convenience to her husband's best friend in order to give her child legitimacy and avoid social scorn.

In return, they'd been supportive of helping her become a doctor. She'd worked at Endell Military Hospital throughout her pregnancy, training beside them and spending all other waking hours studying at the London School of Medicine for Women.

Then, when Alexander had been born, Louisa had delivered him herself and assisted Ginger in her wait to register his birth until he was two months old, in order to dispel any curiosity from their colleagues. Rather than bearing a September birthdate, he had a November one, officially. That detail allowed Ginger and Jack to present Alexander to the world as Jack's son and their secret safe with only a handful of people.

The outbreak of the Spanish flu had been used as Ginger's excuse for staying away and given her extra time to spend in her small room with her son. By the time she'd returned to work at Endell in early spring, no one suspected an irregularity in Alex's age or birthdate.

Mostly the nurses and doctors—all women themselves—seemed surprised to see Ginger back at all. Of course, they didn't know that while Ginger had agreed with Jack to take a loan from him to get her own life started, she'd also made it clear to him she didn't want to rely on his charity for life.

Jack had sacrificed enough by tying himself to her permanently —just as she had. Alexander would never have Noah's last name but Jack had given him legitimacy and his own name, which wasn't a trifle.

And Ginger had also lost her British citizenship by marrying an American, an odd reality that reminded her of the early days of the war, when one of the English women in her town near Penmore had nearly lost everything by being married to a German man. Though Ginger had fared far better, as the Germans seemed universally hated now.

With their arrangement, she was free to have a bank account, free to run her own house, and he was free to have discreet relationships with other women without her permission. They lived separately, but Jack came by more frequently now that the war and the peace talks of Paris had ended and he'd returned.

"I didn't mean to offend you," Flora said, cutting into her thoughts.

Ginger lifted her chin. "Oh—no." She gave a wan smile. "Not at all. You're right. Life is so different now. And I'm eternally grateful to you and Louisa. I don't know what I would have done without you. And Endell."

Flora's eyes misted. They'd just been informed recently that the hospital was to close, and she'd been taking the news particularly hard. "Well, you just continue to change the way things are done." She nodded toward the practice exams on her desk. "Did you find those useful?"

"Very much so." Ginger released an uneasy sigh, reaching for her coat. "I'm still uncertain I'll do as well as I'd hoped. The nights have been long this past month. As though Alex knows I have an important test to take soon."

"It's most likely teething. You could always try my mother's trick of rubbing some whisky on his gums. It may help."

Ginger smiled and thanked her, thinking about her own grandmother's similar advice. Maybe it was their shared Scottish backgrounds. As she left the office and went into the hallway, she couldn't help understanding Flora's heartache over the imminent closing of the hospital. Whereas just months ago, the hospital had swarmed with patients—especially Americans returning from their campaign in Russia—now the noise had dimmed.

The irony of it was that the patients had come from terrible blights upon humanity—the war and the Spanish flu—but their presence had made the wards swim with light and color, flowers, laughing staff and patients who put on shows and sometimes made homemade quilts and decorations that had brightened the wards.

Now, the wards were nearly empty and sterile, the few remaining patients preparing to be sent to other hospitals or home. The monumental task of itemizing and counting supplies lay ahead of them, which Ginger had agreed to stay and do, as it was a perfect complement to the heavier task of completing her studies that lay ahead.

Pausing by the entrance to one of the empty wards, a profound sense of sadness came over Ginger, her throat clenching reflexively.

As the demobilization had proceeded, men from more far-flung and exotic locations had come through Endell Street—partially because of the hospital's proximity to the station and its excellent reputation. Each time a fresh wave of patients arrived from places like Mesopotamia and Egypt, Ginger had combed through the men, hoping against hope that somehow Noah's face would be among them.

But it had been almost two years since the *Aragon* had gone down. Two years since Noah had kissed her one last time and then walked away.

He wasn't ever coming back. He would never meet his son, who looked so much like him, never see him take his first steps.

She couldn't even show Alexander a photograph of him, because she had none. Alastair had sent Noah's trunk to her the previous year, and she'd gone through it, hoping she might find one. Then she'd closed the trunk and pushed it to the back of her wardrobe. The clothes and uniforms inside smelled like him, and there were notebooks with his neat script inside. She'd even found some money and, of course, books and guns.

But no photographs.

Nothing she could point to and show Alexander someday.

Jack promised to track some down—the military was bound to have something—but he had found none yet.

Sighing, Ginger straightened and adjusted the strap of her haversack over her shoulder. She left the hospital, hurrying out to the street. Until July of the previous year, she'd lived with the other staff at Endell Street on the second floor of the building. Strangely enough, there had also been a pregnant doctor in the mix, and all the staff had taken great pains to make certain that the two pregnant women were well accommodated, including giving them orange juice in the mornings to provide vitamins for their growing babies.

By the time Jack was finally demobilized and returned to England, it had been nearly perfect timing for Ginger to move out on her own, under the pretense of returning to her husband. The landlady, a young woman named Olive Jones, had also agreed to care for Alexander during the day once Ginger resumed work at Endell.

Olive was also a suffragette and had no opposition to Ginger's work, which Ginger appreciated. Where women had once been extolled for their help during the war effort, now that most men had returned from the front there seemed to be a pervasive resentment crawling through society, suggesting that women were stealing honest work and wages from the veterans of the war.

The house was only a short walk from the hospital, and Ginger hurried through a fine mist of rain and fog that hung low in the city. She'd never loved London, even as a youth when her family spent the Season here. Always more at home in the country, walking through the wild expanses near Penmore, or taking strolls through the impeccably manicured gardens. Ginger felt bereft of the outdoors here.

Of course, she'd also spent so much time in the sun and heat while in Egypt that the weather at home now felt dark and dour. As much as she missed the warmth, she didn't know if she could ever face going back there. Egypt represented both her most cherished memories and her darkest days.

She made it to the narrow house on Shelton Street where she rented a room and climbed the staircase, trying to dash away the gloomy thoughts. The doorknob practically turned in her hands and Olive greeted her there, holding Alexander on one hip. Olive smiled, in some ways looking more like Alexander's mum than Ginger did —they had matching dark hair and blue eyes.

Alex threw his arms out for Ginger, though, and she caught him as he flung himself from Olive's grip. "You goose." Ginger laughed, lifting him into her arms. "Wait for Mummy to catch you."

Alexander gave her a gummy smile, his face radiating joy. *Oh, my love.* Ginger squeezed him to her chest, cradling him gently. "Mummy missed you."

"He's practically been sitting at the door all afternoon waiting for you." Olive held the door open. "And you have a guest. I let him into your room. A certain husband of yours, back from wherever it is he goes." Olive winked and tilted her head, her eyes twinkling. "Should I put out your plate for supper tonight, or do you think you'll be busy?"

Ginger felt her cheeks warm. "I'll have to let you know," she managed. She started up the stairs, Alexander settling against her own hip. *What is Jack doing here?* They'd seen each other a few days earlier, taking tea together, but they'd arranged it in advance. Jack rarely intruded here at Shelton Street, and, despite their friendship, his being in her room felt like a strange invasion of privacy.

She unlocked the door to her room and found Jack sitting in the armchair near the window. He stood immediately as she stepped in, then gave her a sheepish smile as he removed his hat. "Hi, Red."

Ginger set Alexander down on the rug and then removed her coat. "Jack. I'm surprised to see you here." She held her hands out toward him, and he crossed the room and planted a kiss on her cheek.

"I wouldn't have come but ..." He glanced down at Alexander, who crawled his way over toward them. "My God, he's getting so big." He bent down and lifted Alexander, who regarded Jack with suspicion in his wide blue eyes. "I recognize that scowl."

"I do too." Ginger smiled, sweeping back a wisp of long, dark hair from Alexander's forehead. The unsaid was poignant, and she tried not to focus on the ache in her heart as she took him from Jack. "Give Uncle Jack a smile, darling."

Instead, Alex buried his face in Ginger's shoulder.

"It's all right. He'll smile when he's ready." Jack winked at Alex as he ventured a peek, which caused him to snuggle closer to Ginger's neck.

She peeled him away after a minute, then set him in the corner with some blocks. "He's not used to many men, I'm afraid. Between me and Olive, and all the staff at Endell, and the rare visit with my family—he's surrounded by women. Poor boy."

Not that her family saw much of her. She hadn't seen Lucy in well over a year and had little time to visit Madeline or Gran. Mama came once a month from Somerset to see her grandson, though, which was gratifying, and she'd been pleased that Ginger had married Jack to legitimize Alexander.

Ginger watched as Alex lifted one block to his mouth, testing it against his gums.

Flora's right—he probably is teething.

Forcing herself to look away from Alexander, she clasped her hands in front of her. "What brings you to Shelton Street?"

Jack rubbed the back of his neck and looked at the armchair. "Mind if I sit?"

"Please." She didn't have a wide variety of options for seating in the small room—besides the armchair, she only had a bench at the vanity that doubled as her desk. She and Alexander shared the small bed against the long wall of the room, and the chest of drawers outside of the wardrobe held her books and a small stove where she heated water in a kettle for tea in the mornings and evenings.

Her not having a kitchen and relying on Olive's cook for meals was a blessing—she didn't know how to cook anyway and barely had time for it, regardless. Taking her meals at the house meant a higher rent, but it was reliable and cheaper than dining at a café or restaurant.

She pulled the stool out from under her vanity and sat opposite Jack. The conditions Ginger and Alexander were living in appalled her mother whenever she visited Ginger at Shelton Street. Mama expected Ginger to assume a "normal marriage" with Jack now that he was in England more often, but she'd put off her mother's inquiries about when that would occur by telling her Jack was occupied with the Paris peace talks.

Jack turned his hat in his hands as Ginger settled. If she didn't know better, she'd guess he was concerned. "What is it?" Inexplicably, her mouth seemed drier than it had a moment before. Something serious must have brought Jack here.

"Have you been following the news about Egypt in the papers?"

Ginger's brow furrowed. She hadn't expected him to bring that up. The fact was that she'd gotten into the habit of reading the paper every morning after she'd returned from Egypt—at first scanning the obituaries and lists of the deceased—then simply reading to keep abreast of the exciting news that the war's end might be in sight. "Which part of it?"

"The revolution and the Wafd Party."

Ginger nodded. The Wafd nationalist movement had grown in strength over the last two years—so much so that they'd tried to send a delegation to the Paris Peace Conference. Their leader, Saad Zaghloul, had not only been denied the request but then had been arrested and exiled to Malta in the spring, resulting in riots that had rocked the streets of Egypt for weeks until Zaghloul had been released. "I've read what I can—though, of course, the news is quite biased, as I'm sure you'd imagine. Is that why you were meeting with Winston Churchill?"

Jack sat back in his chair with a sigh. "Yes. Your prime minister Lloyd George is putting together a commission under Lord Alfred Milner to go to Egypt in the winter—assess the situation with the locals."

"But you don't work for the British government anymore, do you?" Ginger quirked a brow. Jack had finished his service in the war as an officer for the Americans—at least as far as she knew.

"I don't. But the thing is—and this stays between us—apparently Lloyd George sent Sir Mark Sykes out to study the situation with the Arabs before his death this past year, and Sykes was adamant that the Arab world has only one ally that they want involved in their affairs right now: the United States. Unfortunately, my country has no desire to be involved in the mess the British and French have created in that part of the world."

"That, and President Wilson threw his weight behind both the British protectorate of Egypt and the arrangements with the Zionists for the Holy Land," Ginger said with a frown. "But they think the locals will trust you more, so they want you to be a part of the commission?"

Jack nodded. "Exactly. They think I'm some sort of expert in that part of the world."

"Well, you are." Then Jack might leave once again. "Will you go?" she asked, searching his dark-brown eyes. Jack had expressed that he had no desire, like her, to go back to Egypt. But, then again, he hadn't been offered a job to go.

Jack set his hat on his knee. "I don't know. I had made up my mind to tell them no, when they decided it might be a good idea to introduce me to some people they've recruited to help them with the commission." Jack cleared his throat. "And it turns out one of them is our old friend Stephen Fisher. He's in London, actually."

Ginger caught a glance of her reflection in the vanity and then diverted her gaze immediately. She didn't need to see the fear she felt at the thought of Stephen being in the same country as her—let alone in the same city. The possibility had always existed, of course, but she'd tried not to think about it, hoping that Stephen might simply remain in Egypt for good.

That Stephen had left her alone the last two years felt strangely purposeful on his part. She wasn't naïve enough to believe that he would ever reform his ways and forget his obsession with her. Stephen had always reminded her of a boa constrictor, slithering his way silently into her life and squeezing the air from her lungs while she hadn't been paying attention.

"Did Stephen acknowledge he knew you?" Ginger managed the question in as casual a tone as she could, her pulse speeding. She touched the scar on her chest, the terror Stephen brought to her manifesting itself in the memory of that horrific moment.

Jack's eyes filled with anger. "Not at first. He barely looked at me. But then someone asked me how my wife was. You have no idea how hard it was for me not to shoot right then and there."

Ginger looked up sharply, her alarm growing. "What did you say when you were asked about your wife?"

"I said she was fine and tried to change the subject. And that's when Fisher looked up at me and said, 'You're married, Darby?'"

Ginger covered her mouth, knowing what was coming. She'd only attended one social event with Jack—mostly for appearances' sake. And she'd been furious when her mother had seen fit to inform the society pages about her marriage to Jack the year before. But the one event where she'd gone to dinner with Jack, he'd introduced her to both the prime minister and Winston Churchill—along with many government officials whose names she scarcely remembered.

Jack met her gaze and gave one nod. "He knows."

She lifted trembling fingertips to her temple. She didn't want to upset Alexander by being visibly distraught in front of him, but fear bloomed in her core at the thought of Stephen being in England.

Why must he continue to breathe while my husband is dead?

"You okay?" Jack asked, his voice low and gruff.

She sat still for a moment, breathing slowly, trying to gain control of her spiraling emotions. Then Ginger stood, her agitation feeling like restless energy mounting in her legs. "Of all people to be involved in that damned commission." She checked over her shoulder at Alexander, then went over toward him and scooped him off the floor, as though to shield him from her own fears. "Why can't he just die?"

Jack chuckled, breaking the tension. "I can't agree more."

Ginger gave him a rueful smile, grateful for his sense of humor. She didn't need to break down in front of her son. Releasing some of her worry in a deep sigh, she said, "Besides my discomfort with the situation, the man has no sympathy for the Egyptians—he's the worst sort to be on a commission to Egypt."

"Yeah, that's about the sum of it. Anyway, I'm sorry. I don't know what—if anything—can be done about any of it, but I figured you ought to know."

"Well"—Ginger hugged Alexander closer—"I suppose if he goes to Egypt, then I at least can rest easier, even if it isn't the best news for the Egyptians." She gave a bitter laugh, trying to shield herself from the terror still clawing at her heart. "How selfish does that make me sound?"

"It's not selfish. You know me. If I'd had it my way, Fisher would be turning to dust in the desert by now. Hell, I'm still trying to think if there's a way I can arrange an unfortunate 'accident' for him now that I know he's here."

In spite of herself, Ginger laughed. She shook her head, unable to keep the smile from her lips. "Jack, you're terrible."

"Am I?" Jack's eyes twinkled. "Terribly useful? Terribly smart? I agree."

"Terribly arrogant."

"You've called me worse before." Jack shrugged, then came over to her side. "Look, I'm not saying there's any reason for alarm—but, you know, keep your eyes open. He's a goddamned bastard, and I wish it wasn't a crime for me to shoot him in public because I would have otherwise." He set his hat on his head. "You still have that pistol I gave you a long time ago?"

Ginger shielded Alexander for real this time, her head feeling light. "Jack, you're scaring me."

He set a comforting hand on her shoulder. "I'm not saying you have to be scared. But you and I both know how Fisher is with you. And don't worry, I'll be looking out for him."

After a gentle squeeze to her shoulder, he dropped his hand. "I should go. If you need anything at all, call my hotel."

Ginger saw him out the door to her room, then closed it, bolting the door shut. She leaned back against it and closed her eyes, breathing in the sweet scent of Alexander's hair.

"Mama," he cooed in a tiny, babyish voice, his chubby hand curling against her neck.

She kissed his forehead. "Yes, my darling. Mama is here. And I will always protect you."

CHAPTER TWENTY-SEVEN

*G*inger woke in the middle of the night, drenched with sweat, then sat up straight. Her hand shot out beside her, and she felt for Alexander. He lay at her side, breathing softly, and she gulped a breath. Then she fumbled in the dark for the lamp beside her bed and turned it on, her fingers feeling clumsy, her desperation to dispel the darkness growing by the second.

The orange glow from the bulb filled the space with warmth and she exhaled slowly, gazing down at her son. His eyelids twitched but otherwise he was a perfect cherub with pink soft lips parted as he slumbered.

In the two days since Jack told her that Stephen Fisher was in London, she'd found herself increasingly nervous, her dreams filled with nightmares. It shouldn't bother her as much as it did—she'd known Stephen was alive and free. But the news had brought back dark memories from what felt like an entirely different life.

Knowing she faced a long night of insomnia ahead of her, she lifted one of her schoolbooks from the bedside table and sat back against the pillows. Alexander would wake to nurse soon enough and she'd have to extinguish the light and put him back to sleep, but for now, her studies could keep her company.

She only had one day left before she would take the exams to qualify for her bachelor of medicine, bachelor of surgery. Louisa, who was still strongly affiliated with the medical school, had seen that Ginger's studies and experience as a nurse be considered for her degree, and she'd been able successfully to test out of classes and expedite her degree. The process had been long and arduous, with little sleep, but she was finally on the cusp of being a medical doctor in her own right.

She swallowed hard, trying not to think of the dream that had jolted her from sleep. She couldn't let Stephen's presence in town rattle her. Not now. Not when she'd worked so hard to get this far.

If she could obtain the degree, she might have a fighting chance of making a proper life for herself. She would have a harder time finding employment as a "married woman"—but she would take any post that came her way. She needed little, she knew that now. It would be several years before Alexander needed space of his own, and she didn't have any need for frocks and expensive clothing as she had before.

She wrinkled her nose. That reminded her of an upcoming gathering William and Lucy had invited her to at Penmore, to celebrate their wedding anniversary, Lucy claimed. They'd gotten married last October, and while they had invited Ginger to the wedding, she hadn't gone. Alexander had only been a few weeks old, and she hadn't been in any condition to travel. Ginger had used the excuse of being unwell to avoid attending the ceremony.

Alexander had been born on the twenty-seventh of September, and Louisa had believed he was late by over a week or more, because of his size, though Ginger couldn't be certain. And though she and Lucy had barely spoken since Ginger had returned from Egypt, Ginger was certain that Lucy knew Alexander was Noah's child, even with the fake November birthday. Ginger didn't care if

Lucy knew—she would say nothing to anyone, for fear of the reper-
cussions it would have on her own social standing—but she loathed
that Lucy looked down upon Alexander as being stained.

Lucy finally had everything she wanted: a life back at Penmore,
wealth, and a title—she was a countess now that she had married
William—but she still resented and blamed Ginger for nearly losing
everything and killing their brother.

Ginger closed her book, running her fingertips over the pages.
She couldn't concentrate—she was too distracted by her thoughts.
She didn't want to go to Penmore with Alexander. Jack had been
invited too, but it was easy enough to explain he already had a
commitment.

She liked her simple life here on Shelton Street, and not because
she felt the need to prove anything to her family. This was the house
where she'd first felt whole again, holding Alexander in her arms for
her first night at home after giving birth. Noah had taken a sizeable
chunk of her heart with him, leaving a wound that would never
heal.

But Alexander had soothed that pain. Even though she'd known
nothing about caring for an infant and had to learn so much by trial
and error, her joy felt bound to him in a way she'd never known
before. He was her world now. There wasn't anything she wouldn't
do for him.

After replacing the book on the table, she turned off the lamp
and settled back against her pillow, inhaling deeply. Softly, she sang
in a whisper, "Let me call you sweetheart, I'm in love with you …"

A tear formed in the corner of her eye as she was transported
back to Malta, dancing with Noah in the Barrakka Gardens of
Valletta. She sniffled and kissed Alexander's cheek, wondering what
Noah would have been like as a father.

Then again, she'd seen him with Khalib, his orphaned Bedouin
protégé who'd followed Noah everywhere. He'd been warm and
kind to the boy. Jack had once told her that Noah had paid for all of

Khalib's needs, giving Alastair—who had taken charge of him—a monthly stipend until the *Aragon* sinking.

At her nearness, Alexander shifted, reaching for her in the dark to nurse. She smiled, wiping her tears away, then curled his warm body against her breast and torso. Within a few minutes, a profound peace returned to her, and she drifted off to sleep once more.

* * *

THE MORNING CAME QUICKLY, and the weight of interrupted sleep fogged Ginger's mind as she left Alexander with Olive for breakfast while she showered and readied herself for the hospital. Sleep would have been difficult enough with just her exam weighing on her mind—but between the stress of her nightmares and being woken by Alexander several times a night, she had felt as though she was back at a Casualty Clearing Station on the front.

She'd just finished dressing when Olive knocked at her door.

Ginger grabbed her haversack and coat, hurried for the door, and cracked it open. "Is Alexander fussing?"

But Olive wasn't holding him. She shook her head. "No, I left him downstairs with June. But"—Olive's eyes were wide—"you have an important guest. Winston Churchill himself is here to see you."

What on earth? How did he find me here?

Why would the secretary of state of war want to ...? Ginger's heart froze, and she set her hand on the door frame. "Is he here alone?"

"No, he came with another gentleman. They're in the sitting room," Olive said in a rushed, excited whisper.

Ginger didn't wait for Olive to tell her more. She brushed past her, rushing down the staircase. If Winston Churchill was here, it had to be about Jack joining whatever commission the prime minister was putting together.

Her footsteps clacked against the wooden floorboards as she

hurried toward the sitting room and opened the door. She pushed her way inside and found Mr. Churchill standing by the window at the front of the house, still wearing a buttoned overcoat and hat, his hand on a fashionable cane.

And in the armchair at his side sat Stephen.

More horrifyingly, Alexander was on Stephen's lap. The housemaid, June, stood a few feet away.

Ginger gasped, her heart in her throat. She gripped the doorknob, staring at Stephen, who bounced Alexander on his knee.

Stephen, who had once held a knife to her breast.

Who had tortured her friend Beatrice, breaking her wrist.

As though darkness incarnate had entered her house, her brain buzzed, her horror growing as Alexander gazed up at Stephen innocently, curiously. Her baby son, fragile and trusting, in the grips of *that man*.

She didn't want to act like a crazed woman in front of Winston Churchill, but, *no. Propriety be damned.* "You can go, June." Unreasonable fury at the poor maid, who hadn't known to whom she'd handed Alexander over, poured through Ginger.

Ginger rushed over toward Stephen and scooped up Alexander, her heart pounding.

"Mrs. Darby?" Mr. Churchill asked, his somber expression unchanging. "How good it is to see you once more. I believe you know Captain Fisher."

She refused to look at Stephen and stepped further from him, not wanting to be within arm's reach of him. In a faltering voice to Mr. Churchill, she managed, "I see you've met my son." She turned toward him. "To what do I owe the honor of your visit?"

The hair on the back of her neck still stood on end, her shoulders tense as she held Alexander closer. Even out of the corner of her eyes, she could feel Stephen's gaze heavy on her. She considered telling Churchill of Stephen's crimes, every cell in her body screaming at her to run. But Churchill obviously thought well of

Stephen, or he wouldn't be with him. He would think Ginger was mad.

"My apologies for calling so early, Mrs. Darby. I think we gave your housekeeper a fright." He gave her a curious look. "I didn't realize you were still volunteering hospital work."

Ginger gave him a polite smile, her heart still pulsing in her throat. He assumed Olive was her housekeeper, rather than her landlady. She had the advantage of knowing Churchill's distaste for women in medicine, but she didn't feel particularly inclined to impress him or have him believe she continued leading the life of a noblewoman. "Actually, I'm about to finish my degree at the London School of Medicine for Women."

Churchill's eyes darkened. "Ah, I see." He cleared his throat. "Well, I won't keep you. But I've come to see if you might prevail upon your husband to agree to help with the commission to Egypt. I understand the tragic loss of your father and brother in the region may be the reason for his hesitation in going. But this commission could use his expertise. He's quite the famed Orientalist, after all."

Ginger blinked at him, surprised that he would see fit to ask for her help with the matter—but she also wasn't convinced that it hadn't been Stephen's idea. And if that was the case, then she wanted Jack as far away from that commission as possible.

She didn't want to contradict Churchill's impression without knowing what excuse Jack had used to express being cool to the proposal, though. "I'm uncertain Jack is easy to sway in any matter, Mr. Churchill. If his mind is made up, I'm afraid there's little I can do."

"I thought suffragettes delighted in trying to change men's minds," Stephen said in a low voice, forcing Ginger's attention to him.

"Perhaps. But only about important issues." Ginger pursed her lips and flicked her gaze back to Churchill. She didn't want to be rude to him, but he couldn't have picked a worse companion to accompany him for the task. Stephen provoked a visceral reaction that was uncontrollable. She wanted him to leave—and now. "I'm sorry I can't be more helpful."

Churchill shifted uncomfortably, understanding that he was being dismissed, and she felt a twinge of guilt. She'd been taught how to conduct herself gracefully in society, but that had been in a different life—one that no longer existed. Right now, the only thing she cared about was getting Alexander as far away from Stephen's presence as possible.

He knows where I live. I'm no longer safe here.

"Very well. Thank you for your time, Mrs. Darby." Churchill gave one somber nod, a flush creeping up his neck. He stalked toward the door and saw himself out without waiting for Stephen.

Ginger didn't look at Stephen, her shoulders bunched with tension as she held Alexander close. She had nothing to say to him. Hurrying to go back upstairs, she'd just reached the doorway when Stephen's voice rang out behind her. "Your son looks so much like his father."

An involuntary shiver rose up her spine. *He means Noah.*

Pausing at the door, she looked over her shoulder. "Stay away from us, Stephen."

Stephen's visage didn't change, but he took a step forward, away from the armchair. "When I heard that you'd married Darby, I couldn't understand it. But it's much clearer now. Funny how Benson left two bastards in the world before he disappeared."

She didn't want to look at him, but Stephen had a way of saying just the right thing to provoke a reaction. *Two bastards? What?* Her heart speeded faster.

He's a liar.

The corners of his lips turned up, because he knew he had her attention now. "Benson was seen taking Lady Victoria Everill up to his room at Shepheard's in November of 1917 by many people. And their romance was well known, after all. I did what I could to save her reputation by marrying Victoria, but his daughter looks just like him, unfortunately. Much like your son."

Victoria and Noah?

Victoria had given birth? She had heard nothing about it—but then she purposely didn't seek information about Stephen.

She felt the blood drain from her face, her mind scrambling back to the memory of that time.

He's trying to goad me—don't believe him.

And yet ...

That small, sinister voice in the back of her head whispered condemningly.

Victoria Everill, Lord Helton's daughter, who had been the source of heartache between Ginger and Noah before.

And she knew exactly when Stephen was referring to. Noah had rescued Victoria from kidnappers and taken her back to Shepheard's for safety. Ginger had come by the next morning and been furious about the matter herself. Noah had sworn there had been no infidelity—they'd already married at that point—but Victoria had been in his bed ...

A sick feeling washed over her.

It's not true. He's lying. He's still trying to destroy my love for Noah, even after all this time.

She'd wondered what on earth could have possessed Victoria to marry Stephen, though Ginger knew, better than most, the desperation of finding oneself pregnant and alone.

Oh, God, no. But it's not true.

She snapped her gaze to Stephen, hoping the hatred she felt shone there. "Don't you ever touch my son again, Stephen. And never come back."

Then she fled up the stairs, her hands shaking, fear enveloping her. She had to find Jack at once.

CHAPTER TWENTY-EIGHT

The last time Ginger had been to the Savoy Hotel in London, it had been before the war. She'd never once felt out of place or as though she didn't belong, but that was no longer the case. Her blouse and skirt, now a few years old, weren't tailored —Noah had purchased them for her in Cairo before they'd had to go on the run.

The women in the foyer seemed to sparkle. They wore beautiful gowns and dresses, elegant jewelry, and exuded expensive French perfume. The red-carpeted entrance to the dining room was teeming with guests arriving for supper, and Ginger tightened her grip around Alexander's body as she spied people watching him. She didn't have a pram to push him around in and, even if she had, he wouldn't have been welcome in this gathering of adults.

A guardsman approached her. "Madam. If you'll kindly accompany me, I can take you to the back entrance for the staff."

He knew she wasn't there for work. No woman arriving—or even applying—for a job would bring their child. He simply meant to get her out of sight.

Ginger's face burned as she ducked her chin. "I'm here to see my husband, who's a guest at the hotel." Even if her appearance wasn't promising, he'd likely recognize that her diction and speech were.

Before he could respond, Jack seemed to materialize out of thin air beside her, wearing a white tie suit. "There you are." He ignored the guard, taking her bag from her and guiding her away. "I meant to meet you outside. I'm sorry I was late."

She glanced over at him. Funny how Jack seemed to fit into this scene better than she did now. "I wouldn't have got very far. That guardsman meant to toss me back out onto the streets." She didn't want to feel embarrassed and released a tense sigh. "I'm on edge, anyway. Thank you for seeing me."

Jack laughed as they drew closer to the lift. "Red ... you're my wife. Even if it's not the most conventional marriage. And your message said it was urgent."

She nodded, then climbed into the lift beside him. She'd tried to get in touch with Jack all day but had been forced to leave him a message that she'd be arriving after her shift at Endell. Too afraid to leave Alexander at home or in Olive's care, Ginger had packed a bag and taken him into work with her. For the first time since the hospital's closure had been announced, Ginger had been grateful there weren't any patients. She and Alexander had spent the day sitting in an empty ward counting linens.

"It is urgent," she said in a low whisper. She didn't dare say much here, with the lift operator in earshot. "About Stephen."

Jack's expression hardened. "What happened?"

She put on a pleasant smile, flicking her eyes toward the lift operator. Once they'd exited, Jack gestured down the hall. "Don't keep me in suspense. My room is down here."

She followed him, settling Alexander against her hip as she walked. Her back ached from the long day of carrying him every-where, but at least he was safe with her. "I don't know how, but

Stephen found out where I live. He and Winston Churchill paid me a visit this morning under the pretext of trying to employ my help in recruiting you for the commission to Egypt."

Jack's eyes widened, horror in his features.

"Did he threaten you?" Jack slipped a key out of his waistcoat as they arrived at the door to his room.

"No." She glanced at Alexander. "But you know Stephen. He has a way of being threatening that doesn't require directness. It horrified me that he found me, and I think I nearly froze with fear. Now that I've had time to think about it, I've imagined a thousand different things I should have done or said."

Jack held the door open for her, and she went inside as he lit the darkened room. The room was opulently decorated, a grandiose space, with a window and balcony. Noah had told her that Jack had plenty of money, but she hadn't expected him to be living so luxuriously while in London. Whatever his plans were to stay here, this had to be costing him a fortune.

Setting Alexander down on a plush rug, she arched her aching back and unbuttoned her coat. "The maid had given him Alexander to hold before I came in. And that's where his attention appeared fixated. I snatched him away, of course, but all I kept thinking was that if I wasn't careful, Stephen might hurt him. And then"—she took a shaky breath—"Stephen said that Noah had fathered a child with Victoria and that was why he had married her. And that the members of Cairo society secretly all knew the baby was Noah's because she looks like him."

A dark shadow crossed Jack's face. "What? What are you talking about?"

"Do you remember—no, of course you don't. They had you kidnapped, too." Ginger took off her hat and smoothed back the stray strands of hair framing her face. "Right before we all left for Malta, when they were holding you at Saqqara, Noah rescued

Victoria from the men that were holding you. They took Lord Helton, and she was terrified. Instead of taking her home, Noah took her back to his room at Shepheard's. I was furious about it, but now the worst of it is that Stephen is claiming Noah fathered a child with her."

Jack's eyes glittered. "He's saying Victoria was pregnant *before* he married her? But it wasn't his child?"

"Yes. He says it's Noah's daughter."

Jack took a few steps away, alarm written on his face. The longer he went on without responding, the more Ginger's nervousness grew. At last, he snapped his eyes back toward her. "And you believed him?"

The disbelief in Jack's voice didn't make her feel any better. All day she'd tossed Stephen's claim around in her head, trying to decide for herself if she could believe such a claim. "No, I—I ... I don't know." She sighed and pulled off her coat.

Noah and Stephen looked nothing alike. The child must have darker hair, like Noah, but that meant little, considering Victoria had dark hair, too.

Jack took the coat from her, then draped it over his arm. He set his hands on her shoulders. "I seriously doubt there's any truth to it. Noah loved you. Only you. No one else."

"Yes, but—he was a man, wasn't he? And Victoria is beautiful. She knew how to play with his emotions, and he cared about her." Ginger shook her head, hardly believing her own logic. "But why would he make a claim that the child he's raising as his own is Noah's? He'd never admit to his wife bearing another man's daughter if it wasn't true—he's too prideful for that. Especially not the daughter of a man he hated."

Unless he'd had another reason for marrying Victoria ...

"You don't think he'd invent something like this to disturb you— just like he has?" Jack quirked a brow. "Come on, Ginger, we're not talking about a good guy here. Fisher's sick. And twisted. He takes pleasure in watching you, probably more than anyone else, squirm. You're the woman he couldn't have, the one who always saw right through him."

Jack lifted his eyes, as though searching his own brain. "Did he say when Victoria's baby was born?"

"No, but if members of society really think she's Noah's daughter, I would imagine she's just a few weeks older than Alexander." Ginger's head spun. "Much as I disliked her, I don't see Victoria as a promiscuous woman—if she was pregnant ..."

Jack lapsed into silence again. "I wonder if Victoria is in England, too."

Ginger gaped at him. "You're not going to go looking for her, are you?"

Drawing a sharp breath, Jack shook his head. "I'm not sure it would make much difference. Fisher may claim not to be the child's father, but he's certainly raising her." He let out a throaty growl. "The thought of that bastard around any baby makes my stomach turn. He didn't threaten Alexander, did he?"

"No, but seeing Stephen holding him was terrifying." Her agitation was still so high that tears pricked her eyes. "I feel so foolish, too. And I didn't want to go back to the house after he'd been there. I'm sorry for demanding you meet with me, but—"

"Hey ..." Jack cupped the sides of her face with his hands. "It's okay. You were right to come to me."

She sniffled, and her eyes locked with his. Much as she wanted to make her own way and be independent, she didn't know what she'd do without Jack.

Something between them seemed to shift just then, an energy she hadn't felt in years, as though the moment was slowly heating. Jack's eyes shifted to her lips and his thumb brushed against her jaw, softly, a caress lingering in his touch.

What if he kissed me?

What if I kiss him?

Her pulse throbbed in her neck, and he pulled her closer still. The thought was in his own mind, she was sure of it. He'd said it best—they were married and there would be nothing immoral about it. Their arrangement had condemned her to a life of celibacy.

Noah wasn't coming back.

But they'd only ever been friends.

Still, Ginger didn't pull away as Jack closed the gap between them, lowering his face to hers. His lips were tantalizingly close and …

Alexander let out a wail.

Startled, Ginger jumped back, then turned to see him climbing along the edge of a sofa in the room. "Oh, darling. How did you get all the way over there?" She rushed to his side, her face flushing, her ears burning hot.

I almost kissed Jack.

Oh, God, *Noah.* The sting of betrayal pierced through her chest. She didn't love Jack. She was lonely and scared, but kissing him would have been foolish.

Jack cleared his throat. "I'll put your coat and bag in the room on the bed. You and Alexander will stay here with me."

Ginger kept her gaze focused on Alexander's face, unable to look Jack in the eye. "I wouldn't want to intrude. And besides, where would you sleep?" Of course, it was this or go back to Endell and beg a room for the night from Louisa or Flora. That would be only a temporary solution, though, as the hospital would soon be closed.

"I'm fine on the floor." Jack's voice carried from the bedroom. "Or on the sofa. I'm not picky."

She held back a laugh. Given the luxury she'd found him in, she didn't doubt that Jack enjoyed his comforts. "Yes, which is why you're staying at the Savoy."

"I said I'm fine with it." Jack walked back into the room, a grin on his face. *Do I see a blush on his cheeks too?* "I didn't say it was my first choice. I slept enough on the ground the last ten years of my life—especially during the war. I'll readily admit I'd rather have a soft mattress and a pillow under my head than mud and rocks."

Ginger lifted Alexander and sat on the sofa, settling him against her knee. "Jack Darby, you've gone soft. And here I thought you were ever the adventurer."

"My adventuring days are behind me." Jack crossed the room and sat in the armchair across from her, a safe distance away. "I've had enough of being shot at and seeing my life flash before my eyes. I'm done."

"Which is why you don't want to go back to Egypt?" She doubted Jack wanted to be anywhere near Stephen either, unless it was to kill him.

"Among other things." Jack looked down, and the smile faded from his face. "Look … Ginger. I know we talked about having separate lives. And if that's what you want, there's nothing to discuss. But if you need more out of this marriage—"

"I don't," she said, too quickly. Her hands tightened around Alexander's waist, as though he were a shield.

Jack winced. "Noted." He exhaled a chuckle. "We don't have to pretend that what just happened didn't happen, Red. I just want to make sure we're both in agreement."

Sometimes she forgot how very American Jack could be. She twisted in her seat. "Jack, I feel terrible having trapped you into a loveless marriage with me, but—"

"You didn't—"

"I know you agreed to it willingly, without my coercion." She held a hand out to stop his protests. "And I'll always be grateful for everything you've done for me. But the fact remains, my feelings haven't changed, and I'll never be able to love anyone like I did

Noah, including you. I think it's best if we continue to live separate lives."

Of course, that doesn't change the fact that I almost allowed that kiss to happen.

Jack leaned back in his seat lazily. "Well, damn, you don't beat around the bush. I take it tall and handsome isn't your type?" He gave her a crooked grin and then winked. "I'm glad that's settled, because as it so happens, bossy and stubborn isn't my type."

She laughed, the tension between them fizzling. Alexander squirmed in her arms, and she put him back down on the floor by her feet. With a huge smile, he crawled toward Jack, then set his hands on the cushion of the armchair, lifting himself to stand. "Speaking of our marriage, my mother sent me another message requesting that you come to Penmore for Lucy and William's anniversary dinner. It's in a week."

"I can go with you. Just tell me when and where." Jack turned his attention to Alexander, standing and lifting him in the air, causing Alexander to giggle. "Someone is having a birthday in a couple of days, isn't he? We'll have to do something special for him."

A pang went through Ginger's heart. *Am I making a mistake?* By rejecting a closer relationship with Jack and keeping him from her life, she also denied Alexander the only chance he'd ever have for a father. Jack had been there for all of Alexander's most important milestones and probably would continue to be.

He'd even come back a few days after Alexander's birth.

Jack had taken the baby in his arms, cradling him with an unease that had made Ginger laugh. "He won't break."

Jack looked up from the baby's face, and his eyes were red and glassy. "He's perfect, Red. You did well."

Ginger's throat tightened. She didn't want to cry, but tears had come so easily the last few days. "I don't know what to name him. All the names I keep thinking of are family names, but I wish I could honor his father."

"You want to call him Noah?" Pain flashed in Jack's eyes.

"I don't think I could manage that." She leaned forward and stroked the shock of dark hair at the top of the infant's hair. "But maybe a family name of his."

"His middle name was Alexander. Did he ever tell you that?"

Ginger shook her head, a peaceful feeling settling over her. There were so many things she hadn't known or asked Noah. "Alexander. I like that."

Pulling herself away from the memory, Ginger watched as Jack tickled Alexander under the chin, eliciting another eruption of giggles.

But the thought of replacing Noah's role with Jack made her profoundly sad. She sighed, sitting back on the sofa and watching Jack as he played with Alexander for a few minutes. The events of the day had occurred with the worst possible timing—she had her exams the next day and no one to watch Alexander yet.

"What do you think Stephen intended by coming to see me?" Ginger asked in an even tone.

Jack kept his gaze on Alexander. "Besides intimidating you? I don't know. I think the circumstances are interesting. Not sure if he's trying to get me to join the commission or to keep me away from it—but my guess would be the latter."

She set her hands on either side of her lap, on the soft velvet of the cushion. "I agree. He would have to know it would frighten me to have you involved with anything he's involved in. But why would he want to keep you out of it?"

Jack set Alexander on the floor, then rubbed the top of his head. He handed him the hotel room key to play with, and Alexander sat down with wide-eyed fascination. "There could be many reasons. Most especially if Fisher has stayed in politics down there, which he probably has. He won't have changed his ways."

"Yes, but why keep you out of this? You could have gone back to Egypt at any point on your own. And you're not the only person who knows what he actually is. Alastair, for one, could just as easily expose him. And he's still in Egypt."

"Alastair won't do anything that could risk the safety of the orphan boys he takes care of. And ... maybe the timing could be inconvenient." Jack crossed his arms. "It might be a good time to put some inquiries out, find out what Fisher's been up to lately. And I wish I could talk to Victoria."

"But what purpose would that serve? Unless you plan on doing something about it."

Jack scowled, then rubbed his face, pinching the bridge of his nose. "You're right. I don't want to know. He can do whatever the hell he wants so long as it doesn't affect us."

She clasped her hands, her agitation flowing back. Noah had been determined to take Stephen and Lord Helton to task for their treachery. He'd died while trying to return to Egypt to do just that. In the time that had followed, she'd tried not to let it bother her that Stephen had ultimately won the game and forced her to flee.

But seeing him made her hate that fact. She loathed that Stephen had continued to live free of his crimes, while Noah's name had been tarnished forever.

She squeezed her hands together. "I should go. You look as though you were heading to supper, anyway. I have my exams tomorrow and need to see if someone at Endell will watch Alexander for me. I don't want to leave him at my home with Olive —not if Stephen could enter so easily."

"If he knows where you live, he probably knows where you've been working, too." Jack came closer and took her hand. "Please stay. There's no reason for you not to. I can watch Alexander tomorrow, and I don't need to go back to supper. We can just order something to the room—you haven't eaten yet, have you?"

"Not yet." She scanned his face. Staying here would be more convenient and take a weight off her shoulders. Jack could protect Alexander better than anyone. "All right. But only until I can plan for something more long term." Without Olive, she would need to find a nanny.

Jack's offer was a relief. She had to focus. Her exams would determine her long-term future. She wouldn't allow Stephen's presence to rob her—or Alexander—of anything else.

CHAPTER TWENTY-NINE

*T*he door to the ward at Endell Street opened while Ginger was folding sheets, and she looked up to see Dr. Louisa Garrett Anderson hurrying inside. A thin woman with dark hair, she had a commanding presence—though not necessarily a welcoming one. Despite that, Ginger felt nothing but affection for her.

But since Ginger had taken her exams a week earlier, she'd been anxious each time she'd seen Louisa or Flora, worried that they might come bearing the bad news that she hadn't passed and wouldn't be able to receive her degree after all.

"Are you in here alone?" Louisa seemed surprised at the quiet in the empty ward. She grimaced. "The others tell me they're too frightened to be in the wards alone. That the whole place feels filled with ghosts."

"Nina was in here just a few minutes ago. But she's worried about three hundred missing sheets and went looking for them."

Lines formed on Louisa's forehead as she lifted her brows. "Three hundred?"

"It might be more than that," Ginger answered with a rueful smile. She finished folding the sheet she'd been working on, then straightened. "Was there something you needed?"

"Yes, your husband is here. And your boy. I understand you're leaving us for a little while?"

"I'm going to Somerset—to my family's ancestral home. My mother has sent notes nearly every day requesting I go to a dinner, and I'm worried she might have something terribly important to tell me."

"Well, I can't think of anyone more deserving of a break than you." Louisa gave her a warm look. "Will you be returning to us afterward?"

"As long as you'll have me. Though I know the work is growing scarcer."

"You'll always have work by my side should you need it." Louisa nodded toward the pile of folded sheets. "But you'd best be off if you have a train to catch. Good luck with your family."

Ginger fought the temptation to give the older woman a hug. "I'll return, don't worry."

She said her good-byes to Louisa and then left, an unsettled feeling in her heart. She'd tried hard the last few days to fight off the feeling of an inevitable march toward the finish line, but that was what this was, wasn't it? Endell would close. Dr. Garrett Anderson and Dr. Murray would return to their old lives.

And if the men in power had it their way, they would reverse any progress women had made in the field of medicine and take away the hard-earned rights they'd fought for. Ginger twisted her lips bitterly. That men in political positions wanted to call them unsuited for the work bothered her less. These women—and all others who had served during the war—had more than proven they could do the work.

What bothered Ginger was that those politicians would rather the sick and infirm had fewer options for their care than have women try to treat them.

She found her way outside, where Jack waited with a car on the street. Alexander wore the new cream-colored romper and bloomers that Jack had purchased for him for his birthday, and Ginger's heart melted at the sight of him on the back seat of the car. "If Lucy doesn't fawn over him in this outfit, I may not forgive her," Ginger said with a laugh, kissing Alexander's cheek.

"Does she fawn over anything that doesn't glitter when it moves?" Jack asked wryly, scooting in as the driver closed the back door.

"How well you know her." Ginger sat back, her eyes drifting over the courtyard of the hospital. She could picture the ambulances or the men gathering to smoke or for boxing and exercise. "Do you think they'll ever allow women to run another hospital like this? Outside of the war, that is."

Jack grimaced. "It's not looking good. Too many people want to return to the way life was before the war and forget what they learned." He lifted the newspaper on the seat beside him. "Just like it's not looking good for any of the Arabs who were hoping for their independence. Faisal Hussein is floundering to get support for the nation he was promised, and it looks like the French will move to take over the administration in Syria any day now. And the Egyptians are faring just as badly." He shook his head in disgust. "Over two thousand Egyptian casualties so far in skirmishes since the spring."

That he'd brought up the Arab and Egyptian plight right now intrigued her. Why was he tying the two together—or was he simply preoccupied with the topic?

Ginger gave him a curious look as they pulled away from the hospital. "Is there a reason you're focused on that now?"

Jack's eyes flashed with humor and guilt. "Not particularly."

She should have known Jack Darby wouldn't be at peace letting Stephen wander back into their lives and then disappear again without consequence. Stephen hadn't made himself known again since that encounter at Shelton Street, and Jack had refused the request to join the commission. Or at least she thought he had.

"Jack." She ducked her chin, narrowing her eyes knowingly. "You've been looking into Stephen, haven't you?"

"If I have, it's only because I want to make sure he's staying as far away from us as possible." Jack gazed out at the passing blur of buildings, not meeting her eye.

"Jack."

He scowled and leaned in, lowering his voice so that the driver couldn't hear. "You know, if you're going to nag me like a wife would, I may have to reconsider our arrangement."

She threw back her head with a laugh. "You're ridiculous. I'm serious. Have you been?"

"All right, yes." Jack lifted his hands in surrender. "You caught me. But I'll have you know, I've discovered some very interesting things. Rumor has it that Fisher and his father-in-law, Lord Helton, have just become major investors on an archeological dig."

Ginger frowned at him. "Why should that matter?"

"Because it turns out that they're partnering with Millard Van Sant—a famed archeologist. And ..." Jack's voice drifted off, then he put his hand on the back of his neck. "You know, never mind. It doesn't matter."

Millard Van Sant. Where have I heard that name before? She knitted her brows in confusion. "I'm sure I've heard of the man, but I can't quite place him."

"Sarah used to work with him." Jack smiled tersely. "Sorry. I shouldn't have brought it up."

That's right—Sarah. Ginger looked away. How long had it been since she'd thought about Sarah and those fateful days in Malta before she'd died? No wonder Jack hadn't wanted to mention it. "I still miss her."

"Me too." Jack's eyes were unreadable. Then he cleared his throat, shifting his attention to Alexander. "So, you ready for a big ride in a choo-choo train, Alex?"

Ginger observed them distractedly. Something about Jack's abruptness bothered her, but she couldn't quite understand it. He had more to tell her—or something had struck him—and he didn't want to share it. Maybe it was because of the driver?

Making a mental note to ask him about it when they didn't have anyone else around, Ginger wound her finger around a loose thread on her uniform. She had other things to worry about now—more immediate confrontations. She hadn't been back to Somerset since 1914, and the thought of going back to the home where she'd been raised felt oddly overwhelming.

Penmore awaited.

* * *

THE SMALL VILLAGE of Penmore had changed little since Ginger had last been there, but as William's chauffeur wound his way through the streets, the houses and shops somehow felt smaller than Ginger remembered. The thatched roofs and stone buildings still held a quintessential charm, but she couldn't see the town without thinking of the ugliness that she'd seen here when the war had first started.

People she'd known her whole life, gripped with fear and spy fever, who had turned against each other. They'd even attacked Henry.

Henry.

She still missed her beloved brother terribly. Would being here, surrounded by the memories of their childhood, make it all so much worse? Henry's betrayal and refusal to help her stop Stephen's treachery had resulted in the most horrifying thing she'd ever had to do: choose Noah's life over Henry's.

She didn't blame her mother and sister for not forgiving her when she really thought about it. She'd killed Henry. Even if she'd done nothing else, that was enough.

Henry's voice haunted her. *"What makes you think Noah Benson can offer you salvation? You don't know him like I do. The man is the furthest thing imaginable from a saint. He's a cold and ruthless killer. It's what he's good at ..."*

Then he'd told her about a German officer Noah had been assigned to assassinate in Constantinople.

"The German officer had a wife. He had his fun with her—like he's doing with you, Ginny—even convinced her to let him into the house when her husband was away. All so he could lie in wait for his true target."

Ginger shuddered. Beside her, Jack seemed to notice the shift in her mood, and he glanced at her over the top of Alexander's head, who was asleep on his shoulder. "You okay?"

"Nervous." Ginger clasped her gloved hands together. She'd changed on the train into one dress Jack had insisted on buying her a few days before, when they'd gone out to celebrate Alexander's birthday. She hadn't been as grateful as she should have been—now that she was just minutes away from seeing her family, she was thankful she was at least dressed for the part. One less thing to face criticism over.

In a hesitant voice, she asked, "What was Noah like before he met me? My brother once suggested he was a ruthless womanizer."

Jack smiled sadly. "Noah could have married any woman he wanted, Ginger. That's true. Even when we were kids, half the girls we knew were in love with him. But he didn't have much patience for romance—or interest in it. He preferred his books and sporting events and anything that was competitive and didn't give any woman the time of day."

"Yes, but I don't entirely mean romance."

Jack made a face. "He wasn't the type to talk about that, if he did. But, look, if you're worried about the whole thing with Victoria—"

"I *am* worried about it. And I hate it." Ginger gritted her teeth. "Jack, I've spent more time with you, known you longer now than I knew Noah when we were married. I don't doubt Noah loved me, but we barely spent two months' total time together, including the length of our marriage. That's why I'm asking you. You knew him better than I did when it comes down to it."

A determined look came into Jack's eyes. "Which is why you should trust me when I tell you I don't believe for a second that Victoria gave birth to Noah's daughter. She might have had someone else's kid, but not Noah's."

Ginger tried to let Jack's words comfort her, but with little success. They passed through the gates of Penmore, and Ginger turned her attention back out the window of the motorcar. In the five years since she'd been back home, ivy had grown thick over the wrought-iron gates. The effect was lovely—but also looked unkempt and wild. Her father wouldn't have been happy with it.

The narrow road to the house was dusty, the old familiar footpaths through the woods and fields were now buried in overgrowth. No one had imagined when war broke out that it would drag on as long as it had—Ginger had barely begun considering marriage offers at the start of it, and now she was both a widow and a mother.

Had William and Lucy tried to bring back the old customs of her family? Garden parties and hunts had been Ginger's favorite events —especially once she was old enough to attend them. From the looks of the grounds, it didn't appear they had.

As the house came into view, Ginger's stomach twisted in a knot, nostalgia and sadness flooding her heart as she gazed up at the grandeur of her childhood home. She'd spent her days climbing those steps to the main doors, skipping along the pillars, and finding cozy nooks in the window seats to read.

She knew where the deep corridors led and had scraped her knees climbing the trees between the tall windows. The roses in the garden had never bloomed so beautifully for anyone as they had for her mother, and they seemed unattended now, their flowers long gone and the trees turning to skeletons for the winter.

The staff of the house had gathered outside in the courtyard to greet them, along with William, Lucy, and her mother, but Ginger was surprised to see how few members of the staff remained. She didn't recognize any of them, but there were only six here ... perhaps more were inside?

Ginger turned toward Jack to take Alexander, then paused. He was sleeping so peacefully in Jack's arms and startling him awake to say hello to relatives he didn't know would likely only end with him shyly burying his face—or being grouchy.

Maybe it was better to have Jack carry Alexander inside. She didn't enjoy pretending they were a family, even if it would make her mother happy, but the appearance would convince enough staff that didn't know them.

The chauffeur came around to open the car door for Ginger and she stepped out, all her former instruction regarding manners and decorum ringing in her ears.

"Cousin Virginia." William came forward first, hands outstretched. "It's so wonderful to see you at long last. I've been telling Lucy for ages that we must see you."

Lucy came up beside him, taking his arm. "Well, you know Ginny. She keeps herself so busy." She was unenthusiastic and unwelcoming as ever.

Ginger greeted them both with a light kiss on the cheek. Lucy looked so much more like a grown woman now, most likely because she styled herself that way on purpose. She was barely twenty. Whether she was truly happy to see Ginger, she did a good job of appearing to be pleased at their arrival. "How was the trip?" she asked, still gripping William's arm.

"Uneventful. Fortunately." Ginger glanced back at Jack as Lucy's attention drifted to him. "And this is Alexander, though he fell asleep as we were arriving. He seemed fascinated with the train ride."

Lucy smiled politely. "So charming. Welcome to Penmore, Jack."

Ginger gritted her teeth. Lucy's disinterest in Alexander was hurtful, but not unexpected. After all, it had been a year, and she'd never met her nephew, which was all the evidence Ginger needed to know Lucy believed Alexander was Noah's son. Swallowing her hurt, Ginger turned toward her mother. *Why did you insist on me coming, Mama?* She forced a smile. "Hello, Mama."

"I can't believe you're finally here," her mother said, embracing her with unexpected warmth. "Each time I visit Lucy, I miss you more and more."

Her mother's candidness made a lump rise in Ginger's throat. "Thank you, Mama. How is life in the dowager cottage?"

"Other than that I feel badly for ever exiling your grandmother there years ago," Mama said with a laugh, "it's fine. Easier to bear the loneliness when I had my garden to tend to, and the winter wasn't rapidly approaching, but I'm content enough." She squeezed Ginger's hand and then moved toward Jack. "Hello, Jack. I'm dying to see my grandson. You don't mind if I wake him, do you?"

Before Ginger could answer, her mother tugged Alexander out of Jack's arms. Ginger stepped back beside Jack, swallowing back the threat of tears. Her mother did appear to be genuinely happy they were there.

Alexander woke briefly, scrubbed his eyes, then snuggled back against her mother sleepily. "Oh, he's had a big day," her mother said with a grin. "Why don't we all make our way inside? Get him out of this chilly weather."

They moved into the house through the courtyard door—the

main door was only used for special occasions—and Jack tugged at Ginger's elbow. "Your mother seems like she's in a good mood."

"She does, doesn't she?" Ginger whispered back. Mother had been courteous to Jack in the past, but never especially friendly or interested in getting to know him. Ginger guessed that it was because Jack was Noah's friend, an American, and far outside their rank. Maybe if she'd known how wealthy Jack was, she would have taken to him more.

Ginger cringed at the guilty, negative thought. *It doesn't really matter what my family thinks of Jack. He's not really my husband in any genuine sense.*

Except that they were legally married. Her son was Alexander Darby, not Alexander Benson.

And Jack is here, by my side, once again.

The thought was a comforting one as they drifted into the foyer of Penmore.

She frowned, a feeling of déjà vu washing over her. She knew Penmore so well she could have practically closed her eyes and described the layout. But some artworks and expensive heirlooms were missing, including an exquisite suit of armor that had belonged to the first Earl of Braddock. Instantly, she was back at their family's home in Egypt, having arrived from the war front. Her father had sold their artworks there to pay off his massive debts —had he been quietly doing it back home too?

"What happened to the suit of armor?" Ginger asked, glancing Lucy's way.

Lucy looked away, not meeting Ginger's eyes.

That's odd.

William rocked back and forth in his shoes. "That old thing was in the way. I like how open the foyer is without it." William looked from Ginger to Jack, then cleared his throat. Going over to Lucy, he set his arm around her shoulder. "In fact, I believe now is as good a time as any to let you know we've decided to sell Penmore. Move on to brighter horizons."

The silence in the room crept in uncomfortably as Ginger's heart rate slowed. From the stricken look on Lucy's face, Ginger could tell that not only was this *not* the time they'd discussed telling Ginger and Jack the news, but that Lucy was devastated over it.

Why on earth would William sell Penmore?

"William. Not now," her mother said, breaking the silence with a tight-lipped smile. She shifted Alexander in her arms. "Should we ring for tea? Lucy?"

But Lucy had still not recovered from the manner in which William had relayed the shattering news. She looked up at Mama blankly, her face pale. "Not now, Mama," Lucy finally managed, then turned and hurried from the foyer.

William shook his head, looking baffled, then rushed after Lucy. "Darling ..." His voice faded away as he disappeared down the corridor.

Ginger's lips parted in shock and she stared at her mother, who had reddened. "Mama? Is this why you insisted I come?"

Her mother swayed, as though to soothe Alexander, who continued sleeping. "I told him not to say anything yet. But, yes. I wanted you to come because this anniversary party is the last party we'll ever have at Penmore." She raised her chin, her lower lip quivering. "And I didn't want you to miss your last opportunity to come home."

She crossed the room over to Jack and handed Alexander back to him. "Why don't you take Jack to the sitting room, Ginger? I'll see if I can find your sister."

As Mama left, Ginger turned toward Jack, her eyes wide. "I can't believe that just happened."

"Slightly awkward. Your family certainly knows how to leave an impression." He winced. "You okay?"

Ginger held his gaze. "I'm uncertain the news has quite sunk in yet."

Whatever William's reasons for selling Penmore, she was certain it had to do with the fact that the estate was failing. Large homes from prestigious families were going up for sale all over the country. Sadness crept through her.

She'd just never expected Penmore to be one of them.

CHAPTER THIRTY

*G*inger found Lucy in a room that had once been her mother's, sitting on the four-poster bed with a handkerchief in one hand. Her nose and eyelids were red from crying, her pale white skin splotchy. When she saw Ginger, Lucy straightened from her slouch, her face pinching. "Why are you here?"

Such a welcoming one, her sister.

Ginger fought the temptation to close the door to the room and go back downstairs. "Mama suggested I find you. That it might be good for us to chat. May I come in?" She rested her temple against the door frame, a tired feeling settling on her shoulders. She'd expected to face some sort of conflict here at Penmore; however, just not so quickly.

Lucy tucked a strand of dark hair behind one ear. "Would you really go away if I asked you to? You have a habit of not paying attention to anything I want."

Ginger checked over her shoulder to make sure none of the servants were within earshot. Then again, there weren't that many servants anymore. Still, it was better to be safe than risk making her sister, the lady of the house, look ill-mannered.

She stepped inside, shutting the door behind her, and rested against the door. "Lucy, I'm not your enemy. And I care about what you want. Very much."

Lucy shook her head, her eyes red. "No, you don't. But it doesn't matter. No matter what I do and no matter what you do, you still somehow always end up ahead. They all always loved you more—Papa, Mama, Henry—everyone. Even my husband would have picked you to marry if he'd had his choice. But you wouldn't have him. You wanted that criminal and left me to save the family."

Lucy dabbed her cheeks with the handkerchief and continued, dramatically, "'Marry William,' Mama told me, 'and all will be well.' It didn't matter that he was ten years my senior and that he bored me; I did what I was told. And what did it get me? He's single-handedly wiped out everything that all our ancestors did, has absolutely no idea how to manage the estate, and now we're so destitute we must sell."

Ginger resisted the urge to roll her eyes. She didn't doubt that William was doing poorly if they needed to sell Penmore, but destitute individuals didn't throw lavish anniversary parties and keep *any* servants. More than likely, they'd be downgrading to one of the cottages William had inherited, which were still large houses.

When Ginger didn't respond, Lucy sniffled and looked her over. "In the meantime, you arrive here, happy as a lark, with a baby and a husband who adores you—and everyone keeps telling me how rich he is—and no one bats an eyelash at anything you do, even though you're a suffragette and in medical school." Lucy made a face. "You always just win, no matter what."

People talked to Lucy about Jack? It seemed so odd, given how far removed from society Ginger felt.

She left her place by the door and came over to Lucy's bedside. "Lucy, at some point or another, take responsibility for the decisions you make and the consequences that follow. You're not a victim. And I'll be the first to admit I made some terrible mistakes in the past. But, the point is, you either learn from those mistakes or you keep making them."

"Wonderful. I needed a lecture from you." Lucy fanned her face. "Don't you understand, Ginny? It's maddening. *You're* maddening. I don't even want you here. Mama and William just struggle while you've coasted through life, doing what you wanted and always winding up happy."

Ginger sighed, her patience wearing thin. "If there's one thing I've always appreciated about you, Lucy, it's your complete and utter honesty. I don't have to wonder how you really feel about me. You just go right ahead and tell me to my face."

Lucy looked away, her jaw clenched.

Ginger stepped back, contemplating leaving. She didn't know why Mama thought she could help, or why she'd agreed to come talk to Lucy. Lucy wasn't about to pour out her heart to Ginger.

Then Ginger's eyes narrowed as she spotted a glass bottle of Lysol on the bedside table. Frowning, Ginger went over to it and snatched it up. The product was sold to women as a douche, especially to prevent pregnancy, but it was dangerous—Ginger had learned in her studies that there had been multiple poisonings from it. Lucy probably hadn't intended to leave something so private in plain view, or maybe she didn't care.

Then again, William had just been up here with Lucy for a while trying to comfort her, though, and the bed wasn't exactly tidy. Despite Ginger's own marriage having been a short one, she knew how quickly comfort could turn into something else. She bit her lip, the thought of William and her sister's private moment making her feel strangely discomfited.

But given that Lucy was feeling the need to be so aggressively plainspoken right now, Ginger may as well return the favor. "Lucy, please tell me you haven't been using this after intimacy."

Lucy's mouth fell open, and she bolted from the bed. "How dare you?" She pulled it out of Ginger's grip. "Get out, Ginny, I'm serious."

Ginger crossed her arms. "I will. I'm more than *happy* to. But I wouldn't be doing my job as a ... woman trained in medicine if I didn't tell you, please, don't use that horrible product. It causes burns and can destroy the uterus. Women have died from it."

"What do you know?" Lucy spat, her face bright red. "You still haven't got your degree, have you?"

"Not yet, no. But that doesn't mean I don't know what I'm talking about. And you may not believe it, but I care about you, Lucy. Whatever reason you have for not wanting children right now with William isn't any of my business, but it is my business to tell you that the way you're going about it—that product—could kill you. It's not only highly ineffective, it's poison. You don't have to believe me if you choose not to, but at the very least go to your own doctor and ask, I beg of you."

Lucy crossed her arms, her jaw clenching.

How much I wish our relationship didn't have to be like this. But she and Lucy had never been close, and the war had interrupted any sisterly bond that might have formed between them. Ginger turned and started for the door.

"I don't love him." Lucy's voice was small and breathy.

Ginger looked back at Lucy, who twisted her handkerchief in her hands, waiting for her to go on.

"I never have. I tolerated him well enough to marry him, but I didn't know ... w-what was expected of me. And I loathe his touch. He wants to have a b-baby and I ..." Lucy's face puckered. "The idea terrifies me."

Surely Lucy must have known William would want children. Much as Lucy's situation was of her own doing, Ginger still pitied her. While society refused to allow women more autonomy, their choices were limited. Survival meant doing what one might not want to do—

Ginger knew that well. She'd wanted so much to strike out on her own after Noah's disappearance, but being a mother had forced her hand. In Lucy's case, she hadn't needed to aim to be a countess or retain Penmore or try to continue a life of wealth, of course. Still, Lucy must have felt desperate and didn't have any skills to recommend her to a life of independence.

She didn't even know what was involved with marital relations.

"Well, don't use that. There's a device you can insert that can help, but if you're too embarrassed to ask for one, you can always come to me." Ginger crossed her arms. "But that's not a long-term solution, either, Lucy. You knew William would want children, didn't you?"

"Yes, but that was before. Now he's bumbled his way through everything—he's an idiot, Ginny. A very convincing fraud. Any money he had, he's burned through. And then he immediately started selling everything *our* family had, to keep up appearances. Now we'll lose Penmore. Whitman Cottage may help us for a short while, but I'm certain he won't be able to keep that, either."

Ginger grimaced. Her sister must truly dislike William if she used such awful terms to describe her own husband. If Lucy was being honest, then her situation would continue to worsen. No wonder Lucy was so angry with her. If Ginger had married William as their mother had wanted, it would be she who was facing this instead of Lucy.

And I knew he was a fraud, didn't I? When William had first arrived in Egypt, he'd come in uniform with his arm in a sling, bearing stories of being an RAF pilot who had fought and lost the use of his arm. Ginger had discovered later that he'd not only been lying about it all, but his arm worked perfectly. She'd insisted he tell her mother and sister, but who knew what excuse William had used to explain his now-functioning arm?

Maybe I could have prevented this.

"When will he sell Penmore?"

Lucy hugged her arms to her chest. "After the party. I'm uncertain when, but he's going to dismiss what remains of the servants then. And then we'll go through the house, choosing a few things to move to Whitman Cottage and sell the rest."

All her family's heirlooms would be lost forever, then.

Maybe she could ask Jack to lend her the money to buy a few items she'd treasured as a little girl.

A heavy sadness wrapped itself around Ginger's shoulders, and she gazed out the window. Her father had been the first to risk Penmore, with his ill-advised investment in an oil concession and other foolish business ventures, but Henry would have known better how to run the estate. Henry had brimmed with ideas to bring the estate into the twentieth century.

And I killed him.

"I'm sorry, Lucy."

Lucy appealed to her with wide eyes. "You know, you could still help. *Your* husband has the money to save us. Maybe he could offer William a loan, keep us from having to leave our family home."

Just how much money was Jack rumored to have? Given the way he'd been living at the Savoy, she imagined Lucy was probably right, but it was odd to her that Lucy appeared to know more about Jack's wealth than Ginger did. "I doubt Jack will be interested in a loan if William is so unreliable with money."

"Yes, but it's *your* fault we're all in this position. You should at the very least talk to him. Leave it to Jack to decide." Lucy tossed the bottle of Lysol in her hands onto the mattress. "You may feel high-and-mighty with your education and not be in need, but our family *is.*"

Arguing would do nothing to warm Lucy to her. This would be a very long next few days if Lucy continued being so angry with her, too. "I'll see what I can do," Ginger said in a flat tone.

She left the room and headed down the hallway, toward the room that she and Jack would share for their time in Penmore.

Mama had tried to insist that Alexander go to the nursery and be watched by a servant, as her own children had been raised, but Ginger had flatly refused. Alexander would stay in the room with her and that was that.

She found Jack and Alexander on the floor of the bedroom and raised a brow at the crib the servants had brought into the room in her absence. "I told her I didn't need one of those."

"Well, she insisted. She's horrified enough at you not having a nursery or a nanny—let her just have the crib. You don't have to use it."

Ginger groaned and sat on the floor with them. "It's hard to believe how little I feel I fit here. I'm fairly certain Mama will find a thousand things in my life to be appalled by before we leave."

Jack lay on his stomach and crossed his arms on the floor in front of him, setting his chin on his forearms. "Imagine how horrified she'll be when she finds out I'm sleeping on the floor." He winked. "Don't worry about your mom and Lucy. I'm not sure I understand how you came from this family, but you go right on being yourself, Red."

Alexander crawled his way toward her just then, but his knee bumped against a block on the floor and he tumbled forward. Both Jack and Ginger reached out to catch him before his chin struck, their hands colliding. Alexander bumped against their hands, then sat, grabbing the block that had impeded him.

With Jack's fingertips against hers, she briefly met his eyes. He didn't move his hand away, *but neither have I.*

Her breath caught, and she looked back at their hands as his fingertips grazed the backs of hers, gently, tenuously. When she still didn't pull her hand away, Jack interlaced their fingers. Her heart thudded, torn with confusion. *Could I allow myself to fall in love with Jack?*

"My sister wants me to ask you for a loan. To save Penmore and William from his incompetency," Ginger said, meeting his gaze again, trying not to think about the fact that Jack was holding her hand and that his touch could affect her.

Jack chuckled, brushing his thumb against the back of her hand. "That sounds like a fantastic business idea."

"Well, I told her I'd ask. I didn't say I would support the idea."

God, help me. She was entirely too distracted by this handholding and what it might mean. Ever since she'd moved into the Savoy with Jack and been spending more time with him, the idea had planted itself in the back of her mind—a proper marriage might not be the worst thing.

Especially if Alexander is ever to have a father.

CHAPTER THIRTY-ONE

*A*fter a relatively quiet first day at Penmore, the house now felt noisy and filled with life—much like Ginger's girlhood days. The morning had been quiet, with Ginger and her mother taking Alexander for a walk around the grounds, while Lucy had stayed in her room. William had made the mistake of inviting Jack to play billiards with him, only to learn the hard way that Jack not only had the complete inability to play a friendly game without demolishing his opponent, but that he was also quite good at it.

Ginger laughed to herself as she remembered poor William's defeated look, feeling guilty about not encouraging Jack to take it easy on the man. Noah had been one of the few people that seemed to go toe to toe with Jack and sometimes she wondered if that was why Jack had valued Noah's friendship. William had made himself scarce at teatime, and now that the evening was approaching, guests were arriving for the festivities the next day.

She carried Alexander down the stairs, Jack just steps behind her. On the first floor, servants hurried through the foyer, carrying suitcases and trunks.

Some guests that were coming to the party were staying at

Penmore, including her aunt and uncle and grandmother. But as Ginger reached the bottom of the grand staircase, she saw another familiar face—one she hadn't entirely been expecting: Angelica Fisher, Stephen's younger sister, and Henry's former fiancée.

Ginger froze, her lungs emptying with a quick exhale. She craned her neck to see behind Angelica. Sure enough, Angelica's parents were right behind her.

And behind them were Stephen and Victoria.

What are they doing here?

Anger at her sister and mother flushed through her. The Fishers had been long-time family friends of the Whitmans, but her sister knew what Stephen had done to her. Why would they have invited Stephen to come?

Ginger gripped the rail and glanced back toward Jack, who had clearly seen them. His eyes were dark, and he set a hand on Ginger's shoulder, holding her back.

They'd failed to bring Stephen to justice, and this was the result. He was free to enter their lives whenever he pleased.

Jack leaned down toward her. "We can leave. We don't have to stay."

Ginger nodded back at him. If her family was going to be so dishonest and care so little about her feelings and safety, then she didn't need to remain.

She started back up the stairs, brushing past her mother at the top. "Ginger! What is it, darling?"

Ginger paused as Jack came up behind her. She narrowed her eyes at her mother. "Stephen Fisher, Mama? How dare you invite him?"

Mama looked at her in confusion, then looked over the rail. Her eyes widened. "I-I didn't know." She took Ginger's arm. "No, you're absolutely right. He shouldn't be here. Come, let's find Lucy."

Ginger held Alexander tight, thinking of the last time she'd seen Stephen. His audacity would be unbelievable if it were any other man. But as Stephen seemed to believe he could do whatever he wanted, he had no hesitation in showing his face here.

When they arrived at the door to Lucy's room, Jack at their heels, Mama turned and took Alexander from her and held him out to Jack. "Take the child, Jack. I think it's time I had a chat with both my daughters alone."

Jack raised one eyebrow in a slow arch, waiting for Ginger's approval.

She pressed her lips together, an uneasy feeling slithering through her belly. Whatever Mama had to say, she could probably say it in front of Jack. But her mother had been gracious since they'd arrived, and Ginger didn't want to seem uncompromising.

At last, Ginger gave a curt nod, and Jack took Alexander. "I'll be right here," he said, his voice flat.

Mama didn't knock at Lucy's door, she simply opened it and ushered Ginger inside. The curtains were still closed, leaving the room darkened, the fading glow of sunset coming in through the gaps between the fabric. Mama shut the door, then crossed the room toward one window, pulling it open wide.

"Mama!" Lucy gasped from the bed, sitting. She blinked, shading her eyes. She still wore her bedclothes. "What are you doing in here?"

Ginger's mother paused by the window, clasping her hands. Impatience twitched at the corners of her lips. "Why are Stephen Fisher and his wife here?"

Lucy, who looked pallid and tired, her hair in disarray, sighed. "What are you talking about? I didn't invite him. Talk to William." She lay back down, turning her back to them and pulling the sheet over her shoulder.

"Oh, no, I won't." Her mother marched up to the bed. "This has you written all over it, Lucy. William is well aware of Ginger's discomfort with Stephen—he never would have invited him. And

get out of bed. The way you're behaving is absolutely disgraceful."
Mama pulled the sheets off Lucy, provoking a shriek.

Lucy jumped up from the bed, her face flushing. "How dare you?
I'm the lady of this house now, Mama. You forget your place."

"And you forget yours." Mama set her hands on her hips. "If your
sister is good enough to beg her to help you salvage this home, then
I suggest you treat her with respect. It's *her* husband who can help
yours, not the other way around."

Ginger clasped her hands, refraining from speaking and shocked
at her mother's forthrightness.

Lucy didn't look at either of them and crossed her arms. "Why
should Stephen be excluded from the guests? We've known him our
whole lives. And I was friends with his wife until Ginger destroyed
that friendship."

A ribbon of disgust threaded its way through Ginger's chest.
"Besides the fact that he murdered our father, nearly raped me, and
carved his initials into my skin?" Ginger set a hand over the scar on
her chest for emphasis. "That's not enough to keep that evil man
from here?"

Lucy squared her shoulders. "That's *if* I believe you, Ginny. You
would have gone to any lengths to protect that criminal you pretended
to call your husband." Her dark-brown eyes sparkled with fury. "You
threw yourself at him, then tried to explain everything away by trying
to convince everyone—probably even yourself—that you hadn't fallen
in love with an evil and twisted man who only wanted to use you. As
though I'm not intelligent enough to read the newspapers. They were
filled with the sordid details of his crimes after you left us in Egypt."

"Those were lies," Ginger gritted through her teeth. "Lies
invented by Stephen and Lord Helton."

Throwing her hands up in the air, Lucy appealed to her mother
with exasperation. "Now Lord Helton is a criminal too? When does
it end, Mama? Don't you hear her lies? She's mentally ill. I think

she's the one who was obsessed with Stephen. Now that he's married Victoria, she's turned to besmirching her father too."

"How dare you?" Ginger shook her head in disbelief. *Is this really what Lucy thinks, or is she just trying to make me angry?* "You don't know what you're saying, Lucy. Either you're being willfully obstinate or just want to hurt me—but, either way, it doesn't make you right. Stephen is a villain who destroyed our family. That you would let him set foot in Penmore is atrocious."

"I don't believe you." Lucy raised her chin and leveled her gaze at Ginger. "I simply don't. And also, you have no proof. I believe nothing you've said about him. And the sad thing is, I don't think anyone does. I don't know how you convinced Jack Darby of your lies, maybe only because he was Benson's friend and he can't bring himself to believe the worst about him."

Ginger set a hand to her forehead. Lucy didn't just seem to want to wound her, as strange as it was. She truly seemed to think the worst of Ginger—and Noah.

"I believe her."

Looking up sharply, Ginger caught the determined look on her mother's face. She stepped closer to Ginger, then set her hand on Ginger's shoulder. "Stephen is and always was a brigand. Your father told me all about how Stephen was blackmailing him and used your father's debt against him to manipulate him. Ginger may not have proof—outside of that scar she showed us—but I know in my heart she's telling the truth."

Lucy guffawed. "Then you believe she murdered Henry, too?"

Mama's eyes misted. "I do. And also, I forgive her." She reached for Ginger's hand, taking it in her own. "I don't know what might have driven Henry to join your father's treachery—though I suspect it was a misguided sense of loyalty—but I'm not blind enough to think he was incapable of wrongdoing. His decision, and Ginger's, will forever break my heart, but I have two living children. *Two.* And

I'm unwilling to lose either of them because I'm incapable of forgiveness."

Ginger stared at her, stunned.

She'd waited so long to hear that her mother forgave her, that she wanted her as a daughter once more. She longed to embrace her, to thank her for the show of solidarity, to feel that she'd come back to the fold even if it was just in her mother's eyes.

But none of that would solve the problem at hand. Lucy would only dig her heels in further if she felt that she'd lost this battle with Ginger. And nothing would change Ginger's position as the prodigal daughter. Being at Penmore didn't change the fact that her life was radically dissonant to the way she'd been raised.

"Well, I appreciate that, Mama, but I'm not willing to stay under the same roof as Stephen. Either he leaves, or I do."

"You know, it's common knowledge that Victoria gave birth to Noah Benson's daughter. Angelica told me." Lucy tossed her messy hair over her shoulder. "Don't you want to ask the mother of your son's half-sister for yourself? I'd think you'd be curious to speak to her."

A dozen ill-tempered curses assailed Ginger but stayed on the tip of her tongue. Her anger at Lucy brimmed to the surface, threatening to bubble over. *Damn Stephen and his vicious lies.* Her mother squeezed her hand in a reassuring gesture, as though to say, "Calm yourself."

"That's not true." Ginger tried to think straight. "And even if it were, I would hardly think it's appropriate for polite conversation. You wouldn't honestly expect me to go up and ask Victoria about any indiscretion she may have had, so once again, I have to assume the only reason you even bring it up is to injure me."

"So everything is just lies. All the terrible claims are sheer fabrications meant to injure you? Goodness, Ginger, do you hear yourself? There are witnesses to Noah Benson's crimes. Men who came forward to say that, yes, he was a traitor and a murderer. People who saw him with Victoria." Lucy gathered herself. "I won't be asking Stephen or Victoria to go."

"Fine, then I will." Ginger started barreling toward the door, seething with rage.

"Ginger, wait—" Mama reached out for her, dashing behind her.

Ginger turned in time to see Mama's foot catch on the tangle of sheets from Lucy's bed. Tripping, her mother fell to the floor with a cry, arms outstretched. Her forehead smacked the wooden floorboards with a loud *thunk*, and her left arm seemed to move out of place hideously. She rolled onto her side with a shriek, cradling her arm with a moan.

"Mama!" Ginger turned and rushed back toward her, arriving at her side at the same time as Lucy.

"Look what you did, Ginny!" Lucy cried out, tears already in her eyes.

Ginger ignored her and turned her attention to the egg-sized knot already forming on her mother's forehead. It was an ugly bruise, but the skin didn't appear to be broken—and fortunately she was conscious. "Ring your maid for some ice. Immediately," Ginger said in a brisk tone.

"I'm going to ring for a doctor," Lucy sniveled, her shoulders shaking with shallow breaths.

"I am a doctor." She helped her mother turn onto her back. "Mama, I need to examine your arm. I think you may have dislocated your shoulder, and I'll have to reset it. Jack!" she called toward the door loudly. "I need you."

The door opened a second later, and Jack came in with Alexander. Alarm registered on his face as he saw Ginger's mother on the floor, and he set Alexander down. "What happened?"

"Mama tripped, and I think she's dislocated her shoulder. Can you come here? I'll need your help to have her sit up so I can remove the blouse."

Mama whimpered pitifully, her teeth chattering with shock and pain. Tears slipped down her cheeks, but she said nothing as Jack bent beside her, helping her sit. Ginger ignored the stab at her gut at seeing her mother in so much pain—dislocations were said to be awful—and focused on her work instead.

With steady hands, Ginger carefully unbuttoned her mother's blouse, exposing the injured shoulder to her view. The dislocation was obvious, and who knew what sort of damage she'd done to the tendons and ligaments there, but her pain would be eased by resetting the shoulder.

"Does your arm tingle at the fingertips? Any numbness?" Ginger asked, checking her mother's arm.

Mama shook her head, her teeth clenched.

Out of the corner of her eyes, Ginger watched as Lucy's lady's maid entered the room and gasped. Lucy went to her side, whispering.

"All right, I'm going to lay you back down. Then I'll have Jack hold your torso while I reset your shoulder." Ginger glanced up at Lucy. "And hurry with that ice. The sooner we have it, the better."

Once Ginger had her mother in place, she positioned herself to reset the shoulder. She'd done it a few times before, as a nurse in the clearing station rather than Endell, where the soldiers already came in patched up from triage and the frontline hospitals. She thanked God for that experience now, which would be to her mother's benefit. Resetting a shoulder while not understanding what to do was frightening.

The shoulder popped into place with surprising ease, and her mother drew in a quick breath. She moaned again, then turned her face toward Ginger, tears in her eyes. "Thank you, my darling," she managed. Her hands still shook, but the relief of the resetting was obvious.

"Don't thank me yet. We'll need to immobilize your arm in a sling and ice your shoulder for quite a while. The more ice, the better right now, to keep the inflammation down. But there's a chance you may have fractured your shoulder or done some other damage." Ginger frowned as she studied her mother's forehead. "And I want to monitor that lump." It had turned an ugly purple. "That's quite a contusion."

She looked at Jack. "Can you take Alexander back to the room and find my medical kit? I have aspirin in it and the materials I'll need to make a sling."

Jack gave her a mock salute, his eyes warm with admiration. "It's a good thing I married someone who knows how to handle a medical emergency. It certainly frees me up to hold the baby."

Ginger fought back a smile. Jack had long had the habit of making her laugh, even in the worst of circumstances. A rush of warmth pulsed through her. She pushed the feeling away immediately, unsettled at how unexpectedly her heart had reminded her she loved Jack's humor. As his footsteps faded, Mama wiped her cheeks with the back of her hand. "He's right, you know."

"He's ridiculous." Ginger managed a look at Lucy, her fury with her put to the side for now. "The ice?"

Lucy wrung her hands together. "It's coming."

"Your servants need to learn the meaning of the word *run*."

Lucy said nothing, but sat miserably beside their mother. "Why don't we help you onto the bed, Mama? I'll have the servants come and change the sheets so you can have clean ones, and you can just sleep here for the night."

Ginger and Lucy helped their mother stand, then moved her toward the bed, where she sat on the edge. Lucy's maid reappeared with ice, and Ginger wrapped it in a pillowcase. Setting it against her mother's shoulder, she tied the extra material of the pillowcase gently around the shoulder, so the ice would remain in place. "I'll need more for her forehead." Ginger glanced at the maid. "And honey, if you have it."

"Honey?" Lucy raised a brow.

"It helps with the bruising. My friend Beatrice taught me that trick when I first became a nurse." Ginger frowned at the large lump. Even if Lucy called a doctor to check on her mother, there wasn't much they could do from the small country hospital.

By the time Jack returned with her kit, she had made up her mind.

"I've decided we should stay for the evening, just to keep Mama in observation. I'll sleep here with her," Ginger told Jack as she pulled the materials for the sling out of her medical kit. She glanced at Alexander. Much as she wanted to have him with her, her mother needed rest, and a clumsy one-year-old who might bump into her wouldn't be a good bedmate. "I'll put Alexander to sleep, and then you can stay with him."

"If you're sure that's what you want." Jack watched her warily. He probably wanted to leave as much as she did. But, if he was anything like Noah, he always carried a gun with him. That was a comfort, at least, and he'd take good care of Alexander.

No, it's not what I want. What I want is for my sister to believe me and to tell Stephen to leave.

But Lucy said nothing, looking away uncomfortably.

She wanted to take care of her mother without the threat of Stephen hanging over her head.

Ginger sighed. "It's what I want."

Hopefully, her mother wouldn't need her longer than a day or two. Maybe Stephen would be gone before then.

CHAPTER THIRTY-TWO

*G*inger had missed dinner, choosing to stay in the room with her mother rather than go down with the other guests. But now that her mother had fallen asleep and was resting, she grew hungry and wanted to see her grandmother and Madeline, who had come up briefly to check on her mother when they'd arrived. They'd only had a few minutes before the dinner bell had rung, though.

Glancing at herself in the mirror, Ginger smirked at her reflection. She'd be terribly out of place if she didn't change into an evening gown, but what difference did that make anymore? After Lucy's denouncements this afternoon, she no longer had the desire to even try to keep up the pretense.

The idea of seeing Stephen, or even Victoria, roiled her stomach, and she traced her fingertips over the scar on her chest. She'd shown that scar to Lucy, poured out her heart and exposed her darkest secrets.

And now, two years later, Lucy had the temerity to look her in the eye and call her a liar.

How I wish I could clear Noah's name, even if he's dead.

The desire burned deep inside her, like a planted seed beginning to sprout. Noah was the love of her life, and, beyond that, he'd been a good man. A man who she'd seen fight against injustice, who'd treated all men and women as equals. He'd gone into the war a patriot and loyal to the Crown and been ejected from it tainted by the crimes of a traitor and ruthless villain. He didn't deserve to have his name sullied any longer.

But what could she do? How could she now prove that Noah was innocent?

Exhaling a heavy sigh, she left the room and headed down the stairs, still wearing her day clothes. She checked on Alexander, who was being watched by Lucy's lady's maid and the housekeeper, then grabbed a quick meal from the kitchen, thoroughly appalling the staff who had been cleaning up after their own dinner.

She headed to the drawing room and found her family and their guests gathered there. A hush went through the room as she entered.

Madeline stood from her seat by the fireplace. "Ginger, darling. How is Elizabeth? You were both very missed at dinner." She held out a hand to her, inviting her approach.

Ginger glanced through the room, where several faces she didn't recognize stared at her. She tried to pick out the ones she did. The Fishers were in the corner speaking with William, eyeing her with polite, blank faces. *How much do they know about their son's misdeeds in Egypt?* They'd always been reserved, especially Angelica, who had the personality of a bag of sand. Still, Stephen's younger sister was pretty enough that she always seemed surrounded by friends and potential suitors.

Jack was just feet away from them with Victoria and Angelica—which didn't surprise Ginger either. Much as Victoria had disliked Ginger, she'd seemed to have a fondness for Jack, even tolerating his teasing. Victoria was just as beautiful as ever, her dark hair elegantly coiffed and her black dress the latest fashion, though she seemed stiff, watching her sister-in-law warily.

Of course, Lucy's right beside Stephen.

Ginger's fingers curled into her hands.

Several people seemed to wait for Ginger's answer. "Mama is sleeping, at last. Her pain is still strong, and she'll likely need to go into London to see about an X-ray. I don't know if there's a fracture, but shoulders are tricky joints."

"We'll take her to London," Madeline's husband, Hugh, said, his brows furrowing. "Does she need to go immediately, or can she go back with us the day after tomorrow?"

"I've put her shoulder in a sling to immobilize it—it can probably wait for a day."

"How very fortunate that we have a doctor in the family," Madeline said and gave Ginger a kiss on the cheek as she arrived at her side.

Ginger held back a laugh. No matter how much Madeline might support her, Ginger wasn't naïve enough to believe that anyone—other than perhaps Jack or her grandmother—agreed with the sentiment. Having a male doctor in the family was perceived to be crude enough. But a woman? Most society families would be ashamed.

"Hopefully my tests went well. And then it will be official." She joined Madeline on the settee.

"As soon as you find out, let us know," Gran said with a firm nod. "I want to be in the front row to see you receive your diploma."

Ginger smiled, thankful for her grandmother's ardent encouragement. Selling that necklace her grandmother had given her when she'd arrived from Egypt had helped Ginger buy some of her first supplies for Alexander. She'd put the money into baby items so that she could always look at them and know who had helped provide for them.

Within a few minutes of Ginger's arrival, some guests retired to their rooms for the evening. They'd been there a while already, of course, and the party was the next day, when even more people would be here. Their absence helped Ginger feel more comfortable as the group whittled away to only her closest relatives.

As she was leaving, Victoria paused by Ginger. "It's good to see you, Ginger." She gave her a polite nod.

Ginger stood, moving away from her aunt and grandmother to step closer to Victoria. She hadn't expected Victoria to be polite, given their tumultuous history together. "And you as well. It surprised me to learn you were here instead of Egypt."

Victoria's dark eyes, which once had seemed to sparkle with fiery vigor, appeared sad and dull. "It's been an adjustment. I spent all my life in Cairo. But with Stephen's older brother passing away from the Spanish flu, he felt it would be wise to come back."

Roland died? Ginger gaped at Victoria. No one had ever told her.

Which also means Stephen is now the heir to his family's estate. He would be the next Earl of Knotley.

And then his triumph would be complete. Everything he'd ever wanted would be his.

Victoria checked over her shoulder to glance at Stephen, who was still absorbed in conversation with Lucy, and lowered her voice. "I just wanted to give you my condolences." A muscle in her jaw twitched. "I never knew quite what happened to Noah, just that you and Jack had married, so I assumed he'd passed." A sheen of tears glistened in her eyes. "He was the best man I ever knew. I'm very sorry."

Before Ginger could respond, Victoria stepped away, heading for the door. Ginger stared after her, blinking rapidly as she tried to process the interaction. Then more cynical thoughts intruded. *The best man she'd known ... known in the carnal sense of the word?*

She didn't dare go after Victoria and ask her. Especially not after Victoria had been so shockingly gracious.

What had changed her?

Marrying Stephen seemed to have softened her, which was strange given that Ginger had wanted to write her off entirely for willingly having married such a horrible man.

Of course, if she was pregnant, then it might not have been entirely willingly.

Ginger wished she could see Victoria's daughter for herself. But if the baby was darker, she might have inherited that from Victoria. Considering that Stephen didn't seem to want to claim paternity, whose child could it be?

After they'd retired from the drawing room, Ginger posed the question to Jack in the safety of their room.

"Do you know of anyone else that Victoria was involved with in Cairo—besides Noah? I know she was in love with Noah, but couldn't there have been someone else?"

Jack shrugged out of his dinner jacket as Ginger laid a sleeping Alexander in the bed. She sat beside him, then changed him. "Victoria's as secretive as they come," Jack said, setting his jacket on the back of a chair. "She never talked about anyone else."

"Hmm." Ginger set her hand on Alexander's soft belly, watching the rise and fall of his breath. She changed the subject, giving him a teasing look. "You seemed to enjoy your conversation with her and Angelica."

"We were talking about archeology. What's not to love about that?" Jack sat in the chair to remove his shoes. "It's the start of the digging season down in Egypt, and, with the war over, people are finally returning to their concessions. She was telling me about Fisher's growing interest in the field."

Ginger tried not to groan. "Why is it that everything he does make me automatically assume he's up to something malevolent?"

"Because he usually is." Jack went over to his bag and crouched beside it. He pulled out a pistol and held it out to her. "Take this tonight when you go over to spend the night with your mother. I don't think he'll be stupid enough to try anything here, but I want you prepared, regardless."

She took the pistol, then wrapped it in a handkerchief. It weighed in her hands as she lifted it. Especially after she'd treated so many gunshot wounds from the war, she'd loathed even holding guns. But they were also protection that would give her a greater sense of security. "Do you think you'll be all right with Alexander? I haven't quite weaned him at night, so I'll have to come and nurse him in the early hours of the morning."

"I'll be fine. And I know where you'll be."

* * *

AT FOUR IN THE MORNING, Ginger roused from sleep beside her mother, her mind thick with slumber. She was accustomed to waking at this hour to nurse Alexander, which meant that he would soon be awake.

Ginger checked on her mother, then pulled on a dressing gown, shivering in the cool dark. Taking the pistol Jack had given her, she exited and tiptoed down the hallway.

When she was only a few doors away from her own room, she heard the sudden creak of a door hinge. Ginger slunk into the shadows, hanging back by an alcove, and the drum of her heart speeded up.

Peeking out, she saw Stephen exit a room a few doors down. She held her breath, hugging the wall more tightly. Then, a girlish laugh followed, and Lucy took a few steps into the hallway behind Stephen. Throwing her arms around his neck, she stood on her tiptoes and pulled him into a passionate embrace, kissing him.

A tingle of pinpricks ran down Ginger's spine as Stephen returned Lucy's kiss, cupping her buttocks with his hands. Then he pinched her, and she gave a muted squeal before she broke away from the kiss and hurried back into the safety of the bedroom.

Stephen slunk away in the opposite direction from Ginger, leaving her alone in the hallway.

A cold, sick feeling filled Ginger's gut, and she covered her mouth, trying to keep her composure.

Oh my God.

Lucy was having an affair with Stephen.

Rage filled Ginger, and she gripped the wall, her jaw clenched tight.

Even if Stephen had somehow seduced Lucy, she'd drawn a line in the sand by doing this. *Stupid, foolish Lucy.* All she could ever think about was herself. And whatever Stephen's motives for getting involved with Lucy, she doubted love had anything to do with it.

Stephen had made it perfectly clear to Ginger: no matter how much she fled from him, he'd continue tormenting her.

It was time to settle the score and destroy Stephen, once and for all.

CHAPTER THIRTY-THREE

*T*he bottle of champagne gave a pop as the cork flew from it, and Ginger grinned as Jack poured the sparkling liquid for the women gathered in the courtyard of Endell Street. After the last few years of hardship and hard work, it was at last time to celebrate: she was a doctor.

A drizzle of rain had started when they'd arrived, but now it threatened to a steady downpour, ominous clouds in the sky above.

Dr. Louisa Garrett Anderson gave a teary-eyed smile as Jack offered her a glass. "We're so proud of you, Dr. Whitman." Flora nodded in agreement beside her, raindrops beading on her coat.

Mama shifted uncomfortably beside Ginger and gave a glance to Madeline and their mother. They'd been surprised that Ginger had kept her maiden name for her professional name, but they said nothing now. Instead, Mama busied herself showing the bubbles in her glass to Alexander, whom Madeline was holding.

Mama had been staying with Madeline and Hugh since she'd come back with them from Penmore a week earlier. Her arm was tightly bound in a sling still, and the bruise on her forehead was fading, but she appeared to have avoided serious damage, all things considered. Her shoulder had shown no signs of fracture, and Flora had been visiting her throughout the week to help rehabilitate it.

Ginger had no desire to think about Penmore now, though, and let the difficulty of that visit throw a shadow on what was supposed to be a happy day. She'd left Penmore before the anniversary celebration, too disgusted with Lucy to pretend to celebrate her anniversary with William—especially not with Stephen there.

Much as she'd wanted to confront Lucy about what she'd seen, it seemed pointless. Lucy had made her decision and chosen her side. The only thing left was for Ginger to figure out a plan to go on the offensive with Stephen before he did anything else. And Jack, whom she'd confided to about Lucy, had agreed.

Finishing the job of dispensing the champagne, Jack set the bottle on the ground and lifted a glass. "To my beautiful wife, Dr. Whitman. Congratulations."

The doctors and staff lifted their glasses in a cheer, and Ginger locked eyes with Jack. He gave her a wink, then downed his own glass of champagne.

She tipped the glass to her lips, the moment surreal. After all the hours she'd labored, the sleepless nights, the seemingly interminable end to her studies and work, she'd not only done what no woman in her family had ever done, she'd also done it as a mother.

Her heart felt light, and the congratulations from the people around her blurred together. Champagne always had a way of going instantly to her head, it seemed, and that was besides the fact that she was bursting with happiness.

"Where are you heading to next?" Madeline asked, coming over to embrace Ginger once again. "We should get Alexander back and out of the rain. It's starting to come down heavily."

Jack stepped up beside Ginger. "I'm taking her to dinner to celebrate. We'll pick up Alexander by ten, I'd imagine."

Gran shook her head. "For goodness' sake, between the three of us, we've all raised children. Just leave him with us. We can watch him for the night—without a nanny, like Ginger prefers. Isn't that right, Elizabeth?" She gave Ginger's mother a sharp-eyed look.

Mama pressed a kiss to Alexander's cheek. "Of course. So long as I get to hold my grandson, I'm delighted."

Ginger hesitated, exchanging a glance with Jack. Much as the offer was kindly meant, the thought of leaving Alexander overnight with them was unsettling. She'd been attempting to wean him since they'd come back from Penmore but hadn't quite managed it yet.

"The rain is coming down pretty quickly," Jack said, then set a hand on her elbow. "It might be safer. He'll be okay, you know."

Ginger's throat tightened as she nodded. The bed without him tonight would be lonely and heartbreaking, but she didn't want to risk his safety for that. "Are you certain you have everything you need?" Ginger asked her mother anxiously.

Mama smiled and kissed her cheek. "I'll be fine. As Gran said, we do have some experience with children."

Ginger gathered Alexander in her arms, smothered him with kisses, then entrusted him back to her mother. As she watched them go to the waiting motorcar, her heart felt heavy.

What if something happens to him?

"As you know, I'm not a mother," Louisa observed, coming up beside her. "But there isn't a mother who doesn't fret about leaving her baby. And you're an excellent mother, Ginger, which I would expect would make the whole notion of leaving your son behind more difficult. But considering that you came from such strong ladies, I'm sure he's in excellent hands."

Ginger nodded, trying not to grow tearful—and not only about Alexander going away with them overnight. That they'd all come to watch her receive her diploma had meant the world.

Ginger said her good-byes to the women who had gathered to toast her outside, not wanting to force them to linger any longer, and then she and Jack headed out. He'd driven them himself and he frowned as they reached the car, the rain coming down in sheets over their umbrella.

"This might require a change of plans." Jack peered out from under the umbrella. "I was going to take you to a restaurant, but we might want to just go back to the Savoy and eat there."

"We'll have to change into something fancier if we're going there." Ginger climbed into the passenger side as Jack held the door for her. "But I don't mind."

The trip to the Savoy wasn't a far one, just a quick trip past Covent Garden. Jack left the car to be parked, and they hurried inside, shaking the rain from their coats at the front entrance. Staying at the Savoy with Jack had become more second-nature now—they still hadn't gotten around to finding her a separate place to live—but after everything that had happened at Penmore, the future felt uncertain.

Despite his misgivings, Jack had agreed to go to Winston Churchill and accept the position on the commission to Egypt. If Stephen didn't want Jack involved with it, then it was a good sign that he *should* be. Either way, it gave Jack the ability to keep a closer eye on Stephen. Also, maybe Jack could do some good and help the Egyptians positively. At least there would be some relief in Stephen being out of England once more.

The thought of Jack leaving again had made Ginger's heart heavier than she wanted to admit, though, and not just because he'd given her a place to stay. She enjoyed his company and friendship, and their time together had been enjoyable. But with the commission set to go to Egypt at the end of November, she'd have to look for another place to live and start her independent path once again.

She could try to stay here in the city, but she was quickly finding that doors were shutting on her face faster than she'd expected. None of the hospitals in London she'd inquired with would hire her —some claimed that if she hadn't been a married woman, they would have considered it, but as she was married, it was out of the question.

Being a country doctor in a small clinic might be her only option. And if that was the case, then perhaps it made sense to go back to Somerset. Her mother wanted her closer so that she could see Alexander, and Ginger didn't want to deny Alexander the opportunity to spend time with what little family he had.

Arriving at their room, Jack unlocked the door and opened it for her. She set her coat and hat down by the entrance. "I'm not sure what I'm going to wear," she said over her shoulder, heading toward the bedroom.

He followed her, as most of his clothes were still in the room. She felt bad for having displaced Jack from his bed, but he didn't complain. He dressed in the bathroom, slept on the sofa.

"Well, whatever you wear, you might want this to go with it." Jack went over to the chest of drawers and pulled out a rectangular, flat box. He brought it over to her, holding it out.

Ginger ran her fingertips over the soft blue velvet of the box. "What is it?"

"Open it and see. It's a present. To commemorate your degree." Jack smiled, then, at her hesitation, he popped the box open.

Inside was an emerald necklace encrusted with diamonds. Her jaw dropped as she stared at it, glittering back at her. "Jack—this is gorgeous." *This must have cost a fortune.*

"It reminded me of your eyes." Jack reached inside the box and pulled it free. "Here, I'll put it on you."

He led her to the full-length mirror, then stepped behind her, setting the emerald at the base of her throat as he clasped it.

Ginger stared at her reflection in the mirror, the beautiful emerald looking out of place against the far less elegant dress she'd worn for the day. In another time, she'd have been dressed to the nines by this time of night or readying herself for supper.

Jack felt like a strange bridge between what she'd once been and what she was now. He had the money to exist in both worlds and the personality to not give a damn about any of the finery she'd grown up with.

And yet he cared enough to make moments like this feel special.

Jack ... who has been more than a friend.

Her pulse crept up, speeding as she lifted her hand to Jack's, setting her fingers against the top of his as he finished with the clasp. He settled his hands on her shoulders, his fingers resting on her collarbone, then met her gaze through the reflection.

Then she let herself step back against him, closing her eyes as his hands slid over her shoulders and down the length of her arms, slipping against her waist and pulling her closer. His lips grazed her jaw as she tilted her head back to receive his kiss against her lips, her heart hammering in her chest.

It was a slow kiss, sensual and bold, and oddly arousing. The thought of being intimate with Jack had entered her mind before, only to be shoved out as quickly as it had come—but now it lingered, wrapping itself around her with a firm grip.

Then, coming to her senses, she pulled away, her face flushing. "We can't—" she gasped, her chest falling with rapid breath.

"Why not?" Jack asked, his eyes dark and filled with sensual heat.

"Because .... b-because Noah. You're his friend and ..."

And he's dead.

Jack ran his fingertips over his mouth, as though her kiss still tingled there in the same way she was feeling. "We're not doing anything wrong, Ginger. I know you loved Noah. For God's sake, I loved Noah. I wouldn't ever do anything to betray him. But this isn't betrayal. This is just two people finding a little happiness in a world that's unfair. What's wrong with that?"

What is wrong with that?

You're married to this man. This isn't an indiscretion. He's your husband now.

Except for the fact that they'd never consummated their marriage.

She'd never been ready for that, and, with Alexander always in her bed, sex hadn't been anywhere on her mind.

But Alexander isn't here tonight.

Ginger released the breath trapped in her chest and searched his gaze. The stinging of her lips told her how much she wanted this kiss. She closed the space between them again and he caught her, his mouth descending on hers with passion.

Her wedding rings weighed heavily on her hands as the kiss deepened, her hands interlacing against his, his tongue stroking hers. She groaned, having forgotten how good a kiss could be, feeling overwhelmed by the sudden need she felt for fulfilment.

She wrapped her arms around his neck, pressing herself against his length. She didn't want to think, didn't want to question this. He was rather good at kissing, and she was enjoying it.

But she also wanted more.

I don't want to be alone forever.

I want to be loved—touched—needed, by a man.

A deep, aching need had grown inside her, throbbing in her core, making her legs feel unsteady. She'd been at the role of mother for so long, she'd forgotten what it was like to have the role of woman.

Lowering one hand to his chest, she walked her fingertips down toward his belt, her hand brushing against the buckle. If he needed a signal of what she wanted, that should be enough.

Jack pulled away, and she opened her eyes, breathing heavily. *Why did he stop?*

He searched her gaze. "Is this what you want? Because ... I want to respect what you want, Ginger, but I'm also a man. And I have to admit, I'm not thinking quite straight. You're beautiful, and I care about you. I don't want to feel later like I pushed you to do something."

She swallowed.

Yes, I'm ready.

Nodding, Ginger pulled away from him, then went over toward the bedside table. She blinked rapidly, surprised that she didn't feel the need to cry, then tugged the wedding rings Noah had given her off each of her ring fingers.

Noah's never coming back. I can't keep living in the past.

A little happiness, with a man who cared about her—whom *she* cared about—wasn't wrong.

Their marriage might not have been conventional, but it was still a marriage. Love could bloom in time. What she'd had with Noah wouldn't be diminished by caring for another man. She and Jack might not be passionately in love, but what they had wasn't nothing either.

In fact, it's everything. Everything I need now. Everything I want.

Desire surging through her body, she drew in a shaky breath and turned toward Jack.

CHAPTER THIRTY-FOUR

Ginger adjusted her earring in the front mirror of the hotel room's foyer, her stomach a flutter of nerves. Jack had lined up ten different girls to come and interview for a nanny position, and the first would arrive within ten minutes. As she finished, she caught sight of Jack exiting the bedroom, already dressed and ready to leave for his meeting.

"I wish you were staying," she said wistfully, coming up to him. She adjusted the lapel of his suit jacket, then stepped on her toes to press a kiss to his lips.

He returned the kiss with a smile, his hand curling around her waist. "I wish I were too, but probably not for the same reason."

She laughed and pulled away, dodging as his hands groped her more friskily. "Alexander is right there." She nodded to her son, who was busy on the carpet in front of the sofa, staring at a book that Jack had bought him a few days earlier. He'd been fascinated with it since Jack had given it to him, reminding Ginger of how much Noah had also loved books.

A twinge of sadness pulsed through her and she lay her cheek against Jack's chest, watching Alexander. Having this comfortable of a relationship with Jack had been easy once they'd admitted their attraction to one another. And with each day, she found her heart surprisingly ready for love, not just physical intimacy. Their relationship had changed by leaps over the last few weeks, and that giddy thrill that came with new love steadily increased each day.

Jack seemed to share her feelings too, even though neither of them dared to say it yet. But she could read the warmth of his eyes, the passion of his kisses. He loved her.

"He's still at it, is he?" Jack gave Alexander a fond smile. "He'll probably be reading by the time he's two. Master Latin and the romance languages by five."

Ginger sighed. "If that's the case, he's going to either need an entire army of tutors or an expensive school." Not that Jack couldn't afford that. She just wasn't accustomed to the idea of having money again. The past few weeks had oddly felt as though she was living someone else's life rather than the one she'd envisioned for herself. She changed the subject abruptly. "How long will your meeting be?"

"I'm not sure. I'll be meeting some men who will go to Egypt with me, and then they'll probably drone on about some boring unrelated subject for a few hours. How did you talk me into doing this again?"

"Stephen is in Egypt again. If we're going to find his weakness and exploit it, we need someone there."

"Spoken like a true mastermind." Jack shook his head. "This could come back and haunt us if we're not careful."

His words continued to ring in her head after he'd left, a tumult of emotions jumbling in her chest. Was she being selfish about asking Jack to go to Egypt? He'd agreed that Stephen was a threat, and his behavior with Lucy had been concerning.

But they couldn't continue to live their lives like this either, wondering how and when Stephen might turn up and throw everything into chaos again.

Ginger sat by Alexander and lifted him onto her lap, then read the book to him, which was a collection of nursery rhymes. He watched each page with serious eyes, clearly enjoying reading by his unbroken attention, but his expression not relaying that enjoyment.

He's so much like Noah.

The thought was a guilty one, especially with Jack in her bed now. They'd wake in the middle of the night to be intimate, and somehow it felt as though she was taking a part of her heart and dividing it once again, leaving Alexander with less. If she and Jack ever had children, he'd be the half-sibling, different from the rest. As much as she knew Jack cared about him, would he be able to look at Alexander the same as his own children?

A knock at the door startled her, and she looked up from the book. An attempt to close it elicited a protest from Alexander, so she set him to stand against the couch, laying the book open and flat on the seat.

The first prospective nanny must be here a couple of minutes early.

Ginger put a pleasant smile on her face and opened the door. "Hello—"

It wasn't a prospective nanny. It was her mother.

And she appeared to have been crying from the redness of her nose and eyelids.

"Mama," Ginger said, drawing a quick breath. She ushered her in, checking the hallway to make certain an interviewee wasn't steps behind her. Shutting the door, she frowned. "What's happened?"

"Your sister. Your sister, of course." Mama dabbed a handkerchief against her nose. She looked around the room. "Is Jack here?"

A feeling of dread formed a knot in the pit of her stomach.

"No, he's just gone out. You must have missed him in the lobby." Ginger crossed her arms. "What about Lucy?"

Mama sobbed into her handkerchief again and Ginger gave her a hug, careful to avoid hitting her injured shoulder still in a sling. "She's run off. She left William a letter telling him she didn't love him and that she was in love with someone else. And she said she had gone to be with her lover." She drew a shaky breath.

Oh, no.

Lucy.

Ginger wanted to hang her head with frustration, but another thought sneaked past. *I should have said something to her—or to Mama.*

"Did she say who she was running off to be with?" Ginger asked, her voice calm.

"No." Mama sniffled. "She didn't. And William is beside himself, of course. He traced her as far as Southampton, but then we don't know where she went."

Ginger rubbed her eyes, her mouth going dry. "Egypt. She's gone to Egypt. To be with Stephen Fisher."

Mama stared at her, frozen with shock. "What? How do you know?"

"Because I saw Stephen leave her room in the middle of the night at Penmore."

"And you said nothing to me?" A look of hurt crossed Mama's face.

"No, Mama, you were injured and in bed. And you saw how things went with Lucy—she's infatuated with him, obviously. I think she's been in love with him for quite some time."

"But he's a married man!"

"And she's a married woman. I don't think vows have much to do with it."

Another knock sounded and this time, Ginger let out a frustrated grunt. She couldn't possibly hold the interviews now. Crossing back to the door, she opened it to find a plain-looking woman standing there. "I'm so sorry. I'll have to reschedule the interview. We've had a family crisis."

She closed the door again before the woman could respond.

"Why did you say that?" Mama's voice was threaded with desperation. "No one can know about this."

"They won't. But I have ten women coming to interview for a job as Alexander's nanny, and I have to get rid of them for now." Ginger hurried over to the secretary by the sofa and pulled out a blank sheet of stationery with the hotel's name embossed on the header. "I'll put a sign on the door. Then we can take Alexander to stay with Madeline and go out from there."

"Where are we going?" Mama asked, confusion written on her face.

"To talk to Victoria Ev—Fisher. She'll know where Stephen is. And once we find that out, we'll know exactly where Lucy is heading."

* * *

FINDING VICTORIA'S address had taken some sleuthing. Ginger's mother had used the hotel telephone to call Lord Knotley and asked his butler. Victoria was in London, but near Cheapside, which surprised Ginger. She would have thought Stephen would have purchased a home in Knightsbridge or Kensington or one of the other fashionable neighborhoods. Cheapside was busy and crowded —not at all where she'd expected to see Victoria settled.

The butler received them and ushered them into the sitting room to wait for Victoria, who appeared a few minutes later dressed simply. Given that Ginger had always seen her in only the highest of fashions, Victoria's appearance was shocking.

"Lady Braddock. Mrs. Darby." Victoria nodded a greeting at them, standing by the doorway. "What a lovely surprise. Please, be seated."

Her tone was monotone and dull, and, just as at Penmore, Ginger had the feeling that Victoria was but a shadow of her former self. As Ginger and her mother sat, she took in the modest furnishings. *What is going on?* Stephen would never live like this. He loved extravagance.

"We're so sorry to call so unexpectedly," Ginger said, trying to think of the right words. She couldn't just come right out with it and tell Victoria that her husband had been having an affair with Lucy, could she? "How's Stephen?"

Victoria paled some, then shifted uncomfortably. "I ... uh, Stephen sailed for Egypt weeks ago."

Ginger searched Victoria's eyes. They'd never been friends, but, seeing her now, Ginger felt nothing but pity for Victoria. She couldn't imagine how loathsome it would be to be his wife. "Victoria ... I know we've had our share of differences in the last couple years, but I also know how highly Noah thought of you. I can't help but wonder, are you well?"

Victoria blinked, then a sheen of tears filled her eyes. She swallowed hard, her gaze flickering toward the door. She lowered her voice to a rushed whisper, her voice so low that Ginger could hardly hear her. "He tore me from my home, brought me here, took my daughter away from me. I have no resources, no money outside of what he gives me. And the servants spy on my every move. I'm not allowed to leave."

Then, quickly, she said, "I'm excellent," in a cheerful, loud tone. "I'm so pleased you're here."

A chill went through Ginger, and her gaze went to the closed doorway. Sure enough, a shadow hung by the bottom crack of the door. A servant must be listening. Victoria was a hostage to Stephen, who probably used her daughter to manipulate her.

I should have known.

Her mother's lips parted with surprise at Victoria's frankness, and she exchanged a look with Ginger. "We just ..." Mama faltered, then recovered. "We were so happy to see you at Penmore. Such a wonderful reunion, and I was so heartbroken that my time with you was cut short by my injury."

Thank goodness Mama mastered the art of pleasant conversation, even under duress.

It took Ginger a moment longer to find her own wits. "Such a shame you weren't able to go to Egypt with Stephen." She rose and crossed the room toward a desk, searching for a piece of paper. She found nothing but a newspaper and quietly tore a slip from the corner. She took a pencil from the drawer, her movements completely silent.

"Yes, it's always so lovely in Egypt this time of year. But I'm happy here in London."

As her mother continued inquiring about topics of no consequence, Ginger scrawled a note. *We need to find Stephen. Urgently. Can you tell us where he is in Egypt?*

She carried the note over to Victoria. "I'm very much looking forward to seeing the snow. I haven't since I was quite little," Victoria said before glancing at Ginger's note. She shook her head no.

Can't or won't? She scribbled the question while her mother said, "It's truly beautiful. You're very fortunate to be here." Mama's eyes darted to the question Ginger had written. "Will you be going to the country for Christmas?"

Victoria's gaze faltered between the question on the paper and Ginger's mother. "I-I can't. Ivy's health is very delicate, so we have her with the best doctors in London."

Ivy must be her daughter. Ginger cringed inwardly. She'd never even thought to ask Victoria her daughter's name.

But also ... she'd provided an answer. Victoria couldn't tell them about Stephen's location—perhaps because she didn't know.

"Do you remember that beautiful cruise we took on the Nile, Ginger?" Victoria said, setting her hands on her lap.

Ginger blinked at her. They'd taken no trip like that. They'd hardly been acquaintances, let alone social companions. "Yes, it was so lovely." She gave Victoria a questioning look.

"That would be the one place I would visit again if I could." Victoria's eyes were hard, narrowing by the corners, her voice not matching her expression. "There's nothing quite like a boat ride in Egypt. I feel as though anything might be found there."

A boat on the Nile.

Stephen must own a boat he used ... maybe for business? Who knew? *And Victoria is telling me it's important.*

Victoria leaned forward and grabbed the pencil and paper from Ginger. "I'm so sorry, but I actually have another guest arriving in a few minutes."

In a quick motion, she wrote, *"The Cursed Valley. Please help me."*

The *Cursed Valley?* That must be the name of the boat. Ginger met Victoria's eyes and saw the desperation hiding there. She nodded. "Oh, of course. We'll have to come back. Just send us a message when."

Just what was it that Victoria knew? The inability to ask her was frustrating, but Victoria had obvious reasons for her silence. And Ginger imagined it had taken Victoria's intelligence and wit to survive a marriage to Stephen.

Then, in perhaps the most shocking move of all, Victoria crumpled the paper in her fist and stuffed it into her mouth. She chewed it and swallowed, then rang the bell on the side table. Victoria tilted her head with a smile as the butler opened the door. "Please come again."

CHAPTER THIRTY-FIVE

*G*inger paced in the hotel room, feeling on edge. She'd picked Alexander up from her aunt's house, then come back to the Savoy, anxious for Jack to come back so that she could tell him about Lucy and Victoria.

But it was nearly four in the morning, and Jack still hadn't returned.

It wasn't like him to leave her worried like this. And no meeting with government officials could have gone on this long.

She had made up her mind to call the police, when the doorknob jingled. She crossed to the door, her heart pounding, and threw it open.

Jack rested against the door frame, his hat and tie askew, the smell of alcohol seeping from his clothing. What had been relief quickly turned to anger as Ginger took in the sight of him. Her jaw dropped, her brow furrowing with outrage, and she let out a guttural breath.

Then, with ire stoking her veins, she turned off the lamp and stalked back toward the bedroom, feeling foolish for having been worried.

"Red, wait!" Jack stumbled inside, catching himself on the wall beside the door. He fumbled with the lock as he shut the door. He turned the light on again.

She turned back toward him with a glare. "Just how drunk are you?"

He rested against the wall, looking at her with red-rimmed eyes. "My God, you're beautiful."

She was too angry to be placated by his words. She'd seen him drunk before, but was this going to be a habit? He'd go off to work and stumble home drunk in the early hours of the morning? She wouldn't stand for it.

She stomped back his way and had almost reached him, when she saw the wet trail of tears on his cheeks. Her heart squeezed, remorse striking her. *Something must have happened.* "Jack—" She set her hands on his waist. "Darling, what is it?"

"Darling," he repeated with a sardonic laugh. "I think that's the first time you've ever called me that, Red."

He was right. *But why is he crying?* She wasn't accustomed to seeing such displays of emotion—especially from a man.

His tears frightened her in a way she couldn't understand, and she put her hands on the sides of his face, leaning up to kiss him. "What's happened?"

Jack closed his eyes, his hands tightening around her waist. Then he pulled her closer, whisky on his breath as his hands smoothed over her curves, his mouth slanting over hers with unbridled passion, as though he clung to her. Surprised by the change in him, she returned the kiss tenuously, then relaxed into his embrace as he dragged his lips down her jaw and over along the tender skin of her neck.

He trailed a kiss down her chest, his hands cupping her breasts over the fabric of her nightgown, then smoothing over her hips as he knelt in front of her. He kissed her stomach then wrapped his arms around her waist, setting his forehead against her. She slid her hands into his hair, waiting for him to continue as she caught her breath.

But he didn't. Instead, she felt the wetness of his tears through her nightgown and against her belly, his shoulders shaking with quiet sobs.

What is happening? She'd never seen him like this.

"Jack, what is it? You're scaring me."

Jack pulled away, rubbing his eyes, then slowly sank to the floor. "I'm falling in love with you, Ginger. I've been falling in love with you for a long time. And now ..."

He never finished his sentence, staring at the floor, as though he was numb.

Why would falling in love with her upset him like this, she wondered.

She joined him and interlaced her fingers with his. If he wasn't ready to share what had him this upset, she would have to wait patiently until he was.

"Jack, you know how I care for you too," she whispered, squeezing his fingers.

He drew in a broken sniff, then gave her a bleary-eyed and sad smile. "I'm not ready to lose you."

Her heart throbbed, and she scooted closer to him. "You're not going to lose me. Why are you saying that?" She raised both brows at him, searching his face. "Is that what has you worried?"

Jack looked away. They sat in silence for what felt like several minutes, with only the sounds of their breath as company. Jack rubbed his thumb over her knuckles, as though lost in thought, swallowing back tears occasionally.

At last, in a rough voice, he managed, "I went to the meeting today—and I met a man. His name is Charles Pointer."

He drew a deep breath, and then continued, "He's American, and they had brought him in to work with me. And I just kept getting the feeling he didn't like me. He didn't hide it, actually—he resigned from the commission at the end of the meeting. So, finally, when everyone was leaving, I caught up with him and asked him about it."

Jack's fingers tightened, and he took another breath. "And he tells me ... he says, 'I know all about you, Darby. I know what sort of man you are.'"

"What sort of man you are?" Ginger frowned, searching his face. "What did he mean by that?"

"Yeah, I was stumped too. So I asked him. And he tells me this story about how at the end of the war he was working with Sarah in Egypt when she went missing ... and he traced her to Malta. Found out that she was with a fugitive."

Ginger sat straight, releasing Jack's hand as the meaning of his words sank in. A cold, restless feeling shimmied through her, her hands growing clammy. *Charles Pointer had been in Malta?*

Then she remembered that incident in the alleyway with Sarah, when she'd been speaking to a man in a Panama hat. "That was him," she gasped. "Charles Pointer must have been the man who killed Sarah." She covered her mouth, feeling sick.

"When he said that, that's what I thought too. But Pointer said he had nothing to do with Sarah's death. That he loved her, even."

She hugged her arms to her chest. "You believe him? Of course he wouldn't admit to killing her. He's not going to tell you he's a murderer. I heard the threat, and then Sarah was killed. We should go to the police—"

"I didn't know what to believe, but, no, I didn't just believe him. I argued with him about it and was prepared to start contacting friends of mine at the State Department." Jack paused, taking a few deep breaths. "And then he told me ..." Jack struggled to find the words.

Ginger's ears were ringing with sudden alertness. "What?"

"He said his only orders were to bring Noah in. That the American government wanted Noah. So he followed us to the *Aragon*, was with Noah when he apparently got hit in the head by a collapsing bunk in his room. He dragged Noah off the ship, took him to shore, then took him to Jerusalem."

The whole earth screeched to a stop.

Ginger stared at Jack, unable to move, unable to blink, only vaguely aware of the slow parting of her lips. *Noah ... hit in the head ... dragged him off the ship ...*

Her heart beat so faintly she wondered if it was stopping, as a slow spread of awareness filled her body, her limbs tingling.

... took him to Jerusalem ...

Then her fingers trembled, the breath she swallowed painful, seeming to stick in her throat as her chest burned.

He's saying Noah's alive.

Ginger felt dizzy, her head spinning.

Oh my God.

Her hands shook as she covered her mouth, trying to keep herself from pitching forward. "Wh-what do you mean? Noah survived the *Aragon*? Jack, what are you saying?" Tears stained her voice, her eyes burning. "He's alive?"

Jack didn't answer, didn't meet her eyes.

Oh, God. No, he must not be. He must have died after that.

Words streamed from her lips faster than she could fully think them through. "B-but—can we even believe this man? How can we know that anything he's saying is true? If Noah survived and was injured, he would have needed to go to a hospital. And Jerusalem is so far from Alexandria." She drew a strangled breath. "Noah would have come back—he would have found me."

"Apparently he was in a coma for a while, then couldn't walk." The strain in Jack's voice was thick, his voice sounding hoarse. "Then, he eventually recovered, and Pointer—who still believed Noah was a criminal—blackmailed him into spying for him on the offensive on Damascus. The British Army discovered them right before Damascus fell, and Pointer managed to get the American government to help him get out of being imprisoned, but he lost contact with Noah."

Ginger put her fingertips to her temple, trying to think. She stood, nervous energy rippling through her, then paced a few steps.

Pointer had to be lying.

But why lie about something like this? For what purpose? And with such level of detail.

But if he wasn't lying, then it meant Noah really was alive.

She held her head, her thoughts cloudy, trying to repeat Jack's words back to herself. Then she fled back to Jack's side, grabbing his arm. "But if the British caught Noah, they would have executed him, wouldn't they? Jack?" She gripped his forearm, the small sliver of hope that Noah might still be alive extinguished. *This must be why Jack is crying.* "Isn't that right, Jack?"

"Pointer didn't know. He couldn't find a trace of him. Didn't know what happened to Noah. But he knew that you and I got married—said Noah told him all about his faithful wife and loyal best friend. That's why Pointer hates me."

Oh, good God. If Pointer knew that she'd married Jack ... had he told Noah?

She nearly gagged, her anguish so visceral that it felt like a sharp blow to her stomach. If Noah knew she'd married Jack, he might not have come back because of that. Tears found their way onto her cheeks. "But how do we know any of this is true? That was it? He had nothing else to say?"

Jack gave a sardonic laugh. "No, actually, I punched him. Split his lip. Told him he was a son of a bitch, because if what he said was true, then he put Noah through hell. All for what? To lead Noah to be captured in the long run? And he said it was all true and that if I wanted to ask someone, T. E. Lawrence could verify that Noah, using the alias of Aziz and pretending to be a Rualla warrior, had been captured with Pointer in Sheik Saad."

That seemed even more unbelievable. *Lawrence?* And Pointer had said he found no trace of Noah. If Lawrence could verify Noah had been captured, then surely he must know what had become of him. "But what happened to Noah?"

Then a chill went through her. If Jack was sobbing, he must have learned something more definitive. *Noah must be dead, and he finally found the proof.*

"I went and caught a train to go to the home of T. E. Lawrence, who was the commanding officer when Noah and Pointer were captured. He seemed like the person who might know best what happened to Noah, and I ... I needed to know."

Ginger gripped Jack's arm, too sick to interrupt now.

Jack met her gaze. "And Lawrence—God, he's in a terrible state —but he remembered. He told me he had never heard of Noah, but he had known a man named Aziz, just like Pointer said. He said the man had fascinated him and that he was a polyglot, who spoke several languages with a fluency and skill he'd never seen before."

Ginger closed her eyes, holding her breath. *Noah. Oh, God. Yes, that would be Noah. His skill in that area was singular.* She felt light-headed and swallowed a deep breath. "Then it's true?"

My God.

If it's true ... then I never should have stopped looking for him.

Or married Jack.

That made her even more ill.

Oh, God, I married Jack thinking Noah was dead ... and if Noah knows ... what must he think of me?

What does any of it mean? Is he even alive?

Jack whispered, "Once Damascus fell, Lawrence drove him to the edge of the desert, gave him a pistol and a single bullet, then wished him good luck and drove away."

Ginger felt as though she might be sick, tears stinging her eyes as she visualized Noah, alone and desperate, in the harsh desert. No wonder no trace had been found of him. Who knew what might have become of him?

But if Noah had survived, he would have immediately come back to her.

Unless he thought I betrayed him.

Or he died in the desert.

"Oh, God. Please just tell me. Is he dead?" She looked up and held Jack's eyes. "I knew, of course, I knew, but I just ..." She broke off, unable to continue.

Tears wet Jack's lashes and he closed his eyes, squeezing them tight. "Lawrence said that about ten months ago he found an envelope in the post. The return address was from Cairo, but there wasn't any message. But he did find—" Jack dug into the pocket of his shirt and pulled out a long, cylindrical metal object. It rolled into his palm and Ginger stared at it, the meaning of it slowly becoming clear.

Then the earth seemed to give way beneath her.

One single bullet.

PART IV

CHAPTER THIRTY-SIX

DECEMBER 1919

CAIRO, EGYPT

*T*he shadowy, dark alleys of the Wazzir red-light district of Cairo were not for men of good intentions, especially not at night. The advantage they provided for someone like Noah was that the upstanding men of the Anglo world—the sort who would never allow themselves to be seen among the brothels—would also refuse to meet here. The police would remain at a distance, and private matters could be discussed without fear of discovery.

Noah adjusted his headscarf, remarkably calm under the circumstances. For ten months, since he'd returned to Egypt after staying with Fahad and regaining his strength, he'd been circling around this moment. His disguise was simple enough—he'd added streaks of silver to his beard and hair, thickened his brows, kept most of his face covered. Thick, black kohl lined his eyes. But Lord Reginald Helton had seen him in a variety of disguises before.

Helton had insisted on the meeting, which both Noah and Van Sant had expected. Since Noah had arrived in Egypt, Millard Van

Sant had been doing most of the work as the face of their opera-
tion. Noah had gone to Van Sant and told him what Sarah Hanover
had entrusted him with in Malta. Fortunately, the grizzled archeologist not only remembered Noah but believed in Noah's innocence. And Van Sant still wanted to expose Lord Helton's
smuggling ring.

The two men had set to work, with Van Sant using an insignifi-
cant and already excavated unfinished tomb in the Valley of the
Kings, KV61, as the backdrop for a farcical find. Then they'd
employed a small—but trusted and well-paid—group of Egyptian
laborers to start the pretense of a dig. In reality, the work that the
laborers were doing was significant: they were building a fake tomb,
one that Noah and Van Sant would soon claim to "find."

Their ruse depended largely on a cache of artifacts that Millard
Van Sant and Noah had found on the island of Malta, right where
Sarah had suggested it might be: in Lord Edmund Braddock's home
there. They were the lost treasures from the tomb of Akhenaten in
Amarna, and they would be used to convince Lord Helton and
Fisher that Noah and Van Sant had indeed discovered something
worth exploring.

But everything depended on Helton and Fisher agreeing to
invest in the dig. Millard had added legitimacy to the project—no
one would suspect that the famed Dutch archeologist was anything
but well-intentioned about a significant archeological find. Now
Noah needed to convince Helton and Fisher that Millard and his
unheard-of excavator, Omar Hassan—Noah—were willing to bend
the law.

Noah's trusted servant, Abdel, peered out from behind the
curtain in the upper room of a brothel. Abdel was one of the few
men that Noah trusted enough to always keep with him. He was
unquestioningly loyal and an expert marksman, which allowed
Noah to sleep comfortably at night in his Bedouin tent while Abdel
kept watch.

Abdel broke into Noah's thoughts, speaking in Arabic. "I think they're coming."

Noah sat on the pillow in the room, the thick scent of patchouli invading his nostrils as three of the women he'd hired pushed through the beaded curtain. They had strict orders to give their attentions only to the *Inglizi*. Helton had always had a soft spot for expensive Egyptian whores, a fact that Noah had ignored when he'd worked for him. Now he intended to exploit it to further Helton's distraction, to keep him from looking too closely at Noah's face.

As the scantily clad women passed him, Noah averted his gaze. Paying brothel owners for their help had long been a part of his job while in British Intelligence, but the more honest contacts Noah had made were unavailable to him now. Instead, he'd had to resort to the more ruthless and conniving in the Wazzir district—men like Ibrahim al-Gharbi, a notorious brothel owner and powerful man. He hated to contribute any money to the man's wealth, while women like these were exploited, though al-Gharbi wasn't the worst of the offenders.

Abdel greeted Lord Helton as he came into the room, followed by Fisher and another man, an Egyptian that Noah had to assume was a bodyguard from his striking size alone.

To think that just a few years earlier Noah would have been in a meeting like this, but allied with both men. The idea filled him with loathing and disgust. He'd kept his distance from both men the last year, both to prevent his discovery but also to keep the impulse to shoot them from prevailing.

I want them both dead.

For a moment, he considered just doing it. Taking out his gun, killing them both. He might not live through it, but it would be over. They would die, and the world would be better for it.

But if they were dead, he would never clear his name. Never be truly free.

Helton blinked in the haze of smoke billowing from the hash

pipe in Noah's hand. The pipe was for effect, but the hash itself had become a relief as Noah had adopted the disguise of Omar Hassan. His headaches seemed to lessen with it, and the sharp ringing in his ears that had come with the nightly headaches dulled to a low din once the drug filled his veins.

"*As salam alaykum.*" Noah greeted the men, taking a deep drag from his pipe.

Both Helton and Fisher had been in Egypt long enough to know the polite routine of Arabic phrases for greeting, and they murmured and bowed.

Helton's gaze snapped to one of the prostitutes as she came toward him. "I assumed we would be alone." His tone was flat and humorless.

"These are the evening's entertainment," Noah said in thickly accented English with a smile. He spoke in a deeper tone than he normally would, to disguise his voice. One of the women passed him, and he stroked her thigh. "Only the best for my honored guests."

"We didn't come for entertainment," Helton said, sniffing. "Send them away. I don't need or want additional ears to our conversation."

Robbed of that small sense of control, acid burned in Noah's stomach but he clapped his hands together, waving the women back out. He gave Helton and Fisher another gracious smile, gesturing toward the pillows on the floor. "Come, sit with me."

Helton and Fisher sat, their bodyguard going to the corner of the room and clasping his hands in front of him, still standing. Abdel came and joined Noah. "Would you all like tea? Or perhaps a cigarette?" Noah pulled a fine cigarette case from his *thobe* and held it out to the two men.

Fisher accepted one, as Noah knew he would, but Helton didn't. Helton continued to stare at Noah, unsmiling, his eyes unreadable and cold. His face was gaunt, his eyes yellow. Either that or the light in the room seemed to give him that sickly appearance.

He can't recognize me. If he did, he would have already pulled out a gun.

It had all come down to this. Either he would be able to take every trick Helton had taught him and use it against him, or he would fail and die trying. The spymaster hadn't gotten to where he was by being gullible, though, and Noah felt as though he balanced on the edge of a knife, unable to control the direction of his fall.

"I understand you've just arrived back here from England," Noah said to Fisher. "Did you have a good journey?"

"Yes, quite." Fisher leaned forward as Noah held out a light. Noah's fingers tensed at the proximity. How easy it would be to simply slice Fisher's throat. The visual appealed in a dark way that Noah dared not indulge.

Fisher took a few puffs, then settled back against the pillow, exhaling a stream of smoke from his lips. "Though the weather here is infinitely better."

"And your wife and daughter—did they return with you?" Noah asked.

He already knew the answer. He'd hired a few boys to follow and report on both Helton and Fisher long ago.

"No." Fisher glanced at Helton. "My wife has no desire to return here."

Noah doubted that. Victoria had always sworn she'd never leave Cairo. He'd always known Victoria was half-Egyptian, like himself. But it was only after he'd returned to Egypt from Jerusalem in the spring that he dug into Helton's past and learned that Victoria's mother had been a prostitute. That Helton had raised Victoria and managed to get her a place of standing in society was a testimony to his ability to hide the sordid details of his own past.

From the way Helton had controlled and used Victoria for spying, though, Noah didn't doubt that he'd made Victoria very aware of her humble beginnings. Noah had thought for so long that Helton had been a devoted father whose weakness was Victoria, due to how much he loved his daughter and the lengths he was willing to go for her.

But the fact that Helton had arranged Victoria's marriage to Fisher had convinced Noah otherwise.

Victoria had been a tool in his arsenal, one that Helton wielded and used like any other tool. He had probably threatened to expose her true roots if she didn't do as he wanted. After all, the consequences to him would be minor—while to her they would be devastating. So Victoria had done his spying, seducing anyone her father wanted more information about, using both her beauty and her intelligence to best her father's enemies.

And when one of Victoria's indiscretions had left her with child and Fisher had found out about it, she outlived her usefulness to her father.

The more Noah found out about Helton, the more Noah hated him.

Because of what he'd done to Victoria, whom he'd loved like a sister.

Hated him for destroying his life.

He sucked in a breath, his pulse steady. The hashish helped with that too. *Yet another thing to control, before it controls me.*

"I understand you have concerns about the dig," Noah said, looking from Helton to Fisher. "How can I help soothe your worries? Was there any trouble with the artifacts we provided you?"

Helton cleared his throat, clasping his hands together. "No, the artifacts you provided were just as you said. And my son-in-law was prepared to invest in your dig. But I couldn't in good conscience go into business with you without doing my due diligence. I'd never heard of you, but I'm prepared to take Van Sant's word that you know what you're doing. But I found a man at the Khan who claims the royal tomb in Amarna was cleared forty years ago, and that the items you provided me were from *that* discovery. Not this new one, as you claim."

Noah had worried about that when he'd turned the artifacts over to Helton.

But that had been the conundrum. He needed unclaimed artifacts, legitimate ones that could stand up to the examination of experts—uncategorized and hard to recognize.

He'd needed previously smuggled artifacts.

He'd found the artifacts he was looking for in Malta in a cellar hidden in a garden in Lord Braddock's home. But what Noah and Van Sant hadn't known, and what they gambled on still, was who else may have seen the artifacts before now.

Dammit. Noah tried to keep his cool, despite the throbbing of a vein in his temple. *This could ruin everything.*

Noah turned narrowed eyes toward Helton. "Well, obviously, your informant at the Khan is lying. The artifacts I presented to you were ones we found just last March. And I can prove it, by being able to continue my excavations this winter. There's more to be found. But not if we don't have the investment for the dig."

"This man claims to have been in Amarna when the artifacts were discovered," Fisher said coolly.

Noah didn't doubt it. He'd heard Akhenaten's tomb had been found—and cleared—by locals ten years before an Italian archeologist had taken credit for the find. But it was also possible Helton had heard that rumor as well.

"How would he know what was discovered in Amarna forty years ago? All of that is rumor. The artifacts Alessandro Barsanti uncovered were meager at best. What *I* am saying is that if that tomb in Amarna was the royal tomb, then it was a poor one. I believe if I continue digging, I will find the tomb of Smenkhkare—and evidence that *she* was Nefertiti. The discovery of the century. All my research leads me to believe I am close."

Noah fought the temptation to hold his breath, chewing on the stump of the pipe instead. Helton and Fisher weren't archeologists, and they couldn't know how bold—or controversial—a declaration that was. But Millard Van Sant, who was so well respected among Egyptologists, had presented Noah as reputable and highly competent. Would they argue with Noah?

Fisher extinguished his cigarette. "If that's the case, then I see no reason for others to profit from our hard work. Why should we invest? The Egyptian nationalists are fighting daily to see their artifacts retained within the country. A discovery this large will attract international attention."

Fisher leaned back lazily, and Noah caught sight of the butt of a pistol, in a holster on Fisher's belt.

Apprehension tickled his throat. His own gun was only inches away and loaded, but he was vastly outnumbered. If Helton or Fisher at any point showed signs of recognition, he'd only have seconds to react.

"Now, gentlemen. I suspect you have a proposal," Noah said, gritting his teeth. "That's the reason you called this meeting, yes?"

Helton watched him warily. "You need us more than we need you, Hassan. Why don't you make the proposal?"

Noah wet his lips with his tongue. "I understand that with your position in the government, you have the means to help us ... *export* some of the artifacts. Have your men turn their faces away from the merchandise and get it to destinations where the bidders will pay a premium."

All that to say, you can smuggle this for us, you son of a bitch.

Helton examined his nails. "What you're suggesting is illegal. Why would I bother?"

Noah turned one of the fat golden rings on his forefinger. "Because I'm in the position to assure you that when we discover the tomb, you will be allowed in first. Have your first pick. In exchange, you shall help me."

It was the sort of opportunity that Helton and Fisher would be fools to turn down. Wealth beyond their imaginings, plus the international fame and legitimacy that came with being involved with such a project. But would they take the bait?

Damn that man from the Khan who had recognized the Amarna artifact. He might have ruined everything.

Fisher leaned toward Helton and whispered in his ear. Then Helton gave a subtle nod.

"We'll give you our final answer in two days." Helton relaxed some, removing his hat. "Now, bring back the girls."

CHAPTER THIRTY-SEVEN

a gentle shaking on Ginger's shoulder was enough to wake her from her slumber and she blinked, trying to reorient herself. A dozen scents assailed her at once—the smell of smoke and cinders from the train, still billowing smoke at the station in Cairo. The warm, earthy scent of the well-worn leather from the seats in her train car. Petrol wafting in from the window, which Jack had cracked open along the journey to bring some relief to the stuffiness of the cabin.

She cleared her lashes of sleep, then glanced at Jack. She'd fallen asleep against his arm, though she hadn't intended to. But she was exhausted. Sleep hadn't come easily to her on the ship passage from England. She'd made the heartbreaking decision to leave Alexander with her mother and Madeline. He'd be well cared for there and safe. She couldn't make that guarantee here in Egypt.

Between missing Alexander so much that her heart felt bruised, and the confusion and agitation she experienced daily when she thought of Noah, each time she closed her eyes to sleep at night, it evaded her. At best, she was sleeping a couple of hours a night.

Jack's distance hadn't helped. After all—who knew what the

future held for them? If Noah really was alive, then what did that mean? She would be an accidental bigamist. Which, if either, of her marriages would be valid? She understood why he kept his distance and agreed it was the best course of action, but she also missed the comfort she'd found in him. Like it or not, she'd started to fall in love with Jack, and being intimate with him had only compounded those feelings.

"We're here," she murmured at last in a rough voice, then cleared her throat. She pulled away from him and sat straight.

I'm back in Cairo.

Of all the places in the world she'd never wanted to return to.

"Looks like it." Jack stood, then grabbed a suitcase from the rack above them. "Ready to get off the train?"

I'm not sure it matters if I'm ready or not. "Yes, I suppose so." She stood, smoothing her skirt. She peered out the window of the train, dirty with a film of dust and soot, watching the other passengers disembark into the station. "It seems the same. Just as we left it."

Except nothing's the same. Everything has changed—including me.

Jack looked over her shoulder. "Fewer people in uniform."

"That's true." Her lips tipped in a rueful smile. "Though, I can't say I really remember Cairo when it wasn't a sea of khaki and olive uniforms everywhere. Even my memories coming here as a girl have been altered by the images I carry from the war."

"You're going to have to be more careful this time. There'll still be some locals who want to milk tips and *baksheesh* from the English, but there are equally many people who don't want your people here."

"Well, I'm not English anymore, am I?" She arched a brow at him. "At least, according to my American documents."

Jack humored her with a chuckle. "You're going to have to learn to pronounce words properly, then."

She passed by him as he held open the door to their cabin. "First you rob us of our colonies, then our language. The audacity of Americans has no bounds, as my father used to say."

Their banter was a relief to the heaviness that had been between them lately, and she flushed as she realized she was flirting with Jack. Her husband. *Maybe.*

None of this makes any sense.

Swallowing hard, she climbed down the steps of the train onto the platform and waited for Jack to catch up. He carried their more lightweight bags, though they'd each also packed a trunk that they'd have to fetch from the cargo. Hers was filled with medical supplies —his with weapons.

The irony of it wasn't lost on her.

Before she had more time to muse on the topic, a sudden flurry of commotion made its way toward them on the platform. A few Egyptian boys, gangly teenagers and some younger, were in the pack, led by Khalib—the youth Noah had taken care of. She hardly recognized him, though. He'd grown so much since she'd last seen him. Khalib approached her with a wide smile and hugged her.

"Khalib, you've grown so tall." Ginger returned his hug, then watched as he greeted Jack with similar enthusiasm. Khalib took one of Jack's bags. The prosthesis on his left arm seemed to work well for him—yet another reminder of the savagery of Stephen, who had beaten the poor boy for helping Noah, causing him to lose the limb.

"I learned English now," Khalib told them both, a proud look on his face.

"Yes, he's one of my star pupils," Alastair said, seeming to materialize in front of them. He must have been just behind the throng of his boys. "Mr. and Mrs. Darby." He shook his head, looking behind them. "You didn't bring the wee one?"

Ginger gave Jack a sidelong glance. She didn't know all the details of what Jack had told Alastair, but she assumed he'd been cautious, given the sensitive nature of their reason for coming. If

Noah really was still alive and somewhere in the region, then he still had the potential to be caught and executed. "Not this time," Jack answered, giving Alastair a firm handshake. "I'll be too busy with the British, and Ginger has some interest in exploring archeological digs, which wouldn't be a good place for a toddler."

"Indeed." Alastair scanned her face quizzically. "I didn't know you to be of an archeological bent. Didn't you just become a physician too?"

"Yes, I did." She gave him a pleased smile. Trust Alastair to keep an ear out for news about them, even from afar. "We'll fill you in on all the details of our itinerary."

"Well, I have a house prepared for you here in Cairo, but if you need me to find you somewhere to stay anywhere else as well, I may be able to help. Or perhaps a boat to live on? Not only will it ease your travel down the Nile, but you'll be free to move around more easily from there."

"That might be a good option." Ginger and Jack allowed Alastair to lead the way to the street, while four of Alastair's boys went to collect the trunks. "You look like a proud schoolteacher with all your pupils swarming around you."

Alastair beamed as he reached a carriage. "They're loyal companions. They give meaning to my life of dreary bachelorhood. Since the war ended, I haven't had nearly the amount of fun I used to."

Despite not knowing Alastair well, Ginger knew enough to understand he exaggerated: the work he did with the orphans he'd taken under his wing was his pride and joy. And he deserved to be praised for it too: all the boys would have been destitute without him. Alastair helped them not only gain education and skills, but a means to make a modest living.

Even though it had only been a little less than two years since Ginger had been in Egypt, she'd forgotten how hot the climate could be compared to England, and she fanned herself. The street in front of the train station was mobbed with traffic—pedestrians,

horse-drawn carriages, carts, and motorcars all competed for space
to get through, all seemingly without a sense of order.

Vendors were on the streets, peddling their wares to the tourists
arriving from the train, the heady scents of kebabs and coffee
mixing with the hubbub of commerce. As they climbed into the
carriage, Ginger felt her chest tighten, overwhelmed by how surreal
being back here felt.

Rather than take them back to his own home in Old Cairo, Alastair drove them to one of the Anglo neighborhoods of Cairo, near to
where Ginger's father had owned a home. She couldn't help
wondering what had happened to that property. William had taken
ownership of it, and Ginger had later learned that it hadn't been
part of the inheritance but that her mother had sold it to him. When
he'd come to Cairo two years earlier, William had expressed a desire
to continue returning to the "City of all Cities"—but who knew
what he would do now, after Lucy's stunning departure.

They hadn't been able to find a trace of Lucy yet, which was
even more alarming. The thought of her being with Stephen was
truly sickening and, though Jack had been asking about the *Cursed
Valley,* his access to information had been limited from England.
Hopefully, now that they were in Cairo, they could learn something
more.

After escorting them into the rented home and introducing Jack
and Ginger to the Egyptian servants he'd hired for them, Alastair
led them to the fully furnished sitting room. "Will the house do?"
Alastair asked, his expression neutral as he sat.

"You did a great job. We can't thank you enough." Jack took the
chair opposite him and removed his hat wearily.

Ginger went over to the window, taking in the view. The Anglo
side of Cairo was quieter and more idyllic, the houses European in
architecture and newer. This would be a perfect house in appearance—anyone looking at Jack and Ginger from the outside would

think they'd simply come to make a home here while he did his work for the government.

"Now, are you going to tell me what changed your mind about coming back to this stinky little city?" Alastair crossed one ankle over his knee.

Jack met Ginger's eye, and she gave him a nod. They'd discussed it in advance: if anyone could help them find Lucy *and* learn what had happened to Noah, it would be Alastair. And he was one of the few people Jack trusted here in Cairo. But the idea of letting anyone in on their secret filled Ginger with dread and she looked away from Jack, setting her fingertips on the windowpane.

"Ginger's sister, Lucy, has run off, we think, to be Stephen Fisher's mistress. We're trying to find her."

Alastair let a slow breath out between puffed lips. "Oh, that's quite a situation. My condolences."

"And ... we've found out some evidence that suggests Noah might still be alive." *There, Jack said it.* Succinctly and without ceremony.

The room filled with silence. Ginger held her breath, waiting for Alastair to respond, and when he didn't, she turned slowly to look at him.

Alastair's eyes narrowed at Jack. "What sort of evidence?"

"An American spy told me he rescued him from the *Aragon*, then took him to Jerusalem. He and Noah were a part of the Damascus campaign. Then Noah vanished without a trace."

Ginger came over to the armchair Jack occupied and sat on the arm of the chair. "And more than that. T. E. Lawrence remembered Noah—they captured him for spying on the British with the American. The American was released to his government, and Noah was released to the wilds of the desert with a pistol and a bullet. Months later, Lawrence received an envelope in the post with the bullet."

She didn't know how she recounted the story with as little

emotion as she had. For the first week, she'd dissolved into tears each time she thought about it.

A bullet, the evidence that her husband was alive—but what did it mean?

And why didn't he ever attempt to find me?

Shame filled her as she imagined Noah learning that she and Jack had married. And maybe before, it wouldn't have mattered. But everything had changed when she and Jack become physically intimate.

Alastair opened his mouth to speak, then shook his head as though in shock. "I may need a minute." He looked from Ginger to Jack. Then his brow furrowed. "But you're married now. And with a babe, no less."

Ginger couldn't quite look at Alastair, heat rising on her cheeks. They'd done a thorough enough job of trying to convince everyone that Alexander was Jack's—they should have thought to at least tell their closest friends the truth.

But, then again, how could they have ever known this would become necessary to share?

"Alexander is Noah's son." Ginger's voice was a whisper. "I only told Jack and a few of my family members. Noah and I never went to the consulate after our marriage, and it had no legal standing. Jack married me—a marriage of convenience—to keep Noah's son from being thought of as illegitimate. We intended to live separate lives."

"But if your marriage to Noah had no legal standing and your marriage to Jack does—it makes little difference whether Noah is alive or not. You and Jack are married now. Unless you could somehow prove the marriage wasn't consummated, which would throw Alexander's legitimacy into question once more."

Ginger squirmed, standing as she felt the discomfort of questions that—from someone else—might be inappropriate. But Alastair likely wasn't asking in order to pry. He was trying to make sense of a terrible situation, just as she'd been attempting to do the last few weeks.

And we consummated it. Our lives didn't end up being quite as separate as we had intended. Fortunately, Alastair didn't appear to question that aspect of their story.

Jack sighed, his face devoid of any trace of his normal humor. "There's going to be a lot to figure out—if Noah is alive. But that's why we're here. Because the letter Lawrence received was posted from Cairo. This is the last known place he was."

"Or so you think." Alastair leaned back. "The Noah Benson I knew would have moved heaven and earth to find his woman. Unless, of course, he found out about the baby and thought you had formed your own family in his absence."

Alastair had said the quiet part out loud.

If Noah didn't return, it was because he didn't want to return. Because he thought I had fallen in love with his best friend.

And that hadn't been true. She hadn't loved Jack.

But ... now?

Ginger clasped her hands, her cheeks burning. Now she could hardly look at Jack. It took little for her to imagine his hands upon her, his lips against her own, their bodies intertwined.

Maybe the first time she'd been filled with lust and need, but they hadn't only made love the one time. Now that reality was like a thorn in her soul, reminding her of what had been—of what *could be.*

And the last thing she wanted was for the love of her life, for Noah, to feel like an obstacle to a different, newer love.

She loved them both. And the reality of this dilemma was horrible.

Ginger hardly noticed that all three of them had lapsed into silence, all of them too caught up in their own thoughts to speak. Mustering whatever shred of composure she could, Ginger drew a breath and met Alastair's eyes. "Will you help us find him?"

"Of course I will. I'm too curious, anyway. I'd be looking even if you didn't ask." Alastair tipped a smile at her. "But are you prepared to deal with the consequences of finding him if he is alive? If Noah doesn't want to be found, he won't make it easy on anyone that comes looking."

"I think so." Ginger hugged her arms to her chest.

Alastair stroked his chin, staring at her. "You know, there may be a way to get Noah to reveal himself. Helton always said you were his weak spot, after all."

Jack shifted in his chair, his posture tense. Whatever Jack was feeling, he had said little about what this was doing to him. Ginger knew how much he wanted to find Noah—but the weight of what that might mean had to be taking its toll as well. "What do you have in mind?"

"I think we should throw you a party, Mr. and Mrs. Darby," Alastair said with a terse smile. "And send the invitations wide. If I know Noah—and I think I do—he may not resist the opportunity to see his *belle femme.*"

CHAPTER THIRTY-EIGHT

The wind howled through the temple at Karnak, and Noah adjusted the *keffiyeh*, sand catching on his lashes. He blinked them clear of the grit, then strode toward Millard Van Sant, who had just finished a lecture to a group of tourists.

The temple complex at Karnak was widely considered by many to be the crown jewel of Egyptian civilization—the stunning beauty of the ancient world found here was breathtaking in a way that even the pyramids, for all their reputation and draw, didn't quite match. Luxor was the world of the dead, where sphinx and stones ever kept their watch, just as they'd done for thousands of years.

Noah skimmed his fingertips over a pylon. Here he felt connected to the blood that ran through his veins, the people who had dwelled in these lands—toiling and bleeding, making love and dying—placing their hope for eternal life in the carvings on these walls and the gods that, in the end, they had abandoned for others.

The metaphor for life was apt. *We make our gods, and then we leave them when they no longer suit us.* He sighed, thinking of the tatters that remained of his own faith. Faith that war and devastation, murder and betrayal had shaken. Noah swallowed a lump that formed in his throat. Faith that had died with a woman.

He pushed the thought of her away, then continued forward, taking careful steps along the pathway that tourists cleared by their constant footsteps.

Millard was one of those men who never seemed to age but who had looked well past his age as a youth. His hair had gone white in his forties, and his face was always clean-shaven. A thin man, he appeared to have the energy of someone fifty years younger, and his skin was tanned and freckled from years spent in the sun. His light-blue eyes were always cheerful, amused.

He saw Noah approaching and removed his spectacles, wiping them with a handkerchief. "You're as stealthy as ever. I barely noticed your entrance."

Noah didn't respond to the compliment. Much as he admired and liked Millard, he wasn't here to exchange pleasantries. "Have Fisher and Helton given you their answer?" Noah asked, standing at his side.

"No." Millard pursed his lips. "And I'm worried. If they're hesitating, it's because they have reason to be suspicious."

"I found the peasant who had filled their heads about the treasure being from Amarna. And I've done my best to discredit him. But that could be what they're worried about. One of my men has been combing through the black market, searching for any of Braddock's former associates in order to silence them."

"Is that worth the risk? Braddock has been dead for three years. If the word gets out that anyone is looking for his allies, you could unknowingly tip off Fisher or Helton."

"I trust Abdel. He's careful."

Millard shook his head. "We can't be careful enough. You and me —we're easy enough to kill. And Fisher won't hesitate. The man is becoming insufferable and brazen, parading around Cairo with a new woman on his arm as though he were Amun-Ra incarnate."

Noah cocked an eyebrow. "And his wife?"

"No one has seen her for months. There are rumors he sent her to an asylum."

Victoria? In an asylum? Stephen was bastard enough to do such a thing.

"That's convenient, given that he's turned his attention to someone new." Noah tried to push away the gurgle of anger he felt. Victoria never should have accepted that she had no other choice than to marry Fisher, no matter what Fisher had used to coerce her. But she had been weak and there would be no saving her from him now.

Millard sighed, his eyes seeming to reflect the sky. "Well, it could be one more thing keeping him content and distracted. He needs motivation."

"I offered him the terms we discussed." That Helton and Fisher would accept the deal had always been the lynchpin. They were greedy, but maybe he'd underestimated their sense of caution. Or they'd become more mistrustful. He'd been worried since their meeting at the Wazzir the week before, when Helton and Fisher had been so unwilling to commit. But now that so much time had passed without a word from either of them, Noah's fears had grown.

"Yes, but if that isn't tempting them, we may need to find some other form of persuasion. Something to put the pressure on Stephen to chance a risky venture. Since the money is chiefly coming from his pocket, he's the one we need to target."

Noah had had a similar thought. Fisher needed sufficient motivation. Maybe if he feared losing the deal, he would take it. Or if he found his other business ventures going poorly.

Fortunately, Noah had spent the last year looking into Fisher's business dealings in Egypt. Besides the smuggling, and working for the British government destroying illegal hashish farms, he had invested money into the lucrative cotton export business. His timing had everything to do with the misfortunes of the Egyptian farmers who grew the important crop—for years now, the British government had been controlling the sale of cotton, preventing them from selling to their enemies in the war.

In return, there had been a glut of cotton and the farmers had lost vast amounts of money. The situation had grown so dire that in the last year of the war, the British Treasury had agreed to purchase the entire cotton crop from the cash-strapped Egyptian farmers, but at a price far below its value.

"Fisher's coffers will grow soon—he offered a few of the cotton farmers in 1918 prices that were marginally better than what the Treasury had given them, procuring their favor. With the new harvest of cotton nearly in, he's set to return to those farmers and make another purchase that favors him. And they owe him, so they very well might take it."

Millard shook his head firmly. "You know I won't agree to anything that will hurt the peasants. They've suffered enough."

"I'm not suggesting that." Noah rubbed his face with his hand, wishing he had more time to plan. "But if a new, upstart cotton company were to come and buy from the farmers at a price that Fisher will never offer, the crop he's counting on to turn a profit could disappear from him. And the Egyptian farmers would benefit in the process."

Millard gave a deep, throaty laugh. "Ah, I like the way you think. But, unfortunately, my lad, I don't have the money for that sizeable of an investment—do you?"

Noah shook his head. "I don't." What little money he'd accumulated since he'd returned to Cairo had largely been spent on this charade. He exhaled a deep sigh. "We would need another investor. And, this time, someone foolish enough to buy cotton for twice its value." The words sounded bitter coming out of his mouth. *A damn near impossibility.*

"Keep thinking. You may come up with something else." Millard gave another laugh, then jerked his head as though startled. "Actually. There is someone. Someone you know, who has a great deal of money, as I understand it. One moment—come with me. Let me show you."

Millard waved him forward, toward the spot where he'd left his leather knapsack during the lecture. Noah followed him, curious but not hopeful. Anyone who would start a cotton company, only to take a loss immediately, would be naïve and gullible. Much as Noah wanted to force Fisher's hand, he didn't want to do it at the cost of hurting yet another individual.

Millard lifted his knapsack and dug through it. He found his canteen first and paused, uncapping it to take a swig. He made a face, his nose wrinkling. "Nothing like the fresh taste of tin to remind you of long days spent in the Egyptian sun." He offered Noah a swig, who declined.

Returning the canteen to his bag, Millard pulled out an envelope. "This came for me before I left Cairo a few days ago. I believe I used to see you running around with Jack Darby when you were young, yes?"

Noah stiffened. He hadn't mentioned Jack to Millard the entire time they'd been working together—or *her*. Millard didn't know, and Noah didn't need to spill his tragedies.

"Yes, we were once friends. We're not anymore." Despite his best effort, Noah couldn't remove the clipped tone of his voice.

"Well. You may want to reconsider. He and his wife are newly arrived in Cairo, and they're throwing a masquerade ball." Millard pressed the invitation into his hands. "I've heard it rumored that Jack found some treasure years ago and has been reaping the benefits of that wealth ever since. And, who knows, maybe he views your former friendship with more fondness than you appear to ..."

Millard's words were lost to the howl of the wind through the pylons. Noah stared numbly at the invitation in his hand. *"Mr. and Mrs. Jack and Virginia Darby cordially invite ..."*

Virginia Darby.

Noah squeezed his eyes shut, not wanting to think of her. Not wanting to see her face in his mind.

Virginia Darby is someone else. Not his love, not *his Ginger.*

His heart thrummed in his chest painfully.

She's in Cairo.

He resisted the urge to crumple the invitation in his fist, listening instead to the mocking laugh in the wind. Jack, who had always had everything—except for love. And now he had that too, and not just love but the heart and devotion of the only woman in the world that Noah had ever given a damn about. No, he would never ask Jack for money.

Not if Jack was the last person alive on earth.

CHAPTER THIRTY-NINE

*T*he masquerade could only be held at Shepheard's Hotel if it was going to look important, and Alastair had wanted it to look like the social event of the season. As Ginger adjusted her mask in the mirror, she threw her shoulders back, trying to look more confident than she felt.

A masquerade for a man who doesn't want to show himself.

A masquerade for a man who once loved me and I him. Who might be dead. Or worse still, who may no longer love me.

A masquerade of who I am now.

She'd come to the women's lounge to catch her breath, needing a break from the social niceties. None of these people were her friends, and none were truly glad to see her.

Most of them she didn't even know. And the ones she did had been more than happy to gossip about her when she'd lived in Cairo.

Since she'd arrived two weeks earlier, she'd only started to receive invitations for social events after Jack and Ginger's own invitation had gone out. She had only accepted a few invitations, and only because they had been former friends of Lucy, who was proving to be as elusive as Noah.

Stephen Fisher had been prowling around all the most exclusive clubs of Egypt, including the Gezira and Turf Clubs. Lucy's friends had also told Ginger that they had seen him at the Opera House with a stunning French ballerina on his arm, but they had not seen Lucy.

What if Lucy hadn't come to Egypt at all? Ginger had no certainty that she'd traveled here, only her instincts. And the only useful thing Ginger and Jack had learned about what Victoria had mentioned was that the *Cursed Valley* was indeed a boat owned by Stephen. The British government had employed him to patrol the banks of the Nile, looking for hashish farms to destroy. But no one seemed to know where the *Cursed Valley* was docked.

Jack was certain that Stephen must be using the *Cursed Valley* for something nefarious, if Victoria had thought to mention it. A boat in any official use by the government would be an easy place to hide illegal business dealings, as it wasn't as likely to be inspected. It may also be a good hiding place for Lucy.

Alastair had scouts looking for the boat and Ginger pinned all her hopes on him finding it.

Ginger sighed, feeling the weight of her frustrations crowding the muscles of her neck and shoulders. She pulled a tube of red lipstick from her handbag, then painted her lips. A costume ball had been Alastair's idea, too. What better way for Noah to come in and out of a crowded space unseen?

But it all felt useless. Noah wouldn't come. If he had learned about her marriage to Jack and Alexander's birth, then he'd known where to find her. Why come to see her now?

She tucked the lipstick away, her eyes looking especially green behind her feathered blue and black mask. Her dress was a black sheath, covered by a sheer navy-blue fabric and decorated with sequins and beads that made it especially heavy. Also, it was a daring style she never would have worn before, with a plunging neckline and a silhouette that hugged her curves.

Ginger tried to collect herself, then headed out of the lounge toward the grand lobby of the hotel. The Moorish style of the lobby had always taken her breath away, but tonight it made her feel the exotic nature of the land she was in, with its secrets and hiero-glyphs, ancient curses and magic.

Alastair was in the lobby smoking, near the draped curtains that framed each side of the foyer, and she approached him, eager for a familiar face in the crowd. He wore a traditional Venetian gold and black mask with a long nose. "If I haven't told you," Alastair said, taking a drag from his cigarette, "you look absolutely ravishing tonight, my dear."

"It'll all be for nothing if a certain man doesn't make an appear-ance," she muttered in a low voice.

"Why, you sound positively bitter and deflated."

She sighed, shaking her head. "I am bitter. And angry, if I'm honest. I never imagined I'd have to attempt to lure my husband out of hiding by playing dress-up like a doll at a ball. And if this doesn't work, what then? I just accept that he may be alive, but doesn't want to see me ever again?"

"Perhaps." Alastair nodded toward Jack, who had exited the ball-room just then. "But don't forget, you're not the only one he didn't want to see. And not all of us married you, dear. His silence, if he is indeed alive, speaks to something else."

As Jack approached her, Alastair extinguished his cigarette and headed back to the ballroom.

He's right. Noah didn't just walk away from her and Jack—he had contacted none of his friends, or at least not the ones that Alastair and Jack had been quietly asking.

Jack reached her, his eyes warm. "I got a little worried when I didn't see you in there for a while. Thought maybe you'd spotted the guest of honor."

"No, I just needed some air." She set her hand on his forearm. "How are you? Enjoying the crème de la crème of Anglo Cairo?"

Jack chuckled. "Oh, you know me. I'm always up for a good social event, so long as the wine is flowing. Speaking of which, I think I owe you a dance. People will probably be expecting my— um, for me to take you to the dance floor at least once."

She finished the sentence for him in her head. *People will expect my wife to dance with me.* The change in little words like that was telling. *His wife.* Jack didn't know what to call her, because their entire relationship had been called into question.

As she allowed Jack to lead her to the dance floor, she gave him a sidelong glance. He was holding up well, all things considered, and tonight he looked handsome in his white tie suit, with only a simple solid black mask that covered a single eye. They'd spent weeks skirting around the topic of Noah, communicating as poorly as only a couple who had everything to lose by speaking could do.

But with his hand on her waist and her hand in his, she released a nervous breath, and he bowed his head, his cheek close to hers. "You okay?"

"I don't know. I keep searching the faces in the crowd, holding my breath, wondering—and sometimes dreading—what will happen if I see him. Because then a new part of my life starts. The part where I have to understand what it all means."

Jack's hand tightened against hers. He pulled her closer. "You know, Red ... I would never stop him from being with you. From being a father to his own son." He paused, as though struggling to get the words out. "No matter how much I might want to."

His words pierced her soul. Would a word from her change his mind? And did she even want that?

When she'd been with Noah, she pictured her life differently than she did now. Noah had saved her—more than once—but Jack had given her life back to her again.

"I-I don't know what to think, Jack. It's all so complicated." She brushed a soft kiss on his cheek. "Let's just dance and forget, for a moment. He's not here. And we won't know if he's even alive if he doesn't choose to find us. It's his choice now."

Jack nodded and twirled her to the waltz, and they seemed to blend into the movements of the other couples on the dance floor. Ginger closed her eyes, her heart beating painfully. Maybe they should have just left well enough alone and stayed in England. She missed Alexander terribly, and being here felt like a fool's errand.

When she opened her eyes, she scanned the crowd, the masked faces around them. Maybe they'd made it too difficult to find anyone. She'd been certain she'd be able to pick Noah out from a sea of faces, but what did she know?

It had been two years.

Who knows how he's changed?

There were some things, of course, he'd never be able to change. His height, for one, and the unique dark blue of his eyes. Not that she could tell the color of most people's eyes from a distance. And with the deeply orange glow of the chandeliers in the darkened room, few things would give him away: his bearing, the way he walked ... his height.

The dance wound to a close, and Ginger's gaze fell to a pillar by an alcove in the room. A tall, masked man wearing all black stood there, leaning against it, watching her and Jack. He had a thick beard that was visible under his metal mask, which resembled a wolf.

It wasn't his height that caught her attention.

Instead, there was a lazy swagger to his posture, a confidence that she'd once found endlessly alluring. He held her gaze, then dipped his chin in one nod before turning and walking away.

Her heart in her throat, Ginger pulled away from Jack, unwilling to call attention to the man in question. If it was Noah, that could be dangerous for him.

If it's not Noah, going after him might be dangerous for me, too.

"I'll be back," she said to Jack, squeezing his hand before leaving him on the dance floor.

She hurried through the maze of round tables in the direction the man had gone.

By the time she reached the exit from the ballroom, she couldn't see the man. *He's gone.* She tugged on the tops of her long black gloves, her heart racing. *It wasn't him. He wouldn't be so obvious.*

But if it is him?

He wouldn't want to be spotted by others. If it was him, drawn by curiosity as Alastair predicted, he'd retire somewhere private. She left the interior of the hotel, going outside toward the terrace, then deeper still, into the garden.

Her heart almost stopped as she saw the tall, masked man in black striding across the lawn, with no intention of slowing.

"Alastair said you would come," she called after him, her voice surprisingly strong.

He stopped in the shade of a tall palm, not turning to look at her.

Her fingers curled into her palms, her mind absorbing each reaction.

He knows my voice.

The moonlight glinted against the grass, a warm breeze catching the leaves of the nearby rose bushes. A sweet floral scent carried and, mesmerized, Ginger took slow steps toward him. When she was only a few feet away, she stopped, her breath choked.

"It's you, isn't it? I didn't want to believe it. But it's true. You're alive."

The man still didn't turn, his posture rigid, and Ginger came around to face him, her heart pounding wildly. His mask made it hard to see his face.

But those eyes ...

She'd know those eyes anywhere. They were the same that had looked at her, once, with love. The same color as those of her son, who'd gazed at her with adoration as an infant on her breast.

Noah.

With a trembling hand, she reached up and untied his mask, then plucked it away in one flawless move. The mask in her hand, she gazed upon the features that no beard or moustache—nothing— could obscure. Her eyes filled with tears and she watched him, unable to move or speak. He didn't move, barely blinking.

He's alive.

And he's here.

In her dreams, she'd lived this moment. Heard his whisper in the tempest, woken with tears on her cheeks when all she'd grasped on the bed beside her was air. She'd sobbed into her pillow, praying that he'd come back to her, hoping against hope.

"You said you'd always find your way back to me," she whispered at last.

Pain, or anger, flashed in his eyes.

When he still didn't speak, she curled her empty hand into a fist. "Noah? Answer me!"

"You're speaking of someone who doesn't exist, madam." Noah reached for the mask in her hand.

She pulled it away, as though stung.

This is the only answer he's going to give me? "No." She shook her head, swallowing hard. "No, that's not good enough. You were my world, Noah Benson, my love, my heart, and you ripped it out of my chest when you left me. And now you're here, and I'm supposed to believe that all we had was nothing? That you walked away and never came back without a reason? Or that you won't give me a reason, at least."

She stepped closer to him and struck his chest with her fist. "Give me an answer. It's been two years. Two years. Answer me, dammit! Why, Noah, why?"

Noah didn't flinch.

Slowly, he encircled her wrist with his hand, peeling her away from him. "Don't use that name again." Letting her hand go, he shouldered his way past her, striding away.

This is how he was going to act? After leaving me alone and pregnant and destitute?

He'd left her on purpose.

She threw his mask toward him. "You unredeemable bastard. First you abandon your wife and son, then you won't give her an answer why?"

Noah turned and looked over his shoulder, narrowing his eyes at her. "What did you say?"

"Your son. Yes, Noah, you have a son. I was pregnant when the *Aragon* went down."

He shook his head in disbelief. "I don't have a son. Jack—the man you turned to in my absence—that's whose son you bore. I came back from the very depths of hell with the singular purpose of finding you. And then I learned you'd borne a son a full eleven months after I went missing. I didn't want to believe it. Even looked to see when his birth had been registered. Don't lie to me to suit your purposes now."

Noah had come looking? Then Alastair was right. He had learned about Alexander and Ginger's marriage to Jack and felt betrayed. But why hadn't he just found her and asked her for the truth?

She gave a sardonic laugh. "Yes." She didn't approach him this time. "That's what the birth announcement and the register says. Because I was able to convince the doctor who delivered him—a trusted friend and mentor—to change the paperwork on my behalf. We didn't legalize our marriage with the consulate, Noah. Your son would have been born a bastard. Jack—your *friend*—saved him from that fate by marrying me and giving Alexander his last name."

Noah's gaze snapped to hers. "Alexander?"

"After his father." Ginger threw her shoulders back. "Whom he resembles closely."

Her words seemed to throw Noah off for a moment, but he regained his haughty expression quickly. "And how can you prove that?"

"You can ask Jack. Or Dr. Louisa Garrett Anderson. Or my mother and aunt and grandmother—who all knew I was with child. I don't have a way of proving it to you otherwise and, quite honestly, I shouldn't have to. I loved you. I vowed to be your wife, and I never, ever would have married anyone else if I hadn't found myself alone and destitute, without options."

Noah closed the space between them once again, searching her eyes. "But you did though, didn't you? You married someone else. Gave yourself to him." His face was in the dark shadow of a grove of trees, his back to the revealing light of the moon, which shone upon her own skin.

She recoiled from him, tearing her eyes away. She couldn't lie to him now if she expected him to believe anything she said. Removing her own mask, she wiped tears from her lashes with the fabric of her glove. "Jack and I lived apart for most of the marriage. It was only supposed to be a marriage of convenience."

"Until it wasn't. I watched him dancing with you in there. I'm not blind. He's in love with you."

She gripped the mask tighter, closing her eyes. She didn't want to have to admit that to him.

Noah leaned closer, his voice in her ear. "And *you* love *him*."

She turned her face toward his, only centimeters away. "That's not fair, Noah. I thought you were dead. You didn't come back for me. You promised you would."

"And you promised you'd love me forever. I suppose we both broke our promises, Ginger."

"You stupid, ignorant man. What makes you think I ever stopped loving you?" She searched his eyes, anger blazing through her like a wildfire. "Death doesn't stop love. I may have thought you died, but my love for you didn't—my heart went right on loving you, no matter how many days went by. I *still* love you."

His jaw clenched, and he grabbed her chin in his hand, causing her to draw a quick, shallow breath. Then he dropped a scorching kiss to her lips, his other arm clamping her against him. Her body arched into his, her senses swimming as his mouth ravaged hers mercilessly—not the tender kiss of a lover, but a man scorned and in agony.

Despite the harshness of his kiss, her body betrayed her, desire sweeping through her as his tongue stroked against hers, robbing her of breath and reason.

It wasn't the sort of kiss anyone should have in the garden of Shepheard's, no matter how hidden by shadow and foliage they might be. She felt dizzy with arousal, a current racing through her body reminding her of the bliss she had once found in his arms. Crushed in his embrace, she wrapped her arms around his neck, forgetting all else.

The kiss went on for a while, a tangle of bruising lips and teeth, and the insatiable need that surged between them, as though Noah wanted to claim her for his own once more, as he'd done in Port Said years before. His hand released her chin, roving freely over the curve of her breasts, then onto her thigh possessively, bunching the fabric of her dress in his grip.

She was his. *Then. Now. Forever.*

Then Noah dragged his lips away, across her cheek, onto her earlobe. "Dammit, we're not alone. Don't look."

It took all her willpower to follow his instructions as awareness came back to her. He sucked in a breath, then disentangled himself from her, her red lipstick on his lips. "Go back to your husband. I shouldn't have come."

Then he backed away, swooping down only to lift his mask from the grass. He turned, then stalked away, leaving Ginger shaking, her knees feeling as though they would give out on her.

Slowly, she swallowed a hard lump in her throat, tears flowing down her cheeks, and looked over her shoulder.

Jack waited at the entrance to the garden. Even from where she stood, she could read the pain on his face.

CHAPTER FORTY

*N*oah flexed his fist and brought it to his mouth, bile creeping up into the back of his throat.

You fool. You absolute idiot.

Coming had been reckless enough. Kissing her ... *imbecilic.*

Who knew who else could have seen besides Jack? Anyone could access that garden. And then months of planning would fall apart, all because he never could control himself with her.

He hadn't gone far when a shadow exited from the street in front of Shepheard's. "I might have known," Alastair said, crossing his arms. "I did know, actually. I told them you'd never stay away when you found out she was here."

"Don't you start with that." Noah kept walking, but Alastair kept up with his rapid pace.

"She loves you. She always has. The moment she found out you might be alive, she came racing back to Egypt, dragging Jack with her." Alastair pulled out a cigarette and lit it, as though they were on a stroll rather than racing away from the most famous hotel in all of Cairo.

"And you believe her?" Noah raised a brow. "I didn't think you were that gullible, Alastair."

"And I didn't think you'd abandon your friends—including Khalib." Alastair shook his head. "What am I supposed to tell him now? The boy was inconsolable for months after you disappeared."

"Tell him the truth. Noah Benson is dead. And must remain so." He narrowed his eyes at Alastair. "If I were to show up now, what would happen? They'd cart me off, execute me by morning. If I'm lucky. And, yes, death would be a mercy at the hands of Reginald Helton and Stephen Fisher."

Alastair sniffed. "Then why are you here? Of all the cities in the world, why choose the one with your enemies?"

It wasn't a bad question. Noah had asked himself the same question many times. *Why bother?* He could have gone anywhere, started a new life. A real one. Not one where he lived in a Bedouin tent at the edge of the desert, waiting like a spider for his prey to fall into an ever-decaying web.

"Because only my enemies have the power to clear my name."

Alastair released a slow puff of smoke. "I see."

Noah said nothing as Alastair continued to keep up with him. Then, at last, he turned toward him, exasperated. "How long do you intend to follow me?"

"As long as it takes."

Noah grunted. "As long as *what* takes?"

"For you to tell me your plan. So that I can help."

"Alastair, if I wanted you involved, I would have come to you. It's safer if you forget that you ever knew me."

"Please stop attempting to be a martyr, Noah. It's very unbecoming. And the fact remains, even if it was safer for me not to know you were alive, the cat's out of the bag now. So you may as well trust me, like you always have, and tell me how to help you—before you lose your life and we all have to go through a period of mourning all over again. Which would be most unseemly."

Noah glanced at Alastair, amused at his unperturbed response. He had missed Alastair.

He had missed all his friends.

"Then you were able to recognize me right away?" He felt a pang of dismay at the fact. He'd attempted to conceal himself tonight, though perhaps not as well as he did when he pretended to be Omar Hassan.

"No, actually. But the red lipstick on your mouth gave you away. I happen to know the lovely lady that is wearing that color on her lips tonight."

Noah rubbed the palm of his hand over his mouth, trying not to recall that moment of weakness. "She looked breathtaking."

"And you couldn't resist. Naturally. *La belle femme* is your greatest strength and your greatest downfall."

Noah gave a contemptuous, scoffing laugh. "She's no longer mine at all."

"That may be the case, and it's really none of my business, but I can't see Noah Benson abandoning his son. Not the orphan boy who had a soft spot in his heart for the fatherless."

This was the trouble with those who actually knew him. They knew too much about him.

Me, a father?

The idea was more than he could comprehend.

"Even if the boy is mine, what right would I have to come in now and destroy his perception of who his father is? They may not have intended it, but Jack and Ginger are a family now."

"The right of a father." Alastair pinched his cigarette between his thumb and forefinger. "And he's barely over a year old, Noah, for goodness' sake. You think he'll remember any of this? There are far more sons and daughters in Europe who waited far longer for their fathers to return from the war, only to have that hope dashed. You should consider yourself lucky."

Much as Noah wished that Alastair's rebuke couldn't penetrate his exterior, it was too late—Alastair had already volleyed his arrow true by bringing up Noah's own dead father. Scowling, Noah turned and grabbed Alastair by the collar, dragging him into a nearby alley. He pushed his back up against a wall, roughly, so that the shorter man's feet barely touched the ground.

"I'm not interested in having to be witness to Jack and Ginger as they grow their family. It's good that you found me instead of Jack, because I don't know that I could have restrained myself with him. Tell Jack and Ginger to go back to England and get on with their merry lives and leave me to ashes, where they were only too happy to cast me." He released Alastair, giving him a menacing glare.

Rather than appearing intimidated by him, Alastair set his hand on Noah's shoulder, clearing his throat and coughing.

"I-if you lose her, which may be entirely up to you, then you'll have only yourself to blame. But I-I don't believe that's what you want. Why would a man who's lost the only person he deemed worth living for be fighting to repair his reputation? Yes, you're angry, Noah. And that's logical. But don't let your anger get the better of you now, old friend."

As though sensing a weakness in Noah's armor, Alastair shrugged his shoulders and continued, "She was pregnant with your child. They both believed you were dead. We all did. Jack did what he thought was honorable, what he thought you would have wanted —to care for your wife and your child. Is it really that difficult to believe that he would have fallen in love with her in the process?"

Noah stepped back, his pulse pounding at his temples. He'd been foolish to threaten Alastair, who always carried brass knuckles in one pocket and a pistol at his waist. But it was yet another example of how he wasn't thinking clearly right now.

He stumbled backward, his hands shaking. Then, with his back to the other side of the alley wall, he slid down to the ground, cradling his forehead against one palm. "I can't think straight," he said, blinking up at Alastair. "I've had headaches since the *Aragon.*

Nightly, it seems. And Ginger makes me mad. Helton was right about her effect on me. Maybe not about anything else, but he knew she wasn't any good for me."

"You're going to let that gormless bastard be right? You *have* changed." Alastair crossed the space and sank down beside him. He pulled out a cigarette case. "Would you like one?"

"I've found more relief in a hash pipe as of late."

Alastair guffawed. "No wonder your mind is addled. You know, *la belle femme* is a doctor now. I hardly think she'll approve of that disgusting habit."

Ginger ... a doctor?

Then she'd done it after all. She'd succeeded and flourished without him, it seemed.

"I can't keep talking about her, Alastair." Noah rubbed his eyes. "Our love isn't optional for me. Like the air I breathe, the food I eat. It sustains me—and sometimes poisons me."

"Do you remember how I used to call you *Se Osiris*—the boy magician who could read sealed scrolls without unsealing them? Because you were so good at all that intelligence work you did."

Noah's lips formed the hint of a smile. "Yes, I remember."

"As it turns out, I should have dropped the *Se*. You are simply Osiris, battling with his brother Seth, needing to have his body stitched back into pieces by Isis so that they can happily raise little Horus together."

This time, Noah's laugh was genuine. The analogy was ludicrous, though well meant. "Your fondness for nicknames leaves your comparisons without merit in this circumstance."

"Well, it was worth a try. And it got you to smile." Alastair gestured with his forefinger. "That alone was worth it. Now, are you going to trust me with your troubles, or are you going to insist on forging bullheadedly onward?"

Noah leaned back against the wall.

He was exhausted.

Not since he'd left Fahad's house in Jerusalem had he felt the security that came with genuine friendship.

Sarah's voice, from two years earlier, rang through his head.

"You have to do it alone."

From that moment, he'd been spiraling. Trying desperately to do everything on his own. And so many times, when he'd felt on the cusp of breaking loose from the whirlpool, he'd found himself sucked back in, deeper than where he'd started.

Maybe that had been his mistake from the start.

CHAPTER FORTY-ONE

The drive home from Shepheard's had been an uncomfortable one, the silence between Jack and Ginger terse and heavy—and that was after Ginger had been forced to endure the end of the ball, attempting to be a gracious hostess.

Jack had every right to be hurt. His first time seeing Noah alive had been under the worst of circumstances.

To make matters worse, it appeared Jack hadn't been the only one to see Ginger follow a man into the garden. Or witnessed the kiss. By the time they'd left the ball, Ginger had heard the whispers swirling around her, seen the looks thrown her way.

Some things never change.

She had heard no one identify Noah, thankfully, and his face had largely been in shadow, even during their kiss. But the rumors must have reached Jack's ears in some form, and as they arrived at the house, he exited the motorcar, then held the door for her.

"Jack." She followed him inside, her gut churning. "Jack, please, talk to me."

He was already on his way up the stairs. "About what? You came here for one purpose—you accomplished that goal, congratulations.

Now that my services are no longer required, I'm going to make myself scarce." He gave a mocking bow.

She gritted her teeth. "Then what was all that about not wanting to stop us from being together?"

Jack ran his fingers through his hair, and they stumbled on the tie of his mask. He removed it and tossed it over the rail in frustration. "I don't know." He took a few steps down toward her. "I know what I said and I know—I know you would never choose me over him, but that doesn't mean I'm not flesh and blood, Ginger. And I guess I thought it would take more than two minutes for you to jump right back into his arms, as though everything we had meant nothing to you."

She didn't want to feel guilty.

But I do.

She didn't want to feel selfish and horrible. As if Jack was an obstacle.

Everything we had ... not just a friendship, not just a marriage. Love too.

Tears escaped her eyes, and she wiped them away. "I didn't think, Jack. I didn't mean to kiss him. He was so angry with me, so hurt. And I told him about Alexander—which is precisely why he didn't come back, by the way—and he barely believed me. All he could focus on was us. Because, yes, I know there's an *us* to worry about. I lived those moments with you, too."

"No, you didn't. They weren't the same for you as they were for me." Jack's eyes were red. "And I told myself that it didn't matter. That you needed time. We had the whole rest of our lives, after all. But you didn't lie to me either. What was it you said? 'I'll never be able to love anyone like I did Noah, including you.'"

She swallowed a shaking breath, her chest trembling with the falling of her tears. "I wasn't trying to hurt you."

"No, but that doesn't really matter, does it? That won't stop you from choosing him in the long run."

In the long run? Noah didn't even want her. *"Go back to your husband,"* he'd said. He hadn't given her a way to find him, the opportunity to ask questions. And he probably wouldn't make the mistake of showing up again.

She pulled off one glove, then swiped the tears from her cheeks. "Don't do this right now, please."

"No?" An infuriated look crossed his features. "Not now? Then when? When you need to contact me for what—a divorce? An annulment? Our lives together can't be so easily dissolved as shaking hands and going our separate ways. You owe me a conversation, at the very least."

"At the least?" Tonight wasn't the best night to have allowed herself a few glasses of champagne. She could never think quite as clearly afterward. "What's that supposed to mean? That you didn't get what you bargained for when you married me? You got everything, Jack—including access to my bed. Which never should have happened."

Jack grabbed her by the bicep, pulling her closer to him. "Maybe it shouldn't have, sweetheart, but you wanted it as much as I did. Sorry if that's inconvenient for you now. I love you. That's what it comes down to. Noah coming back doesn't just make what I feel for you disappear."

His words had the unfortunate effect of both reminding her of the intimacy that had briefly existed between them and castigating her enough that she calmed. *He's right.*

She set her hand on his, easing herself from his grip, which was harder than he probably intended. "And you love him. Which is why I'm begging you to give me time to think about this. I know he's your best friend and—"

"Don't you get it?" Jack's eyes were glassy. "The minute I slept with you, Noah and I stopped being friends. We're never going to be friends again, Red. He will never forgive me for that. You, maybe. But not me. So now I lose you both. And ... while you're still here,

I'm begging *you*, please. Just talk to me."

Jack and Noah, not friends? The idea made her ill. They'd been friends since childhood, when Jack's father had been brought into a dig in England and the two boys had stumbled across each other.

Jack, who'd fled from his home country and spent his days with Noah in Egypt and the Levant. Who was the one person Noah had trusted blindly.

The certainty of their continued friendship had never faltered. They would be friends for life.

Until I risked their friendship.

She backed away from Jack numbly, wishing she could escape the heavy, elegant ballgown that felt as though it suffocated her. Going to a settee near the staircase in the main open foyer of the house, she sank onto it, then removed her shoes and gloves. "I suppose that never really entered my mind. Or I was so preoccupied thinking about Noah and myself that I didn't think about that."

Jack followed her and sat beside her, keeping his distance. "It's what's the worst part of all of this. I ... I hoped he was alive, of course. That he somehow had survived. But I didn't think it was possible. If there had been any doubt in my mind, Red—I-I don't think I would have married you. Or maybe I would have, but not ... you know." He palmed his face.

They both lapsed into silence. *What now?*

I'm acting as though I have a choice. What if Noah gives me no choice?

Noah couldn't live a normal life with her and Alexander. And just what had he been doing the last year?

I can't believe he's alive.

Or that I kissed him like that.

She hadn't been thinking clearly—she still wasn't.

He had been so ... different. Trying to find the man she'd married in him was harder than she'd expected it would be. His appearance was not only altered, but more. *He's not the same.*

Then again, neither am I.

She'd changed the last two years, hadn't she? What she'd been through after losing him had changed her, as had motherhood and becoming a physician.

... and finding myself falling in love with Jack changed me, too.

She glanced around the foyer, thankful that the servants had left them to themselves, not interrupting their conversation. They were probably in bed—it was already the middle of the night—and Alastair had assured them he'd hired not only the most discreet individuals he knew but also ones who knew to only give help when required, which was Ginger and Jack's preference.

Alastair's work with the Egyptian orphan boys had earned him the loyalty of many locals, a fact that Ginger was ever grateful for, now that she and Jack were having such a sensitive conversation. Still, she lowered her voice, not wanting to be overheard.

"I don't even know who I'm legally married to. Noah may procure the paperwork from the Coptic church and prove that our marriage was before yours and mine, but will the British court accept that? And, if not, Noah's Catholic. He can't marry a divorced woman."

"Then that's the plan, right? So long as we can figure out a way to fix this disaster, you'll just go with him and we all part as former friends?"

Was he hoping she would choose him over Noah? She hesitated, torn by her conflicting emotions. "I don't know, Jack. I don't know if he's even going to come back again. He walked away tonight. And he may never forgive me, either." In which case, would Jack want to remain married, knowing Noah was alive and she'd have chosen him if Noah hadn't rejected her?

Because Jack was right about that, too.

Her heart would always choose Noah.

And yet ... what if she and Noah couldn't repair the damage they'd inflicted on their marriage? Would every disagreement turn into an exchange of *"If you'd just come back to me?"* and *"If you hadn't married my best friend?"* They'd both unknowingly wounded each other deeply. But the justifications they'd had couldn't make the pain of it go away.

"He'll return. And he'll forgive you." Jack released a slow sigh. "Maybe not right away. But eventually. He didn't kiss you tonight like a man ready to let go." His voice was tinged with acid.

She'd humiliated him with that kiss. And his reputation.

It had been stupid and thoughtless ... and cruel. After everything Jack had done for her, the very least she could have done was not to allow Noah to kiss her like that in a place they could be seen.

"I'm sorry for that kiss, Jack. It was reckless, and I shouldn't have put your reputation at risk." Ginger reached forward and clasped her fingers around his.

His shoulders hunched forward. "That's the problem, though. You didn't just risk what we have—you risked Noah too. Other people saw you. They may not know Noah's identity, but I guarantee those rumors will get out quickly. And who do you think Fisher—or Lord Helton—will conclude you were with?"

"That's precisely what I said," Alastair's voice came from the shadowed back corridor. His footsteps were silent as he came into the foyer.

Noah was only steps behind him.

CHAPTER FORTY-TWO

*S*eeing Jack holding Ginger's hand was enough to make Noah's temper flare, nearly undoing the last few hours of calm conversation he'd managed with Alastair. Ginger looked stricken as their eyes met, and she released Jack's hand instantly, rising to her feet.

"What are you doing here?" Ginger asked, her face paling.

Noah had never allowed himself to think of what he would say to her if they ever came face-to-face once again. But with Jack just steps away, his eyes boring a hole into Noah's, his thoughts felt muddled and unclear. Alastair had spent a long while coaxing him to return here with him.

"This needs to be settled amicably and with care, Noah. You may have been mistaken about the circumstances before, but you're not now. You can't simply walk away again."

And though Alastair was right, it didn't make any of it any easier.

An awkward pause lingered in the air. Then, clearing his throat, Noah pushed the acerbic rage down and said, "It seems I left my wife in the arms of someone else."

Ginger's lower lip trembled, and she ducked her chin down and toward her shoulder, as though unable to respond.

"Well, that's putting it mildly," Alastair said, sauntering further inside the foyer. "Can I suggest we all retire to the sitting room? My dear, follow me." Alastair held an arm out to Ginger, who took it, helplessly. He led her away, clearly assuming Noah and Jack would follow. Instead, neither man moved, both staring at each other boldly. The mistrust seemed mutual, the discomfort palpable. Finally, Jack broke eye contact. "Noah, you have to understand—"

"I don't think I do." Noah didn't move, his eyes roving the space. Unconsciously, he was already looking for an escape. He didn't want to be here. But he'd invited this trouble upon himself by going to Shepheard's tonight.

Jack went on, his voice faltering. "She was pregnant. And you know, if it hadn't been for that, I would have left her in England and probably not seen her again for a while. She didn't need me to survive, really. She got herself over to a military hospital, found a doctor to give her a job and help her get into medical school, and a place to live. I gave her a loan, but she's almost paid all of it off. But I didn't want your son not to have a future."

Noah took a few steps toward Jack, slowly, deliberately, his eyes glaring. "Giving my son a future didn't mean fornicating with my wife." Neither of them were being rational, though maybe that wasn't what was needed right now. Noah's fury was quickly burning into a conflagration.

Jack's face flushed with color. "Goddamn it, that's not how it was." His hands curled into fists. "And I love her, Noah. Like it or not, I married her. I didn't dishonor her." Then Jack's pride seemed to blaze. "And I didn't seduce her. I didn't *touch her* without her permission."

That was enough to break his composure. Noah's hand curled into a fist, and his punch was so quick, with so much force, that Jack didn't have time to duck. His hand made contact with Jack's face, his knuckles erupting with pain, a hideous crack from the contact.

Jack fell back with a cry, holding his face, and footsteps raced in behind them.

Ginger brushed past Noah, racing toward Jack. "Noah, what have you done?" She knelt beside Jack, pulling his hand away. Blood dripped from Jack's nose, which was already bruising and red. "Oh, God, you brute. You broke his nose."

Alastair paused beside Noah. "You couldn't just follow me?" he asked, shaking his head.

"Alastair, call a servant to fetch me some ice. I'll need my medical kit, too." Ginger cradled Jack's cheek with her hand, inspecting it.

"I'm fine," Jack said, pulling away from her. He sniffed, then wiped his nose, leaving a streak of blood on the back of his hand. He pulled out a handkerchief and held it to his nose. "I deserved it."

"No, you didn't, though you often say more than you need to when you're angry." Ginger's voice was irate, and she swiveled her gaze at Noah. "He didn't deserve to be punched. And none of us deserved anything that's happened. Now, this has gone far enough. I'd rather live *my* life with *my* son alone than to continue in this madness. This is a horrible situation, and anger and frustration and resentment are only going to make it worse."

Then she shot a furious look at Alastair. "And you knew exactly what you were doing by bringing Noah here tonight. Are you happy with the result? Grow up, gentlemen."

She stood, then wiped her hands on her skirt. "I'm going for my medical kit. When I come back, I expect all of you in the sitting room and Jack to have some ice on that nose." Ginger stormed up the stairs, leaving the three men in the foyer.

Blood continued to drip from Jack's nose despite the handkerchief. Alastair blew out his cheeks. "Well, she's certainly turned into a mother, hasn't she? Let me go and see about that ice." He slipped away.

Noah's knuckles throbbed painfully, and he rubbed them with the opposite hand, gazing up the stairs in the direction she'd gone.

She seemed different, though he'd barely spent enough time around her to know.

If it had been any other circumstance, he would have helped Jack get up from the floor, offered a grumbled apology, and all would be well between them. But this wasn't the sort of situation that Noah knew how to navigate. Anything else he could have forgiven.

Jack falling in love with Ginger—and worse still—her loving him wasn't in his power to so easily overlook.

Without a word, he stalked away in the direction he'd seen Alastair take Ginger before. The corridor led to the sitting room, where the lights were already on. He still wasn't convinced he should be here, and, in many respects, it felt as though he was dreaming. What was worse, he couldn't decide if it was a nightmare or not.

He sank onto a sofa, sullen and lacking any desire to talk, but knowing that if he left now, it would only make everything worse. His shoes felt strangely claustrophobic—he'd worn nothing but sandals for years now, and even the western clothes he'd once been at home in felt restrictive.

Jack came in behind him and sat in an armchair, tilting his head back to staunch the blood flow. "I'd forgotten how fast you are. I think the last time my nose got broken, it was you who'd hit me."

"Was it?" Noah rubbed his eyes, unamused.

Jack nodded. "In Spain ... or was it Italy? I don't really remember. I just remember it was after some festival and a girl was involved."

Noah knew exactly when Jack meant. The gaps in his memory that had come with his head injury from the *Aragon* had faded recently, though his recall still wasn't what it had once been. "Italy. We were staying with a family who had a daughter about our age. You snuck into her room one night, and the father kicked us both out."

"That's right. I was an ass." Jack cringed.

Hence why Jack—though Noah had always trusted him—was the

last man he'd want to see with his wife. Thinking about that would only lead to more irritation, though.

Alastair reappeared with two bundles of ice. He handed one to Jack and another to Noah. "I thought you might need to ice those knuckles."

"I do, thank you." Noah set the ice on the back of his hand, wincing. How long had it been since he lived anywhere with an ice box? He had a camel and a horse. A few servants who he trusted and who kept watch when he was gone or slept.

"Now, before Ginger comes back, I'd like to advise we do our best to avoid discussing the more temperamental aspects of this delicate situation. There are more important things to sort right now." Alastair sat across from Jack and laced his fingers together. "I wouldn't have brought Noah here tonight if I didn't think it was absolutely vital."

"Is that the excuse you're using?" Ginger's voice came as she pushed open the door and came in. She'd changed into a far more practical outfit—a brown corduroy skirt with wide pockets and a cream-colored silk blouse—and she had her medical kit slung over her shoulder. She breezed over to Jack and squatted beside him.

Alastair shifted. "I hate to be the voice of reason in all this, but Noah has spent the last year working on a plan to clear his name. Your arrival in Cairo may have been poor timing, but to make matters worse, because of a very unfortunate kiss, everything that Noah has done may be ruined. Helton's reach in Cairo is longer than before, and he has spies everywhere. He'll find out about Mrs. Darby's illicit encounter, and then what?"

"If I've done my job well enough, they won't connect Sheik Omar Hassan to me," Noah countered, shaking his head. He and Alastair had been through this earlier. "Why would they?"

"Who's Omar Hassan?" Jack asked as Ginger examined his nose with an endoscope.

"They will connect you immediately if you're caught looking like that," Alastair said, nodding his head at Noah. "That beard and long hair must go. You can easily enough don a wig or fake beard if you need to parade around as Hassan."

"Well, the good news is I don't see evidence of a septal hematoma," Ginger said, shutting off the light of the endoscope. She shook her head, dabbing the blood away from Jack's nose with a piece of gauze. "Once the swelling has settled, we'll have a better idea of how crooked that nose will be. Constant ice and five grains of aspirin ought to help."

Noah nearly smiled. She'd always been competent, but, despite everything, it gave him pleasure to see her so effortlessly take control of the situation. She glanced at him and seemed to catch the warmth of his gaze, her expression faltering. "I should look at your hand, too."

Noah drew his hand further toward his chest. "You don't need to."

"Yes, I do." She came over to him and sat at his side. He'd noticed how clean and fragrant she smelled when he'd kissed her earlier, and his shoulders hunched. His own ability to bathe was more limited. He felt like a barbarian beside her, and she, ever the angelic healer, radiated cleanliness in contrast to his grime.

She held out her hand to him, and, hesitantly, he offered his for examination.

Noah felt Jack's eyes on them as he looked at Alastair and returned to their previous conversation. "Even if Helton hears Ginger was seen kissing someone in the garden of Shepheard's, he has no way of knowing it was me. That may be his suspicion, but I hardly think he'd make any immediate conclusion. It's far better if I simply stay in disguise as Hassan and allow the rumor of Noah Benson's resurrection to disappear."

"So you're Hassan, then?" Jack squinted from behind the bag of ice, no doubt still trying to piece together Alastair and Noah's conversation.

"Better still would be to allow Hassan and Noah Benson to be seen—coincidentally—in some location at the same time. If you're worried about Helton and Fisher having their doubts about this entire plan with Van Sant, then one way to offer security is to clarify that one of their newly reappeared enemies is unrelated to that plan," Alastair said with a sigh. "Anyone close to your size and stature can don the look of Hassan. Only you can appear as yourself."

Noah was having a hard time thinking with Ginger's proximity. Her fingers were soft, gentle against his hand as she smoothed an ointment over the torn skin. She didn't react to the conversation around her, her brows furrowed in concentration.

Jack straightened in his seat. "Of course. I should have known." He released a throaty growl, then tilted his head back again. "I should have known you were involved with that. That should have been my very first clue you were alive."

Furrowing his brow, Noah gave Jack a suspicious look. "What have you heard?"

"Just that Millard Van Sant and some archeologist I've never heard of had been digging at the Valley of the Kings and may have found something in KV61. Fisher and Helton are investors, I take it. I heard they were asking around about the dig from archeology contacts I have in London."

"They haven't invested yet. They were on the verge, but then a black-market dealer from the Khan recognized one artifact we'd given them to authenticate as the treasure from the missing Amarna cache."

Ginger lifted his hand, wrapping a bandage around it. She was unusually quiet. In the past, she'd always been inquisitive, asking them for details about any topic they discussed in front of her she was unfamiliar with. But she said nothing now.

"Fisher, it appears, may need some persuasion to invest. If he does, the dig at KV61 will resume—it's currently stopped for lack of funding. At which point, Noah, as Hassan, will locate the supposed hidden burial chamber immediately and allow Fisher and Lord Helton inside and unguarded to have their first pick. And then, in exchange, Helton has agreed to help Hassan smuggle some of the treasure out," Alastair explained, his gaze focused on the neat bandaging job Ginger was finishing.

"And then you'll expose him. Makes sense." Jack raised a brow. "It's not a half-bad plan."

"The credit doesn't go to me. Sarah Hanover came up with it in Malta before we set sail on the *Aragon*."

That drew a reaction from Ginger, whose green eyes darted toward him, the corners narrowing. Having finished with the bandage, she dropped his hand and stood. "Good night, gentlemen. Best of luck with your plans."

She started toward the door, and Jack gave her a baffled look. "Aren't you going to stay? Hear what's going on?"

Ginger paused. Without turning back, she drew a deep inhale. "I no longer want to be included."

"Wait—" Alastair stood, one hand out. "Don't go yet. If I'm not mistaken, doctors frequently carry hair clippers in those magical bags, yes?"

Ginger tossed Alastair an impatient look. "Yes, I have hair clippers. They were often necessary for surgery."

"Wonderful. Now, you wouldn't mind giving our Colonel Benson a trim, would you? Our Samson is desperately in need of his Delilah."

She gave Alastair a cutting gaze. "If I'm not mistaken, Delilah was Samson's nemesis. Caused him to lose everything and be ultimately killed."

"A very apt metaphor, I'd say." Alastair could hardly keep the laugh out of his voice as he set both hands on the back of the armchair.

"Hilarious, Alastair." She scowled, her lack of humor showing through. She took the hair clippers out and held them to Alastair. "Do it yourself."

Alastair wrinkled his nose. "I wouldn't cut the hair of my enemy, let alone my friend. Trust me when I say I don't feel competent."

Ginger's lips pursed, and she looked over her shoulder toward the exit before glancing back at Noah. "Do you want your hair cut?"

Noah's chest tightened. The idea of her cutting his hair felt oddly unnatural and discomforting. But Alastair might also be right. If someone else could adopt the role of Hassan while Noah revealed himself to Fisher or Helton, he might erase any link they'd make between the two personas. A wig or a fake beard was never as convincing as the real thing, but he'd made a mistake and now he had to undo some of it.

He nodded, begrudgingly.

"Then come upstairs to the bathroom. I'd rather not make a mess in the sitting room." Ginger's voice was flat and unenthusiastic, and she hurried away as soon as she'd finished speaking.

Alastair cringed. "In the meantime, I'll think of a few people who might take your role as Hassan—though you may have just broken the nose of the most obvious choice. And we'll come up with something to pressure Fisher into investing in your plan."

Noah stood slowly, feeling strangely nervous. He ignored Jack, hoping, once again, he hadn't made a mistake by coming here. Being in a room with Jack was strange enough—they'd been friends for so long that Noah could read the haughty look on Jack's face. The anger just beneath the surface. *As though he has the right to be angry with me.*

"Just remember what I told you," Noah said to Alastair. *I don't want Jack's help.*

Alastair gave a lengthy sigh. "Yes, yes, I remember. And you take care around those shears. An angry woman with a sharp object is never a good combination."

CHAPTER FORTY-THREE

Ginger leaned over the water of the bathtub, testing the temperature with her hand. Noah looked like he needed a good bath, though he didn't smell poorly—but like a man who spent most of his time outdoors. She certainly wasn't about to cut his hair without him washing it.

The door to the bathroom creaked open and Noah stood there, practically filling the doorway. She'd forgotten how tall he was, how his presence always seemed so commanding.

She'd forgotten more about him than she'd realized, it seemed.

Like how vulnerable I feel near him. He had the capacity to either make her smile, set her at ease, or make her want to cry with a single glance.

"I drew a bath for you," she said in a steady voice, avoiding his gaze. "Everything you need is beside the tub. Once you finish, put your trousers back on, but leave your shirt off. You don't want hair getting in your clothes."

Her cheeks had grown hot as she spoke, and she drew her hand out of the water and dried it on a towel beside the bath. "I'll return within ten minutes."

If Noah had something to say to her, then he could just say it. If not, they could just continue in this uncomfortable silence, each of them wallowing in their own pain.

He said nothing, so she dipped her chin in a nod, then brushed past him. She closed the door behind him, leaving him alone, then stopped, setting her hand over her heart.

If only Alexander were here.

It was a selfish thought, but right now, more than ever, she wanted to scoop her son into her arms and hold him to her chest, burying her face in the intoxicating wonderfulness of his innocence. Her days on Shelton Street with him after his birth had been some of the happiest of her existence. Simple days without all the complication that grown men seemed to bring into her life.

She stayed outside the bathroom until she'd regained her composure, the exhaustion of the evening fraying the edges of her patience. More than anything else, she wanted this long day to be over.

When she entered the bathroom once again, Noah was at the bathroom mirror and he had helped himself to the tools she'd laid out before he'd arrived—including Jack's straight razor and scissors. His beard was nearly gone, the skin underneath paler than the tan of his cheeks and neck. But the change was striking.

Gone was nearly any hint of that stranger from the garden.

Noah—*her Noah*—was there at the mirror, calmly shaving his face, wearing only trousers, as she'd instructed him to do.

She gripped the door frame, dizzy at the sight of him.

He paused when he saw her there, his blue eyes flickering at her, locking with hers through his reflection.

Ginger sucked her lower lip, a torrent of emotions threatening her demeanor. In some ways, it was as though they'd only just parted. But the rational part of her mind tried to tell her it wasn't true. The experiences they'd had in the interim had likely changed them both. Maybe they were both unrecognizable to each other now.

To begin with, Noah had always been muscular and lean, but somehow his shoulders seemed broader and the finely carved muscles of his torso seemed larger and more defined than before. His skin was golden tan and a broad swath of tattoos, from his left shoulder down to the wrist of his left arm, marked the skin that had once been spotless. She could no longer see the English regimental tattoo of his youth—now he looked more like an Arabian prince than a polished British officer, especially with his long, dark hair.

She felt her pulse puttering unsteadily. "You can finish," she finally managed, tearing her gaze away.

"I was planning to." His full lips curved in a half smile. He leaned toward the mirror, scraping the straight edge of the razor along his strong jaw.

"I can come back." She looked over her shoulder, the impulse to escape growing stronger. Whatever magnetic, physical pull she'd always had toward him hadn't diminished—the kiss in the garden had proven that much. And in the intimacy of this space, watching him shave, it felt even stronger.

"No, stay. I won't be long." Noah nodded toward the stool she'd set out for him. "You can have a seat if you'd like."

She swallowed, trying to moisten the dryness of her throat, and then sat. The sound of the gentle scraping of his razor filled the air, and she clasped her hands in her lap, looking down at them. Desperate to find anything to talk about, she finally said, "I understand you finally met T. E. Lawrence."

Noah paused, glancing over his shoulder. Then he resumed the shaving. "It was that bullet, wasn't it? Either that or you've had a run-in with Charles Pointer."

"Both actually." She gave a wistful smile. *But not me. Jack.* She didn't dare bring Jack into this now, though. That topic felt far too fraught with pain.

Finishing, Noah rinsed his face in the sink, then washed the surface of the razor blade. He dried his face with a towel, turning his back toward the mirror. "Yes, over a year ago. Seems like a decade."

She had so many questions she wanted to ask him. So many stories to tell. And didn't he want to know about his son? Hear anything about her? Being here with him, in the confines of this space, she found she didn't have the words for any of it. She stood, gesturing toward the stool. "It's your turn to sit, I suppose."

He folded the towel by the sink, then ran his fingertips through his wet hair. "I can't say I've enjoyed a hot bath for a while. Thank you."

His hair had some natural wave to it, and as she stood behind him combing it, she tried to focus on the top of his head rather than on their reflections in the mirror and the feel of his gaze upon her. "You have lovely hair. I hate to cut it."

He gave her a taut smile. "I can't say I'm thrilled to cut it, either, but I trust Alastair. He's a meticulous planner, with good intuition."

"Then why didn't you come to him before now? Why do all your plotting here in Egypt alone?" She finished combing his hair, which was well below his shoulders. She had little experience trimming men's hair outside of speedy trims on an operating table. But hopefully that would suffice.

"After Sarah ..." He paused, shifting in his seat. "I didn't want to risk anyone else's life. Being dead gave me a freedom that I wanted to take advantage of."

Her stomach twisted. Had that been part of his hesitation in coming back to her? "I suppose we've ruined that for you now."

Noah didn't answer, his lips pursing. She didn't want to imagine what he'd been through. Since Jack had told her the details Charles had relayed, she'd spent many nights tormented by her imagination. As a physician, she knew the struggle he must have gone through to recuperate his strength if he'd been in a coma for so long. And who knew what lingering side effects he had from his injuries?

But, somehow, those struggles were dwarfed by the other parts of Noah's story that she'd heard, and his somber demeanor seemed to reflect that.

She went to the counter and fetched her trimmers. "You certain you trust me to cut your hair?" she asked with a tense smile.

"I trust you with that, yes." The subtext was clear enough—he didn't trust her with other things.

So we're back at that.

The beginning of their relationship had been rocky, with neither fully trusting the other. She returned to her place behind him and started trimming, holding her breath as she started. *Please let me do a good job.*

Despite the tension, she felt the pressing urge to speak growing within her until she was nearly bursting with the feeling. She settled on the only subject she thought he might want to know about—his son. "Alexander was born on September twenty-seventh, last year. I think he was a couple of weeks late," she said in a calm voice. "He had a head of dark hair and eyes just like yours."

As his hair fell to the floor, she flicked her gaze at the tattoos on his back for a moment, then continued, "And ... he was serious. He still is serious. He loves books. Stares at them as though he's discovered something magical. But when he smiles"—her throat clenched—"it's like sun after a tempest. That break in the clouds that puts all other sunny days to shame."

Noah didn't reply, continuing to study her through the mirror.

She felt her insides growing weaker. *Does he want to know any of this?*

"The first few days with him at home alone were the hardest. I had a bassinet that I bought, and I placed it beside my bed but then woke twenty times throughout the night to check on him. Finally, I fell asleep for a few hours, and when I woke again, his little arm felt so cold that it frightened me. And he's slept in my bed ever since. Leaving him with my mother and aunt in England to come here is one of the most difficult things I've ever had to do."

His silence was deafening. At last, she ventured, "Do you have anything you want to know about him?"

Noah raised his chin, meeting her eyes through the mirror. "I enjoy listening to you speak. It calms me. Reminds me that this isn't a dream. Your voice was never quite right in my dreams."

Oh, my love.

Her heart pulsed achingly, filling her with a fragile hope, and she tried not to overreact. What if she frightened him away? The thought seemed absurd, but everything about their interactions now felt wrong. Somehow, the man who'd once known her best was a stranger to her again.

She looked away and kept trimming. Half his hair was gone now, and her confidence with the cumbersome instrument was growing. "Speaking of my family, my sister Lucy may be here in Cairo, too. She's married to William, the new Earl of Braddock, but I witnessed her having an indiscretion with Stephen." She swallowed hard, knowing they still had this in common. Stephen had done evil things to them both. "I-I'm terrified she's run away to be with him."

Noah's brow furrowed. "When?"

"Just recently. I'm not sure why he's entangled himself with her, but I worry that, whatever his reasons, they can't be good. He's married to Victoria Everill now."

"Yes, I know." His features hardened, his eyes darkening.

She hadn't intended to bring Stephen's claims about the paternity of Victoria's daughter into the conversation now, but if they were going to be having such stilted, difficult conversations, she may as well out with it. "In fact, Stephen paid me a little unexpected —and terrifying—visit in London. He told me that Victoria's daughter is yours."

Noah's expression didn't change. "And you believe him?"

"No, I—"

"I was never intimate with Victoria. Not once. You may have to speak to your other husband if that's something you find unappealing in a spouse. If I remember correctly, Jack and Victoria were friendly."

Ginger gasped, her clippers falling to the floor with a clatter. *Jack has had sexual relations with Victoria?* Her face burned as she retrieved the clippers. "Are you implying the child might be his?"

"It could be, but I doubt it. Victoria wasn't exactly a nun. And her father threatened to reveal her origin as the daughter of an Egyptian prostitute if she didn't do his bidding. My guess is that Victoria had some indiscretion with a man that Fisher found out about and used it to blackmail her."

Ginger stepped back from him, still shaken. Why hadn't Jack told her about his history with Victoria? Distractedly, she brushed a few stray hairs from her skirt. She'd already let Noah know how much that had unnerved her, but she didn't want to take the bait of discussing Jack.

I don't even know if I can believe him. Suggesting that Jack had a romantic dalliance with Victoria was a cheap way to get a rise out of her—and to cause strife between her and Jack.

"Whatever means he used, she's completely controlled by him now. He took her daughter away from her, placed her in the care of his father with a nanny. There are rumors swirling that she's gone mad, but the truth is that he won't let her leave the house to which he's confined her in London."

Noah looked away, his jaw flexing. "There's a reason I've made it my life's goal to destroy him. Even if I die in the process."

That didn't surprise her. Noah had always had courage and tenacity—but, most importantly, a sense of honor that was so pervasive to his thinking that it made him willing to take risks to keep it.

"Goodness, I missed you." She nearly whispered the words, tears threatening her voice as she straightened and moved back to finish the haircut.

He looked down and only a thumb twitch seemed to give away that he even heard her.

He doesn't want to hear it. He doesn't care.

When she'd finished, she lifted his chin to see that she'd trimmed both sides of his head evenly. The face that looked back at her was so familiar that her knees felt weak. She brushed the hair from his shoulders. "A few days in the sun ought to even the tan on your face," she said, strangely wishing she could extend the moment. "I'm not a barber, but hopefully I did all right."

He plucked some hair from her skirt, his eyes not reaching hers. "You have the Midas touch. I'm certain it will be perfect."

Considering how contemptuous he'd been earlier, the fact that he was being so amiable now felt encouraging. She didn't move away, her fingertips tracing the intricate tattoos on his left arm. "Was this painful?"

"Not very. But given how foolishly I'd marked myself in my youth, they seemed necessary."

Still, as her fingers grazed his bicep, goose bumps rose on his skin. He was keeping her at a distance, she understood that much, and perhaps maybe she should do the same. But he was the one who had spent over a year feeling betrayed and rejected by her. "Noah, I know words mean little after everything that's happened, but I never wanted to be separated from you. I should have told you while we were on the *Aragon* that I thought I was expecting, but you had so much on your mind and I didn't want to add to your burdens. And I never should have stopped looking for you, no matter what anyone told me. I'm sorry. For that and ... for everything." Her words fell flat. Nothing she could say felt good enough.

He pushed the stool back and stood, rubbing the back of his neck. "Thank you."

Her heart fell, crushingly.

He doesn't love you anymore. He's put you out of his heart.

A small flicker of self-preservation fired through her as he gathered his shirt from the bathroom floor. "And, for the record, I'm not a bigamist. I may have married two men in an honest mistake, but I only have *one* husband. Considering you called me your wife earlier—unless that was solely to injure Jack—it may do you good to remember only one of my marriages is legal. If you want me to be your wife again, Noah, you're going to have to do more than just throw poison arrows at the man who scooped me off the ground when I had no one else—out of love for you."

Noah paused, still bent over, then slowly straightened, his eyes dark.

Now I've done it. Damn. He'd cracked the cool exterior she'd been trying to project.

He ran his hand over his smooth jaw, as though adjusting to the newness of it, and she hated how manly he appeared with that gesture. "What would you like for me to do, Ginger?" He stalked toward her, his hips swaying, the slightest scowl on his lips. "Bend you over that bathroom counter and reclaim you as my wife?"

Oh my God. The outrage of his remark, coupled with the effect it produced on her, shook her to her core. "No." She backed away until her backside hit the counter and she held onto it, trying desperately to remember any defiant comment to combat him with. She moistened her lips. "No, that's not what I want."

Had she noticed before how low the trousers hung on his hips? Or maybe she'd tried not to stare at his chiseled abs, the sheen of dark hair that trailed low ...

She sucked in a breath as he paused in front of her. He seemed to notice how her breath quickened near him, and he smirked. "Are you enjoying what you see, then?"

Miserable bastard. She gritted her teeth as he leaned closer, dipping his face against her hair, inhaling the scent of her. Now he smelled of clean soap and an earthy ruggedness that made her head spin.

He turned a hand, trailing the backs of his fingers down her cheek, gliding them along her jaw seductively and slowly as she arched her back, raising her face toward him. His hand plunged into her hair at the base of her head and he lowered his lips to her ear, his voice a husky whisper. "You know what I see when I look at you? I see the most gorgeous woman I've ever known, the only woman I've truly loved, the mother of my son—apparently."

His words made her faint, her heart slamming into her ribs.

He drew his head back, his face inches from hers, his lips full and flushed. He searched her gaze. "I see you ... beautiful Ginger ... with *him.*"

He let her go, backing away.

Ginger had to hold herself up to keep from collapsing, his words colliding with her body with a sickening blow. She hugged her arms to herself, her heart feeling as though it might burst. If he'd driven a stake into her chest, it would have been less painful.

She sank onto the floor as he pulled on his shirt, as though giving no notice to the way he'd flattened her.

He's gone. My love is gone, gone ...

This cruel man couldn't be her Noah. Not the man she'd loved.

She covered her face as the tears she'd been holding back flooded her.

Then footsteps clattered up to the door. The door opened, and two of the Egyptian servants stood there. "Hurry. Hurry. This way," one of them said.

Ginger brushed her tears away. "What is it?"

"The police. They've come to search the house."

The police? Ginger wiped her tears away, sniffling as she scrambled to her feet.

That was faster than any of us expected.

Noah stiffened, then looked at the mess of hair on the floor. "This has to be cleaned. It won't do any good for me to have shaved my beard and cut my hair if they find this." He gathered the hair into a towel.

"I'll clean," one man said, jumping into the bathroom. "Now go. You and the *Sitt*. You are in danger. *Effendi* Alastair sent us."

Ginger looked at the servant in confusion. She was in danger, or just Noah? Had Alastair and Jack felt it necessary for her to leave? This was the house she and Jack were living in, after all—why shouldn't she be here?

"Go now!" the Egyptian cleaning the floor ordered.

Her questions would have to wait. If she delayed, she could risk both Noah's life and her own. She grabbed her medical kit as she bolted for the door, Noah just steps behind her.

"This way, this way." The other servant held a finger to his lips, and Ginger heard the commotion of heavy, booted footsteps below them. He led them to the end of the corridor, then pushed on a panel on the wall. It moved, revealing a passageway, and he led them inside.

How had I never noticed that?

Most likely it had been built as a servant's passage, but she hadn't seen it used. She didn't doubt Alastair knew about it, though. She couldn't help wondering if he hadn't picked the house precisely because of it.

Once the servant had reset the panel, the space darkened and she groped in the darkness, finding his robe. He held her hand and led her down the stairs. Noah said nothing, seeming to find his way without her help, and they raced down the stairway until they reached the ground floor. The servant cracked open the door there, a sliver of light coming through.

As the servant opened the door more widely, Ginger's hands shook, fully expecting someone to jump out of the shadows and surprise them. But they appeared, thankfully, to be alone. "That door there leads to garden. *Effendi* asks you find him at the home of Van Sant, tomorrow at noon."

The servant pointed to a doorway opposite to where they stood, and Ginger understood his meaning—he wasn't coming with them. Ginger found the servant's hand and squeezed it with gratefulness. "Thank you," she choked out.

Then she and Noah hurried toward the door and fled into the night.

CHAPTER FORTY-FOUR

*T*he last thing Noah had expected this evening was to be riding on horseback past the Pyramids and into the desert with Ginger. Her arms were curled around his waist, but she was stiff and silent. None of the pleasant conversation she'd made during that damnable haircut.

He'd hurt her, drawing blood like a wounded viper, and he regretted it. But there was little to be done about it now. She had barely spoken two words to him after they'd taken off by foot, then caught a cab and been driven toward Mena House Hotel, near to where he'd left his horse in a stable.

And if she didn't want to go with him—which he imagined she very well may not—she said nothing when they'd mounted the stallion and started toward the dwelling he kept near Cairo. His man here, Abdel Salah, would be surprised to see him with his hair cut and face shaven like this, but he would say nothing.

Still, with the Wafd party quickly turning so many of the locals against the English, he hoped he wouldn't alienate the few men he relied on and who were so integral to his plans.

The outline of the tent formed as they drew closer. It was so late that it was nearly morning. By the time he drew the stallion to a stop, Abdel was waiting for him outside the tent. He raised a brow when he saw Noah, then frowned when Ginger dismounted from behind him.

"It's a long story," Noah told Abdel in Arabic as his feet hit the ground. He handed him the reins. "Water the horse and keep watch. If anyone approaches, I want to know immediately."

Ginger adjusted the strap of her medical kit, gazing into the barren desert landscape. "This is where you live?"

"At times." He was too tired to go into a lengthy explanation now. "But it's where we can sleep for the night."

He led the way into the tent and she followed. The first night he'd ever spent with her had been in a Bedouin tent, and he'd been tempted—tortured, really—by lying beside her. He wouldn't make that mistake again. He grabbed a pillow from the rug on the floor and went to the corner, where another rug was rolled up—the one Abdel used when Noah wasn't here. He spread it out, then set the pillow atop it. "I'll sleep here. You can take the other rug."

Her face was in shadow now and she stood still, unmoving for a moment. Then she set her bag on the floor and lay down without a word, turning her back to him.

She's not my concern.

I don't love her anymore.

He'd already made up his mind as to what he would do: if he lived through the next few weeks and reclaimed his name, he'd see what he'd have to do to divorce her. If their marriage had no legal standing before, he might not have to do anything. He would send her money for the child and maybe visit him a couple of times a year and that would be that. He had no desire to take the boy from his mother, and he would be a terrible father for an infant.

Even if the boy was his, he most likely already thought of Jack as his father. Jack could provide for them in ways that Noah never could, anyway.

She could live happily with Jack.

A few minutes of silence passed, and he heard her crying softly. He stared at the ceiling of the tent, blinking. Her tears had always had a way of provoking guilt. Two years hadn't changed that, it seemed.

"Do you need a handkerchief?" he asked after a moment. A neutral comment, not especially interested—*that's what's best.*

"No, thank you."

"All right then, good night."

He gritted his teeth. He needed to brush his teeth, actually—he was diligent about that. But if she was going to spend what little remained of the night sniveling, then he would face an enormous headache. A smoke might do him good, then he'd brush them.

He rose and crossed the tent toward the longest side of the tent panels, where a small table held a drawstring bag of hashish mixed with tobacco and a pipe. After lighting a candle, he prepared a pipe for himself, then lit it and sat back, closing his eyes as the smoke filled his mouth.

Ginger sat up and turned to face him. Wiping her cheeks, she scanned the tent, her eyes settling on him before they narrowed at the pipe. "You're smoking?" She raised a brow.

"Yes." He calmly took another drag. "I have headaches. Nightly. This helps."

"What is *this*, exactly?"

"Hashish."

She blinked at him, her expression dark. Then, like a lioness about to strike, she rose and crossed the space toward him. She snatched the pipe away, then dumped the burning contents out on the floor and stamped them out with her shoe. "Disgusting habit. You're more of a fool now than I thought."

He almost laughed. Her outrage was so typical for her. Taking his pipe back, he lifted the bag of hashish from the table. He'd just refilled it when she seized the bag. This time, she stalked toward the entrance to the tent, then pushed her way outside.

Noah sighed and followed her. She'd already wandered several feet away and stopped. Untying the drawstring, she scattered the contents to the sand and wind. Standing in the fading moonlight, the brilliance of the Egyptian night sky behind her, she looked breathtakingly beautiful, like a porcelain statue, trails of tears still wet on her cheeks.

He crossed his arms, stopping just behind her. "You do know I can get more."

"I know. But while I'm sharing your tent, you won't be smoking beside me."

The gesture, though done in anger, made his stomach flop strangely. He thought of Brother Wagner, then Nasira.

The last two people who had cared for him. And that had been well over a year earlier.

He'd spent so much time alone that he hardly remembered what it was like to answer to anyone other than himself. And not since they'd been together in Malta had he experienced the loving touch of a woman.

She turned to go back inside, and he caught her hand by the wrist, his grip firm.

Stiffening, she stopped, looking down at his hand. She said nothing, her brows forming an indent between them.

"I shouldn't have been so blunt earlier. I'm sorry."

Ginger lifted her eyes to his. "After you disappeared, I was certain I couldn't ever experience anything more painful than living in a world where you were dead." She swallowed hard, her eyes glistening with tears. "And now I know I was wrong. It's far, far worse to live in a world where you're alive but no longer love me."

Yanking her wrist out of his hand, she let out a tearful breath. Instead of going back to the tent, she strode further onto a sand dune, then sank down, drawing her knees to her chest and wrapping her arms around her legs. She buried her face against her knees, her head bowed in defeat.

Noah raked his fingers over his scalp, then halted. He'd forgotten he no longer had long hair, and the sensation was strange. Maybe he'd allow his hair to grow longer once again when this was over.

Go and sit with her, fool.

He hesitated.

"It's far, far worse to live in a world where you're alive but no longer love me."

Her words rang through his head, and his heart twisted. He knew that agony. He'd lived it, thinking that she no longer loved him. Only to find out that if he had just gone to her, perhaps he could have met his son a few months after he'd been born ... before she and Jack had lived as man and wife.

After a few minutes, he sighed, then went to her, dropping beside her. "There could be scorpions out here."

"I don't care." She didn't even budge, her voice weary.

He checked the sand behind him, then set his hands on the ground, leaning back on his arms. "September twenty-seventh last year, while you were bringing a new life into the world, I was at Tafas, near Damascus. There I not only witnessed one of the most horrific massacres of a civilian population, but then I killed more men in one day than I've ever killed before. We gave no quarter to the Turks. Took no prisoners. Shot the wounded, and those who surrendered."

She studied his profile but said nothing.

He'd never spoken about the events at Tafas, and he didn't know why he did now. Except that it had always been the way between them. She was an angel of mercy. He, a harbinger of death. Opposite in nearly every way. "It was a dream, Ginger. To think that we fit together. We don't. And we never did."

She set her chin on her knees, her eyes on the desert. "All right."

He did a double take.

She sat straighter. "If that's what you want, then so be it. I've already mourned you once, Noah. I don't know that I have the strength or desire to do it again. I came to Egypt to find you, and I did. I'd rather keep my good memories than to have this imposter you've become ruin them. I have no desire to spend my days running from police or trying to outwit a monster. All I want now is to find my sister, if she's here, and then go home to my son."

Even though he didn't quite know why, he struggled to find his own voice. "Then we agree."

"Yes ... yes. We agree. We can divorce or inquire if it's even necessary." She stood, then dusted herself off. "I'm going to sleep. If you need to smoke or whatever it is you do now, then I just ask you do it out here, where I don't have to breathe it."

Then she crossed the sand back toward the tent and disappeared from view.

There. That was amicable. The conversation needed to be had, and there was no reason to prolong this torture.

But if I no longer care, why is it torture at all?

* * *

GINGER DIDN'T SPEAK to Noah at all in the morning or on their horse ride back toward Giza, other than a nod or a shake of her head to answer his questions. He tried not to be affected by her silence—this was what they had both chosen. Separate lives, separate hearts.

But as they approached Millard Van Sant's home, only a mile from the Great Pyramid, Noah felt a tug of remorse. Should he have spent their time alone more wisely? It had been two years, and the only things he knew of her life during that time had been what little Alastair had shared, or she'd said to him during the haircut.

He chided himself. She was exiting his life once again. *None of that matters.*

He'd given her a burqa to wear, in order to cover that bright red hair and fair complexion, and he'd donned a disguise as well. They rode into the courtyard at Millard's house and were greeted by a servant who took the horse.

Noah led Ginger into the house, following the route he normally took—the servants's entrance, up the back staircase, then down the corridor into the library. Millard was the first to come into view, sitting in his favorite rocking chair. A large old sheepdog named Dirk sat at his feet. He immediately noticed Noah's arrival and pawed his way toward the door, tail wagging as he walked.

Jack and Alastair were further in the room, both standing, their backs to the door.

Noah leaned down to pat Dirk's gigantic head, receiving a slobbery swipe of a tongue as a response. Then he stopped short, looking beyond Alastair and Jack.

What on earth?

Seated in a chair in front of them, a blanket around her shoulders, was Ginger's sister, Lucy.

CHAPTER FORTY-FIVE

The stiffening of Noah's shoulders had alerted Ginger to the fact that someone surprising was here, but it took her several seconds before her brain seemed to fully comprehend that Lucy was, in fact, truly seated in the middle of Millard Van Sant's library. Of course, she had to assume that the elderly gentleman in the rocking chair *was* Van Sant, but she was more concerned about her sister than requesting a proper introduction.

"Lucy!" Ginger dashed past Noah, her heart in her throat. She removed her burqa and ran toward her, then embraced her, even though they'd parted practically as enemies. *But that doesn't matter now. At least she's not with Stephen.*

Lucy shrank in her seat before dissolving in tears against Ginger's chest, clinging to her. "Oh, Ginny ... I'm so sorry. So sorry." She trembled in Ginger's arms and wept.

With her back to the men in the room, Ginger couldn't gauge their expressions or reactions, but Alastair and Jack, closest to her, said nothing. She heard Noah speaking in Arabic in a low voice to, she assumed, Van Sant.

When Lucy had settled somewhat, Ginger pulled away and cradled her cheeks in her hands. "What happened? I was worried sick about you."

Lucy's eyes were red, her nose stuffy from crying. "You were right. About everything." She hiccupped, her eyes darting up as Alastair approached with a teacup. "Thank you so much," she said, taking it from him.

Ginger stood and looked from Alastair to Jack. She cringed at the bruising under Jack's eyes, the swelling of his nose. *Noah didn't show him any mercy, did he?*

Then again, he hadn't shown her any mercy, either.

"What happened? How did you find her?" She couldn't quite meet Jack's eyes. What must he think had transpired between her and Noah the previous night? She was more ashamed than ever of that kiss at Shepheard's. If her marriage with Jack was going to survive this episode, then she needed to think of him as her husband and ally and forget all else.

"We didn't find her. She found us," Jack said, crossing his arms. "She's got a story to tell, but maybe we should give you two some privacy? We can find another room to talk."

Ginger nodded. Wordlessly, the men started for the door. Ginger called, "Wait, Jack."

Jack paused, giving her a questioning look.

She hurried to him, then took his hand. Dropping her voice, she sidled closer. "I just want you to know you have nothing to be worried about. Nothing happened between Noah and me, and nothing will. We've come to an agreement about that."

Jack sucked his cheeks in and squeezed her hand. "We can talk about that later. But I'm glad you're safe. I didn't sleep much last night."

"I have my medical kit if you need more aspirin, by the way." She tapped the bag at her side.

That provoked a laugh from Jack. "That doesn't surprise me. There could be a fire, and somehow you'd find a way to bring that damned bag with you." He winked, then touched her cheek gently. "Sure, I'll take some aspirin soon." He left, closing the door behind him.

Lucy was watching with curiosity. "If Noah's alive, aren't you married to him?"

Ginger sighed and rejoined her, taking a seat on a chair beside her. "I don't really know. But it doesn't matter. Noah and I have moved on from each other, it seems. And it's for the best. But"—she reached for Lucy's hand—"all of that isn't important now. What happened to you? Alastair's been sending men everywhere in Egypt to search for you—no one could find a trace of you."

Lucy's lips puckered. "I ..." She looked down at her hands, her eyes closing as color crept up her neck. "By now, I think you know I ran away to be with Stephen."

"Yes, I heard." Ginger tried to keep any tone of judgment from her voice.

Lucy looked up, her gaze directed out the large bright window nearest to them. "When we were all at Penmore, Stephen and I started talking, and then he—he came and visited me late at night. We made love and ... *Ginny* ..." Lucy squeezed her eyes shut. "I'd experienced nothing like it. I thought I was in love with him."

Much as Ginger didn't want to imagine that, she felt a pang of sorrow for her sister. Wrong as she'd been, Lucy had never experienced falling in love, nor genuine romance. She had to assume Lucy hadn't told this part of her story to Alastair and Jack.

"He asked me some questions while we were lying together afterward—I thought it wasn't terribly important—just about Papa and whether I'd ever seen him bring any antiquities through the house in Cairo. I told him I had, and he asked if I ever knew what became of them. And then he mentioned casually that if I ever remembered or learned if those objects had gone to William, he'd very much like to see them. He said he was interested in buying them."

Ginger rolled her tongue against the roof of her mouth, trying to keep herself from interrupting. She had a feeling this had something to do with whatever treasure hunt Noah was flaunting in front of Stephen. Maybe she should have taken the time to ask more about the details of that the night before, but she'd been too irritated to show interest.

"Anyway, we parted, and after everyone had gone and Penmore was sold—"

"William sold Penmore so quickly?"

"Yes." Lucy gave Ginger a baffled look. "Didn't you know? Jack bought it."

Jack bought Penmore?

Her lips parted. This was one reaction she couldn't control. *When? How? And why hadn't he told her?*

Lucy saw Ginger's shock and wrinkled her nose with remorse. "I hope I didn't ruin the surprise. He bought all the contents too. Said he wanted to preserve our family's home for you and Alexander."

Oh my God.

Now she really felt guilty about that kiss with Noah. And more than that. The instant Noah had appeared, she'd stopped thinking of Jack as her husband, her heart leaping to return to Noah.

Jack's angry scolding from the night before rang in her mind. *"Our lives together can't be so easily dissolved as shaking hands and going our separate ways. You owe me a conversation, at the very least."*

She certainly *had* owed him a conversation.

"Go on," she said, distractedly, rubbing her fingertips along her forehead.

"Anyway." Lucy exhaled, dabbing her eyes with a handkerchief. "Once Penmore had been sold, I felt so alone. So desperate. Stephen had told me that Victoria was half mad and that he was going to divorce her soon. And I thought he loved me. So I took what little money I had and bought a passage to Cairo so that I could surprise him here. He'd given me a means to contact him about that antiquities question, and I thought he would look forward to my arrival. Only..."

Ginger nearly sighed, the reality of Lucy's situation making sense at last. Stephen must have gone to Penmore *only* to find out about those antiquities, and Lucy had been a means to an end. "Only, he wasn't happy to see you."

"No." Lucy sniffed, her eyes shining and red. "No, he wasn't. He seemed angry that I'd come empty-handed. He said he didn't have need for another mistress and no use for a married woman who couldn't help him."

"But it's been weeks—where have you been in the meantime?" Lucy wasn't exactly the type of woman who knew how to survive. She had no skills and little experience outside of her cushioned life.

"I didn't have any money." Lucy wiped her eyes. "And I asked Stephen if he would lend me some, so that I could return, but he said no. Said he'd lent enough money to the Braddock clan, and he'd seen nothing back from it. He said if I was going to earn my passage back to England, then I needed to *work* for it first."

Rage filled Ginger as she looked at her sister. *Stephen had prostituted her?*

Oh, God. She wanted to cut his heart out of his chest.

Lucy caught the look on Ginger's face and held out a hand. "I didn't know what that meant at first, and then when I understood, I told him I wouldn't. But then he wouldn't let me leave, wouldn't allow me to call anyone or do anything. I was terrified. So I told him I would pay off my debt to him and him alone."

Ginger suppressed a shudder. Her poor sister.

"The man is evil incarnate, Lucy. Even if he accepted that, I can't imagine anything you've gone through has been easy."

"It's been horrible." Lucy sobbed, broken. "I'm such a fool. You told me what he was, but I wouldn't listen. And I did my best to make him think I was still besotted with him, telling him how happy I was that we were together and had come around to the idea of me being his mistress, because I thought that might help protect me, but he's repulsive."

"It probably helped protect you on some level. Stephen's arrogance can get the best of him." Ginger scooted her chair closer to Lucy and wrapped one arm around her shoulder.

Lucy wiped her nose. "Anyhow, once he heard you were in Cairo, it was all he could talk about. He's as obsessed with you as you said he was. And then, when he heard you were having a masquerade at Shepheard's, he decided he needed to be there, even if he wasn't invited. So he rented a room at the hotel and he took me there with him last night."

Ginger shrank at the thought of Stephen there, watching her. Had he seen Noah? Goose bumps rose on her skin.

"Last night, he was like a man possessed. Then he returned from the dance in the middle of it, saying he'd seen you go into the garden. He hadn't got a good look, because Jack was there, but he'd heard whispers someone had spotted you in an indiscreet moment with another man. And he was sure it was Noah. Then he immediately left, and, in his distraction, he left me unattended." Lucy sniffled again, her tears still flowing.

She might have guessed that Stephen would be there.

Both Noah and I were completely reckless. Though maybe something good had come from their recklessness, if Lucy was here.

"I didn't know how long I had, so I ran out of the room, even though I only had this nightgown." Lucy gestured to her outfit. Ginger had hardly noticed it under the blanket draped over her shoulders. They'd need to find her something to wear right away. "I ran to the ball, stole a mask that had been left unattended on a table, then went to the coatroom and helped myself to a coat."

Ginger raised a brow, impressed by her sister's resourcefulness.

"You showed some quick thinking. Why didn't you come and find me immediately, though?"

"I wanted to, but I was afraid that Stephen was keeping such a close watch on you that he'd see me, too. So I waited outside the hotel on the terrace until I saw you leave. Then I tried to follow on foot, as best I could. But I got hopelessly lost. A few hours later, I saw several police cars heading in one direction, and it occurred to me it could all have to do with Noah. So I followed and waited outside the house until they'd gone. Then I knocked on the door, and Captain Taylor answered."

To think that Lucy had probably been around the corner of the house when Ginger and Noah had fled from it the night before. She'd shown an impressive amount of courage and shrewdness—more than Ginger had given her credit for. But Ginger didn't doubt that it would take a very long time for her to overcome the trauma of the last few weeks.

Ginger rubbed her shoulder, comforting her. "You're here now and you're safe. The men are working on a plan to see that Stephen faces consequences for his reign of terror in our lives, but in the meantime we'll see to taking care of you. Starting with getting you a bath and proper clothing. I'm surprised Alastair didn't fetch you anything out of my wardrobe."

"We didn't stay there long. Jack was afraid Lord Helton might make some excuse to see either of them arrested. So we came here instead."

All things considered, Jack was right to be cautious. It also likely meant that they'd taken care to come here unseen.

Ginger spent a few more minutes trying to console Lucy before she left her to find Jack and see what accommodations they could make for her sister. She found him in the dining room with Alastair and Noah, who appeared to be arguing. She held back a few feet from the doorway, watching them.

Jack was nearest to the entrance, sitting back lazily—as he often did—his long legs stretched in front of him. Normally, his posture was accompanied by a look of wry humor, but he wasn't smiling now.

Noah stood at the other end of the table, both hands on the surface, leaning forward. "This is precisely what I forbade, Alastair. You went flagrantly against my wishes."

"Your wishes be damned. You're going to get yourself killed just to spite Jack? No, I won't allow it. Just thank him and be done with it. Your pride has nothing to do with this. So long as the result is the same, the means shouldn't matter." Alastair dusted his shoulders as though to show his finality about the subject.

"Well, there's nothing to be done about it now, my boy." Van Sant entered the scene, edging closer to Noah. He'd been out of sight, but he appeared to have been quietly listening in. "If Jack has already sent emissaries to purchase the cotton, what's done is done. I think it's a brilliant plan, to be honest."

Noah scowled at Van Sant. "No. Not this way." He turned his attention to Jack, narrowing his eyes. "Call the men off."

Jack shrugged. "What if I happen to be in the market for cotton right now?"

"At three times its value? Don't be imbecilic. Call it off, Jack. I want no more favors from you."

"I don't think I will."

Noah pounded his fists on the table in frustration. "Goddammit, Jack. There's nothing humorous about this. If I succeed in this, I don't want it to be because of Jack Darby. I don't want to live with that for the rest of my life. Maybe it's pride, yes, but that's all I have left and very little of it. So please ..." Noah's voice nearly broke. "Call the sale off."

Ginger moistened her dry lips, a thick lump in her throat. Jack's words played in her head: *We're never going to be friends again, Red. He will never forgive me ...*

Jack set his hands on his face, then shook his head. "Even if I sent riders out after the men we dispatched this morning, there's no way they'll catch up to them. Just let it go. I'll stay out of your way from here on out."

Poor Jack. Yet again, helping an ungrateful Noah. Her ire at Noah increased as she watched Jack's handsome face, worn with sadness and consternation. A feeling of loyalty to Jack flared within her. *I do love him.* He'd been wonderful to her. If Noah couldn't get over his childish pride and understand what a staunch friend Jack had been, then she had a straightforward answer as to who was the better man for her, anyway.

The current between the two men seemed more charged than ever, and Ginger cleared her throat and stepped forward, knocking on the open door with the back of her knuckle. "Pardon me ... Mr. Van Sant, is it?" She breezed toward him, hand outstretched. "I'm trying to inquire if I could send someone into Cairo for some clothes for my sister."

Van Sant kissed the back of her hand. "I believe Captain Taylor has already made arrangements. The clothes will be taken to the room where your sister slept within the hour."

Ginger gave Alastair a grateful look. "Thank you, Alastair."

"I sent for clothes for you too," he answered with a nod. "How is she?"

"Shaken, and I should probably return to her. If you're in the market for someone to go and shoot Stephen Fisher, I'll happily apply."

Alastair chuckled. "I think we'd all gladly do that, so long as we could guarantee it wouldn't ruin Noah's chance at a pardon." He sighed wearily. "No, what I'm in the market for is someone who can convince Stephen and Lord Helton to invest in Van Sant and Omar Hassan's dig. Pity he doesn't trust any of us."

She couldn't look at either Jack or Noah, growing uncomfortably aware of them looking at her. "That is too bad. I'd volunteer to convince him, but I think he'd do the exact opposite of what I suggest." She started for the door.

"Although ... he may yet trust your sister," Alastair said.

Ginger tensed and gave him a sharp look over her shoulder. "Meaning?" Much as she liked Alastair, he was a schemer, too. He seemed to possess the ability to think like a criminal at times, sometimes scarily so.

"Meaning that she could be useful." Alastair's gaze was thoughtful, and he looked at Jack. "What if your purchase of that cotton was a touch more *personal*? That you made it very clear it was you trying to undercut him?"

Noah seemed to have already caught on to what Alastair was suggesting, while Ginger felt she was trying to leap ahead to understand. "I hardly think it fair to ask anything of the girl. She's naïve and inexperienced. One crack in her resolve and we could all be ruined."

"I'm not so sure about that. She's shown she's resilient." Alastair drummed his fingers on the tabletop. "And she's the only one among us that could work as a double agent."

Is Alastair suggesting we send Lucy back to Stephen?

Ginger turned fully now, holding up her hands. "Gentlemen, please. My sister is not a pawn in this game of yours."

"Aye, she may be more like a queen if we're comparing her to chess pieces. She can move stealthily, in multiple directions," Alastair said.

"Ironic. I'd think she would be more like a knight, only capable of moving in an *L* shape, like her name," Jack mused, his lips turning up in a smile.

"Jack, stop it." She shot him a hard look. Then she stepped toward Alastair. "This is non-negotiable. She just escaped that monster. She is not going back, even if it's to help destroy him in the long run."

"Not just destroy him, dearest. There's so much good that will come if we can see Stephen Fisher and Lord Helton face justice." Van Sant spoke up at last, his voice earnest and gentle. "Including clearing Benson's name from the hideous tarnish they placed upon it."

"If Lucy could go to Stephen, tell him she left us only to spy on us and gain his favor, she can do two things." Alastair held up one finger. "Tell him that Jack intends to purchase cotton from the farmers he'd secured last year—and outbid him."

Alastair lifted his second finger. "Then she can say Jack is meeting with Omar Hassan and Van Sant tomorrow in the morning, to see about investing in the dig. All she has to say is that Jack wants to ruin Stephen and has a personal vendetta against him. That Jack's been busy trying to discover what Stephen is up to and then plans to come along like a thief and usurp his business. When the cotton sale turns out to be true, he'll panic and assume he's about to lose the dig too."

The room was quiet, all the men staring at her. She had to admit it wasn't a half-bad plan. "Except for the fact that your plan involves risking my sister," Ginger said with a ludicrous guffaw. "She's terrified, Alastair. We could never ask such a thing of her. It would not only be wrong but immoral to do that to a woman who's been badly used by that demon—I couldn't live with myself."

"It may be the only way," Alastair countered.

Ginger appealed to Jack with wide eyes. "Jack, please. Convince Alastair this is a horrid idea."

"It's not the idea that's horrible, Red. The truth is—"

"Oh, God, not you too." She looked in Noah's direction, though she didn't meet his gaze. But she knew just where to hit him too. *At least, what would have moved him before all this.* "Noah? Are you all right with this? Putting an innocent woman at risk in order to save yourself?"

Before Noah could answer, a soft voice came from behind her. "I'll do it."

Ginger whirled around to see Lucy come into the room, the blanket wrapped around her like a shawl. "Lucy, no."

Lucy's face was still puffy from crying, but she lifted her chin. "I didn't hear everything, but I think I heard enough. And if you need my help in order to destroy Stephen, then I'll gladly do it."

CHAPTER FORTY-SIX

The door to the Van Sant's stable swung open, and Noah glanced up from the stall where he was brushing his horse's coat. Resheph stamped his feet in awareness of the trespasser, his ears pricking forward. A moment later Ginger darted inside, then slammed the door shut behind her.

She didn't appear to see him; her hands were clenched in fists at her sides, her brow knitted. She was obviously vexed. Noah doubted she would have come in here if she knew he, too, had fled to the relative privacy the stable provided. The stable was a good walk from the house, sheltered by fencing and guards to keep out intruders.

He said nothing, watching as she paced and took calming breaths. Returning to the smooth strokes he made with the brush, Noah frowned. He understood her frustration. Jack, Alastair, and Van Sant had overruled both of them. Noah had been so angry that he'd left before her, coming here to calm himself by grooming Resheph.

She must have finally given up as well.

Ginger went a few stalls away, toward where Millard's white nag had looked out in curiosity at her, and she patted its whiskery nose. "I wish I had an apple or a carrot for you," Ginger said. "But, sadly, I've come empty-handed."

"Hatshepsut likes bananas," Noah said in a low voice, not looking up from his work.

Her sharp intake of breath was indicator enough that he'd startled her, and she didn't respond. After a minute, she came toward his stall and peered over the gate. "You might have announced you were here, rather than frightening me."

"I just did." Noah met her gaze, a smile on his lips. "But, my apologies, milady. Next time I'll ring a little bell and tell you you're not alone."

"Oh, stop it." She scowled, then pushed the gate open, coming inside with him. "I can't believe you're letting them just take over everything you've planned the last year. You've got to put a stop to it. Risking my sister is ludicrous. She's not thinking straight right now."

Finishing with the coat, Noah set his brush on a wooden bench near the door and grabbed a pick. He lifted one of Resheph's front hooves and cleaned it. "If it were that simple, I would have put a stop to it. You heard me arguing in there, didn't you?"

"Yes, but—"

"But they've made up their minds. That's the problem with involving others. Your opinion diminishes considerably, especially when other people—like Millard—have something at stake."

Ginger crossed her arms, huffing angrily. "What's he have at stake? I can't understand why he's involved at all."

Noah nodded toward the brush. "Hand me that brush, will you?"

She lifted it and brought it to him.

"Millard's passion is Egypt. Its archeology, its customs, its people, its preservation."

"But he's not even Egyptian."

"True, but he still cares deeply for this land. It's his adopted homeland. His wife is Egyptian, his children are all half-Egyptian, and he'll die here. He's long been an advocate for keeping Egypt's treasures in Egypt, and he sympathizes with the nationalists who feel so betrayed by the British government. Men like Lord Helton are exactly the type of vultures Millard has been battling against for years, who take greedily from the land, impoverishing the locals through the broken system of colonialism."

Ginger wearily sat on the bench near the gate. "Proving Lord Helton's guilt won't stop all that, though, Noah. Surely, he must know that."

"Sometimes fighting injustice means being at peace with accepting one small win at a time. Stopping the smuggling ring that Helton has been operating for years would be a victory, whether it ends the British protectorate in Egypt or not. Besides"—Noah picked a small pebble from Resheph's hoof—"the Egyptian people have found their own voice. I don't think this Wafd movement is going anywhere. The war only made it clearer to the peasants that the British didn't have their interests at heart."

"The British haven't been *all* bad." Ginger frowned. "They've helped in several ways, too. Shouldn't the good be recognized along with the bad?"

"It should, but life isn't a utopia. Emotions aren't always logical. Sometimes it's necessary to forget about the good, just to survive." Noah brushed the hoof he'd just cleaned, his throat tightening. Inadvertently, he'd switched topics, and she was clever enough to know it.

"Like you forcing yourself to hate me?" Her voice was empty and quiet.

Hate her?

He set Resheph's hoof down and held Ginger's gaze. "I don't hate you."

"You just don't love me." She twisted her skirt onto one fingertip, her voice sounding empty.

He watched her hands, feeling a tug at his heart. He'd noticed immediately the previous evening that the wedding rings he'd given her were gone. She wore no replacement, but she'd taken them off. That was a bold statement.

"Or worse," she said quietly, "you're indifferent. Which is harder still because it means you feel nothing toward me."

She stood again, then stretched, setting her hand on the small of her back, arching forward. A maternal stretch that he imagined she might have done when she'd been pregnant.

The thought nearly undid him. He didn't have to use his imagination to think of her naked body, but the idea of her belly, round and swollen with their child, was a state in which he'd never seen her. If he had, he might have worshiped at her feet, wrapping his arms around her hips at the wonder of her beauty.

But he'd missed it.

He'd missed the birth of their son. While she'd been doing God's beautiful work, bringing life into the world, his world had been cloaked with murder and filth.

He'd missed the sight of her nursing their son.

Then his ugly words to her the previous night hurtled back toward him, burning his ears, throat, and eyes with acerbic cruelty and self-awareness.

He'd been wrong all along. She'd done what she had to do to survive. And he'd treated her as though she'd taken every good and beautiful thing that had existed between them and trampled it with glee.

I'm the fool.

How could Jack *not* fall in love with her? She was an angel. Not only gorgeous, but tenacious and clever. Headstrong to a fault but willing to change and learn from her mistakes. Loyal and fierce.

Her desirability was even the one thing that he and Fisher could agree upon, disgusting as the thought was.

He set Resheph's hoof down, then put the brush on the ground.

"Ginger."

She tilted her head to the side, her eyes locking with his. "Yes?"

"I just wanted ... needed to say—"

The door to the stable opened, and Jack ventured inside. "Ginger, are you in here?"

Ginger turned away from Noah, exiting the stall. "I'm right here." She crossed her arms, her anger flickering back. "Are you done trying to ruin Lucy's life?"

Jack grimaced and came forward hesitantly. "Please try not to think of it that way." He stopped short as he noticed Noah in the stall, his gaze darting toward Ginger.

Noah looked away, the intimacy of the space gone, his heart beating painfully. He lifted the pick and started on Resheph's other hoof.

"How else am I to think about it, Jack? You want to send Lucy back for a full night with that despicable demon. Who knows what he'll do to her? And if he doesn't believe her, he will kill her."

"Not a full night. We've refined the thing." Jack glanced back at Noah once again, clearly uncomfortable with his presence. "She says they've been primarily staying on a boat. You'll never guess which."

Ginger looked up sharply. "The *Cursed Valley*?"

Jack smiled. "Victoria was right. And it's docked in a grove on the Nile—Lucy knows where. That's most likely where Fisher is, but we don't want to risk him setting sail before we lure him out to witness me meeting with Millard and the man Alastair has found to impersonate Hassan."

Ginger didn't answer, her arms still crossed, and Jack took a few steps further inside. "So, we thought we'd set up the meeting on the terrace of Shepheard's tomorrow. Lucy will go in the morning to the boat, tell Stephen about what she's learned, and—if we're right—Stephen will already know that I've stolen his cotton sale out from under him and be furious. We're hoping he'll leave immediately to put a stop to my stealing his opportunity to invest in the dig, and then you and Noah can make a show of 'rescuing' a very reticent-to-leave Lucy from the boat. That way, Noah can be seen at the same time as the meeting."

Noah hated the fact that it wasn't a poor plan. In fact, it had merit. *No wonder Millard wants to do it.* But Ginger was also right—the risk to Lucy was still grave. And to them all if Fisher learned they were trying to use Lucy against him.

"The time Lucy will be with Fisher is reduced significantly, then?" Noah asked quietly. Talking to Jack directly at all was painful and strange, but he'd involved himself so much in Noah's affairs now that he had no other choice.

"Yes, hopefully only a few minutes, if we're lucky. An hour, if Fisher is slow to action."

Ginger's eyes flashed at Jack with anger. "If it were your sister, would you risk it?"

"No, but—"

"But nothing." Any calm Ginger had found in the stable had dissolved. "I don't know whom I'm angrier with—Alastair for coming up with this idiotic idea or you for not supporting me. I'm your w-wife," she finished flatly.

Oomph. Ginger's words hung in the charged air like a current and Noah slunk back, closer to Resheph. *This is what I agreed upon. What I told her I wanted.* He was the interloper now, intruding on a marital spat with his presence.

Setting the brush on the ground, he slipped out the other side of the stall, locking it behind him as he strode away and into the mid-afternoon heat.

Will I ever be truly able to accept a world where she's his and not mine?

He'd spent the last year doing it, but it hadn't been easy. Seeing her now only made everything he'd buried bubble to the surface—so much so that he could hardly remember why he'd ever believed he should give up and leave her and Jack to be a family.

Noah's own father had killed himself with grief when his mother had been murdered, leaving Noah and his younger brother as orphans. Maybe in time his father would have accepted that she was gone, but when faced with a future without her, his reaction had been strong and visceral—he'd rather have no life at all.

Is that what I've been doing?

The life he'd been living had been reduced to a singular purpose: to take his revenge and reclaim his name. But it wasn't a life, really. There was no joy in it, no love. And once he'd accomplished his purpose, what would he do with himself then?

He wouldn't marry again. He had no desire for anyone else but her.

And even if their marriage wasn't legal, it had been valid in the eyes of God, hadn't it?

No wife meant no family. With his brother dead and his friendship with Jack gone, the chance of feeling part of a family was further reduced. He could do something like Alastair and raise his own troop of orphans, but Alastair had spent years gathering the funds and resources for something like that.

Meanwhile, his wife and his son would be with Jack.

The soft crunch of earth behind him alerted him to the fact that someone had followed.

He turned, praying he could control his temper, and found Jack a few feet away.

"She told me earlier she's choosing to be with me. And I won't try to talk her out of it—she doesn't deserve to feel like neither of us wants her now—but I wouldn't be a very good friend if I didn't ask you what the hell you're doing."

"I'm uncertain you meet the requirements of a very good friend, Jack." Even as Noah said the words, he felt the resentment and hurt curl up from deep within him. And a fresher and deeper emotion, too—guilt. That Jack claimed to have married Ginger out of friendship to him. That he'd cared for his wife when she'd needed it the most. That Jack would spend the money to buy that cotton—a losing investment for him—without hesitation. He didn't want to owe Jack anything else.

"No? You asked me to take care of her, remember? I did what I did because I was—and still am—your friend. And I love her, Noah. I couldn't help that. It's killing me to force myself to even have this conversation with you. It would be so much easier to pretend she would rather be with me. I want her to be with me. But I won't stand in your way either, and she knows that. And now you do too. I couldn't live with myself if I didn't tell you."

Noah's shoulders bunched, and he tried not to look at the bruising on Jack's face, from the savage punch Noah had unleashed the night before. An obvious sign of how very affected he was by this. *And more to feel guilty about.*

Jack pointed back to the stable. "You want that woman? You're going to have to go and get her. You should be *begging* her to be with you. And if you don't want her, then you're the biggest goddamn fool I've ever met."

Then Jack walked away, as quietly as he'd come.

Noah watched him go, hardly able to breathe.

He hadn't been able to admit to himself why he'd been unable to stay away from Shepheard's the night before ...

... or why he'd kissed her.

I won't let myself admit it.

Admitting it was like a burning poker thrust through his lungs and heart.

If he walked away from his wife and son, all because of misunderstanding and pride, then he would be to blame for all the pain he'd gone through the last year. He had failed them both. All the hope he'd crushed and the life he'd thrown away had lain like a wounded soldier on the sands of Tafas, hands outstretched, begging for mercy.

Instead of bestowing it, he'd aimed true and pulled the trigger.

Just as he'd done to the heart of the woman he loved.

CHAPTER FORTY-SEVEN

The Nile River sparkled in the light of the early morning, beckoning with its beauty, but Ginger faced the day with an increasing feeling of dread. Riding along beside her in the covered carriage, Lucy wore the coat that she'd stolen from Shepheard's earlier, and she shivered despite the warm air.

Lucy had directed them to the place where the *Cursed Valley* was docked, which turned out to be along the riverbank, in a local fishing dock tucked near a grove of palms. Though there were other boats and small fishing vessels nearby, there wasn't much human activity yet and Noah had ordered his man to stop the carriage while they were still at a distance.

"You can still change your mind, Lucy. You don't have to do this," Ginger said, ignoring Noah watching them, across from her. Jack and the others were already at Shepheard's, leaving her an unwitting participant in this madness. Even if Noah didn't approve, he appeared to have resigned himself to it and had offered no further protest.

Just like everything else—the fire I knew in him is gone.

Noah would have fought against this before, if she'd asked him to. Now, she would have to fight alone.

The night at Millard Van Sant's house had been a strange one of preparation, quiet whispers, and awkward encounters. Noah had even taught Lucy how to fire a gun. Ginger had opted to stay in Lucy's room for the night, which may have been the strangest thing of all. She hadn't spent the night in the same room as Lucy since she was a young girl, and it reminded Ginger of how much she'd missed in her younger sister's life.

Whereas Lucy had been brash and outspoken before, she was penitent and withdrawn now. She listened to the instructions Jack, Alastair, and Noah gave her with care, like a studious pupil, but saying little.

Her teeth chattering, Lucy gripped Ginger's hand. "It's just— harder now that we're so close to Stephen again." She shook her head. "What if I can't do it? If I can't convince him? I might fail, and everyone is counting on me."

The pressure Lucy must feel was enormous.

"No one will blame you if you don't." Ginger squeezed her hand. "It was brave of you to offer, but they'll think of something else."

Lucy closed her eyes, resolve filling her face. "No. This needs to end, sooner rather than later. Before he hurts anyone else."

"If I may, Lucy," Noah said, leaning toward her. He looked handsome in his trousers and loose white cotton shirt, a fact that Ginger was trying hard not to notice. "The Whitman women are among the bravest, most resilient that I've met. You're entirely capable of anything you choose to do. And we can have you on a ship to England by nightfall, if all goes according to plan."

That was kind of him, considering how little Noah had cared for her sister. *Then again, she's saving his plans.*

"Yes, but—" Lucy's eyes filled with regret. "What about after? What am I supposed to do then? Go back, hat in hand, to William and tell him I was with Stephen for weeks? I suppose my life is over anyway. There's no reason for me to really be afraid."

"William loves you. You might find he's willing to forgive what you view as unforgivable. Love has a way of doing that. It just takes courage."

Ginger stared at Noah's face, her mouth going dry. *Just like you forgave me?* She wanted to rebuke him, call him a liar, but he didn't look at her, his gaze entirely focused on Lucy.

"No one is making you go back to William, either." Ginger held back the bitter tone that wanted to come forward. "Though there's a great deal to consider—carefully—unlike your hasty marriage. William hasn't been honest with you, either." Now it was her turn to feel Noah's eyes on her.

Yes, I'm speaking to you, too, Noah.

Lucy dipped her chin, then straightened her shoulders. She gave Ginger a tense smile. "Wish me luck, Ginny. And if I fail, please forgive me. For everything."

Noah's man, Abdel, who had been driving the carriage, opened the carriage door and let Lucy out. Without a backward glance, she started toward the dock, her head held high.

Ginger waited until she'd gone about twenty feet, then she wrapped a headscarf around her hair. "I'm going to follow at a distance. See that she makes it to the boat."

"Ginger, you could be seen." Noah scrambled behind her, grabbing her by the elbow. "This is in the open."

Ginger pulled her arm away. "She's my sister and I'm going. And if you'd like to stop me, then get out of this carriage and stop me. Risk being seen yourself. That's of utmost importance to you now. Your pride, your name, your scheme that's hinging on the back of an injured woman. But, if you're unwilling, get out of my way."

Unsurprisingly, Noah released her arm, his eyes troubled. Ginger raced forward, past Abdel, trying to keep Lucy in her sights. She kept a rapid pace, not daring to look back at Noah. It wouldn't take long for him to see what she was doing, and, if she timed it poorly, he might just try to stop her again.

She closed the gap between her and Lucy before she was in sight of the boat, then took her by the elbow.

Lucy gasped, turning to look at Ginger with alarm. "Ginny, what are you—"

"As though I'd let you get within ten feet of that man alone." Ginger pressed a gun into her sister's hand not a moment too soon. "Point the gun at my back and keep walking. I'm going to be your hostage. We're almost there, yes?"

"But this isn't what we planned." Lucy pressed her lips together nervously, the gun limp in her hand.

"Then improvise. Tell Stephen you've brought me to him. I'll play along." Ginger squinted into the sun, the standing water near the docks stinking of rot and refuse. "That's the boat?" she asked, gesturing with her head as the largest boat moored to the dock came into view. She didn't see the name on it. A massive Egyptian man was loading a crate up the gangplank.

Lucy paled and nodded.

"Look confident. And hurry, before Noah can catch up to us." At least, the Noah she'd known would be relentless in trying to stop her. Enraged with her, even.

The Noah I know now may not even care.

Lucy tightened her grip on the pistol, then held Ginger's arm awkwardly by the elbow. She didn't know how to escort someone at gunpoint, but Ginger couldn't blame her for that. They had barely reached the gangplank when a shadow leaned against the rail, looking down at them from the boat.

The sun was directly behind Stephen and Ginger couldn't make out his features, which was disconcerting in a way she couldn't explain. "Well, well, well. This is a surprise," Stephen said, straightening.

No matter what bravado Ginger tried to show with the man,

every time she saw him, a slick feeling of sweat broke out across her back. A shiver went through her.

"You said you wanted me to be useful. Here I am. Being useful." Lucy released Ginger's elbow, setting her hand on her hip. Amazingly, she sounded much more confident than Ginger had expected her to, scarily so.

"Lucy, please." Ginger turned toward her, doing her best to sound terrified, though it wasn't too hard, given that she was in the presence of someone who truly frightened her. "Please don't do this."

The sound of Stephen's footsteps coming down the gangplank made Ginger flinch, and Lucy smiled smugly. "I told you, darling. I'll do anything you want. And you wanted Ginny, so I got her for you." She smiled prettily at Stephen, then sidled over to him, slipping her arms around his neck. "Aren't you proud of me?"

If Lucy really had been holding Ginger at gunpoint, then she would have done a terrible job of it—she'd lowered the gun already. Stephen knew Ginger well enough to believe she'd fight back, so she may as well pretend she was trying to do just that. The large Egyptian would likely stop her.

Quickly, Ginger darted forward, as though to jump into the water on the side of the dock. A solid wall of muscle blocked her, and Ginger fell back dazed.

The large Egyptian man had stepped in front of her. He wrapped an arm around her, pulling her into an ironclad hold. Fear crept up her spine, any semblance of control slipping away. *I should have expected this.* "No, please," she said. This time the trembling of her voice wasn't feigned at all.

Stephen stepped closer. "Masud, take our guest up to one of the rooms." He turned toward Lucy, then dropped a kiss to her lips, taking the gun from her hands. "You've done well, darling. I'm very proud."

Lucy beamed at him as Masud lifted Ginger. She struggled

against him, clawing and trying to free herself—even screaming. That proved to be a mistake, as Masud's dirty hand clamped down over her mouth.

She'd brought a knife with her, strapped onto her thigh, but now she wished she'd brought another gun too. Lucy had given hers up already. It wouldn't have made sense if Ginger had been found with it, but she hadn't mentally prepared herself enough for the reality of being taken captive. All she'd known was that she couldn't send Lucy back here alone. Not after the harrowing experience she'd been through. This was more believable, anyway, and if necessary together they could devise a plan to get out of this.

... if he doesn't kill us both.

Please, God, let Noah still be watching.

He would be, wouldn't he? He wouldn't have just let her slip away sight unseen as he'd been prepared to do with Lucy.

He will. He'll follow.

Once aboard the boat, Masud carried Ginger to a sleeping quarter that felt more like a hovel, then tossed her onto a bed. Either he didn't know his own strength or he didn't care—the air was knocked out of Ginger's lungs and spots flashed in her vision as her eyes adjusted to the darker surroundings. The only light came from a small porthole, and the room was stuffy.

The door closed behind Masud, a lock sliding into place, and Ginger struggled to sit up.

The bed took up most of the space, and Ginger saw a trunk in the corner, with Lucy's initials embossed on the surface. This must have been the room where Stephen had kept Lucy all this time. She hadn't expected Lucy to be separated from her so quickly. But she had to trust in what she knew. Stephen didn't love Lucy, and he'd be far more preoccupied with Ginger's presence now. He'd pay less attention to her sister.

Shaken but undeterred, she hurried to the door and pounded on it. "Let me out of here," she cried, coating her voice with desperation.

Not all her apprehension was false though.

The last time she'd been taken captive by Stephen, he'd made quick work out of carving his initials in her chest. He was as unpredictable as he was brutal, and this could very well be a huge miscalculation on her part. But that had been her worry with this plan all along—Stephen had a way of doing the unexpected.

She hoped Jack wouldn't throttle her later, if she survived. He could be irascible, but she deserved his anger for this. *Of course, if he'd just been on my side and helped me stop this ridiculous plan, I wouldn't have felt the need to protect my sister.*

The door opened, and Ginger slunk back until the backs of her legs hit the bed. Stephen strolled in with Lucy on his arm, as though they'd just come in from a seaside stroll rather than the ugly scene that had occurred. A chilling thought struck Ginger: how very different it would be if Stephen had loved Lucy. They were similarly haughty. Would he have manipulated and twisted her to do his bidding if he hadn't used and hurt her?

"Lucy tells me she's been on quite an adventure." Stephen's ice-blue eyes roved over Ginger. "And I'm eager to hear more. I'm especially interested to learn just how it is you convinced Benson to share you with his closest friend. I can't fault you for your proclivities. You always had an appetite for sensual pleasure, didn't you?"

"You ignorant maggot. I thought Noah was dead—as everyone did—until a few nights ago. He's betrayed and abandoned me." Ginger rubbed the backs of her arms. "Please, Stephen—just let me go. You have Lucy and she loves you. You don't need to keep me here. Aren't you exhausted from all this?"

"Exhausted of what, precisely? I have a foothold in every major industry and export of this country, beautiful women at my beck and call, and the wealth to do anything I want."

Ginger resisted the urge to roll her eyes. *Yes, your power is most impressive.* But Stephen wouldn't be amused by her defiance. For now, it would be better to bide her time, let Lucy relay what she'd learned, and catch him off guard later by being calm.

I simply need to remember to stay calm and wait. Noah will help soon.

"Ginny's always shown a strange distaste for money, darling." Lucy left Ginger's side and approached the bed, then sat on it with ease. She was doing a marvelous job acting, Ginger had to admit. "She proved long ago that she preferred a common life. But she's telling the truth about Benson. Ginny ran off with him again, and now Darby is walking around with a broken nose—I think they brawled. So disgraceful."

Maybe Lucy is selling this a little too well.

Stephen quirked a brow. "Darby and Benson at odds? How delightful."

Ginger looked away. Even though Lucy was embellishing for her story, the comment struck Ginger through the chest. She wished she could pretend Noah and Jack were still friends and allies, but that was far from the truth. Noah hardly looked at either of them, growing sullener and more silent as the previous evening had passed.

She had the feeling that Noah wanted nothing more than for all of this to be over so he could remove himself from any association with them. Her heart hurt for Alexander, who didn't even know he'd been so summarily rejected by his father.

"Yes, it's especially awful of Ginny, given how much money Jack has spent on trying to win her favor." Lucy leaned back on the pillows as though it were an expensively furnished divan rather than a sparsely outfitted bed. "He bought Penmore, and I even over-heard him saying something about investing in cotton and some promising dig in Luxor. All that and she still throws herself at Benson like a whore."

"You go too far, Lucy," Ginger shot in a hard voice. Lucy had been clever though, and Ginger appreciated how well she'd improvised, given how Ginger had switched everything on her at the last minute.

Stephen stiffened, a dark shadow crossing his face. "What do you mean, a dig at Luxor?"

"I don't know. I didn't get the details." Lucy shrugged, then examined her nails. "Darling, can we please go out tonight? I think I've earned an expensive dinner, yes?"

Stepping toward Ginger, Stephen narrowed his gaze at her. "What dig, Ginny?"

"I don't see what difference it makes to you."

Stephen's slap struck with such speed and ferocity that Ginger fell back dazed. An explosion of pain on her cheek followed and she held her face, this time her fright quite real.

Her ears rang as she held her throbbing cheek, her jaw already sore, and Stephen glowered down at her. "Don't be a little bitch, Ginny. You'll find I no longer have any patience for your antics. What dig is Darby investing in?"

Ginger drew herself up, mustering all the determination she could. "The one at KV61 that Millard Van Sant has been heading. Even now, Jack is meeting with Van Sant and the Egyptian archeologist at Shepheard's. And you want to know why?" She glared at Stephen. "Just so that you can't. You'll also find that the cotton farmers you were counting on selling their harvest to you this year have already sold to Jack. So maybe your position in Egypt isn't quite so secure after all."

Stephen lifted a hand to strike her again, and she covered her head.

The blow never came.

Instead, Stephen grabbed her by the hair, lifting her head with an agonizing yank, then caught her chin in his hand, forcing her to look at him. He stepped closer still. "Listen to me and listen closely, Ginny. If you think I'm unprepared to deal with you, you're very mistaken. You think I don't know that Benson's little bastard isn't at your aunt's home in Kensington? Your mother and aunt take him for a walk in the park every day. They put him to bed at seven each night."

A chill of terror snaked its way up from Ginger's gut, curling around her spine. *Alexander ...*

"I never leave myself exposed to my enemies or without resources. If you think Darby's pathetic attempts to sabotage my business dealings will do anything other than force me to retaliate, you're mistaken. And, as I hear, infants don't float too well in the Thames."

Oh, God. No.

God, please, no.

The very idea of it made her ill.

"You stay away from my son, Stephen," Ginger gritted through her teeth.

Stephen pushed her back onto the bed, then stalked away, slamming the door to the cabin behind him. Lucy instantly scrambled toward her, placing a shaking hand on Ginger's shoulder. "Oh, I've never seen him so angry. I think he would have killed me if I had been the one to tell him."

Covering her mouth, Ginger choked back a cry.

Maybe she had spared her sister from further harm ...

... maybe.

But instead she'd put the target on someone far more precious to her.

Tears slipped out from her eyelids.

What have I done?

CHAPTER FORTY-EIGHT

The minute Fisher had disembarked from the boat, Noah had found his way onto it.

Noah had been forced into the water in order to climb onto the boat while there was still a line available to use. He'd intended to follow in a rowboat with Ginger if necessary, but now Abdel was in the rowboat, watching at a distance, and Noah had squeezed himself into a crevice in the hull with the boat's anchor, waiting while he surveyed what he might be up against. What was worse, the boat had now set sail.

It had taken every ounce of restraint in Noah's body not to go after Ginger immediately, but she'd been clever enough to disguise her intentions until the last moment. If he'd intervened too quickly, it could have proved deadly for them both.

Why, why didn't she stay the course?

And, yet, it was also entirely unsurprising. He'd forgotten how determined she could be—sometimes to her own detriment—driven by her heart at times when her head needed to prevail.

I should have predicted this. I should have been prepared for her to do something like this.

What was worse, Noah couldn't trust Lucy not to switch sides once again. Who knew what had happened in the time he had been waiting here? Yet another failure on his part. Ginger had been in the hands of the man Noah had sworn he would never allow to touch her again.

There were at least six members of the crew that Noah had counted, not including that giant Egyptian that counted as two men. Noah could count on Abdel to follow at a safe distance, but they still outnumbered him seven to one. And he doubted either Ginger or Lucy were armed or, if they had been, that they still were.

He couldn't think about that. The further they got from Cairo, the more the risk to Ginger and Lucy grew. Isolated in the middle of the crocodile-infested waters of the Nile was not a good position to be in.

If it were nighttime, Noah could move with more stealth, but he didn't want to risk the wait.

When he was certain that none of the crew members were in sight, Noah slipped out from his hiding place. He was still soaked, his cold clothes clinging to his skin, and he unbuttoned his holster, wanting quick access to his gun. A gun wouldn't be his first choice of weapon for now, though. It would instantly announce his presence.

A knife would have to suffice.

He'd removed his shoes before climbing into the river and was grateful for that fact now—he could slip across the wooden deck boards soundlessly. He had one goal—to find where Ginger was and get her the hell off this boat.

He never should have allowed this plan to continue, not when Ginger had been so against it.

The boat was larger than Noah had expected it to be with spacious dimensions along the lines of the royal yacht *Britannia*—and it had an expensive and ultramodern motor. Unlike the *Dahabiya* houseboats and *felucca* sailboats, which relied on wind to make the passage up and down the Nile, the noisy motor helped reduce the time necessary for lengthy trips on the river. The thrum from the engine was both an ally and foe. It masked his movements, but it made it harder to hear.

Finding a small stairwell that led further into the hull, Noah hurried toward the sleeping quarters, hugging one side of the darkened corridor. He had nearly reached the room when he saw what looked like a potato sack in front of one door.

Then the sack moved.

Noah froze, realizing that it was a boy, no older than six, squatting and head hunched forward as he played jacks. To Noah's dismay, he lifted his head and looked straight at him.

Noah lifted his free hand in a slow, calming gesture, but the boy's eyes were fixed on the knife in Noah's other hand.

Then he cried out loudly, in Arabic, "He's here! He's here with me!"

Dammit.

Noah rushed toward the door, determined to shove the boy out of his way, but it opened and the large Egyptian filled the frame, his face dark. Just beyond him, further in the room were Ginger and Lucy.

They're alive, thank God.

The Egyptian repelled Noah with a sharp blow to his stomach, sending him crashing back against the wall behind him. Noah nearly vomited, pain searing through his gut as he doubled over, one arm clutching his abdomen. He wobbled, trying to stay upright, then stepped onto one of the sharp metal jacks and pulled his foot back.

The boy had taken off running down the corridor, and footsteps alerted Noah to the fact that other men were now coming in his place. The Egyptian slammed the door shut, closing himself inside with the women as Noah turned to face the new arrivals.

No point in a knife now.

Letting the knife fall with a clatter, Noah whipped his gun out from the holster, then fired four shots quickly. Both men fell flat.

A woman's scream followed.

"Stay away from her!" Noah recognized Lucy's voice. A soft moan followed, together with a *thump.*

Ginger.

Noah braced himself for impact and then kicked the door. Now would be an appropriate time for boots. The door boomed against his blow, shaking. Three more kicks and the door frame broke away, the door splintering inward.

Noah paused for a moment, trying to survey the scene. The Egyptian seemed to have cornered Ginger, his hands on her throat. Lucy lay on the floor, not moving. A sudden *woosh* of a blade slicing close to him forced him to duck.

One of the wounded men had come hurtling back and had menaced with a knife—maybe even the one Noah had lost. He tackled Noah, knife aimed at his face, and Noah lifted his hands to shield himself, losing his grip on the gun. They both tumbled to the floor, just past the broken doorway, struggling over the knife.

Out of the corner of his eye, Noah saw Ginger flailing. The Egyptian had lifted her from the floor, choking her. She gripped his forearm with one of her own and a knife was in her other hand, but she couldn't reach beyond his elbow as his arms were significantly longer than hers. Whether he was choking her to force her to drop the knife or to suffocate her, Ginger had little time.

Noah tried slipping his legs under the torso of the wounded man above him, but he fought like a hellion, his eyes equally filled with rage as with pain. With the dominant grip on the knife, he was winning, the knife coming closer to Noah's chest.

A soft moan sounded, and Lucy lifted her head, stupefied.

"Lucy, my gun," Noah cried, then nearly squeezed his eyes shut as he gripped the blade of the knife, a last attempt to keep it from plunging inside him. He gave an agonized grunt as it sliced into the meat of his palm, blood dripping onto the blade and his clothing.

Lucy scrambled from the floor, leaping for the gun. She kicked it toward Noah, who groped for it with one hand and grasped it, then fired three more shots, trying to reserve one for the large Egyptian.

The man above him nearly collapsed on him but continued to move, like a demon spawn that refused to die.

Noah fired the remaining shot straight into his heart, and the man stilled at last.

As Noah stood, he reached for another magazine from his waist-belt, his hand shaking from the pain of his cut palm.

Ginger thrust the knife in her hand into the Egyptian's bicep, as her face turned redder still. She pulled the blade back out and dropped it. A stain of blood erupted on the Egyptian's arm, then spurted forward in a gush.

The Egyptian dropped to his knees, holding his arm, horror written on his face. Within seconds, he collapsed, a large pool of blood gathering below him.

Ginger sank back against the wall, holding her throat, gasping for breath and coughing as color returned to her face.

A curdling death rattle rasped from the large Egyptian's throat, then he stilled.

Lucy stared at the carnage in horror, her face pale save for an ugly bruise that was forming on her forehead. "What did you do?" she asked Ginger, her eyes wide.

Ginger breathed heavily, her shoulders heaving. "B-brachial a-ar-rtery." She cleared her throat, climbing onto her hands and knees. She swallowed hard. "If severed, it's n-nearly irreparable. Instant death."

Noah crossed toward her, then pulled her up into his arms. Trust Ginger to use her medical knowledge to her advantage. *His brilliant wife.*

He fought the temptation to kiss her. *She isn't mine to kiss anymore.* "Are you all right?" he asked, touching her neck gently.

"I'll be f-fine." She coughed a few more times, then pulled away from him. "You, on the other hand, need stitches." She grabbed a sheet from the bed and tore a strip from it. "Let me wrap your hand."

"We have to go; there are others."

She ignored him, wrapping the cloth twice around his hand, then tying a knot. She was shockingly calm, nothing like the terrified young woman he'd rescued from the Turks years before, neither in need of consolation nor him to support her. "We should search the boat. Victoria mentioned to me that it was important to Stephen, but considering the difficulty we've had finding it, who knows what else might be here," Ginger said in a low voice as she dropped his hand.

The cut throbbed, but covering it helped. Then he reloaded the gun and grabbed Ginger's hand, leading the way as they exited into the hull. "I don't know that we have time to search the boat. They obviously know we're here."

"How many more of them are there?" Lucy asked, holding onto Ginger's other arm, terror streaking her face. Noah hadn't remembered until now that they were supposed to be trying to remove her under duress. He hardly gave a damn about it now, but if the others witnessed her clinging to them, they might tell Fisher.

"Four. But one of them is likely to be piloting the boat, so three. Plus the boy." Noah turned to Ginger just before the stairwell. "Can you walk?"

"Yes." Ginger's hair was disheveled, and she squinted against the sunlight coming in through the opening in the stairwell. "But where can we go? The boat has put out."

Noah didn't answer and went to Lucy. In one swift motion, he threw her over his shoulder and she stiffened. As he did, the old injury from his lower back flared, throwing a spasm of pain down his leg.

"What are you doing?" Lucy asked, twisting her body.

"Putting on a show. Apparently." He ignored the pain in his leg and started up the stairs, his gun secured in his free hand. Once outside, he hadn't gone far when running footsteps and shouts in Arabic sounded.

This time the three men had come prepared, but with an unusual weapon. A burst of flame leaped across the deck, and Noah jumped back to avoid getting singed, holding Ginger behind him with an arm. Flames already licked the entrance to the stairwell.

What the hell?

"They have a flamethrower," Ginger gasped beside him. "They're going to burn the whole boat down with their recklessness."

"They're trying to keep us from being able to leave the hull." Noah fired toward the men as the flames shot forward again, blazingly hot. Without a proper sightline, he missed all but one of his shots.

"Or maybe they're trying to burn it down on purpose," Ginger shot back. "We shouldn't leave without checking to see what else is here."

A conflagration had broken out on the deck, though, and the men backed away from it. "There's no time for that now. We have to run!" Noah shouted to Ginger. "Straight to the rail and into the water."

Frustration was written on Ginger's face but she grabbed his shirt as he pushed forward and fired at the fleeing men. He shot one of them, the other two leaping over the side of the boat.

Once at the rail, Noah set Lucy down. "You're going to have to jump."

"Jump? Into the Nile?" Lucy appeared panic-stricken. "There are crocodiles!"

"Would you rather take your chances here?" Noah was already

climbing the rail, Ginger behind him, when a bullet whizzed past him. The last member of the crew was firing at him, and Noah turned, eliminating him with one shot.

"Go," Noah said to Ginger, helping her climb. "The fire is spreading."

Ginger shook her head. "I'm not jumping without you. The last time you asked me to jump from a boat without you, I lost you."

Lucy continued to hesitate, then her eyes fixed on the deck a few feet away. The boy who had been playing jacks was huddled in a corner, arms wrapped around his legs. She pointed toward him. "We can't leave him here."

"He may try to drown you," Noah gritted through his teeth. He'd known more than one child during his time in the war who wouldn't hesitate in malice, having been raised by ruthless men. He doubted this boy was an exception.

"I don't care. I'm not leaving a child." Lucy ran back and grabbed the boy's arm.

For the first time, Lucy reminded him of her sister, and he raised a brow toward Ginger. She gave Lucy an approving glance. "There was a time you weren't quite so cynical. You wouldn't have hesitated to grab that boy."

She's right.

The boy struggled with Lucy as she dragged him toward the rail, then helped him climb.

"I can't swim," the boy cried in Arabic, tears on his face. He shook.

The heat from the fire drew closer.

"Jump," Lucy said, then took his hand. "Here, hold on to me." They went over the side together.

Noah glanced at Ginger and then reached for her hand. Together, they jumped from the side of the boat and into the water. Noah sucked in a breath before he hit the surface, the cool waves engulfing him in a swirl of bubbles. His hand tightened around

Ginger's, and he tried not to think of the actual danger lurking in the waters. Lucy was right, after all—crocodiles patrolled this river —and they preferred the open water to anything else.

They came up together, bobbing at the surface. Noah shook the water from his eyes. He searched for Lucy, who was struggling with the flailing boy. He fought against her like a cat, pushing her head underwater as he tried to climb onto her like a raft. He would drown the girl at this rate.

Leaving Ginger's side, Noah swam toward Lucy and grabbed the child. He encircled the boy's chest with a firm arm. "Stop flailing," he said in stern Arabic. "You'll drown us both."

Something brushed against Noah's leg, and he drew in a sharp breath through his nose, unable to see into the murky water below him.

If it was a crocodile, the movement had probably drawn its attention. Shivers broke out on Noah's skin and he shifted the boy onto his back, searching the water for Abdel and the rowboat. Drifting away from them, the *Cursed Valley* was engulfed in flames.

A familiar scent filled the air. "Is that hashish?" Ginger asked as she swam closer, staring at the burning vessel.

Lucy nodded, paddling her arms in circles. "Stephen uses the boat to smuggle hashish down the Nile into Cairo."

Ginger narrowed her gaze at Noah. "It's always a wonder to me that anyone would use that vile drug and line the coffers of the criminals who still smuggle it."

"Now I understand why there was a flamethrower on board." The burning boat had continued moving in the water, and was now a safe distance away. "Fisher probably sends his men to burn the hashish fields of competitors, in the name of the law. All while smuggling it himself." It appeared he'd learned Helton's techniques well.

"If there wasn't a demand for it, he'd make no money at all," Ginger countered with bitterness.

Her rebuke stung, but before Noah could answer, Ginger sucked in a breath. "I think something just touched my leg."

Goddammit.

Lucy let out a shriek, scanning the water below them. "Oh my God. We're going to be eaten by crocodiles."

"Stop moving," Noah barked. "Move as little as possible. If you do see one or if it grabs you, try to gouge it in the eyes and nose."

"We're going to die." Tears streamed down Lucy's face.

Ginger set a hand on his arm, fear in her gaze, her expression somber. Noah locked eyes with her. "If one grabs you, don't stop fighting."

"Have I ever?" she asked, her breath rising and falling at a rate that betrayed her panic.

Good God, I still love her.

However foolish it was that it had taken this macabre, horrible circumstance for him to feel that rush of love toward her, he wanted nothing more than to be holding her, keeping her safe from the deadly creatures that he knew he had little hope of protecting her from.

The boy's arms tightened around Noah's neck, nearly choking him.

"No," he said, his voice low. "You never have. So don't stop now." *Don't stop fighting for me, either, my darling rohi. Don't give up on us.*

Abdel drew close to them at last, and Noah helped the boy in first, relief at his neck as he drew in a clear breath. He helped Ginger and Lucy next, then started to climb in, when the rowboat bumped as something large passed underneath it, rocking it.

A large pair of yellow eyes approached, just at the surface of the water, all teeth and scales and horror.

"Noah!" Ginger screamed, throwing her hands out toward him.

Time seemed to slow, then a shot rang out, splitting his eardrums. Abdel stood on the rowboat with a shotgun.

Beside Noah, the water bubbled, a stream of blood sinking away.

Noah flung himself into the boat, pulling his legs safely inside it. Ginger's arms were around his neck, holding him as tears shook her shoulders.

"I thought I had lost you for sure this time," she sobbed against him.

Noah's arms tightened around her, his body shaking. His life had flashed before his eyes, it seemed, and he could still practically feel the scrape of the crocodile's scales against his legs.

"I'm right here, *rohi*. I'm sorry, my love. I'm so sorry."

She let out a breathy cry, then pulled away from his chest, tugging his face down toward hers. As their lips met, Noah closed his eyes, not caring who saw them or what they might think as he returned her kiss.

No matter how he'd tried, he couldn't stop loving her.

But how can I live in a world where she's no longer mine?

CHAPTER FORTY-NINE

*T*he mood at Millard Van Sant's house in Giza was somber, despite their apparent victory with their plan at Shepheard's. Stephen and Lord Helton had agreed on Hassan's offer, and the dig was moving forward.

But the *Cursed Valley* had burned. Any evidence of Stephen's misdeeds that had likely been on it had burned with it.

Worse still, despite their best efforts, they hadn't been able to contact Ginger's mother or aunt in London. They had wired but gotten no response.

Ginger sat on the sofa beside Noah, stitching his wounded hand, trying to swallow the panic that poured through her. For the first time in ages, her fingers didn't feel steady enough to be stitching like this, and she had to will herself to continue. The cut was deep, but it was clean thanks to the sharpness of the blade. He'd have a scar there for life, though. *One more to add to his collection.*

Normally, concentrating on her work brought her calm. But now all she could do was think about the threats that Stephen had made against Alexander. And that had been before the *Cursed Valley* had burned with the load of hashish it had been carrying. Stephen was likely to be enraged and itching for revenge.

Lucy had already retired to bed for the evening, thoroughly spent from the ordeal, and Alastair had taken the boy they'd rescued back to his house in Old Cairo. Thank goodness Van Sant was still here. He and Dirk made the uncomfortable tension between her, Jack, and Noah bearable.

"I want to go back," Ginger said, keeping her stitching even. "If anything happens to him, I only have myself to blame."

"It'd be weeks before you got there. You can't possibly arrive in time to help," Jack said gently. "We just have to trust that Alastair's friend in London can find them and get them to safety. Fisher's a lot of talk sometimes too. Pulling off a kidnapping and attacking two high-class women all the way from here would be a feat."

"I don't care." Ginger didn't meet his gaze. That kiss with Noah on the boat earlier was seared too closely to the surface of her memory for her to properly talk to Jack. "I'm his mother. I shouldn't have left him vulnerable like that."

"Jack is right about this, Ginger." Noah's voice was quiet. "And if you go, you could expose yourself too. Fisher has far more reach here in Egypt. It's not safe for any of us right now."

"I agree," Van Sant said, patting Dirk's head. "The best course of action is to move forward our timeline on the dig at the Valley of the Kings. We can set sail for Luxor in the morning, arrive in a week, and send word in two weeks that we've found something. Any sooner than that will be suspicious."

"It may be suspicious regardless, but there's little to be done about that," Noah said.

"But that means doing nothing for almost three weeks." Ginger pressed her lips together, her anger with herself growing by the minute. She'd done this. She had put Alexander in danger. "Because it'll take Helton and Stephen another week to get down there, and then what? Days before you settle everything. It could be a full two months before I can hold my son in my arms again."

"Not nothing." Jack ran his hand through his hair. "I've got to report to Alfred Milner, resign from the commission. I haven't even bothered to show my face in the office for several days."

"You shouldn't resign," Van Sant said with a shake of his head. "You might do some good. The Wafd party has been telling everyone not to cooperate with the commission, but I believe it's a mistake. They need someone advising the British government to make clear how much the Egyptians desire independence and the lengths they will go to get it."

Jack's brows perched low. "Maybe. I'm not sure I have a whole lot left to give any mission right now."

An awful feeling of dismay weighed heavily on Ginger's shoulders. *This has all been so unfair to Jack.*

She cared for him so much. Their friendship, his humor, and his teasing had meant everything to her, especially when she'd been at the lowest points of her life. Tears filled the corners of her eyes, blurring her vision as she thought back to that last happy morning they'd spent, before their world had turned sideways.

He was a dream of a husband, and she was lucky to have him.

... except he's not Noah.

He didn't deserve for her to be disloyal.

She had told him she and Noah had decided to move on from their marriage, that she was choosing to be with him. And, yet, when she was beside Noah, nothing between them felt finished.

Neither of them would have chosen for their marriage to end willingly.

He'd called her *rohi* today.

"I'm right here, rohi. I'm sorry, my love. I'm so sorry."

And her heart had broken at the sound of his words. He hadn't called her that since she'd seen him again, and it had been his term of endearment for her always.

Noah still cares for me.

The thought of that nearly undid her. He'd kissed her tenderly in that boat, not with the anger and need he'd expressed in the kiss at Shepheard's. Not with the vitriol that had spewed from him afterward.

She'd hurt him, deeply. Even if he loved her though, it didn't mean he could forgive her.

And after everything he'd said to her, after how callous and hurtful he'd been, she didn't know that she ought to forgive him either.

Millard interrupted her thoughts when he set his hand on his cane and stood. "Darby, you're an adventurer. You'll perk right back up again soon enough. And, who knows, maybe after this nasty business with Fisher and Helton is done, I can find you a real dig to explore. Though, I doubt I'll be allowed to here in Egypt." He winked and headed for the door. "Good night. May your youthful energy help you with all these calamities. I find rest is often the best solution."

As he left, Ginger frowned at Noah. "Why wouldn't Millard be able to dig here in Egypt?"

Noah shifted in his seat. "The Department of Antiquities is likely going to be furious about what we've done in the Valley of the Kings. We've tried to take every precaution, but the fact remains that we're disturbing an important archeological site. If we're successful, we both might be banned."

If Noah was right, then he'd never go back to his chosen field again. His career as an Egyptologist could be ruined, as well as Millard's.

"But if you're successful, you'll also have done the Department of Antiquities a great service. Helping to stop a smuggling ring is no small trifle. Keeping the treasures of Egypt here should be admired, shouldn't it?" Ginger asked gently.

"Perhaps. But either way, Millard is willing to make the sacrifice of his reputation and career for that goal. Though it probably helps that he's an old man."

That's true.

Ginger tied off the last stitch, then snipped the thread. She reached for her ointment, then laid a strip over the cut and started the bandage. "I'll have to cut the stitches for you in a few weeks. Try to be gentle on your hand in the meantime."

"It's my dominant hand," Noah said with a grimace. "But I'll do what I can."

Ginger felt Jack's eyes on her as she shifted away from Noah. Guilt flushed her as she stood and lifted her medical bag. "I don't know that Millard's solution will work for me. I doubt I'll have any sleep at all until I hear that Alastair's man found Mama and Alexander."

"They'll be safe." Jack tipped a smile. "It's Kensington. Anyone out of place there would be noticed."

She knew Jack said that to make her feel better, though he might not truly believe it.

"Ginger has every right to be afraid," Noah said tersely and stood. "Frankly, more thought should have been given to the boy's safety before you left London. Fisher has a long history of taking advantage of the most vulnerable members of that family."

Noah's words were barbed and Ginger winced, feeling them in her gut. He meant the insult toward Jack, but it hit her deeply too. *He thinks we were careless.*

Jack reddened, his posture changing as he leaned forward in his seat. "We gave Alexander's safety a lot of thought. Don't even try to suggest you would have done better."

"I wouldn't have left him in the hands of unprotected women where Fisher had just been lurking recently, no." The corners of Noah's eyes tightened as he glared at Jack. "Not even if I thought Fisher was halfway across the globe."

"Glad to hear you're finally taking an interest in your son," Jack shot back through clenched teeth.

"That's right, Jack. As you say, *my son*. Or would you prefer we go back to me not having a voice?"

Not this again.

Ginger pressed her fingertips to her eyes. "That's enough. Both of you. This is ridiculous." She lowered her hands, feeling drained of energy. "While I appreciate the support, I can't take much more of this bickering. All I want is to go back to England and live a quiet life with *my son*. Whether or not I have a man at my side."

She gripped the strap of her medical kit. "In fact, that might be the best solution for all of us. I can take care of myself. We've clearly made a mess of things, and I don't know if I can be with either of you without one hating the other. That's not what I want."

Jack stood, some of his familiar swagger in his stance. "I don't think it's possible for Noah not to hate me, regardless if I'm with you, Red. I committed the unforgivable sin of loving you."

Noah flinched at Jack's words.

Unforgivable. Ginger looked from one to the other, her heart breaking. She appealed to Noah with a pleading look. "Noah, please. Can't you understand how confusing everything was in your absence? We're all adults. We can discuss this amicably. Jack had no ill intent."

Noah rubbed the bandage on his hand as though the cut bothered him. "Do you know one of the last things Jack said to me before we left Malta, Ginger? He said that everything that had happened was my fault. Including Sarah's death. Look him in the eye." Noah pointed toward Jack. "Ask him if maybe, just maybe, he resented me for what happened with Fisher and didn't care if I lost as much as he had. He knew the only person I cared about was you."

Ginger glanced at Jack, who lowered his gaze, guilt flashing on his face.

This isn't fair.

"But that's why he tried to protect me, Noah. To keep me and my name—and your son's name—from being dragged through the mud." Ginger shook her head in disbelief. "I don't see how that's so hard to understand."

"And I don't understand how a woman who begged me in Malta to go to America with her and start a new life was suddenly so swayed by the dictates of the society she claimed to loathe. Jack couldn't have loaned you money? You couldn't have gone somewhere else—somewhere safe—and claimed to be a war widow? Widows abound in Europe right now."

That was all true. But it would have meant losing her family entirely, her chance to become a physician, and more pain. More struggle. Alone.

Was I just not strong enough? She felt so weak now. So foolish.

"If you want to wound someone, I'm right here, Noah." Jack stepped closer to Ginger, protectively. "Stop taking your anger at me out on her."

"No, he's angry with me too." Ginger's throat clenched. "In which case, I'm going to have to ask you to keep your hands off me the next time you're overcome with feeling. You made your feelings to me perfectly clear a few nights ago when you told me you wanted our marriage dissolved, Noah. It's not fair to do that and then turn around and ..."

Her face flushed. *This is too complicated.* That kiss this afternoon had been anything but the kiss of two people who didn't care about each other.

"Maybe I've changed my mind." Noah crossed his arms. "And I believe it was you who kissed me."

What?

Her heart lurched, and she felt unable to breathe.

"You were saying?" Jack asked in a low voice, raising a brow toward Ginger.

"She kissed me. Today." Noah stepped closer still, his eyes glittering. "Maybe I'm not willing simply to roll over and allow you to have the woman I love *and* my son without a struggle."

The hurt in Jack's eyes was measurable.

I can't do this.

I can't continue hurting them both.

She'd known she shouldn't have kissed Noah. But he'd almost been swallowed by a crocodile, and she'd been terrified and ... *it was inexcusable after I told Jack I was choosing to be with him.*

But should I even have told Jack that?

It wasn't that she didn't know which man she loved more. There was no denying the passion she shared with Noah. Theirs was a love that had felt otherworldly. Indomitable. Unbreakable.

And yet ... here they were.

The love she felt for Jack had come about through friendship and time. Comfort. Security.

Different.

"Jack, I'm sorry," she whispered, looking away. She raised her chin, aware that they both watched her closely, but wanting nothing more than to be away from them. "I can't continue like this. I love you both. In different ways. And I'm sorry ... I apologize. To you both." Her heart squeezed in her chest as she said in a strangled voice, "I shouldn't have kissed you, Noah. And we can never survive a marriage if you can't completely forgive what happened with Jack. I-I don't know if you're capable of that. I think it's best that I just remove myself now and go home to Alexander."

"No." Jack drew a deep breath. "No, I don't think you should. It's too dangerous for you to go anywhere alone. If anyone should exit this situation right now, it should be me." His face was still red. "I-I need some time to think. To fend for myself for a little while. I know what you said about us being together, Ginger, but I stand by what I said too. I won't get in the way of you and Noah. So I'm the one that should go. And when this is all over, maybe the chips will fall right where they need to." He turned and started for the door.

"Jack—" Ginger hurried after him. That she'd wounded him this badly made her want to be sick.

Jack looked over his shoulder, pausing at the door. "Just trust me on this one. You stay here—you'll be safe. Noah will make sure of it." Then he gave her a wink, his face overwhelmingly sad, and left.

Tense silence followed. Ginger heard Noah's footsteps behind her. She stiffened as he came closer.

"I want you to know ... when we were apart, I thought only of you. I love you. I always will."

How I wanted to hear those words.

Had he said it even two days earlier, she would have believed him.

... but I can't.

"If you love me," she whispered, "then find a way to draw Stephen to Luxor right away. Before he hurts anyone else."

"I will. I promise."

She closed her eyes and listened to his footsteps fading. Sighing, she glanced at the empty room.

Alone had never felt like such relief.

All that mattered now was finishing this plan Noah had set in motion and getting back to Alexander.

Noah found Jack in the stable, saddling a horse. His face was in shadow, but from the way his shoulders bunched at Noah's approach, it was clear Jack was aware of who had followed him there. "What do you want?" He didn't turn, tightening a strap.

"We have to talk." Noah braced himself for another argument, the muscles in his neck taut.

"I think I'm done talking, Noah." Jack took a few steps over to a bench, picked up a bag, then carried it to the horse and started tying it on.

"I know I haven't been fair to you but—"

"Is that what you think I care about?" Jack turned and scowled at him. "I don't give a damn. We've had our fights before—never like this, but bad enough. And, believe it or not, I'll be fine if you never forgive me. Because I know I did the right thing with *her*. You can't say the same thing."

Jack was clearly goading him, and Noah drew a breath to keep his head clear. "Is that so?"

"Damn right it is. I haven't been able to figure you out since I found out you were alive. But what you did today really takes the cake. Because I don't know what the hell you were thinking letting Ginger get on that goddamn boat with her sister."

The pain in Noah's hand was nearly intolerable as his fingers flexed. "I didn't let her. She said she was going to follow Lucy for a few feet. Next thing I knew she was getting on the damned dock with Lucy aiming the pistol at her."

"Don't give me that bull. You *never* should have let her out of your sight. Not for a second. And now the whole damned boat has burned down besides everything else. Did Ginger tell you Victoria said the boat was important? That we'd been looking for it for weeks? You might have found something on that boat that would have helped prove Fisher was a criminal and ended this once and for all. And then you *jumped* in the Nile? Wait—that's right—you also kissed her. After you told her she should forget you and stay married to me. And that you didn't give a damn about being a father."

Noah stared at Jack, the tension in his shoulders growing.

Jack had never had any problem telling him exactly what he thought. Why should he be surprised by this?

Because I was careless. I didn't fight Ginger hard enough when she said she was going after Lucy. Didn't listen to her when she told me about the boat.

I haven't fought for Ginger at all.

Or my son.

He wanted to fight for her now. Wanted more than anything to have her be his. He'd been a fool to think that anything else but her really mattered. If he could go back, he'd willingly sacrifice his name and everything he thought he'd lost before he left Malta.

None of it compared to having lost her.

... to having lost *them.*

The thought of a son that had never known him filled him with such a profound sadness that his breath hitched, his heart aching.

Which makes what I have to say to Jack that much harder.

Jack shook his head in disgust. "You know what? I take back what I said yesterday. You don't want her? Fine. You're an idiot. But stop interfering with me—because I'm not going to let her go to someone who clearly doesn't deserve her anymore."

Noah's jaw clenched and he looked away, focusing his gaze on the twitching of the horse's ears. He tried to steel himself to calm, knowing how easily incensed this might make him. That Jack should have a say in this at all was hard enough to stomach.

But it's worse knowing I did some of this to myself.

I let her go.

Jack shook his head in disgust at Noah's silence. "I guess you don't have that much to say after all." He grabbed the reins to lead the horse from the stall.

Pushing back the bile rising in his stomach, Noah stared at Jack as he moved past him. In a low growl, he finally managed, "I need your help."

Jack slowed and stopped. "Oh, do you?"

"Yes, I do." Noah came up behind him. "Because Alexander is in danger. And Fisher is clever. The more time we give him, the further he'll slip out of our grasp. We need to draw him to Luxor right away and I have a plan, but I need you. And it would be risky."

"So now you need me." Jack removed his hat and turned, setting a hand on the horse's neck. "I don't think I have any more favors in me. They haven't ended so well."

Noah ducked his chin, studying Jack's expression The fact that he hadn't said no outright was encouraging. Jack had a right to his pride, after all, and Noah had behaved badly.

"I'm pleading with you, not for myself. But for her. And for Alexander." Noah's stomach roiled as he stepped forward. "And if you do, I'll go away quietly after this is all done. I don't deserve her. Not anymore. But I ... I do love her. I never stopped, even when the thought of her with you was unbearable. It still is and I can't help that. But all that matters to me is that she's safe. Even if she's not with me."

Jack held his gaze for a full minute, not speaking.

Then his shoulders dropped with a heavy breath. "What's your plan?"

CHAPTER FIFTY

*I*f not for the men that Noah was meeting inside the Winter Palace Hotel in Luxor, the day couldn't have appeared more beautiful. The January weather was perfect, with feluccas drifting down the Nile with white sails billowing in the warm winds. Set on the banks of the river, the hotel was spectacular and modern, catering to the needs of the cream of British Anglo society and international tourists.

Two staircases gracefully flanked the main entrance as carriages unloaded in front of it, ladies and gentlemen drinking in the sights from the east bank of the Nile. The Luxor Temple was only a ten-minute walk from the hotel, and, even from here, the feeling of being close to antiquities usually produced a thrill in visitors.

Noah glanced at the river, his thoughts going to Jack and Ginger, who had left over a week and a half earlier with Alastair and Lucy to make the journey down to Luxor aboard a houseboat. By now, he hoped Jack would be meeting Lord Alfred Milner at the train station. Having an influential witness to the events Noah had planned for the evening was crucial, but his ability to communicate with Jack and Ginger was limited now that Helton and Fisher had arrived in Luxor.

"Hassan." Van Sant's voice came from behind him, and Noah turned to see him climbing from a carriage. He wore a linen suit and used a polished black cane, the crook in the shape of Anubis's head.

Noah bowed his head in greeting. He still regretted the shearing that Alastair had encouraged, feeling less at ease in his fake beard and wig. But Noah had replicated the look remarkably well, though he was uncomfortable meeting with either Helton or Fisher. It felt riskier now that they knew he was alive.

Van Sant stood shoulder to shoulder with Noah, gazing at the west bank of the Nile. "All will be well, my boy, you'll see. Things are coming along swimmingly, given the hiccups we've experienced."

Noah stood straighter, his eyes narrowing toward the dusty wasteland of the Valley of the Kings. Thankfully, most of the tourists that came to Luxor stayed on this side of the river. With the Luxor and Karnak Temple complexes to keep them occupied, few showed much interest in the wadi valley cut into the limestone cliffs of the desert. Little had been found there of note recently, and many archeologists believed the valley had already spilled its secrets.

The tomb Noah and Van Sant had settled on as the backdrop for their scheme, KV61, had been previously cleared in 1910 and found to be an unused and unfinished tomb. That had been to Noah's advantage, as his men had then dug a shaft from that site, tunneling deep into the ground and digging out another small tomb.

They'd even built an antechamber to the fake tomb, which was where Noah had set up the treasures he'd found in Malta at Lord Braddock's home—the Amarna cache. The result had been a brilliant fake. The photographs he'd been able to give Millard to tempt Helton gave every appearance of an undisturbed tomb from antiquity.

But for every ounce of meticulous planning, Noah couldn't help feeling that he hadn't been diligent enough. Too many people knew now, and too many things were out of his control. And Noah didn't like that Ginger would be close by. "If my— If Ginger weren't here, I'd feel more confident."

My Ginger. My wife ... no more.

Giving her up once again might prove the hardest thing he'd done yet.

He'd seen little of her since they'd left Giza. But things were as they needed to be. Ginger and Jack needed to present a unified front.

Van Sant's mouth tipped in a frown. Noah had explained the private matter to him, and he knew the old man was sympathetic. "She's a competent woman. And clever. I wouldn't worry about her."

"It isn't just her. I'm concerned that we overplayed our hand— that the imposter for Hassan might be suspect." Noah himself had supervised the costuming job Alastair had done on Hassan, and it had been impressive. And they'd allowed Millard to handle most of that meeting at Shepheard's, still worried that the imposter would be spotted.

The fake Hassan had only shown himself briefly, dropping by the table during the confusion when Helton had arrived to intercept the meeting, having been sent by Fisher. Fisher had never actually shown up to the meeting at Shepheard's, which Noah was thankful for, since Fisher had more reason than Helton to feel suspicious right now.

"Only time will tell. Have faith." Van Sant checked his pocket watch. "Shall we proceed inside? They'll be impatiently waiting."

They made their way up the hotel stairs and went in through the main entrance. The high vaulted ceilings, ornate chandeliers, and wide-open interiors were detailed with luxury. *Just the sort of place Fisher and Helton would want to stay.* Noah's last visit to the hotel had been during the war, when the hotel had been requisitioned as a convalescent home for injured soldiers. They were long gone now, but Noah still felt the presence of those wounded men hobbling on crutches or pushed across the verandahs in wheelchairs.

The sights and sounds and smells of a war that would never be truly over for him.

He pushed away the memories of those times and focused his gaze on a far dark corner of the lobby, where Fisher and Helton waited.

His arms flexed, his gut twisting with disgust at the sight of them.

Van Sant greeted them with all the warmth of a business partner happy to see his investors, while Noah hardened his face to a mask. His loathing of both men increased each time he saw them. He hated their audacity, their immorality, their freedom.

When Noah had started this, he'd wanted his revenge. Thought it could bring him justice and clear his name, that he could find satisfaction.

But now—especially after Ginger and Jack had found him—he knew it would never be enough. What they'd taken from him could never be restored.

Noah stayed standing, moving into the furthest, darkest corner of the room. He was certain his eyes would betray him if he looked at either of them too closely.

Helton was holding a newspaper, a look of profound displeasure on his face. "Van Sant. Hassan." He held up the paper. His voice was thinly veiled with contempt, barely above a low growl. "What is the meaning of this? We agreed that this would be handled with discretion."

Noah fought the urge to smirk at the emblazoned headline on the paper: *New Tomb Discovered at KV61!*

The leak to the newspapers had been Noah's idea, a tactic he'd learned from the war and the Arab Bureau's diligent use of the news media to control the narrative. Except, in this case, it was to motivate Lord Helton and Fisher to hurry to Luxor, which they'd done. The story had broken in the papers the previous evening, and, within the hour of publication, Helton had sent Van Sant a telegram demanding to meet him at the Winter Palace Hotel today.

Considering the speed with which Helton and Fisher had arrived, they must have boarded the train directly after they'd learned of the leak.

Journalists and eager tourists—all wanting the first glimpse of a possible new find in the Valley of the Kings—would soon pour into Luxor, making for a messy situation.

Van Sant held his hands up. "Calm yourself. We don't know who released this information, but it wasn't us."

"It was Darby. I'm certain of it," Fisher said with a sour expression. "The man has been a plague to me since arriving in Egypt."

"If anything," Noah said in his accented English, "this presents a problem to us. We've yet to breach the tomb beyond the antechamber. And we had to set up extra guards around the perimeter, to protect our find from thieves."

"Then we go tonight." Helton's eyes narrowed. "See the find for ourselves. Before this becomes a spectacle. You made promises, gentlemen."

Noah's jaw clenched as a surge of victory rushed through him. However, he couldn't afford to show any delight in Helton's predictability. "Not tonight," he said in a throaty growl. "There hasn't been time to—"

"We had a deal." Fisher leaned back in his seat. "It will be tonight, or you won't receive another pound from us."

"The shaft may not be secure enough for visitors," Van Sant said with feigned alarm. "We are dealing with antiquities that have existed for thousands of years. It could be a danger to you until we've had time to ensure all is structurally sound."

"My men will take care of everything," Stephen said finally.

"Including guarding the place. We wouldn't want any interruptions, after all."

Van Sant glanced toward Noah. That would be problematic, simply because it would change the balance of power. But rejecting Fisher's terms could also cause him to be suspicious.

He would have to send word to Jack and Ginger, though. Let them know they would have to approach with stealth and caution.

Noah kept his gaze low, his mouth going dry. It also meant that he couldn't allow Van Sant to take the risk of going into the tomb they'd dug. If something went wrong, Van Sant could be caught in the crossfire. He'd given Noah enough already.

Van Sant would likely protest, but Noah wouldn't give him the option.

At last, Noah nodded. "Tonight then. Just after midnight. Meet us on the west bank. We will ride in together."

The men said brief good-byes, then went their separate ways.

Van Sant smiled at Noah as they stepped back out into the golden sunlight. "You see—nothing to fear. Your plan will go well. Once we have them inside the tomb, the trap will be set."

Noah wished he could share Van Sant's optimism.

Tonight he would ride into the valley of death.

CHAPTER FIFTY-ONE

*A*s colonial secretary, Lord Alfred Milner had more to do in Egypt than be concerned with an archeological dig in Luxor—he'd been a signatory at the nearly disastrous Treaty of Versailles, and his commission to Egypt was failing badly.

Which was why Noah had asked Jack to go to Milner and request him to come to Luxor to catch a known fugitive. Traitors operating against the British government were worthy of notice, even if it meant that Noah might lose everything if he couldn't prove his innocence.

Ginger hadn't learned of Noah's request until after Jack had already made it, and as she waited on the bank of the Nile on her horse as Milner and the local police disembarked from a boat, her stomach churned with anxiety.

Noah had offered himself up as bait.

Milner's men were here to capture him.

Jack was settled in the saddle of his horse, while Ginger rode on Resheph, at Noah's insistence. "He's an Arabian stallion," Noah had said before they'd parted in Giza. "The fastest horse I've ever ridden. I want you on a horse I trust as much as a friend."

Ginger's face must have been lined with worry because Jack looked at her and frowned at her expression. "Try to relax."

"Relax?" Ginger gripped the reins more tightly. "I don't know that I can, Jack." If Noah couldn't force a confession out of Stephen or Helton, or if anything went wrong, he'd be executed.

Her nerves were running high, as she knew they would be, and she thought of her comfortable room on the houseboat, where Lucy and Alastair were waiting for their return, despite it being one in the morning. If only returning to her life was as simple as returning to the boat.

There could be no return. Alastair's man had found her mother and Madeline and taken them to safety with Alexander—but they couldn't live like this either. Who knew when Stephen might turn up, threatening them? And then there was Victoria, who was desperate and relying on Ginger for help.

Stephen needed to face justice.

Lord Milner came toward them on horseback. He blinked at Ginger in surprise. "Mrs. Darby. I didn't expect to see you here at this late hour." He said nothing about the trousers she wore, which she'd purchased in Cairo before leaving. They would be the most convenient for whatever terrain she might have to travel through here. *No wonder Sarah had enjoyed them so much.*

"The criminal in question was accused of killing my father and brother, my lord. I have a vested interest in seeing him caught." How she longed for the day when people would know she referred to Stephen as that criminal rather than Noah.

"Quite right. But I'll expect you to stay back, my dear. This is a messy business, and we can't guarantee your safety."

They started toward the wadi entrance into the Valley of the Kings, a deeply cut path worn by water through the limestone cliffs over millennia. Towering above the valley was a pyramid-shaped mountain called the Qurn, which Jack had told her was part of the Ancient Egyptians' homage to the sun god, Re.

A barren desert with no signs of life, the valley had entombed the great pharaohs of ancient Egypt. Despite the hope of being able to make their way to eternal life and the underworld in this quiet, morose expanse, the tombs built here had instead endured centuries of grave robbers and thievery.

Noah had sent word that Stephen's men would guard the perimeter of KV61, and that made her fret. Noah and Van Sant would be outnumbered and surrounded by enemies who might turn on them before they understood what was happening.

"The scouts I sent earlier said that Benson entered the wadi just after midnight, accompanied by several men—they believed the number to be eight. Three went into the tomb after arriving there."

"They must have felt the need to clear it after the newspapers published the discovery," Lord Milner said and gave Jack a pleased smile. "You were wise to tell the press. It forced Benson's hand. We'll have to approach surreptitiously." He spoke over his shoulder to the local police inspector. "Tell your men to be armed and ready for anything."

It had been relatively easy for Jack to convince Milner of his desire to see Noah brought in for justice by claiming the outrage of a friend who had been betrayed and deceived. He'd confided to Ginger that he'd considered telling Milner the entire plan and hoping he'd be reasonable enough to want to investigate claims against Helton and Stephen, but their reputations and places in society were too strong.

Milner glanced at Ginger once again. "You might stay here, Mrs. Darby. In fact, I insist. You can't possibly be anything but in the way. We'll allow you to see the scoundrel before we drag him away in chains."

Rather than argue, Ginger gave him a pleasant smile. "As you wish." She pulled the reins back and met Jack's questioning gaze. "I'll see you when you return."

Jack raised a brow, then continued forward. As Milner and his men passed her, Ginger walked Resheph back a few paces. Arguing with men was pointless. She'd learned that by now.

Staying back afforded her the freedom to do what she wanted anyway.

She dismounted when they were out of view, then brought Resheph to the side of the wadi. At least this way the horse wouldn't be in danger. She patted his neck, then reached into her saddlebag and dislodged the second gun she'd stashed inside.

Hurrying on foot, she moved with speed, her heart racing. The eerie sound of distant jackals, probably close to the shoreline, made shivers go up her spine. She wasn't in more danger than Noah or Jack, though. Jack was riding into a group of armed men that wouldn't hesitate to shoot him.

And Noah ...

She tried not to think about him in that tomb with Helton and Stephen. Anything could go wrong, not the least of which was Stephen and Helton realizing 'Hassan' had duped them.

Time was of the essence, and now that she didn't have a horse, she didn't have a moment to spare.

She ran, the sound of her steps surprisingly light against the soft earth.

Then, a gunshot.

Oh, no.

* * *

NOAH LOWERED the sledgehammer Fisher had insisted he use to smash through the wall to the fake tomb, his head lifting sharply.

Gunshots.

Only seconds later, two of Fisher's men came tumbling out of the shaft, yelling.

Helton and Fisher leveled accusing gazes at Noah, as the men panted.

"The police have arrived!" one of them said.

"How did they know we were here?" Fisher snarled at Noah.

Noah rested his hands on the top of the sledgehammer, breathing heavily. "It was you who insisted we come tonight." He wiped his forehead with the back of his sleeve.

He needed to keep them busy. Noah had expected this might happen. No need for alarm yet. Hopefully, Jack and Lord Milner would be along soon enough.

Fisher's face was red. "How convenient that the police managed to find us, Hassan. First you take our money, then you renege on the deal—is that it?"

Noah scowled. "And how would that help me? I'm here with you. It's just as illegal for me to steal the treasures."

Helton glanced toward the entrance to the shaft, his brow furrowing. "We're trapped in here. All they have to do is wait out there for us to come out."

"Unless they come in," Fisher said, then crossed the small space toward a crate. He opened it, displaying a variety of guns and ammunition, even dynamite.

Perhaps he was planning on blowing open the entrance to the tomb if we couldn't smash it quickly enough.

Fisher grabbed a fistful of bullets. "Let them come in. We'll wait here for them and shoot them one by one."

Noah didn't doubt it.

He lowered his hand from the handle of the sledgehammer, his palm creeping closer to the butt of his gun tucked in a holster under his *thobe*.

Move slowly.

They were distracted, watching the entrance, both with guns at the ready.

He couldn't kill either of them, no matter how much he might want to, especially not at this juncture. Milner might be surprised to find them here, but he wasn't coming for them.

But I can wound them.

His fingers slipped around the handle of the gun, tightening as footsteps and light approached down the tunnel. One of Fisher's men watched him closely, his eyes focused.

Would Fisher wait to see who approached before he shot?

* * *

HER HEART IN HER THROAT, Ginger broke into a sprint.

More shots sounded, their ear-splitting familiarity echoing through the walls of the canyon. *God, please help them.*

And her medical kit was strapped to Resheph. *Dammit.*

She drew closer to the sound of gunfire, then shouts, some in Arabic, some in English. What was happening?

As she turned a corner, she pressed herself against the face of a cliff, venturing slowly. A horse tore around the corner, galloping past her, carrying a man fleeing. Another pursued—one of Milner's men. They must have confronted Stephen's men.

Please.

Let Jack be safe.

Let Noah be safe.

Could she get there fast enough to help?

A moan nearby caught her attention.

* * *

WHOEVER WAS COMING through the shaft was almost upon them.

Noah raised the gun and aimed toward Fisher's kneecap and fired, before quickly retraining the gun on Helton. Fisher fell back with a cry just as Jack burst out of the shaft, his gun at the ready.

Helton was frozen in place, but one of Fisher's men fired carelessly, the bullet ricocheting from the walls of the tomb before he ducked behind a crate. The other man dropped his gun, lifting his hands in surrender as he backed toward a wall.

"Am I late?" Jack asked Noah as he walked over to Helton and disarmed him.

Lord Milner followed Jack, stepping into the dimly lit tomb, his expression somber. "Which one is Benson?" he asked Jack.

Fisher rasped a breath, his chest heaving as he held his bleeding leg and writhed. Helton's eyes swiveled toward Noah, and Noah raised his hands in mock surrender, not releasing his gun. "I suppose you've found me."

"What?" The agony in Fisher's features was only outdone by the shock in his wide blue eyes as he struggled to his feet, grasping the wall of the tomb. Helton shrank, his body sagging. Their breathing, dulled by the enclosed walls of the tomb, was the only sound for a few seconds.

Milner looked from Fisher to Helton, faint recognition on his face. "Aren't you—"

"Lord Milner." Helton seemed to recover, the sick expression on his gaunt face lessening as his normally cool exterior prevailed. "Thank goodness you've come. Arrest this criminal. We were informed he'd be trying to rob our claim here tonight, but, as you can see, he wounded Captain Fisher and threatened our lives."

Noah chuckled, peeling the beard from his face, then the wig. He dropped them at his feet before he retrained the gun on Fisher, who still had his gun in his hand, though he held it limply. "Odd, that I could evade your capture, when you and Fisher's men outnumbered me eleven to one. Or perhaps those crates at your feet are evidence enough of your true purpose here tonight, Helton."

Milner turned toward Jack, a sudden nervousness in his movement. "Darby, what is the meaning of all this?"

"You didn't know?" Helton answered, his eyes narrowing. "Darby and Benson are lifelong friends. The very best. They even share the same wife. Despicable."

"That's rich coming from someone who used his own daughter like a whore to spy on his enemies." Jack's voice was laced with contempt. "Lord Milner, I wasn't entirely honest with you about coming here tonight. I brought you to capture a traitor. Two of them. Lord Reginald Helton and Stephen Fisher."

* * *

A MAN she didn't recognize lay on the path in front of her, curled on his side, hugging his arms to his chest.

The burning scent of gunpowder grew stronger as Ginger pushed herself past him. She nearly stumbled over the body of another man, slipping in the blood pooled on the dust beneath him. His eyes stared up at the stars lifelessly, jaw slack.

She didn't have time to be a doctor or a woman of compassion right now.

Throwing aside her instinct to help, she continued forward, then ran headlong into Millard Van Sant.

Millard grabbed her by the shoulders, then shone an electric torch at her face. "My lady. What are you doing out here like this?"

She scanned his face, stunned to see him out here at all. "What am I ... what are you doing here? Where's Noah? And Jack?"

Millard shook his head, beads of sweat on his forehead. "Noah didn't allow me to go with him into the tomb. He's there with Helton and Fisher—but Jack and Lord Milner have gone in after them. Once the shooting began, I ran for cover. I think Fisher's men have all fled, though."

If Noah had gone in there alone with Fisher and Helton ... *they might have killed him when the shooting started.*

No.

She swallowed the acid rising in her stomach, burning the back of her throat. *I can't lose him again.*

Ginger reached for the torch. "Show me where the entrance to the tomb is, Millard. I'm going in after them."

* * *

"Enough of this," Helton snarled.

Keeping his gaze level with Lord Milner, Helton pointed toward Noah. "This man murdered women and children, plotted to destroy Abdin Palace, sold secrets to the Germans during the war, operated a smuggling ring—not to mention murdering Lord Edmund Braddock and his son. His list of crimes is well established."

Did I ever truly admire this man? Think of him as brilliant? If Noah had, those memories had been so tarnished that now all he saw was the filth of Helton's soul, even when they'd been allies.

"Except that Fisher is responsible for a good deal of what you mentioned—and you're responsible for the rest of it." Noah saw Fisher shift, his hand tightening on his gun.

Fisher might have more guns, but Noah also had to be careful. *Kill Fisher or Helton too quickly, and any chance at freedom I have will die with them.* "Don't even think about lifting that gun, Fisher. You have a whole other knee for me to aim at."

"Benson, put the gun down." Lord Milner's face was rapidly growing darker and more flustered. "There can be no dignified communication while weapons are being wielded."

"I respectfully decline." Noah moved closer to Fisher, then snatched the gun from his hand. "You don't know these men like I do. They wouldn't hesitate to shoot you, either, if they thought they could evade the consequences."

"You have no proof of your claims." Fisher lifted his face, defiantly.

That was true. Noah needed them to confess. And, right now, Milner didn't appear convinced that Noah wasn't the criminal Helton had painted him to be.

"No, but I do."

Noah's heart lurched. He'd hoped she wouldn't come down here.

Ginger stepped out from the shaft.

* * *

GINGER SURVEYED THE SCENE, taking careful steps. Stephen and Helton both appeared disarmed, and one of Stephen's men cowered near a crate. Stephen was bleeding, favoring one leg and bracing himself against a wall. Her pulse buffeted her eardrums, mostly from the exertion of racing through the wadi.

"Virginia Whitman. Of course." Helton's voice was strangled, and Ginger dared a look to see his expression. Even though the only light in the small tomb came from overly orange oil lamps on the floor, his visage appeared a sickly, deep yellow.

If she didn't know any better, Helton had malaria—either that or he was suffering from some disease of the liver, like hepatitis or cancer.

"Mrs. Darby, what on earth?" Lord Milner's outrage was clear enough. "This is no place for a woman."

"This is precisely my place." Ginger's gun was steady in her hand as she turned her attention back to Helton, curious about his appearance. She hadn't seen him before now, but she wished she had.

She doubted he had malaria because he would have other symptoms that would be more noticeable. Most likely he'd contracted hepatitis during his time in Egypt, and now the disease had caused liver failure.

Which means he's dying.

As a doctor, she would normally feel sorrow for a patient in this state, but, oddly, she felt nothing—neither satisfaction nor dissatisfaction. Noah had told Ginger about Helton's proclivities and abuse of prostitutes, and he'd likely contracted the disease due to his behavior. It seemed a fitting punishment for him.

A derisive scowl twisted Helton's lips. "You're quite the little bitch, aren't you, Lady Virginia? Always turning up in my life with a stink about you, like you've spent too much time in the gutter where you belong."

"And you're quite the bastard. At least once in my life I thought some good of you—you seemed devoted to your daughter. Only I found out that you used her the most vilely of all. But that's precisely who gave me the evidence I needed against you both. Lady Victoria Fisher, Lord Helton's daughter, is prepared to testify against both men. Which, considering they're her father and husband, should be damning evidence."

Helton stiffened, his yellowed eyes turning feverish. "Lord Milner, my daughter is mad. My son-in-law has been forced to take her to England and placed her in an asylum."

Stephen watched them like a cat, his eyes like slits. "Yes, it's sad but quite true. She didn't take well to motherhood. And she can't be legally required to testify against me. I'm her husband."

"She won't be required," Ginger said in a quiet voice. "She'll do it willingly." She held Stephen's gaze, her eyes hard. If they didn't succeed, what she said here could cause Victoria more harm, but it was the only ace in her pocket. "She is the one who told me you were holding her against her will. Then she confided in me that I could find damning evidence against you on the *Cursed Valley*. Which is why Lucy helped me get on board."

Stephen's lips parted, his forehead shining with sweat, and his fingers were shaking, his face pallid. His body was probably experiencing trauma from the wound in his knee. For the first time, genuine fear showed in his eyes. She cursed the fact that she'd never had the chance to search the boat. But Stephen didn't have to know that.

Jack, Noah, and Lord Milner watched Ginger intently as she

looked back at Helton. She felt oddly calm and in control. "Stephen has taken Victoria's daughter from her too. You've robbed her of everything by marrying her to that man, Lord Helton. She's not mad, but she's been hurt."

Helton's eyes darted toward Stephen. "You said she—she didn't want to return to Egypt."

Interesting.

Ginger saw a chasm forming between the two men, one that perhaps she could take advantage of. Maybe not all of Helton's feelings toward Victoria had been fake. "Stephen has the servants spy on her every move. Has her living in a modest house, which she's not allowed to leave. He took the child and now uses her to blackmail Victoria into doing everything he wants."

Helton's hands formed into fists, his lips quivering.

"You're dying, Lord Helton, aren't you? Wouldn't you like to see your daughter one last time? Hold your granddaughter? She's the only thing you have left at the end. Your only true legacy. Maybe even the only person who's ever truly loved you."

Helton bowed his head, squeezing his eyes shut. "What do I have to do?"

* * *

OUT OF THE corner of his eye, Noah saw Fisher's man take aim.

Turning, Noah fired three rounds, aiming for the man's head. Missing could be disastrous and this man had already proven he would fight for Stephen.

He fell down, dead.

Jack bolted from his spot beside Helton. "Noah, watch out! Fisher!"

In the chaos, Stephen had pulled another gun.

Noah swung around to shoot him.

A single shot rang out, a burst of blood and brain splattering the walls.

* * *

GINGER LET OUT A STARTLED CRY.

Helton fell to the ground, blood seeping from the back of his head.

"Good God," Lord Milner cried, covering his mouth.

Ginger lifted her gaze toward Stephen and saw him staring from behind the barrel of a gun.

Oh, no.

With Lord Helton dead, what hope could there be of Noah's name being restored?

Oh, God, no.

A dizzy feeling crested in her skull. She'd pushed too hard. Been too close.

Noah came up behind Stephen, pressing a gun into his neck. "Give me the gun, Fisher."

Stephen smirked with satisfaction, but didn't lower his gun. "Or what? I'm the only one who can clear your name now, Benson. If you kill me, the charges against you will stand. You won't live a week."

"Fine." Noah shot Stephen in the arm, forcing him to drop the gun.

Noah kicked it away as Stephen gasped, his breath shallow. His face turned a deep red and he stumbled back, further against the wall, blood seeping from the wound on his arm.

"Put the guns down." Milner stepped away from the slow seep of blood spreading from Helton's body across the floor. "Do not let this madness prevail, please. Darby, this is outrageous. Had I known that you intended to bring me into this-this lie—"

"The only one lying here is the same person who just killed

someone in cold blood." Jack's eyes darted to Noah. They all knew the same fact: without a confession, this was all for nothing.

Jack scooped up one artifact from the antechamber—a small clay tablet. "These are all stolen treasures. From a cache discovered in Amarna at the tomb of Akhenaten, many years ago. Unfortunately, they found their way into the hands of a smuggler. Lord Helton, who was busy operating his own smuggling ring, took notice of the competition and ordered Noah to find evidence to accuse the other smuggler of treason."

"Those are all lies," Stephen breathed through his teeth. "You have no proof."

"I didn't know, of course, that Helton was a smuggler." Noah still trained his gun on him. "I was a simple intelligence officer, loyal to the Crown and wanting to do my duty. And, in attempting to do that, I learned Fisher was a spy for the Germans. He murdered the other smuggler in cold blood, then fled, only to come back and strike a deal with Lord Helton to accuse me of all his own crimes, rob me of my good name, and force me to flee or be executed."

"What evidence do you have of this?" Milner asked, his hands fisted at his sides. "These are bold claims."

"He has none," Stephen snapped. "He's a deranged criminal. And Virginia Whitman, who you know as Mrs. Jack Darby, is his lover." His hands shook harder now.

Now Milner's head swiveled toward Ginger.

With Lord Helton alive, with the lie Ginger had told about Victoria, she'd felt hope. Stephen didn't know she didn't have evidence from the *Cursed Valley*, but if she couldn't get him to admit anything else, they were out of options.

Most of what Stephen had done was void of proof.

Except ...

Releasing a slow breath, she unbuttoned the top button of her blouse, then pulled the fabric to the side, showing the scar on her chest. "Three years ago, Stephen held me down at knifepoint and carved his initials into my chest, Lord Milner. You can see here. He did this to me before murdering my father in cold blood. I'm the evidence. This scar that he gave me so that I could never be free of him is the evidence. I carry it with me always."

Lord Milner's wide eyes fixed on the scar.

Stephen drew a deep breath, and she turned her eyes back toward him and held his gaze. "You remember, Stephen?" Her eyes misted with tears. "You held me down, kissed the blood from your handiwork. You wanted me to be yours. And you failed. Because no matter what you try to do, I belong to Noah Benson and him alone."

The words left her lips before she'd thought them through entirely.

A stab went through her heart. *Jack.*

I wasn't thinking ...

The corners of Stephen's lips turned up in a smile, the pallor in his face increasing. "That's not true," he whispered, his eyes unblinking. "You're mine, Ginny. You always were. All I wanted to do was take you away from all this, give you everything you deserved. I gave your father that money because I loved you."

Pushing her emotional turmoil to the side, she tried to gather her senses.

"And then you used his debt to make him do your bidding." Ginger took a step toward him, sensing that his strength was fading.

"He ... owed ... me ... you." Stephen bared his teeth, his jaw clenched. "Everything was for you."

"All the spying?" She raised a brow, her heart feeling sick. "The smuggling? The murder?"

"Benson didn't deserve you. I did. He never should have *touched you.*"

His face dripped with perspiration, his body trembling as he slumped against the wall. He panted, leaning his head back, as though he was doing his best not to writhe.

"Everything I did was for you, Ginny." Stephen smiled weakly.

"Don't you see? Until my miserable brother died, I was simply the spare with no true legacy, my darling. If Germany had won, I could have secured property for us of untold value. Titles, too. The life I could have given us, that the Kaiser himself promised me, would have given you every luxury in the world."

Ginger held her breath at Stephen's revelations, hoping it would be enough. His eyes looked glassy, as though he was losing whatever fragile tether on restraint he might still possess. "You really thought murder, treason, and spying could win my heart? And implicating an innocent man like Noah? How could I forgive that? And you murdered my father."

Stephen coughed, blood seeping from the corner of his lips. "Innocent? Benson *took you from me.* Disgusting half-blood. He needed to be removed. And your meddlesome father—I only shot him because he turned against me too. I would have done anything for you, my beautiful Ginny. You're *mine*—"

He lunged for Noah at the same time as Jack slammed into Ginger, pulling her to the ground. Noah's gunshot was only a split second later.

Ginger hit the ground painfully, Jack's weight knocking the wind out of her.

Then Stephen slid down the length of the wall, leaving behind a bright stain of blood.

Time seemed to slow as she saw the lifeless look in those pale blue eyes that had haunted her for so long.

He's dead. Oh my God, he's dead.

She focused on Lord Milner, who gripped the wall closest to the shaft, looking as though he might vomit. Jack rolled off her.

And Noah ...

A bright burst of light from the corner of the room caught her eyes—Fisher's remaining man had lit a fuse on a stick of dynamite in the crate beside him.

Time seemed to slow as more gunshots rang out.

We have to get out of here.

She turned to see Noah standing, unhurt and firing the gun at Fisher's man, who stumbled back, his hand tightly fisted around the dynamite.

Her ears rung, sharp pain from the noise of the gunshots in the small space clouding her thoughts.

"Get out of here!" Noah shouted at them. "Go, now!"

Milner bolted into the shaft without hesitating.

Jack grabbed her hand, tugging her to her feet and pushing her forward as Fisher's man fell, dead.

I can't go without Noah.

The stick of dynamite, the fuse still burning and getting lower, rolled out onto the floor and continued rolling, into the corner of the room.

"Noah!" Ginger cried out.

Noah started toward the shaft. "Run. There's not much fuse left on that." He practically shoved Ginger inside, crawling behind her. Jack was at his heels.

They were only seconds into the shaft when the explosion sounded behind them. The earth shook, then the wooden framing at the top of the shaft began to collapse, falling onto their backs.

Fear clawed at Ginger's heart, but she kept moving, as fast as she could. She had to make it. *Alexander. Please, God, I want to see my son again.*

She could hear Noah's breath behind her, and she focused on that.

Noah is with me.

Jack is with me.

And we're going to live.

A wooden plank landed painfully on the top of her head, the ground continuing to tremble, dirt and pebbles raining down on them.

Ginger dug her fingers into the dirt, the crust filling her nails.

Thank God she'd worn trousers. She coughed as dust filled her nose and mouth and lungs. Sand and dirt collected on her eyelashes—she could barely see.

Just keep going forward. Keep going.

Stephen is dead.

Milner heard him confess.

She wiped her eyes, then pressed forward as she saw electric torches up ahead. The exit was close.

Stumbling, she crawled out, a cloud of dust following her. She coughed, wiping her mouth on her sleeve, trying to catch her breath. Up ahead, a disheveled Lord Milner sat in shock and bewilderment, surrounded by his men.

Van Sant grabbed her by the arm. "Ginger. Where are Benson and Darby?"

Ginger gasped and turned around, looking for Noah. "He was right behind me," she managed, then tried to rush back. A cloud of pebbles and dust poured from the exit.

Van Sant clutched her. "No, you can't go back there."

Coughing again, Ginger's knees went weak. Why weren't Noah and Jack coming?

I know Noah was with me.

Oh, God, not Jack too.

Almost a full minute passed. Ginger pushed back against Van Sant. "I'm going after them. Jack is in there too. We have to do something, Millard!"

Then, through the cloud of dust, she saw the dark forms of Noah and Jack making their way out of the shaft. Jack's arm was wrapped around Noah's shoulder and he limped, Noah supporting his weight. They were encrusted with dirt and dust, coughing, and heaving for breath.

Ginger rushed to them. "What happened?"

"The tunnel collapsed. I had to dig him out." Noah set Jack on the ground, and Jack looked up at her, dazed.

"Y-you were brilliant in there, Red." Jack coughed, reaching forward and pulling her into his arms. "But you have to stop walking up to men who are aiming guns at you."

Ginger sagged against him, her heart churning with guilt. *He's all right. He's safe.*

He's my husband. He was worried about me. And I just told him my heart belongs to Noah.

Stephen hadn't been the only one to make a confession in there.

She looked toward the tunnel as the dust settled.

Helton and Fisher were entombed there.

They're dead.

They're both dead.

She shook, her relief uncertain, and she rested, dazed, against Jack. She avoided Noah's gaze, her cheeks burning with shame.

Milner appeared to be in a heated discussion with Millard and the local police chief, no doubt trying to decide what to do about the situation.

Had it been enough?

Jack drew himself to a seated position, still coughing. He pulled a handkerchief out and blew his nose, shaking his head at Noah. "Hopefully that counts for something."

Noah sat beside him, tilting his face toward the moonlight. "I haven't thanked you enough for your help, Jack. And I should have. Because you've been the best of friends—and, more than that. A brother to me. And you have my word with what I promised in Giza."

He took Ginger's hand, then kissed the back of it. "Thank you, Ginger."

Not the kiss of a husband.

The kiss of a man who intended to let her go.

She wasn't about to let that happen. Not now.

Noah rose, wiping the dust from his eyes, and turned to go toward Milner.

Don't go.

"What did you promise in Giza?" She looked from Jack to Noah.

Noah's eyes were dark. "I—"

"He promised we would be friends again." Jack stood abruptly. "And not a moment too soon. Let's go talk to Lord Milner, shall we?"

Ginger watched them both as they walked away. She was too mystified to be happy, too overwhelmed to think clearly.

The ringing in her ears continued and she closed her eyes, pressing her fingertips to her ears as she tried to rid herself of the sound.

Over the cliffs of the Valley of Kings came the howl of a jackal. She shivered, looking toward the shaft once again, thinking of Anubis, the jackal god of the dead.

It's finally over.

CHAPTER FIFTY-TWO

"*I*f I ever marry," Alastair said from his perch on a chair on the deck of the houseboat, "I've decided I will marry a doctor. It may be the most useful tool to have in one's back pocket, besides a loaded gun."

Ginger glanced up wryly over Jack's head, tucking her stethoscope around her neck. "You may be hard-pressed to find a lady who will want to marry you once she has her degree. If the English government has its way, at any rate."

"You aren't married?" Lucy asked curiously, seated beside Alastair. They had been playing cards when Ginger, Jack, and Noah found their way back to the houseboat—after spending an exhausting morning dealing with the authorities. Lucy thumbed the cards she'd set down when they arrived. "I would have thought you would be."

Oh, dear. Please don't let that be a glimmer of interest I see in my sister's eyes.

"Alastair is determined to be a bachelor," Noah said, sipping the glass of water Ginger had insisted he drink when he'd returned from bathing. He had escaped the shaft with only minor scrapes and bruises, to her relief.

Jack had fared well also, but Ginger worried about him differently.

Standing in that tomb with them both, it had been clearer than ever to her. She loved Noah. She could only be his. And when the two men had embraced as brothers, she'd dared to hope that Noah might forgive her too.

... and now I have to tell Jack.

She set her hand on Jack's shoulder. "Your lungs sound fine, Jack, but I want you resting the next few days. Who knows how much dust and dirt you inhaled when that tunnel collapsed."

"Yes, ma'am." Jack gave her a lazy smile. "That won't be a problem. For the first time in a few years, I can finally close my eyes and sleep soundly."

"Cheers to that," Millard said cheerfully from the door of his room. He'd been standing there, listening to their chatter quietly while the sun had risen over the water. Even though she'd spent a few days with him, she thought of him in a grandfatherly fashion. He raised a drink in his hand. "And cheers to Jack, who had the foresight to join a commission with Lord Milner. It was a true stroke of genius, my boy. The ultimate piece to the puzzle that we needed."

"Genius is what I do best," Jack said with a wink.

His good mood made Ginger's heart feel heavier. The last thing she wanted to do was take away his ebullience.

"How exactly did you find your way into Milner's service?" Alastair asked, leaning back in his seat as he took a puff of his pipe.

Jack shrugged. "I'm an American. People are always begging for my help."

"That's true," Noah said with a hint of a smile. "Though maybe it's because of your competence rather than your nationality."

"I'll accept that." Jack grinned, stood, and stretched as Ginger packed her bag. "Am I all done, Doc?"

"All done." She gave him a warm smile.

"So what happens now?" Lucy asked, looking from Ginger to Jack. Ginger couldn't help wondering if Lucy was curious about the disaster of her marriages or if she meant something else.

"Lord Milner has sent word up to Cairo of Stephen's confession in the tomb and his murder of Lord Helton. And he's going to see that Noah is cleared of all charges against him. With any luck, we'll be able to brush off all the journalistic interest in the dig as mere rumor, and speculation about the ill-fated KV61 will quietly disappear," Millard said, a pleased look on his face. He looked directly at Noah. "You finally have everything you wanted, Benson."

Noah gave Millard a smile that didn't quite reach his eyes. "Yes, I'm grateful. To you all."

His gaze flicked toward Ginger, and she felt frozen in the weight of it.

He doesn't have everything he wanted.

Her heart squeezed, and she tore her gaze away.

Noah cleared his throat. "I should go to my tent. It's been a long night. I need some sleep before the sun is too high in the sky and my tent is too bright."

Ginger raised a brow at him. "You're not staying at the house?"

He gave a regretful smile. "Believe it or not, I've spent so long sleeping on the ground that I have trouble sleeping in a bed. And I need rest—my head hurts worse when I haven't slept."

She slanted a suspicious look at him as he left. *He probably just wants to go and smoke in peace.*

"I'm going to go turn in too," Jack said, then gave Alastair, Lucy, and Millard a mock salute. He glanced at Ginger. "Could you come help me with something?"

Feeling oddly exposed, she gave a mute nod. That everyone on this boat knew the difficult situation she was in with Jack and Noah made it all the worse. Saying good night to everyone, she picked up her bag and followed Jack back to the cabin where he'd left his bag earlier.

When they went into the room, Jack closed the door and turned on a light, glancing at her with an odd look. "You—" He rubbed his jaw. "You left something at home in England. I came across them when I was packing my bags."

Left something?

Jack went to his trunk and popped it open, then dug inside it. He took out a small pouch, then tossed it to her, and she caught it deftly. "Good catch," he said with a gentle smile.

She gave him a curious look, then untied the drawstring. Emptying the contents into the palm of her hands, her heart gave a painful thump.

My wedding rings.

Her eyes misted, and she scraped her dry tongue over her lips, not knowing what to say to him.

Because I know what I have to say.

"Thank you, Jack," she whispered, unable to look up at him.

Jack crossed the room and then drew her in to rest her against his chest. It was a comfortable pose, an intimate one that spoke of their comfort as husband and wife.

He set his nose against her hair, breathing deeply. "Your hair smells nice. What'd you put in it?"

"I'm not quite sure. Some concoction that Millard's servant gave me. I think it might have had jasmine in it though." She sniffed and pulled away from him.

Goodness, I'm going to miss Jack.

The thought seemed to bubble out of nowhere, but it had been brewing at the back of her mind all morning.

She hoped he would always be in her life—and in Alexander's— but she knew how much this all might hurt him too. He would need time and space to heal. She truly loved him …

... just not as much as she loved Noah.

It wasn't a fair contest. She couldn't ever love anyone as much as Noah. And even Jack—*sweet, honorable, charming Jack*—had known from the start he'd lose.

She took his hand. "Jack, I have to tell you something." Nervous energy poured through her, a knot tightening in her stomach.

Jack looked away, his hand loose against her grip. "You want to be with him, right? I know." A muscle in his jaw twitched. "That's why I gave you the rings. They belong on your fingers. And you belong with him."

Of course he knows. Her heart felt as though it was breaking, tears threading her voice. "I love him. I'll always love him. And even if he didn't want me, it wouldn't be fair for me to continue in our marriage while loving him as much as I do. I can't be a faithful wife to you if my heart belongs to him."

Jack swallowed, closing his eyes briefly. "Good, then you made your choice. I knew you had." He shifted away from her. "And it's the right one. No matter how miserable it makes me."

"Jack, I want you to know—"

Jack stopped her, holding up a hand. "Red, I—" He met her gaze, just briefly, his eyes blurry. "I'm happy for you. Both of you. I've never cared about two people more. But I ... have to have a smidge of self-preservation too. So let's not say anything that we can't unhear at this point. I'm going to go to Cairo in a few days, do some digging, see what we can do to annul the marriage. Or, if not, I may have to file for divorce, so long as you don't hate me for having to claim adultery—because I think that's the only way."

Adultery. She rubbed her eyes, grimacing. *One more label to add to the sordid list.*

But she knew the truth too. She'd married Noah first, in the eyes of the church, even if not approved by the law. She was no adulteress. And the truth would have to be sufficient.

Wiping the tears that formed on her lashes, she nodded. "I understand."

"And I, uh—" Jack ran his hands through his hair. "I bought Penmore. So, I'm going to put it in Alexander's name, but under your guardianship, if that's all right. You can do whatever you want with it, but I figure that's the best way to handle it, for Noah's sake. I'll always be Uncle Jack, but I'm sure Noah and I need some time apart too."

She covered her mouth, stunned. "Jack, that's too much."

He shrugged. "It's what Alexander deserves. And you too." He backed away. "Good-bye, Ginger."

Ginger rushed toward him and pulled him into her arms, hugging him tightly. She wept against his chest. Her heart shattered as he wrapped his arms around her. "I owe you everything, Jack. My whole life, really."

He didn't answer but kissed the top of her head. Then, releasing her, he swallowed hard. "You should go to him. I have a feeling you two are going to be just fine, after a while. He's never loved anything or anyone as much as you."

Ginger wiped her eyes, sniffling. *Why does this have to be so difficult?*

She felt more alone than ever.

After the incident with the crocodile, when Noah had kissed her, she'd felt for the first time that true flicker of hope that Noah could still love her, still want her.

But he'd said nothing since they'd left Cairo and kept his distance since then.

"Good-bye, Jack," she said, struggling to force herself out the door.

"Get going, Red."

She turned and hurried from the room. Thankfully, it appeared the rest of their party had retired to their own rooms, and she found her way off the boat without having to speak to anyone else.

Maybe they all sensed the need for privacy.

Ginger hurried toward the desert and found Noah's tent out in the open, a singular sign of life amid the dry landscape at dawn.

Her hair was tied back with a simple ribbon and she released it, pushing it over her shoulder.

"Don't stop fighting ..."

She shivered, thinking of his words in that water, when a crocodile had clearly been stalking them.

But had he meant something more?

What if he didn't want her to stop fighting for him?

He'd been arrogant and cruel when she'd told him she loved him and missed him. But he'd been fighting like a wounded dog, baring his teeth at the person he believed had hurt him the most deeply.

The last thing their relationship needed was more pride.

The magic of the Egyptian morning was enough to bewitch her, but she'd always felt as if the earth was transcendent here. Maybe the ancient Egyptians had cast their spells well enough, gripping their lands in their enchantments.

The pouch Jack had given her was still in her hands and she paused, taking the rings out again. She put one on each of her ring fingers. Maybe that alone would tell Noah how she felt.

The sweet scent of jasmine carried from her hair as she drew closer to the tent. She spotted Noah standing just beyond it.

"Noah."

He turned toward her, and a smile hinted at his lips. "I was praying."

"Praying?" She raised a brow, approaching him until she was a few feet away. "Not smoking?"

The corner of his lips turned into a smile. "I may have given that up. A very knowledgeable doctor I know is adamantly against it."

"Not to mention it being illegal, but, yes, all the literature about it is alarming. The colonial doctors have seen a thirty percent increase in insanity related to hashish ... " She was getting off topic.

Ducking her chin, she said, "I'm glad you've stopped. What were you praying for?"

"That you'd come." He dropped to his knees in front of her. "Because I need to beg your forgiveness."

She grew teary-eyed once more, then stepped closer, setting her hands on his shoulders. "No, you don't. I forgive you, Noah. I love you. I always will."

He took her hands, kissing her open palms, then, seeing her rings replaced, he kissed them and pressed his face against her palms for a moment. Pulling away, he whispered, "I do have to beg. Because I don't deserve you. I don't deserve your love, my beautiful darling *rohi*. I'm not worthy of you."

She pulled her hands away and dropped to her knees, lifting his chin. "Noah. Stop it." She searched his eyes. "I don't know what you went through in the time we were apart. And maybe someday you'll tell me about it and I'll weep, because I can't imagine any of it was easy. But you have *always* deserved me. Because you are a good man and the only one that I deem worthy of my heart and my soul. I choose you, my love."

Tenuously, Ginger leaned forward, brushing her lips against his.

Noah dipped his head down onto hers, receiving her kiss and deepening it, his mouth opening against hers, seizing it with passion. His tongue invaded her mouth, stroking her own and she groaned, heady with desire for him, yearning for his touch.

Her arms were around his neck again in an instant, pulling him toward her with ferocity. "I love you, my beautiful Ginger," he managed, his lips catching her jawline as her mouth found his.

She coaxed him into a deep kiss once more, his hands roving over her curves, unbuttoning the waistband of her skirt. His hands moved to her thighs, then he lifted her onto his hips, her arms sliding around his neck.

Tears fell from her cheeks as he kissed her. "I love you too, Noah. I always have. And I always will."

Her words were lost to his kisses.

Pulling her upright, Noah swept her into his arms, then carried her back into the tent. The early-morning light threw a warm glow into the space, and he set her down on her feet in front of him, tugging her skirt away. Her body throbbed with hunger, wanting nothing more than to feel his hands on her skin. "My love," she breathed.

His fingers deftly unbuttoned her blouse, then he tore it away and sighed with dismay at her corset. "I thought the war had ended the need for these damned contraptions."

She laughed lightly, then unlaced it herself and shrugged out of it. "Better?" She raised a brow.

"A thousand times." Noah's hands cupped her naked breasts, sending shivers of delight through her. He set her down against the rug, then finished disrobing her, his eyes roving over her with a lust that made her want him even more.

He slipped out of his own clothing, and she watched him with fascination. Both of their bodies had changed in some ways since they'd last been together—and it felt like so long. A thrill of nervousness went through her. What if she disappointed him now?

He knelt between her legs, and her pulse speeded. "It may not be the long lovemaking that we indulged in in Malta," he said in a deep tone, his fingers sliding past the curls between her legs, parting her for his view. "But I promise to make up for it later."

She let out a shattered breath, her lips and face flushing with heat. "I don't care about that," she said, holding his gaze. "I just want you now."

She arched against him as he teased her with his fingertips, dipping deep inside her as she moaned. "Darling, please," she begged. She wanted to be filled by him, to experience the sensual heat of his body inside hers.

Noah guided himself to her and pushed in slowly, releasing a low, husky groan. Her heart slammed against her chest, and she ran her fingers over the hardened muscles of his back, savoring each jolt of sensual pleasure as he drove further inside her. "I love you, Noah ... my husband." She breathed the words, her chest nearly bursting with joy. *My husband. The man I've loved like no one else. Here with me, at last.*

He smiled, his palms skimming over her hips, then trailing higher still. "I love you, my gorgeous wife."

She reached for his hand, intertwining their fingers as he stretched himself over her, joining their bodies more deeply. He kissed her once again as they found a rhythm together, their souls connected, lost in the union of their bodies.

Unexpected tears slipped from the corners of her eyes, sliding down her face and pooling in her ears as she wrapped her arms around his neck, raising her hips to receive each thrust of his body.

My love ...

... my life ...

This felt like a dream, one she didn't want to wake from. Too many nights she'd dreamed of him, only to open her eyes and find herself alone. *I love this man, like no other. I can never lose him again.*

If she'd ever had any doubt that they should be together, those fears shattered like glass as her body broke through to bliss in his arms and she moaned against his shoulder. Then he cried out, pouring himself inside her.

He stilled against her, both panting, then he lifted his head, kissing her lips again. "Thank you," he said with a hint of a smile.

"For making love to you?" She laughed as he rolled to his side. "There are benefits to me as well."

He shook his head, his eyes dark with love. "For being my wife." He interlaced his fingers with hers, then kissed the back of her hand. "And I promise that for the rest of my life I will never take that for granted again."

"Well ..." She traced the thin bandage on the back of his hand. The cut on his palm must have hurt, even if he didn't show it.

"Thank you for rescuing me today. And when I foolishly climbed on Stephen's boat. You've played my hero quite a bit recently."

He gave her a wry smile. "I didn't. You rescued yourself. I think we've moved beyond the days of you needing my help with most things. You've exceeded my own levels of competence."

"I prefer to think we make a perfect team, each complementing the other."

She closed her eyes, the soft sounds of the desert morning filling the air.

They'd both found their way home to each other, at last.

CHAPTER FIFTY-THREE

*T*he Great Hypostyle Hall of the Temple of Karnak was an unusual place for a celebration, but given that Millard Van Sant had such influence among Egyptologists, an exception had been made.

Dinner was served on a long table that had been brought in between the pillars, local fare that suited the palates of the men in Ginger's life who had all grown to love this land. As Ginger sipped a glass of wine, she sat back at the table, listening to the cheerful chatter amongst her friends and Van Sant's family, who had joined them for the celebration.

A few seats away, Lucy practically glowed in the company of Alastair Taylor—a shocking development. Maybe it was their shared interest in saving Egyptian orphans. *Poor William.* For that matter, poor Lucy. She doubted Alastair shared her interest. But somehow Ginger had the feeling her sister wouldn't be the one to make the Whitman sisters look like women of unimpeachable character.

Jack cleared his throat, standing as he lifted a glass. "I'd like to make a toast," he said as the group hushed.

"To Sarah Hanover. Without whom we might not be here tonight celebrating."

Ginger set a hand over her heart and lifted her glass in a toast. *Sarah.* She still missed her friend so deeply. *I may never have another friend like her again.*

She released a deep sigh, then settled back against Noah, whose arm was outstretched against the back of her chair. "It seems impossible to believe that it's already been two years since she died."

Noah kissed her cheek, murmuring in agreement. "She sacrificed a great deal for us all."

"Once again, you Brits can thank your American friends for swooping in and saving you," Jack said with a satisfied stretch. "Not just in the war but now this too."

Millard chuckled. "Speaking of which, I hear you're heading back to America, Darby," he said from the other side of the table. "Maybe you'll finally put down your roots?"

"Maybe so." Jack grinned, then winked. "But I'm not in a rush to settle down. There's a whole world out there to see."

Ginger's heart hurt for him. Even though he made light of it, she knew how much Jack yearned to find someone to love—someone who would love him the way he deserved.

A local played the lute, and as puddings and sweetmeats were served, Ginger reached for Noah's hand. "Care to go for a stroll with me?"

Noah nodded and they stood, then slipped away from the group. They wandered down past the towering ruins carved with mysterious and beautiful hieroglyphs, and Noah pulled her close against his chest, holding her hand. "Are you having a good evening?" he asked in a low voice. "You look sad."

"I am sad. I don't know when we'll return here. And Egypt feels like such a huge part of our story." She nuzzled her head against his shoulder. "But I am also eager to leave, to see Alexander. And to have him meet you."

Noah squeezed her hand. "I'm nervous—can you believe that? After all I've seen and done, the thought of holding a child feels oddly disconcerting."

"You'll adore him. And he'll adore you." She stopped, the gentle breeze of the

Egyptian night sweeping past them as she turned toward him, holding his hands. "Just like I do."

Noah lowered his face closer to hers and smiled. "And I love you forever, my Ginger."

Their lips met in a kiss, and Ginger's heart swelled with love for him.

Time would continue forward, the tempests of the desert wearing away at the ancient stones around them until they were gone, just as someday she and Noah would be. But she would never forget this moment, in the land that had brought them together, torn them apart, and then healed them both.

* * *

THE LAST TIME Noah had really spent any length of time in England had been six years earlier, and so much had changed since then.

Most especially me.

The last time he'd been in London, he'd been little more than a boyish upstart, pleased with the commission his uncle had gained him in the military, dreaming of adventure, determined to prove his honor, certain that he'd be back within a few months.

Now, as he stood in the library of Ginger's aunt's home in London, waiting while Ginger and her mother were upstairs with Alexander—who still was asleep when they'd arrived from the train station that morning—he felt like an entirely different man. Ginger's mother had received him graciously enough, which had surprised him, and she'd even thanked him for his help in finding Lucy.

Not that Ginger or Noah had convinced Lucy to leave Egypt. Whether it was her sudden interest in Alastair—which Noah wasn't certain he relished the thought of—or the fact Ginger had helped her find a job working as a secretary for a newspaper in Egypt, Lucy had been determined to have her freedom and pave her own way.

But it wasn't the reversal in his mother-in-law's treatment of him that made Noah feel so different. Or that he'd grown more cynical, harder, and less enamored of polite society.

It was that he was on the verge of another role entirely, one that he had little experience with. Having lost his father so young, he'd never really had one of his own.

He didn't know how to be one.

As the door opened, Ginger came through and Noah's head lifted, his heart racing in his chest as she came closer.

She held a young child—no longer an infant but still very much a baby, though he watched the world with bright blue eyes that held an intelligent, analytical look.

My God. Noah's breath caught. *He does look like me.*

His mouth dried as Ginger came closer and he watched the two of them, a sense of wonder growing in his chest.

She'd never looked more beautiful.

"Noah, I'd like you to meet your son," she said, her eyes shining with tears. She tried to smile, and happiness was in her face but something else too. The pain of the time they'd lost, perhaps. Maybe the surrealness that this moment had come about at all. "Alexander, this is your papa."

Ginger stopped only a few feet from him, an arm's distance away, and Noah found he couldn't move.

Alexander. It had been his grandfather's name, too.

A name that meant warrior.

Hopefully, the battles he fights will never be like the ones I've endured.

Alexander held his gaze, his cherub lips parted as he stared at Noah with the same fascination that Noah seemed to have. Noah reached out toward him, brushing the back of his knuckle against the smooth, soft skin of his cheek, as though to remind himself that this beautiful, focused child was real. After a moment, Alexander tore his eyes from Noah's, then reached toward the floor, pulling away from Ginger and from him.

Ginger set him down and gave Noah a wistful smile as Alexander ducked behind her skirt. "You can try picking him up if you'd like. He's a bit shy."

"Maybe he just has good judgment," Noah said wryly and squatted in front of Alexander. Blue eyes peeked out from behind Ginger's skirt before immediately hiding again.

He swallowed hard, then reached for the bag he'd brought with him into the library. "I have something for you, Alexander." Noah pulled the small wooden box out and flipped it over. After winding the key, he opened the lid, and the soft tinkle of metallic music sounded. "It's a music box. It was my father's."

Alexander peeked again, his eyes finding the box. He didn't look beyond it, clearly avoiding Noah's gaze.

Noah smiled tenuously, then set the box down, closer to him.

"Alexander, your papa wants to meet you," Ginger whispered, trying to peel him away.

The action only made him scramble away, ducking near the closest armchair.

Ginger stood, a look of frustration and sadness on her face. "I should have warned you about how reserved he is. This isn't how I wanted the first moment of you meeting him to go."

Noah stood and reached for her hand. "It'll be all right." He squeezed her fingers, then lifted her hand to his lips, kissing the backs of her knuckles. "He has a long time to get to know me."

Ginger stepped closer to him, setting her hands on his shoulders. "He has a wonderful vocabulary for his age. But he's shy and doesn't speak unless he feels comfortable."

Noah kissed her gently. "He'll come around."

The soft trill of the music box sounded.

Ginger and Noah both looked over. The box had vanished from where Noah had left it, an astonishing feat since it had been grabbed with such stealth. Noah chuckled, then took a few steps over to peek behind the armchair. Alexander stood there, brow furrowed in concentration as he held the music box.

The music played, the melody as familiar to Noah as the sound of his own breath. After his parents had died, he'd played the tune repeatedly, as he dreamed of them.

When the music stopped, Alexander's frown increased.

Noah approached him, squatting again. He held out his hand. "You can wind it on the back."

If he didn't know better, his son was scowling at him.

Noah laughed and flipped it over, his hand on Alexander's. "I won't take it away from you. Here, look. I'll teach you." He guided the chubby little fingers toward the wind-up key. "Twist this." He helped him wind it a few times, then turned it over and opened the lid again.

As the music started again, Alexander's eyes lit happily.

"Can you say thank you to Papa for the box?" Ginger asked, coming closer.

Alexander's smile vanished, and he hugged the box closer.

"Alexander, say 'Thank you, Papa.'"

His lower lip puckered.

Noah dropped back. "I think he's worried I'll take it away." He stood, giving Alexander the space he sensed his son wanted.

As he turned to go back to Ginger's side, a tiny voice said, "Papa."

Noah's chest tightened around his heart, and he glanced back. Alexander looked up to him, hugging the music box firmly.

Unable to resist the temptation further, Noah bent and pulled Alexander into his arms, the burning sensation of tears pricking his eyes. "I'm sorry it took so long for me to meet you, Alexander. I should have been here eighteen months ago when you were born."

Oddly, Alexander didn't fight him and Noah pulled back, a tear trickling onto his cheek as Alexander searched his gaze again.

Ginger sniffled from beside them, and they both looked at her. "I'm sorry if I'm weepy. I just—never thought this dream would come true." She smiled through her tears, then leaned down, kissing the top of Alexander's head.

Noah laughed as Alexander squirmed away, then held the music box out to Noah to wind it again.

"I think he likes it." He wound the box, then stood beside Ginger, still holding Alexander in the crook of his arm. *This feels so natural. Easy.* "It may not be a whole estate like his Uncle Jack gave him, but it might do."

Ginger wiped her cheeks. "We have you, Noah. That's the best gift of all."

Noah pulled her into his other arm, a prayer whispering in his heart.

Thank you, God, for this woman.

She'd made the journey to find him. To rescue him. And, because of her, their love would go on, in their hearts and in their children.

Always.

EPILOGUE

NOVEMBER 11, 1922

SOMERSET, ENGLAND

The icy wind whistled over the cliff side, curling its fingertips over the tall grasses. Ginger shivered, tightening the shawl around her shoulders. She closed her eyes tightly, the first rays of sun on her face. Mornings like this grew more seldom as winter approached, but she couldn't sleep as the day broke.

Just four years earlier, the war had ended on this day. She hadn't expected to be here, so close to where she'd been when it all began, but somehow it all made sense too. When the war had ended, there had been parades, celebrations in the streets, champagne and whisky. Despite the excitement, she'd never been able to muster the same sense of joy. The war had taken so much from so many and changed them all—all for what?

Her father, Henry, Sarah.

She whispered their names and opened her eyes again.

Yet, even now, as the light broke on the horizon, change was in the wind. The British government had been forced to declare Egyptian independence earlier in the year, which had brought a fragile peace to the region—and ensured that Howard Carter's sensational new finds in the Valley of the Kings, found at KV62, would stay in the country.

And in Arabia, a tacit resolution had been found as well. Despite the betrayal he had endured at the hands of the British, Faisal Hussein had finally been given some of the lands he had been promised. T. E. Lawrence had helped to design the borders of the new nations, and, for now, the world seemed to hold its collective breath as new kings took their thrones among the tribes and nations that had been warring in those lands for centuries.

Noah watched it all with quiet fascination, never saying much, but Ginger had the feeling her husband longed to return one day to the Arabian lands he loved, if only to say one final good-bye.

She sighed, rubbing her arms in the cold, and looked back at the sea beyond the cliff.

It seemed calm this morning.

She headed back to her house, trekking over the dusty path. The sun lit the front of the small, thatched farmhouse, and she smiled at the sight of it. She opened the gate and slipped through, shutting it tightly behind her. Three hens scampered past as she went up the walk to the front door. She opened it as quietly as possible and went inside.

She hung her shawl on a hook by the door and slipped off her shoes, then went through the hall into the bedroom in the back. The door was open a crack. She tiptoed toward the bed and stopped at the edge. Soft light filtered through the curtains and illuminated Noah's sleeping figure. In the crook of one of his arms, their eleven-month-old daughter's gossamer red hair jutted against his bicep. She smiled, chuckling at the way it stuck up. Her profile faced his, her cherub cheeks rosy and lips parted slightly.

In his other arm slept Alexander, who grew to look more like Noah by the day.

She slid into the bed beside them. Noah opened his eyes for a moment. "I was wondering where you went," he said in a low voice.

"I kept thinking of the armistice. It's been four years already," she said, leaning forward to kiss him. "How's Clara?"

"She barely moved while you were gone. She smiled in her sleep."

She laid her head on the pillow and stroked Clara's cheek. They named their daughter for Ginger's grandmother, much to Gran's delight. Ginger's fingertips trailed over to Noah's face. "Doesn't it make you feel guilty—all this happiness—when so many men never came home?"

Noah opened his eyes. "If I were to add up all the things I feel guilty about, that wouldn't be one of them." He held her gaze. "I never feel guilt about you. Or them." He nodded toward their children.

Clara startled in her sleep, her little fingertips spreading before they curled gently back.

Ginger kissed the top of her head. "They are the best thing to come out of all this."

Noah slipped his pinkie into Clara's palm. "Besides, the future is all any of us has. If we don't take the time to celebrate the good moments, we'll never make it through the bad ones. You should get some sleep. The hospital needs its head surgeon ready to face the day in a few hours."

Ginger smiled at the ceiling. Of all the changes in her life, that one had been, perhaps, the most satisfying. They'd turned Penmore into a mother-and-children's hospital and a home for single mothers and orphans: *The Darby Hospital and Mother/Child Home at Penmore*. On the day they'd opened the doors, they'd found a familiar face coming up the drive: Victoria Everill and her daughter, Ivy—a sight that had made Ginger truly happy.

Instead of Noah and Ginger living at the main house, they'd moved their own family to a small farmhouse on the grounds, near the edge of the sea, which was more than enough for them.

Clara shifted, this time turning her face toward Ginger. She blinked, her eyes opening. Her dark-blue gaze held her mother's. Ginger kissed her again, and she settled against Noah's arm, listening to the gentle sound of her children breathing softly, her heart at peace.

ACKNOWLEDGMENTS

When I was first beginning college, I started writing Ginger and Noah's story. Almost everything about it changed—except them. It was always Ginger and Noah, no matter how many drafts I wrote, no matter what else changed.

For years, I dreamt about the day that I could share their story with readers and when that opportunity finally came true with the publication of *Windswept*, it was an act of sheer perseverance and stubbornness. I also knew that I would never write another book I loved as much, nor characters I knew as well. Ginger and Noah have been with me—a part of my mind—for over twenty years now.

Ginger and Noah were my outlet during some of the hardest times of my life. Writing their story helped hold me together and brought me through those moments.

And as I drew closer to writing the end of the WWI portion of their story, I realized I had a monumental task in front of me: ending their story well.

I always knew who they needed to be at the end of this journey. That their love would be tested by fire. But writing this book is the hardest thing I've ever written. I never knew just how difficult it would be to put these characters I love so much through so much.

So to everyone who told me from the sidelines how much they were looking forward to reading this ... you have no idea how much you helped.

And Susanne Lakin, my wonderful editor, who agreed to deal

with my crazy writing method … thank you for all your hard work on this.

To my wonderful copyeditor, Robin Seavill, who was kind and sympathetic, encouraging and flexible, thank you so much.

To the Word Slayers team for agreeing to help me when I had my deadlines upside-down—I can't tell you how lifesaving it was.

A huge thanks to my proofreaders, Julie and Amanda—it's been wonderful having you on my team.

Patrick Knowles knocked it out of the park with this cover, which is my favorite one yet. Can't you see Ginger coming into her own front and center here?

Lisa Boyle—my writing bestie—this book might not have happened without you allowing me to pester you at all moments with my dumb questions, haha. Thank you. I'm so grateful to the Instagram algorithm for recognizing that we needed to be good friends.

Thank you, thank you to my team of Mother's Helpers made it possible for me to write this when I was woefully short on time.

My darling children were a huge source of inspiration for Ginger's story in this and the reason I do everything. Without them, this book wouldn't be here in this form.

Lastly, to my husband Patrick for his patience, for teaching me what true love is, for encouraging me, and for always giving me Jack's best lines.

ABOUT THE AUTHOR

Annabelle McCormack writes about timeless love and unforgettable journeys. A bit of a misfit who always feels slightly out of place (no matter how extroverted she is), she now champions misfits in the characters she writes, hoping to bring a smile to her readers, hopefully some laughter, and maybe a few tears, too. She is a graduate of the Johns Hopkins University's M.A. in Writing Program. She lives in Maryland with her beach-hating husband, where she spends her days convincing him to take her and her five sun-loving children to the beach as much as possible.

Visit her at www.annabellemccormack.com or http://instagram.com/annabellemccormack to follow her daily adventures.

Milton Keynes UK
Ingram Content Group UK Ltd.
UKHW012203080923
428326UK00005B/533